Wendy Perriam was born in 19 and was expelled from her convent boarding-school for heresy, and escaped to St Anne's College, Oxford, where she graduated in History Honours. She then worked as a barmaid, nanny, artist's model, carnation debudder, social worker, and researcher in the British Museum, before embarking on a successful career in advertising, which she combined with writing poetry and short stories. She now writes full time.

Her previous novels, which include *After Purple, Born of Woman, The Stillness The Dancing, Sin City* and *Devils, for a Change*, have been acclaimed for their explosive combination of sex and religion, humour and hang-up. She is at present working on her ninth novel and some new short stories.

By the same author

*Absinthe for Elevenses*
*Cuckoo*
*After Purple*
*Born of Woman*
*The Stillness The Dancing*
*Sin City*
*Devils, for a Change*

WENDY PERRIAM

# Fifty-Minute Hour

Paladin
*An Imprint of Grafton Books*
*A Division of HarperCollinsPublishers*

Paladin
Grafton Books
A Division of the Collins Publishing Group
8 Grafton Street, London W1X 3LA

Published in Paladin 1991
9 8 7 6 5 4 3 2 1

First published in Great Britain by
Grafton Books 1990

Copyright © Wendy Perriam 1990

ISBN 0-586-09082-7

Printed and bound in Great Britain by
Collins, Glasgow

Set in Bembo

For God the Father Almighty
(Clapham Common Branch)

It almost looks as if analysis were the third of those 'impossible' professions in which one can be sure beforehand of achieving unsatisfying results. The other two, which have been known much longer, are education and government.

Sigmund Freud: *Analysis Terminable and Interminable* (1937)

Who, if I cried, would hear me among the angelic
orders? And even if one of them suddenly
pressed me against his heart, I should fade in the strength
of his stronger existence. For Beauty's nothing
but beginning of Terror we're still just able to bear,
and why we adore it so is because it serenely
disdains to destroy us. Each single angel is terrible.
And so I keep down my heart, and swallow the call-note
of depth-dark sobbing. Alas, who is there
we can make use of? Not angels, not men;
and already the knowing brutes are aware that we don't
feel very securely at home
without our interpreted world.

Rainer Maria Rilke: *Duino Elegies* (1912–22)

# I

'Hallo. This is 246 2321. John-Paul is not available at present, but if you leave your name, address, phone number and a short message, after you hear the tone, he will get back to you as soon as possible.'

Liar.

'Hallo. This is 246 2321. John-Paul is not available at present, but if . . .'

Not available. That means sleeping, shirking, eating Garibaldi biscuits. I buy them now myself.

'He will get back to you as soon as possible.'

He used to say not 'he', but 'I' and even 'we'. Royal we. He never phones me back. I rarely leave a message, though I think he knows it's me. I have a special way of breathing, of putting down the phone.

'John-Paul is not . . .'

I like to hear his name, especially when he says it. His voice is rich and dark, like those jams they sell in tiny pots at twice the price of normal jars, then call 'preserves', to justify the cost. John-Paul is 'preserved'. Old, but not admitting it. I think he wears a toupee. His hair (or hairpiece?) is very dark and straight. I often want to tug it, to see if it comes off, but his first rule says 'No touching', and the rules are very strict. He'd never touch me, ever, not even if I'd just been mugged or gangbanged, or crawled out of the wreckage of a near-fatal bloody car-crash – no arm around my shoulder, or brief squeeze of my hand. I've been wild to touch him all these last six months; dreamt about it, fantasised, embraced him in my mind, even heard his heartbeat thumping into mine, though in cold and cramping fact I've not so much as brushed against his jacket-sleeve, or jogged elbows when I'm going in and out. You can die from lack of touch. John-Paul, John-Paul, John-Paul, John-Paul.

I chose him for his name – half Mayfair hairdresser and half Vatican incumbent. It was difficult to choose. There were hundreds on display, all with blurbs and selling-points, strings of letters after names, countries where they'd studied, universities which had granted them degrees; perversions, specialities, suicides, successes. He had the shortest blurb, the simplest name, and was by far the smallest there. He's not a dwarf, but near it. He thinks he's tall, but most men do, regardless of the facts. Just last year, a leading diet foods company in Welwyn Garden City commissioned a new survey on body-image. Seventy-seven per cent of women of normal weight described themselves as worryingly obese; eighty-seven per cent of men below five foot six regarded themselves as 'average', if not tall. Which makes me somewhere near a giant. I'm five foot ten in flatties, which I never wear, in fact. Tall girls in flat shoes seem to be apologising. I suppose I should say sorry all the time. I'm loud, large, dark, big-boned, and was twenty-six last birthday, and any woman worth the name should be small, slim, fair, demure and under twenty-five.

I don't know John-Paul's age. I know nothing much about him, not even the colour of his eyes. He wears dark glasses all the time. It may be affectation, or chronic conjunctivitis, or a need to get attention, stand out from the crowd. Does he sleep in them, I wonder? I imagine him at night, taking off the glasses, removing his dark suit, the silk tie with its tiepin (a pearl one – probably real), the old-fashioned stiff white shirt. Nothing ever creases on John-Paul. His shoes look always pristine, never scuffed or stained. I dreamed about his shoes once. I was crouching at the bottom of his wardrobe, surrounded by a thousand pairs of shiny black size sevens. I was smaller than the shoes, and very flat and thin. Perhaps a sort of shoehorn. 'Phallic,' John-Paul commented, lighting up a Chesterfield, which itself was surely phallic, then droning on about the 'obvious connotations' of the word horn, and the fact it went 'inside' a shoe. He finds it very difficult to stay away from phalluses. I dreamed about dead mice once, and he said they were limp pricks.

I remove my lemon Chewit, dial his number – seventh time.

'If you leave your name, address, phone number and a short message . . .'

I leave someone else's name and an extremely lengthy message, which the answerphone cuts off. It's fairly safe if I give my name as Mary. He specialises in Marys – nice quiet unassuming girls who have problems with religion, and still live with their parents, and are sweetly fair and small. I meet them on the stairs. They always smile and lower their blue eyes. I glare, and keep on glaring.

I put the phone down, count the minutes till ten past two on Monday. Three thousand, one hundred and sixty-four. Weekends are just lost time. My week starts on Monday, when I see him; stops on Friday, when I don't. Monday, Tuesday, Wednesday, Thursday, are all living breathing days, not golden, but alive. Friday dies and shrivels. Saturday is putrefied. Sunday tugs the rotting flesh from bones. Monday resurrects again. The whole world hates a Monday: black Monday, back-to-work-day, end of the weekend. Not I. I bless them, hail them, pant and groan and thirst for them. Even winter Mondays, with snow above and slush beneath, and hold-ups on the tube, I'm singing psalms and swinging thuribles.

It's half past nine on Saturday, so things are very bad – not winter, but October, which is worse. Summer's over, the snow and slush to come. Poets love the autumn, but they lie. Words like 'mellow fruitfulness' are simply syllables. Things are actually rusting, breaking down. Grazes scar the countryside, scabs form over ponds. Farmers burn dry stubble, gardeners burn old leaves. You can smell the whole world scorching, even in the towns. The bones begin to show beneath the flesh – bones of trees, of leaves.

I haven't got a garden, though my bedsit's called a garden flat, which really means a basement looking out on dustbins and a dreary square of concrete. The windows are all barred. So are John-Paul's windows. I like to think we have some small things in common. I tried to make a list once, though I didn't get that far: dark straight hair; heavy brows, which look better on a man; long nails; long slim fingers (his are stained with nicotine); Garibaldi biscuits and the bars.

I fetch my purse and shopping bag and set off for the butcher's. I haven't got a car. John-Paul drives a hearse. It may be affectation, like the glasses, or something more symbolic to do with Thanatos. Or perhaps his father was an undertaker and he was left it in the will. You can drive a hearse extremely fast if you're not carrying a corpse. John-Paul speeds. I dawdle; kill off fourteen minutes. Three thousand, one hundred and forty-four to bear.

I live on a main road in what politicians call the Inner City, which means poverty and problems, but also Yuppies sniffing around. There seems to be a natural cycle with most areas of London – splendour, slow decay, downright squalor, then back to almost splendour. My own patch is still decayed, though a hundred years ago, or less, it was stately-smug and fashionable, and there are still relics of that grandeur left: a self-important town hall and assembly rooms, its Corinthian pilasters flaking like dry skin; half a naked lady still clutching half her drapery with one dock-fingered hand; a granite clock-tower erected to the memory of one Albert Henry Basing, now spidered with graffiti and stained by drools of urine, mainly dogs'. The clock has stopped. It's always half past twelve. John-Paul's clocks never stop. They go faster than any clock I know. Or slower.

I trudge along the grey and dingy street. Albert Henry Basing would not have liked the litter, nor the vulgar Dixon's with its rash of shouting signs, nor the launderette which smells of Madras curry, nor the stale and fetid air. Inner City air is always breathed-out air, expelled from sickly lungs. No young and frisky oxygen. And you can hardly tell one season from another. There's very little sky left, and trees are luxuries. The only green is mulched and rotting cabbages chucked into the gutter from the market stalls. Keats would never have written *Autumn* had he lived here, only *Melancholy*.

There's a queue at Bullock's, but Wilhelm lets me jump it. I wouldn't say we're friends, more business partners. We trade in dreams, not meat. I don't like meat, especially not in Bullock's, where decapitated rabbits swing from hooks, pathetic scraps of fur still patchworked to their twisted bleeding carcasses. A few last desperate feathers cling round naked turkey necks; livers and intestines coil black in neat white trays. I prefer to eat things which have neither lived nor died. Even lettuces can scream when they are shredded. Cheese and milk are safer: strawberry-flavoured milk in plastic cartons, or very mild white babies' cheese mushed up in silver foil. No mould or rind or oozings, no strong sour smells reminding me of cows.

'Hallo, pet,' says Wilhelm. His accent is quite thick still, though he's lived in England since 1956. He must be seventy-five now, and rumour says he was an SS guard at Auschwitz, who escaped reprisals and set up home in Twyford with Welsh collies and an English wife, then moved to London after his divorce. His dreams are like the rumours – shocking, very violent, and drenched in blood and guilt. My own dreams are far too timid: drab

13

and grey and often just fragmented shreds and wisps. Not gas chambers, but 1930s wardrobes; dead mice instead of decimated Jews. I've been making much more progress since I borrowed Wilhelm's dreams. Not borrowed – bought. I pay Wilhelm in sex. He rattles off a dream or two while he's still slicing tongues or gouging eyes from calves' heads, then he takes me out the back, where the sawdust's damp with gore and later sperm. I'm meant to swallow it, but it's not that hard to cheat. We're restricted to fellatio, since both time and space are short. The room is very cold and full of corpses. You can hear noises from the shop: meat-saws hacking thigh bones, choppers cleaving breasts. Afterwards, he adds a few more details, or even a new dream, and also gives me luxuries like veal or T-bone steaks, which my landlord's wife accepts in lieu of rent. It's a complicated system, but it works.

Wilhelm's very tall (which makes me less conspicuous), and also very bald. As if in compensation, other hairs luxuriate – fierce dark hairs in nostrils, long grey hairs in ears, jutting shelves of eyebrows meeting in the middle, hairs sprouting from his shirt neck and tangling with the medal, coarse hairs on wrists and thumbs. He wears white, like a doctor, but blood-stained white to match his blood-stained hands.

I unzip his blood-stiff trousers, kneel down in the saw-dust, coax his foreskin back. He hates it if I bite, so I draw my lips right down until they're covering my teeth, keep them firm and taut, like a schoolgirl's small tight cunt. I try to build a rhythm, as much for my sake as for his. Once my mouth and hand are moving up and down, up and down, more or less together, more or less in time, I can slip away to Shropshire. I was born in Ludlow, where autumn was dramatic, even as it died, and winter had a grandeur in its cold and splintered cruelty.

I flick my tongue up and down his frenulum, climb the hill beyond my childhood home. The bank of oaks

14

and beeches is so bright it seems on fire, blue smoke choking from the pyre of golden leaves, the sky bleeding in reflection. I can't smell fire, but chestnuts; leaves rotting underfoot; the sweet pink smell of dolly-mixtures clutched in my hot hand. I can hear a nut-hatch chiselling at beech mast, splintering the shells, snatching the soft kernels as they spray into the air. Other sounds intrude: Wilhelm's German gaspings (he always comes in German); a woman talking sausages, whose shrill and discontented voice soars out from the shop. 'The beef are far too salty, and those pork are solid fat. Heart-attacks with mash.'

I close my eyes, concentrate on Wilhelm. He's taking far too long, yet the one mingy dream he gave me was brief and even boring. He's less generous than he used to be, or maybe just too old, so his memories are dulling, the nightmares tailing off. I increase the pressure slightly, use my other hand to graze his testicles, nails scratching, almost clawing. He likes me to be rough, so long as it's not teeth. He comes, at last, with a great guttural German cry. His sperm tastes bloody, and is tepid on my tongue. I hold it in my mouth while he straightens up his clothes and fusses with the sawdust, which we've scuffed and disarranged. Then I spit it out, guiltily and furtively, pretending just to cough. Impossible to swallow it, to have Wilhelm's guilt inside me, churning through my bloodstream. Already I feel tainted – a quisling, a collaborator; Wilhelm's hands my own now, as I whip the naked prisoners to their camps. How could I have done this for a dream? Would I *murder* for John-Paul, exterminate six million?

Yes, I think I would. I suspect he found me boring before I had good dreams, and it's essential that he likes me, doesn't cast me out. I'd shave my head if he said it made me pretty, lop it off completely if he preferred to see me with just a gaping neck. He seems excited by the dreams, says I've stopped repressing all my violence. I remember as a five-year-old crying one whole Sunday

15

because I'd found a wounded bird. I'm not well-trained in violence, but I have to make an effort, fight to be more interesting than all those bashful Marys, who probably dream of bloodbaths every night.

I shudder as Wilhelm passes me the limp and soggy package. Sweetbreads? Maybe brains? I never check until I get back home. That would make me seem a prostitute, counting out my coins.

'Same time next week, *mein Schätzlein*.' I try to nod and smile. My mouth tastes bloody still. I can hear the cries of butchered Jewish children. 'And I hate those herbs you put in them,' the sausage woman nags. 'They look like specks of dirt.' Why is she still there? Years have passed, whole decades. She should be old by now, or dead. Shrivelled like a sausage skin.

People shift and mutter as I pass them in the queue; see I haven't paid. I long to shout, 'I *have* paid.' Far too highly. I sneak out with my head down, limp along to Waitrose. It's a very large exotic branch which sells Israeli pomegranates and ewes' milk with no additives. I buy two pots of instant noodles and a yogurt labelled 'passion fruit', and John-Paul's Garibaldis. I sent him two huge crates once. He never thanked me, though he crunched them every session, which I suppose was thanks enough. He has a problem with orality and eats or smokes continuously.

I use Waitrose for my exercise. It's cheaper than a gym and less solitary than jogging. I trot up and down each aisle a dozen times each weekday, and twenty on a Saturday; sometimes with my trolley, sometimes not. Young men often follow. I never feel attractive, but people say I am. I think it's just my hair, which is very thick and heavy and reaches well below my waist. I've never cut it in my life. John-Paul says I keep it long to establish my identity as female. I began life as a male. For my whole nine months in the womb, both my parents assumed I was a boy. And even after the birth my father was still boasting about his 'son'. He stopped boasting when he saw me. I was large and bald and ugly and quite obviously castrated. I try to quash the memory, which is upsetting in a supermarket, especially on a Saturday when everyone's in families – fathers pushing trolleys, fathers holding daughters whom they might even have wanted, young couples arm in arm. I gave up all my boyfriends when I started with John-Paul. It seemed unfaithful, somehow, and they didn't like it, anyway, when I called them by his name. My brain just plays the record, needle in the groove: John-Paul, John-Paul, John-Paul, John-Paul, John-Paul.

I dial his number as soon as I get back, leave another message from another (meeker) Mary, ape her simpering voice. I check the clock, a tiny ugly plastic one which came free with a computer and was a present from a client. I've done quite well: Monday's session's nearer by one hundred and seven minutes. I suppose I ought to eat, though it's not easy on my own. I drag upstairs to Sasha, hand her over the package (brains *and* sweetbreads), ask her very casually if she'd like to come to lunch. I know the answer before she spits it out. Sometimes I ask strangers, odd people in the street. 'Come and share my lunch' – or tea or dinner. The answer's always no. It reminds me of that story in the Gospels, when the guests declined the wedding feast. My parents weren't religious. I had to read the Bible like other adolescents read porn, or violent comics – under covers in the dark. I still remember that chilling phrase in Matthew: 'Many are called, but few are chosen'; imagine John-Paul saying it in his jam-and-granite voice.

I climb another storey to invite the man in number three. We all have numbers on our doors, which gives us more identity, except mine is zero and therefore blanks me out. No reply from Three. Four is fasting, Five works nights, sleeps days. I trail all the way downstairs again and pour boiling water on to basil-flavoured noodles. I had a friend called basil once – yes, lower case. He always signed his name without the capital. I could phone him, I suppose, ferret out his number from my five-years-old address book, ask him if he's free, but he'd probably only refuse, like all the rest.

The noodles mulch and soften, slip down very easily. I can't taste basil, can't taste anything. I drink water from a cup, which is a completely different sensation from water in a glass, and makes it more like milk. I've bought a piece of cheesecake for dessert. I like the name – my two favourite foods combined, yet tasting unlike either. I sometimes dream of cheesecakes – those heavy soggy foreign ones with moisture-logged sultanas which sink down near the crust. I never tell John-Paul. He prefers Wilhelm's dreams to food ones, and, anyway, I've given most foods up. Eating's so one-sided. The food never loves you back. It's like John-Paul again – passion unreciprocated. Even now, I'm sinking teeth in curd, tonguing up cream and cherry topping, and the cake itself just sits there getting smaller. No emotion, no response. basil was like that in bed – passive, uninvolved, and always dwindling.

There's no washing-up, except two teaspoons and the cup. I ate the noodles from their pot, the cheesecake from its carton. All the same, I run a bowl of water, froth up Fairy Liquid. Rituals are important, help to pass the time. Three thousand and seven minutes now. I wish it were two thousand. The three thousands are quite frightening, especially on my own.

I pass the afternoon rearranging my collections. I collect anything that's small and doesn't die. I like to keep the different piles neat and clearly labelled. At five-thirty Howard rings and we do it with the light on. My bedsit's always gloomy, even in high summer. Howard's not a boyfriend. He helps me pay the bills. Which means mainly John-Paul's bills. John-Paul writes them out himself on stiff white damask paper (old-fashioned, like his shirts), and times them to arrive on the first of every month. I don't know how he does it. I find the post erratic and have sometimes missed a birthday by as much as half a week, but maybe John-Paul has a patient who's Someone in the Post Office.

I decide on early bed. If I swallow enough pills, I can sleep for thirteen hours, which is nearly eight hundred minutes off my load. I hate sleeping on my own, though my divan bed is so narrow, there's not much room for partners. My clients are all small. I never take John-Paul to bed – not now. The once I did, I woke with bleeding hands. He was made of glass underneath his clothes and when I tried to fondle him he shattered into pieces, and I scarred my fingers badly. *On* my bed is safer than inside it. Sometimes he's my father, watching by the womb, praying for a girl. Sometimes he's the chaplain in a hospice, helping me to die. Chaplains can hold hands. Their rules are very different. I checked it with St Christopher's, where people die quite regularly anchored to a chaplain.

I die at least five times, lingeringly but bravely. No morphine, no self-pity. The final time is real, if sleep is death.

*Adieu.*

# 2

'Make sure you take your raincoat, Bryan.'

'I've got it.'

'And those shoes won't like the rain.'

'I'll change them.'

'Do you have to leave so early?'

'Yes, Mother.'

'You never used to, did you, dear? Other firms don't start at seven o'clock.'

'It's the management consultants. They want more productivity.'

'Don't the other staff object?'

'Not really. Just the older ones. Must dash. I'll miss the train.'

'Don't I get my kiss?'

He moved a step towards her, let his lips graze empty air. He didn't like her smell: powder over sweat, hot flesh in cold silk knickers. Peck and gone. He heard her calling after him until he turned the corner – alarm clock for the neighbours. 'I put fish paste in your sandwiches. I need the cheese for supper. Don't be late. Macaroni spoils.'

At least the train was empty. He'd caught the eight-thirteen for seven years; other people's newspapers thrust across his own, other people's briefcases slammed down on his feet. The six-ten was his exclusively. If he'd had the voice, he could have sung. No one to report him, and he was feeling almost well. Monday was a good day – well, better than the rest, since there were still another four to go before he spent another weekend with his Mother. Weekends took their toll.

He opened his blue notebook, still hadn't dared the

red one. He'd touched it in the shop, returned a dozen times, nervous fingers stroking down its shiny crimson cover. No lines inside at all, just blank and dangerous paper, with no limits, no restraints. His blue book had ruled margins as well as neat ruled lines, and was labelled 'narrow feint', which sounded like a description of himself. He was narrow top and bottom, longed to have broad shoulders, be less what he called an '-ish' man: smallish, fairish, slimmish, youngish, with mousish hair and lightish hazel eyes.

'GOLD STARS', he wrote, in his neatish faintish writing, drew a line beneath it with his pen. He couldn't think of many stars at all. He'd bought a coloured shirt, but hadn't dared to wear it. He'd stood up to his Mother on the matter of the mushrooms, but spent all next day apologising. He'd plucked up courage to say hallo to Avril in the office, but his voice came out so softish, she hadn't even noticed, let alone replied.

'BLACK MARKS', he wrote, but didn't underline it, just covered two whole pages, and was still writing very swiftly when he arrived at Fenchurch Street. Thank God he lived in Upminster, rather than Ponders End or Cheshunt, which would mean arriving at King's Cross. People said the bodies were still down there – bits of bodies, charred and twisted limbs.

He'd started a Disaster Scrapbook since 1987. Zeebrugge, then Hungerford, the Enniskillen massacre, the King's Cross fire just ten days later. His Mother believed in an English God who punished Jews and foreigners. But these were God's own people, normal decent British, shopping in a Berkshire town, or stocking up on duty-free on the Coffin of Free Enterprise. Or commuters like himself, merely earning livings, travelling up and down towards their pensions. And even the weather had been weird and overwrought that year – the coldest January since 1940, the wildest storm since 1703. Statistics helped a little.

Fifteen million trees destroyed seemed somehow much more bearable than his one ripped-up Cox's Pippin.

But the horrors had continued – through '88 and '89, and into 1990: Lockerbie and Hillsborough, the Clapham Junction train smash, the British Midland air crash, the *Marchioness* disaster, kidnappings and hijacks, fatal gas explosions, avalanches, mud-slides, constant rapes and muggings. And then the ozone layer. He'd forgotten the statistics, but the hole was getting bigger all the time. He'd thrown away his aerosols, never bought anything in polystyrene cartons, but other people did, despite the scares and warnings – irresponsible people who still lit up in tube trains despite the ban on smoking, or bought guns without a licence, or made love without a Durex. He'd never made love, ever, not in thirty-one long years. Nobody had asked him, and he'd probably never get a Durex to stay on. He'd watched a commercial on TV where they gave a demonstration, using a banana. Bananas weren't quite fair. Who'd ever seen a limp one?

He checked his watch, relieved he'd bought a digital. It made time more precise. He could see the tiny figure two changing into three. 6.33. Exactly. He walked swiftly down the escalator, which not only saved more minutes, but prevented him from lingering on the underwear advertisements, especially the graffitied ones which turned women into men, jumbled all his boundaries. He found underwear upsetting, even on a man.

The station smelt of heat and urine, overlaid with damp. Last night's litter huddled into corners, or clung round grimy bench legs, as if desperate for shelter or support. There was no one else around, save one old dosser sleeping on his coat, a disaster in himself. Bryan walked the other way, towards the black hole of the tunnel, heard angry muffled roarings, glimpsed sudden sparks and flashes, but no actual solid train. Not the time for suicide. You could decide to jump and wait so long you'd change your mind again. Decisions weren't his forte. He could write out 'PROS' and 'CONS', underline them both, divide the page right down the middle with a thick-ruled vertical line, so that nothing overlapped, and still be left completely paralysed. He imagined a decision would look like a banana, if he ever got that close to one to check. Something firm and solid, which stood up on its own; something healthy and exotic, yet commonplace for some.

A train roared in, at last. He moved closer to the edge, was tempted just to jump, forget decisions, pros and cons, simply act, for once, become part of all that speed and force, spend his next life welded to a tube train. Too late. The doors were opening and he stepped in, still alive. No one in the carriage.

'Hallo,' he said. 'Just practising.' Nice to speak to someone; ask the time, even though he knew it; comment on the weather, as people had when he'd lived much further out. It wasn't safe to speak in London. A guard might be a gunman, a tramp a terrorist. A girl had asked his name once, a total stranger on the eighteen-twenty-two.

'Bryan,' he'd told her. 'Bryan Payne.'

'*Pain?*' she'd said, half-mocking. He'd known she wouldn't like it. People never did.

'Yes.'

'Pain like hurting?'

'No. Payne with y, n, e.'

'Those funeral directors are called Payne.'

'Yes.' He knew, resented it. 'It's a different spelling, though.'

End of conversation. Women never lasted. One was getting in now, thighs straining through her flimsy scarlet skirt. Open provocation – that flesh, that curvy red. He put away his notebook, didn't want her snooping, reading his black marks. She was sitting far too close to him, which seemed suspicious, anyway, with all those empty seats. He sat on both his hands, prayed she'd get out first. The

23

fear was building, building; always did as the time moved close to seven. He couldn't even run through what he'd say. You weren't allowed to practise, had to be spontaneous, which was often even harder than decisions. 'Free association', it was called – which meant you said what sprang into your mind, without censorship or straining. John-Paul had told him once that Freud's own phrase – '*freier Einfall*' – was far better than its inexact translation. He didn't speak German, spoke no languages at all except Mother-soothe and English and a phrase or two of Welsh, but he suspected that word '*Einfall*'. It contained the idea of 'eruption', John-Paul had pointed out, those sudden extemporaneous thoughts which burst into your head.

'Eruption' sounded frightening. There were enough eruptions in the universe, things exploding, breaking up. And he'd spent years and years fighting to suppress all personal eruptions, physical as well as simply verbal. Belches, farts, or rumblings were all abhorrent to his Mother. His body was so quiet now, it might as well be dead. It was John-Paul who made the noises – suckings, shiftings, sudden flares of matches, long deep exhalations, hoarse unhealthy coughs. He worried sometimes that he'd die of cancer from all that passive smoking: hours and hours each month inhaling John-Paul's Chesterfields.

The sessions always ended with his Mother, where they invariably began. He saw it as a Circle Line – no progress, endless loops. Even his dreams hardly varied in their content. He was always wrapping up his Mother in a parcel, sending her off to Benares or Peking. Before he woke, the parcel thudded back again, landed on his doormat, marked 'Return to Sender', and often half-undone. He'd tried changing the addresses, chosen far-flung islands with corrupt or useless postal systems which wouldn't send things back. Except they always did, even tiny foolish islands such as Ponape or Tuitula, which he hadn't known existed until he found them on the map. John-Paul said they couldn't stop the sessions until the parcel was delivered as addressed. It was costing him a fortune, in stamps, in John-Paul's bills.

He'd been going four whole years now, four years of so-called therapy, which had made him worse, not better; adding new oppressive guilts about the bills – alarming, never-ending bills which got higher every year and which meant giving up all luxuries, even cutting back on basics. He didn't mind the privations for himself – no holidays, no clothes, no car, no treats or trips or outings, but his Mother had the same restraints without the actual bonus of John-Paul. Could he call it 'bonus' – the shameful sodden Kleenex, his amputated mornings, the need for endless lies?

'Why are things so tight, dear? I thought you'd had a rise?'

'No. They . . . changed their minds.'

He invented crises, pay cuts, money lost in corporate frauds, his wallet stolen – yes, *again* – impending mergers, friends who borrowed money and then fled. Or he told her he was saving – saving for her funeral, so he could do things with some style; saving for a Ford Granada to drive her down to Eastbourne at weekends. Weekends he made his lists, in his other bigger notebook, which had an index at the back and a page in front headed 'Personal/Financial', nicely ruled and subdivided into Business, Bank, Medical and Accident, Insurance, Car and Notes. A shame about the car – all those unfilled spaces – its registration number, his driving licence number, his car insurance number, his AA/RAC number. But he'd filled in all the rest, reread it each weekend to make sure he hadn't changed: his name, address and telephone number; his national insurance number, the name of his GP, his next of kin, his blood group. 'In case of accident, please notify . . .' He'd left that blank, deliberately, didn't want his Mother poking his remains, criticising the way he'd been run over, telling him he should have done it *her* way, or at least warned her in advance. Meals didn't cook themselves and she could have saved the time, not wasted best rump steak.

Not that they ate steak – not now – not since the last increase in John-Paul's hefty fees. (He upped the fee each January – the worst time of the year, when everybody's finances were already wrecked by Christmas.) He couldn't eat much anyway, with the constant pain, the heartburn. He avoided his GP, feared a diagnosis. He'd seen an ulcer once, on *Your Life In Their Hands*, writhing in full colour on the lining of a stomach. The television surgeon had pierced it with his scalpel and its red lips seemed to scream.

The girl got out at the stop before his own. He could see her thighs still gaping on the seat – a different seat – the one right opposite. Her red and writhing lips were opening wider, wider, as he peered up her thin skirt, pierced it with his scalpel. He fought to change the images before he arrived at John-Paul's rooms. Safer to talk Mothers, over-sixty-fives.

He stood ready at the doors as the train shuddered to a stop. Seven and a half minutes and he'd be lying on the couch, breaking into fragments. The terror hadn't lessened, not in four long years. John-Paul was his surgeon, made the diagnoses. 'You see me as your feared and hated father.'

He'd never had a father. His Mother's husband had been unreasonable enough to die before his birth, *and* without insurance. He'd spent much of his brief childhood trying to draw fathers: pin-men, matchstick men, squiggles with no substance and no eyes. There'd been no males at all – no grandfathers, no uncles, no brothers or best friends. Yet now his world was full of males – cloned and cut-out males, sharing the vast office, or jostling in the gents, stamped from the same stiff grey polystyrene as the desks, the plants, the chairs. He hated BRB –

a twenty-storey tower-block firm with eyes instead of windows, swivelling up and down the whole of Greater London, tracking workers' movements. Their spies were everywhere, pretending to be traffic wardens, or guards on trains, or tourists. He could see one now – Fletcher from Accounts, doubling as the ticket collector, the man who worked the lift. The lifts were automatic, and anyway he wasn't due at work yet. Two hours to go – free time. Except time was never free, always tied to Mother, Mother or John-Paul.

He backed away, dared not risk the lift. Fletcher might report him, guess where he was going. He'd spent four years avoiding people, skulking to and fro, not even crossing John-Paul's road until he'd checked on all the roadsweepers, the loiterers at bus stops. It had often made him late. 'You must be well aware, Bryan, how much time you're losing in your therapy by arriving late like this, and how in a sense it's burning money, which at other times you often seem to grudge.' John-Paul's voice was low – accusing low, sarcastic low. Did all fathers speak like that?

He edged crabwise down the passage towards the ancient spiral staircase, labelled 'Emergency Exit Only – Ninety-Seven Steps.' You could die of steps: be struck down with a heart attack or overstrain your lungs. 'In case of accident, please notify . . .' He should have put John-Paul. John-Paul would pick his corpse up, arrange it on the couch, start explaining why he'd done it, why he'd chosen to collapse. There were no accidents with John-Paul. Everything was chosen – illnesses and nightmares, even fear or farts. Everything had reasons. Which was partly why he went.

It had all started with a *Reader's Digest* in the dentist's waiting-room – a quiz entitled 'How Neurotic Are You?', which he'd filled in, twice, while waiting for his annual scale and polish. The highest you could score was fifty. He'd scored sixty-three, then sixty-five.

Two days later, he was in another waiting-room (the doctor's, with an abscess) and reading *Woman's Realm* – 'Do You Suffer From Panic Attacks?' He'd had one on the spot, rushed sweating, shaking, stuttering, into his GP's consulting-room, emerged with Ampicillin and a referral to a psychiatrist.

The psychiatrist was young and keen, believed in psychotherapy, not drugs; offered to refer him to a private psychotherapist, which was where his problems started. He'd simply never realised how many brands of therapy existed: Reichian, Rogerian, behavioural and cognitive, feminist and primal, rebirthing, hypnotherapy, and several dozen more – not to mention psychoanalysis – Freudian or Kleinian, Jungian, Lacanian – transactional analysis, psychosynthesis, bioenergetics and Gestalt. It had been impossible to choose, or even grasp the differences. The indecision got so bad he could neither eat nor sleep, staggered back to the psychiatrist, who cut through all his dithering, phoned a colleague there and then, to fix up an appointment. The colleague was John-Paul, who was what was called a psychoanalytical psychotherapist, which sounded most alarming with those two 'psychos' tagged in front. In fact, he never would have gone at all if he'd known what it entailed, known what lay ahead; realised just how wrong he'd been in his simple expectations.

He'd imagined his neuroses bursting like the abscess, clearing in a week or so; all the pus and suppuration draining safely out. But instead they'd swelled and festered, sprouted secondaries, infected his whole system. And still no cure in sight. Four years was only 'minimal', according to John-Paul. Some patients kept on coming after a dozen years or more – and three or four times weekly – still struggling with resistance or repression. His own fears had bred new (deeper) fears, as expounded by John-Paul. His panics on the underground, for instance, weren't simply the result of the recent King's Cross fire, but went right back to the womb, reflected his pre-natal fears, his sense of claustrophobia as he'd laboured through the birth-canal, panting to push out. And the labels he'd been saddled with since childhood – 'lazy', 'clumsy', 'self-ish' and 'bone idle' – were now augmented by more serious ones – 'obsessional', 'compulsive', 'alienated', 'anal' and 'aggressive'.

He shook his head violently, as if to dislodge those shaming tags, started toiling up the staircase, counting steps to calm himself. Eighteen, nineteen, twenty . . . The steps were made of stone, decayed and chipped like teeth. Twenty-three, twenty-four. Drops of dirty water were oozing down the tiles; the clammy black iron balustrade wet with condensation, slippery from his sweat. Thirty, thirty-one. He stopped a moment to puzzle out a damp patch on the wall. It looked like a small island, with the tide seeping in and out of it; a forgotten lonely island. Perhaps he'd send his Mother there, string her up tomorrow, mark her 'Airmail, Urgent'.

'Keep left,' the notice said. Safer to obey it. People might be spying, even here. There were always rules, rules for stairs and staircases, even rules for dreams. He paused to listen. Silence. He'd begin to hear the screams soon – screams of bloody victims, struggling from the wreckage, fleeing from the bombs. He must keep counting, climbing. Thirty-seven, thirty-eight. There were squiggles on the walls, daubed in chalk and paint. Hieroglyphics? Arabic? Non-existent fathers?

'DANGER! HIGH VOLTAGE,' shrieked another larger notice, which covered a square cupboard recessed into the wall. There were cupboards in his mind like that, doors he dared not open, things which might explode. The silence sounded darker now, more threatening altogether. He dropped a penny, just to hear it fall. It seemed to fall for ever, echoing and whimpering, never touching base.

'*Waste!*' his Mother peeved. 'If you save the pennies, the pounds will . . .'

Forty-eight, forty-nine. He stopped, alarmed, as he realised what the numbers meant. If there were ninety-seven steps in all, then he was exactly halfway up now, one foot on the upper step, one foot on the lower, which meant no chance of a decision if he needed to go down. He could see the black backs of the stair-treads coiling up and round, precisely the same number winding down and down. Two armies in his mind.

He was late already, one whole minute late. It was eleven minutes past, and he should be stretching out on the clammy leather couch with its mean thin-bellied pillow, its freshly laundered head-slip. The laundry must cost pounds. John-Paul saw his patients from seven-ten in the morning till ten o'clock at night; exactly fifty minutes allotted to each one – what was called 'the fifty-minute hour'. Strange how that profession always cut time short. If every hour he'd ever lived had been docked to fifty minutes, he'd be only twenty-six now – almost a young man. He couldn't remember ever being young. He'd been old and shrivelled in the womb; spent ages wrestling out of it, as if he hadn't got the strength; kept his Mother waiting even then. His limbs were aching now, but he must move, up or down. It was wicked to waste anything, especially John-Paul's time; book sessions and then break them, especially that first session, which other patients craved. John-Paul was better value at seven in the morning – no one else's terrors clogging up his mind, no one else's Mother bursting through her string.

He moved an arm in preference to a leg, pretending to be waving, pointing out a vista. 'You can see the whole of Surrey on a clear day. That's the spire of All Saints church glinting in the sun, and if you look down to the left . . .' Sweat was sliding down his stomach, prickling on his scalp. 'Bryan,' he said. 'Bryan Pain,' tried to hold himself together with his name. He was in danger of disintegrating, could feel the process starting, brain-cells shrinking, blood-cells drying out. 'John-Paul,' he called. 'Please help me!'; knew he wouldn't hear. He'd had a nightmare once, where he'd been abandoned at the bottom of an endless plunging mine-shaft, with John-Paul at the top. 'Pull me out!' he'd shouted, but his voice was trapped as well, couldn't scale the tunnel of his throat.

He moved his foot a fraction, put it back again. An inch could mean decision, and decisions locked you in. Endless steps above him, endless steps below; steps coiling to infinity, infinity of fear. He rummaged in his wallet, clawed out his identity – credit cards and bank cards, BRB security pass, season ticket, library card. He must exist, surely, if those documents endorsed him; all of them official, some of them with photographs, signatures, addresses. Or were they all unreal themselves, only shadows of identity, like his shadow on the wall?

He touched his shadow, watched it wince and shudder; still kept his feet exactly where they were. 'Bryan,' he said. 'Bryan Real.' The fear was closing in now, squeezing round his throat. Only fear was real. He could hear his Mother's voice: 'Worked my plundits to the bone; cold teat Monday, boiled tid Tuesday, turned sheets side to muddle, eked out grisk with crimplings. Thirty hours in labour, and then you got tangled in the cord. Always were ungrateful, even as a midget. Don't walk across the midwife, please keep off the cheese, don't touch don't think don't breathe don't don't . . .'

'I didn't, Mother, *didn't*. I wasn't even there.'

'Don't you lie to *me*, lad. You've been telling lies for years. A Mother always knows. Lies come from the Devil, Bryan, and we know the Devil, don't we? He's the one who tortures little boys, throws them down the mine-shaft and leaves them there for ever.'

'John-Paul!' he cried. 'I'm coming. I've packed her up in

31

cardboard and stapled all the joins. I'll move house, leave the district, set up home abroad, so even if they send her back, I won't be there to see.'

He crammed all his cards and passes back, began to run – three steps at a time now – stumbling, tripping, grazing hands and knees. 'Please wait for me. I'm coming, I'm only seven minutes late. Don't cancel my appointment. Don't rub me out. I'm *here*.'

John-Paul couldn't hear him. He was running down, not up; down down into the tube again, season ticket ready; running all the way to Fenchurch Street, all the way to Upminster, back to Ivy Close, voice roaring with the train.

'I'm coming, Mother, coming. And I'll never leave again.'

# 3

'Pass the butter, can you, dear? Thanks. I like the tie.'

'Half-price in Simpson's sale. Do you think it's a bit bright?'

'Well, just a fraction, maybe. You could keep it for weekends.'

'I don't wear ties at weekends, Mary.' James picked up his fork, peered at it suspiciously, as if it were stolen, or not clean. 'Another letter from Jonathan? What's wrong with him, for heaven's sake? We only heard on Thursday.'

'He's homesick, I suppose.'

'It's time he settled down. The others never made that fuss. And why can't he write to me as well? I'm his father, aren't I?'

Mary didn't answer, drank her coffee scalding, totted up the pain. Not quite a three, but a fraction more than two. Two and a quarter, she jotted on her Pain Score. She glanced across at James, who was examining his bacon, jabbing at the glazed yolk of his egg. His face looked red and angry, as if she had boiled it in a saucepan; his hair was grey, and sparse. She had fried the egg in sunflower oil, hoped it wasn't greasy. Three years ago, they'd been pushing polyunsaturates as healthy. New evidence had proved they gave you cancer, recommended olive oil instead. She kept on buying sunflower.

James took one small mouthful, wiped cancer off his lips. 'I'm late, you know – again. We're always late without the boys to wake us. Can't we get up earlier?'

'I'll reset the alarm.'

'It's broken.'

'I'll buy another one.'

33

'You said the same last week, Mary.'

'I'm sorry. I was busy, dear.'

'*Busy?*'

She apologised again. Only men were busy. His father had been ill, that's all, *and* the aunt who lived with him, and she'd had to visit every day, do their chores and housework, as well as just her own, cook them tempting meals. She could still have bought the alarm clock – on the way, or later.

James pushed back his chair, took a last fierce swill of coffee, then clasped hands with his briefcase.

'Don't you want your toast, James?'

'I haven't time for toast.'

'I'll fetch your coat. The black one or the grey?'

'The black – and my umbrella.'

She kissed him, twice, kept waving as he drove away – fainter, fainter, fainter – returned to her own toast. Only half a finger left. The problem with their marriage was they ate at different rates. James regarded food as something dangerous, which must be checked and probed and scrutinised before he actually transferred it to his mouth. She tried to arrange it nicely on his plate – the fried bread at an angle, the halved and grilled tomatoes lined up two by two. But he'd poke at things, disrupt them, shift his egg around, yank up a bacon rasher with his fork, as if he suspected it was harbouring something unpleasant underneath. When, at last, he got around to eating, he proceeded with great caution, cutting off small pieces, raising them very slowly to his mouth, then lowering his fork again, as if he'd changed his mind, the mouthful still untouched. It made her very nervous. She would hold her breath as his fork moved slowly upwards, find herself perspiring as it returned to base, still loaded. James rarely finished any dish. There simply wasn't time. Sometimes he would shut his eyes in the middle of a meal, fall completely silent, one hand on his fork still, face creased up in suffering.

34

At the beginning of their marriage, she had blamed it on herself, enrolled for cookery classes, continued for six years, progressing from Beginners' Basic to Hostess Entertaining. But even when she presented James with *Symphonie de la Mer aux Perles de la Gaspienne*, with a lobster *coulis* and an exotic mix of vegetables, he had still shied at the okra, resisted the mangetout, removed the grapefruit garnish as if it were a bomb, and asked her why she'd mixed up sweet and savoury. Her own unease at meals increased, so she began to eat too much too fast. She didn't really want the food, hardly even tasted it. It was just a way to fill the silence, calm her agitation. She reached for James's toast, crammed it in and down, devoured his cold congealing egg, then went out to the kitchen, shared the uncooked bacon rinds with Horatio, the dog.

'Good boy,' she murmured vaguely, stroking his broad head, wished he could reply. It was deathly silent in the house, as if it expired once James had gone.

She checked her watch, a gift from James, who liked her to be punctual and kept his own watch fast. Still only half past seven, which meant a good twelve hours at least before James was back again. Horatio had returned to sleep (and wheezing), his fat French-mustard-coloured flanks bulging over his basket, a trail of slobber necklacing his chest. He'd started life as simple Ben – James's mother's dog – had moved in with them a year ago, following her death. Her eldest son had re-christened him in honour of his latest hero, Nelson (and some fellow in his Latin book she'd never actually heard of, but who was courageous and dynamic like Lord Nelson). The new name didn't suit him. Horatio alias Ben was an idler, an asthmatic, and a thief. All the same, he did provide some company, another presence in the house, and if he didn't talk, he listened – which was more than could be said for the four other males she lived with.

Nice to have a daughter, someone really close to her,

who might share long cosy chats, and who wouldn't go to boarding school, wouldn't be as busy as James and the three boys. Even Jonathan was busy, at seven and three-quarters, busy with computer games, or chess or maths or cricket. She tried to count her blessings (as she counted sheep at night), work out her own routines, volunteer for rotas, take on more good works. Every day was really much the same (well, all except for Fridays, which were in a class quite on their own) – empty and too long – but she did her best to make them short and different, gave them special names: Ironing Day, Church-Cleaning Day, Old Folks Afternoon.

Mondays were the worst. She'd known it was a Monday the second she woke up. That sense of almost dread at starting a whole week again – seven days stretching to infinity. God had made the world in seven days, which only went to prove how long a week was. It was important to keep busy, though, everybody said – her mother said; the Bible said; James's mother used to say, before her tragic death. She often washed the sheets by hand, since it took far longer than using the machine, or cleaned the stairs with just a tiny hand-brush, instead of the over-eager attachment on the Hoover. Both also gave her backache, which could be added to the Pain Score, and so meant a double bonus. The Pain Score was important in itself, consumed a lot of time: working out the numbers, comparing steady aches with sudden pangs, crushed fingers with burnt tongues.

She cleared the table slowly, one thing at a time, tried to force a smile. She always had the feeling that someone might be watching her – God's eye in the ceiling, or in the television set, checking on her cheerfulness, her face. 'I believe in one God,' she whispered to herself. 'The Father Almighty, Creator of heaven and earth . . .'

'What's heaven?' Jonathan had asked, when they'd first taught him the Creed. She hadn't known the answer, had let James fill the void with clouds and angels. James's God was different – Anglican and friendlier, with a different set of (vaguer) rules and less stress on sin and hell – which made another problem in their marriage. The boys were at his own old schools (preparatory and public), instead of at the Catholic ones he'd promised. She missed her youngest son. Seven was too young to board, though she'd been packed off at that age herself, and James had gone still earlier, at the tender age of six; insisted it had done him only good. The house felt far too big without the boys. No cakes to ice, no knees to bathe, just one unrumpled bed to make, with no hidden cache of sweets or bears or toys. She stared down at the sheets. She'd changed them only yesterday, but they still looked not quite clean. Who knew what emissions seeped from their two bodies in the night – discharges or dribbles, perspiration, phlegm. It wasn't sex which fused you, just the passive sharing of a double bed: dead cells falling from James's scalp to hers, his loose coarse greying pubic hairs straying through the gap in his pyjamas, their breaths and bad smells mingled. Last weekend, they'd been away to Bristol, slept in single beds. She'd been cold all night, but clean.

She tucked in all the blankets, smoothed the counterpane, polished up the silver frame of their wedding photograph – James with hair, and smiling. She touched his curving mouth and the one eye that was showing. Her eyes were blue, as his were, but a different sort of blue – more summer sky than winter sea, though his had faded anyhow and now looked slightly dingy, as if a badly trained window-cleaner had left smears across the panes. She had changed far less than he had, could still claim a waist and cheekbones, and her fair hair was still natural, not Tru-Blonde from a bottle. She wasn't even lined. What James had called her convent-girl complexion had somehow stuck out thirteen years of marriage without withering or shrivelling.

She was frowning in the photograph, gripping her

bouquet so tight it could have been a gun. Her period had started the morning of the wedding, a whole eight days too early. 'Nerves,' the doctor shrugged, when she'd returned from honeymoon. She'd been terrified she'd leak – red patches on those yards of virgin white. She'd remained a virgin five whole days. James detested periods. If men were women, he'd exploded on day three, they'd have found a way to stop them, turn off that crimson tap.

'Wilt thou take this man as . . . .?' Her mother had complained that she'd mumbled all her answers, but she'd been too shy to shout. She wasn't keen on weddings. All that heat and noise and fluster, and the bubbles from the Moët skulking in her stomach throughout the honeymoon. And the service so alarming – talk of poverty and sickness and leaving Mother and Father and cleaving unto a large and loud-voiced stranger till death did them part. That meant no divorce. She had never lost her faith, never jibbed at the Church's line on the indissolubility of marriage; just wished God were a shade less large and strange Himself. She presumed He must be busy, like all men; had more important things to do than listen to her feeble prayers about abolishing all prep schools so that Jon could come back home, or persuading James to buy new (single) beds.

She switched on the radio, listened to the news. Everyone so busy once again: attending Disarmament Conventions, shooting Irish Protestants, winning by-elections, marching for Black Power. There was a riot in Peshawar. Where was Peshawar? East or West, theirs or ours? She went to fetch the atlas, looked it up. She had to make an effort to improve her general knowledge, mainly for the boys' sake. Oliver knew words she'd never heard of, words like byte or fianchetto, and Simon read the business news, at ten. She'd enrolled for a new evening class – not soufflés or choux pastry, but 'Science and Society'. She

38

was finding it a struggle, and no one laughed and chatted or borrowed flour and raisins, as they did in cookery.

She slipped into the spare room, the fourth and empty bedroom they'd been saving for their daughter, the one they'd never succeeded in conceiving. She drew the curtains, lit the candles at the little shrine she'd set up on the dressing table, turfed out a wilting aster from the votive vase of flowers. The flowers were not that special, just bits and pieces from the garden, a few dwarf gold chrysanthemums, the last full-bodied rose. It was the spiritual bouquet which really counted; that offering of penances and prayers she'd first learnt to make at her convent boarding school, and which had been presented to their Reverend Mother General on her annual summer feast-day – the equivalent of orchids, or rarest hothouse lilies. Her own bouquet was almost ready now, lacked just one final bloom, something which took courage, tested her devotion. She'd be presenting it on Friday, wanted it to please.

She removed her shoes, unbuttoned her blue blouse, unhooked her brassière, let her breasts spill out. Her breasts were large and firm still, despite suckling three big babies (and even James, as well, once, since he'd been jealous of the first child and had insisted on his share). She reached across for the tallest lighted candle, then stretched out on the bed, held the candle poised across her chest. She tipped it at an angle, closed her eyes as the hot wax seared her flesh. She moved it lower, lower, so the flame was on her nipple, held it very steady, while she counted up to five. Excruciating. Wonderful. She must pray, must keep on praying, however fierce the pain. 'I believe in one God, the Father Almighty, Creator of heaven and earth and of all things visible and invisible. And in one Lord John-Paul Christ, the only begotten Scourge of God . . .'

There was a ringing at the doorbell, a crescendo from Horatio. She replaced the candle, buttoned back her blouse. The rough cotton fabric chafed across the burns. She jabbed at them deliberately, as she returned downstairs, opened the front door. Mrs Clarke from down the road, collecting for the RSPCA. She looked like her two beagles: long jowls, short legs, bright brown trusting eyes. Mary went to fetch her purse, unfurled a five-pound note. She was extremely fond of animals. It was James who was allergic to all household pets and pests, only tolerated Horatio because he'd been his mother's dog.

Mrs Clarke's tail was wagging, as she took her paper bone. 'Thank you, dear. That's generous. Would you like our magazine? It's another 50p.'

Mary glanced down at the cover, ready to decline, shuddering at the photographs of tortured cats and dogs, some with severed ears, some with cigarette burns. She almost wept with pity, hated anything to suffer save herself. She peered closer at the pictures, taking in the details. They might give her new ideas: livid cigarette burns on a spaniel's legs and chest, even on its genitals. She hadn't thought of cigarettes, let alone of genitals. She could buy a packet right away when she left to clean the church – Chesterfields, of course.

'Yes,' she said. 'I'll take one. Lovely weather, isn't it?'

# 4

Just one hundred and sixty minutes left. That's bearable, endurable, and at least I'm now alive. I first got dressed two hours ago, but I've changed my clothes completely several times. I'm still not happy with this stupid dreary dress, but it's so hard to know exactly what he likes – pastels or bright colours, trousers or tight skirts? I lard on several perfumes which I can't really afford, but keep for just the sessions, then use four deodorants – foot, vagina, underarm and mouth-spray. It would be unthinkable to smell, though perhaps he wouldn't notice in his haze of Chesterfields. I apply my lash-extender, then tie a white crêpe bandage round my leg. It's a bigger one than last time, since he didn't notice that. I started with just Band Aids, but even when I stuck them on each and every finger, plus huge ones on both knees, he still never thought to ask me how I'd come to hurt myself. I suspect I'm wasting bandage and that even if I tourniqueted all four of my limbs and added splints and slings he wouldn't say 'I'm sorry' or 'What happened?' I went once with laryngitis, and still not a word of sympathy for all my croaks and grunts. He simply said that a lost voice was a common hysterical symptom and I was probably trying to suppress some forbidden line of thought, or frightened of expressing hostility or rage.

I never miss my sessions, even if I'm ill. I've limped there from the hospital after x-rays of the bowel (which required two days' fasting followed by two enemas and left me feeling as if I'd lost my whole insides) and when I'd promised the radiologist I'd go straight home and rest. I've gone with various viruses and once with gastric 'flu;

quite like the thought that I'm infecting him with germs, so that at least we'll have bacteria in common. I keep praying I'll get chicken pox, or measles, so we can share our spots, itch and scratch together.

I needn't really leave for a good hour or even more, but I leave in any case. I always go by foot now, although it's several miles of slogging through some pretty grotty streets, but at least I'm not held up by traffic jams or busmen's strikes or trouble on the tube. I was twenty minutes late once because a toddler fell onto the line at the Elephant and Castle and all the trains were halted, but John-Paul still suggested that maybe I was late on purpose to prove I didn't need him, which was what he called a reaction-formation against extreme dependent-attachment need.

I slam the door as I remember, step out into drizzle. Even walking has its disadvantages, especially in the rain – splashes on my dress from passing motorists; my hair in limp black rats'-tails. Just my luck. It was sunny earlier on. I even heard a man say 'Lovely morning'.

My nerves begin to build before I've walked a hundred yards. They always do, and worst of all on Mondays. Weekends are so hazardous. John-Paul might have died or disappeared. For all I know, he may have dangerous hobbies – hang-gliding, ballooning, motorcycle racing. Even as I fret towards his rooms, he could be in intensive care, or chilling in a mortuary. I stop a moment, fight a wave of nausea. If he died, I'd have to die as well. Life would be impossible without him, like trying to survive without oxygen, or water. I struggle on, imagining our deaths. There must be *some* way of ensuring we could be buried close together, in the same cemetery or churchyard. Or if I collapsed near his mortuary, I might be shunted to the shelf-space next to his.

I'm so involved with corpses, I splash right through a puddle which I didn't even see, ruin my white shoes. Those shoes are almost new. I found them in the Cancer Shop, two sizes too small, but they make my feet look slimmer, so all the pain's worthwhile. I expect his wife has tiny feet – if he has a wife at all. The thought is so upsetting, I murder her immediately, then annul the marriage on the grounds of non-consumption. Which leaves him free for me – or all those ghastly Marys with their prissy size three feet. I've murdered a good million wives since I started with John-Paul, though I suspect he isn't married, so the crimes are pretty pointless. I know he wears a ring, but that doesn't mean a thing. It's probably for protection. I had a doctor-client just a month or so ago, who although a lifelong bachelor, said he always wore a ring to save him from his patients' wiles and wooing, and had even borrowed a family photograph to set up on his desk.

I dispose of the dead body, then stop at the big sweet-shop on the corner of Beech Road. If there were ever any beeches here, they've long since been cut down, or used to make the *Sun*. I've tried all the different sweet-shops and this one is the best, sells expensive Belgian chocolates and fondants packed in velvet. I've bought him both of those, *and* the handmade chocolate truffles and the mint and Drambuie creams. He says I give him presents as a way to get attention, buy myself more love, or as 'bribes' to twist his arm, make myself more special than his empty-handed patients. A gift is never just a simple selfless offering, a way of giving pleasure, or just giving for its own sake – or not in John-Paul's book. Yet he always snaps them up, I notice, never hands them back. I've already bought him biscuits, when I did my shop on Saturday, but they don't seem quite enough. Nothing ever seems enough, especially not his love. If I could make him really love me, I wouldn't need another thing on earth – not food, not work, not sleep, not legs or arms. I'd be content to be a stump. So long as he kept telling me I was the most special and exquisite stump he'd ever met or dreamed of.

I examine all the chocolates, trying to work out which he'd like, finally choose Ferrero Rocher, mainly for their name and the exotic golden wrappings which swathe each nut-rich cluster. Those he won't resist. He's never given *me* a thing, not even good advice. Advice is almost a dirty word for analytic therapists. You could tell them you had planned to kill your boss, or had a date with Jack the Ripper, and they wouldn't try to stop you, or suggest you took some Valium and put yourself to bed, but just sit there droning on about your sadomasochistic trends and their probable connection with your suppressive controlling mother.

Sometimes I imagine him giving me mink wraps, or diamond rings, or Porsches. I'm afraid I'm not original when it comes to thinking of presents. I suppose there's nothing much I want really, except John-Paul to myself.

I'm relieved to leave the sweet-shop, continue down the street. I was beginning to feel queasy surrounded by rich chocolates, jars and jars of sweets. I haven't eaten anything all morning, rarely do the days I see John-Paul. There's too much fear and longing in my stomach to leave room for eggs or toast. Though the whole damn rest of London appears to be indulging, judging by the smells – curries and fried onions, Kentucky Fried, kebabs. Someone's jabbed me with their cornet and smeared ice cream down my sleeve, and I've trodden on the belly of a discarded ketchupped bap. Walking in London requires very special skills. You could probably do a course in it – how to dodge umbrellas, or lighted cigarettes, how to glare at lovers who insist on holding hands, how not to fall down manholes, or waste small change on homeless drunks with placards. Five years ago, the homeless slumped on benches and left the world in peace. Now they're into Protest, waylay you with their outstretched hands, their broken scraps of life-story crayoned on strips of cardboard. 'Mick from County Cork. Homeless, hungry, penniless. Two kids back in Ireland. God bless you for your help.'

I toss him two pound coins, though I doubt if God will bless me. If He cared enough to bless people, He'd have put a stop to homelessness before it got this bad, and then reversed the Marriage Feast of Cana thing and turned the alcoholics' hard stuff into water.

There's water water everywhere, swirling in the gutters, sneaking down my neck. I wait at traffic lights to cross a huge main road. Lorries pant and rumble past – more splashes on my skirt – a bus disgorges passengers; a cyclist in a yellow cape weaves in and out of cars. Who are all these strangers – fellow human creatures, co-travellers on the Road of Life? Balls! They're rivals. Rivals for the living-space, the oxygen, resources. Rivals for the miracles, the lucky breaks, the love. Rivals for John-Paul.

I'm just three streets away now. The fear is near unbearable. I've already passed two accidents, assumed each one was him. He won't be there, I know it. I'll collapse. They'll cart me off, confine me in a straitjacket. I won't even be able to die, or join him in a burial plot. You can't swallow all your sleeping pills with your arms strapped round your body.

I try to calm myself by walking round in circles. I'm far too early anyway. It's only one o'clock and still his lunchtime. I presume he breaks for lunch. I often hang about and watch the other patients coming in and out, but at one-ten on a Monday, things are pretty quiet. He can't be very hungry if he's been sucking sweets all morning and suppressing any last frail shred of appetite with nicotine. Perhaps he does his filing then, or puts money on a horse. He must be pretty rich by now. All those fat three-figure cheques just for sucking sweets.

I slip into the College of Technology, which has the perfect combination of a near-moron at reception and a loo on the ground floor. I use the loo eight times each week

– before, to do my hair and face, and after, to throw up. No one seems to notice, or asks me to enrol. Even now, the moron's more concerned with picking out the chutney from her cheese and chutney sandwiches than with ousting an intruder. I dive into the ladies, dry my hair on yards and yards of toilet paper, scour my shoes and legs, then collapse onto a toilet seat for a good half-hour or so, listening to the voices, as folk come in and out. I've heard a lot of secrets in that toilet: adulteries, divorces, abortions, even shrinks.

At last, it's time to leave, though I'm so keyed up I can barely move at all now, and feeling almost feverish by the time I turn the corner to the tower. I never tell a soul I see John-Paul, but if I did confide, then went on to mention that he practised in a church tower without the adjoining church, they'd assume I was unhinged, but that's the honest truth. The tower is genuine Gothic, complete with pointed arches, buttresses, finials and turrets, even grinning gargoyles with chipped teeth and snaky hair. I take my usual minute to admire its sheer dimensions, its soaring upward thrust; crick my neck to gaze up at the steeple, which seems to rip right through the low and timid clouds, its triumphant cross pointing straight to God. I'm back in the late twelve hundreds, when God was still alive and all creation owned Him and His rules; when cool monastic refectories gave sustenance to travellers, in place of stifling Wimpy Bars, and the only serious traffic noise was the clack of hoofs on cobblestones, not Kawasakis tearing up the tarmac.

I let my eyes creep lower, wince, as always, at those incongruous modern office blocks with their glass and concrete facings, which squeeze the tower both sides, though are nothing like as dramatic or as high. The tower looks short of breathing-space, beleaguered and castrated without its nave and chancel, as if it's been captured by a smaller race and left a silent prisoner in the barbaric twentieth century, which doesn't speak the language of faith or aspiration, and where the only gods are dwarf ones like John-Paul. I imagine there were yew trees once, symbols of eternal life, and moss-encrusted gravestones, to guard the bodies of immortal souls returning Home to Father; now only litter-bins. I haven't yet discovered what happened to the rest of it. If somebody destroyed a church to make more room for offices, then why not its tower, as well, and how the hell did John-Paul lay his hands on it? Can you buy towers, just like houses, or rent them by the hour, and do they count as consecrated ground?

I'm sure John-Paul's not religious (which disappoints me, actually), so it's probably just a hang-up on his part – a phallic one, quite clearly, though a tower is so damned obvious I'd have thought he'd have the savvy to avoid it. Or maybe it's a power thing. I know he's very short, but all the same it seems a bit extreme to add two hundred feet to your stature by working in a tower. Unless it's simple swank. Other shrinks are content with rooms in Harley Street, or a snazzy Hampstead mansion in Freud's own NW3. Trust John-Paul to have to be unique. I suppose it also helps to keep away the boring geriatrics, the old or weak or crippled, who couldn't cope with all the stairs. Actually, his rooms are less than halfway up, but the stairs are steep and spiral and sometimes I can hardly cope myself. I take a minute's breather while I'm still safely on ground-level, then press the buzzer on the high-arched Gothic door, which opens straight on to the street with no path or fence or garden, not even any notice warning 'Church' or 'Shrink', 'Beware!'

Silence, shocking silence. I've pressed the buzzer twice now, but he hasn't said 'Come up.' I freeze, burn, faint, choke, expire. He's dead and buried – I knew it all along. My fingers shake and tremble as I lean them on the bell-push, then the entry-phone suddenly replies.

'*Yes?*' it says, in that steel-and-truffle voice of his, which registers displeasure while it oozes charm and breeding.

'It's Nial,' I stammer out.

'Come up, Nial,' he answers, as if he hasn't died at all, caused me all that anguish, made me a near-wreck. He had trouble with my name at first. A lot of people do. Nial is a boy's name, a fifth-century Irish king's name, which my father chose before I'd quite materialised. Nial comes from 'Niadh', which means 'champion', and I suppose my poor unlucky father was into wish-fulfilment and could see me with an athletics blue or crowned with laurel wreaths. He wouldn't change it anyway, though my mother added 'Maureen', to show I was a girl. Second names are hopeless, unless you're an author, or American. No one even knows them – just louses up your first one. Nobody can spell Nial, or pronounce it. You say 'ni' like 'nice', and not like 'knee'. John-Paul told me once that he thought my name might actually have contributed to my sense of unreality, since it's the stressed and central syllable of the word annihilation.

I suppose I should be grateful he uses my name at all. Classical psychoanalysts often avoid all names on principle, because they interfere with their famous blank-screen image, and may distort the transference (which is a sort of buzz-word with them, and feeds their self-importance, since it means you see them as your father, mother, brother, sister, lover, teacher, God). I had a client just last spring, who'd been in Freudian analysis for over twenty years, and the shrink never once used his name in three thousand five hundred and eighty-seven sessions – except on his endless bills, of course. That poor (anonymous) sod, who didn't know his own name by the time he quit at the age of sixty-five, was one of the main reasons I started analytic therapy myself. He made it sound so painful and frustrating, any natural masochist couldn't fail to be enchanted.

I start dragging up the endless stairs, up and round, up and round, with a sudden view of toytown streets from one

48

deep-embrasured window and the echo of my footsteps rising to John-Paul; then pause outside his rooms – one private where he naps or wanks, and the dim-lit round consulting room which I suppose is meant to represent the womb. Actually, the first time that I saw it I felt something close to awe. It *did* look like a womb, dark and claustrophobic, with all the curtains tightly drawn, so there seemed to be no windows, and that deep-hush carpet the colour of old blood, and the curving shielding walls. I seemed to recognise it, felt I'd been there long before, floated there nine months, in fact, lolling, dozing, sprouting hands and feet.

The door (or cervix?) is open, but I knock, to be polite. John-Paul never greets you, never says 'Hallo,' like any normal person would; let alone 'How are you?' It's all so damn impersonal – no friendly smile or hand-shake, no cosy little chat before you start the session, about the weekend or the weather, or what you did last night. It's part of their whole system, which I've started mugging up; dipping into Freud, or reading books on psychoanalysis, where before I read Nabokov and Paul Auster. Their aim is to be 'neutral' – neutral personalities, neutral in their attitudes – though you might translate the term as meaning aloof and uninvolved. They even have this so-called Rule of Abstinence, which is all to do with frustrating your deep longings for basic human contact, refusing to gratify your hunger for comfort or support. (They love words like 'gratification' – so long as they're withholding it.) They're basically just cold machines which give interpretations – no heart or hands – all head. Forget sympathy or friendship or even fellow feeling. I doubt you'd wrest a word of reassurance from them if your entire extended family had been wiped out in a nuclear attack.

I stand in rigid silence, eyes fixed on the floor. If I can't bring myself to raise my head, I've no proof he's there at all. That buzzer could be just a trick, a recording of his voice. I do look up, in fact. I've had enough bad scares already and it's the only glimpse I'll get of him the whole damn fifty minutes. I hold his gaze for one heart-stopping second; check his hair, his glasses, his suit, his shirt, his shoes. Yes, all complete, all there – even the pearl tiepin and the half-smoked cigarette. No heart, no warmth, no word, but then I'm used to that by now. Funny, though, it's still a shock every time I see him. It's as if it's never really him, not the him I've loathed or worshipped all those hours and hours, nor the one who gets entangled in my dreams, nor even the one I saw last week – or just the day before.

I hand him both his presents, try not to see his ring. It makes me mad, that ring. Oh, I know it's only sham, but you'd think he'd trust us, wouldn't you? I mean, all his female patients are hardly going to leap on him just because he's single. It's actually deceitful to pretend you're married when you're not, not to mention hypocritical, when you're a fully trained professional who's always stressing the importance of the whole and naked truth. One rule for the patients, another for the shrinks. He knows absolutely everything about us – our infatuations, fantasies, our dreams, our sexual oddities, our eating and excreting habits (even at the breast), our toilet-training, hobbies, hates and crimes – and we know almost nothing about him. Is he gay or straight or celibate, a solitary masturbator, or a wild polygamist? Does he vote Conservative, or sign petitions for the Greens? Is he constipated, anxious, scared of heights or moths? Does he do the washing up, or kick cats and dogs in private? Does he love his mother? Does he sail or jog or swim?

I snatch a quick glance at his tie. Ties are phallic symbols, so it's like examining his prick. The tie looks limp and drab, and has little squiggles on it which remind me of dead sperm. I kick off my wet shoes, lie down on the couch, and suddenly he's gone again, sitting right behind me, but removed now from my view. It never fails to screw me up, that strange and frightening moment when his face and body disappear, but his voice and mind and presence swoop dangerously nearer, seem huge and overwhelming, so that I myself shrink to just a pinprick – a flea, a mite, a speck, a dot, an ant. I'm a creature with no backbone, a mollusc with no shell, just a dab of limp pink protoplasm smeared across his couch. All the things I'd planned to say ooze and leak away. I haven't got a larynx, let alone a tongue.

I suppose I should talk molluscs if I were following the rule – their famous Fundamental Rule, which means you undertake to tell your shrink whatever comes into your head, without any reservation or exception, including murderous thoughts, sheer drivel, or outrageous sexual fantasies. It's a crazy sort of system, and would cause sheer bloody mayhem if you used it in your ordinary daily life – lose you all your friends in half a day. Actually, I often just ignore it, or sometimes deliberately confuse the issue by breaking it on purpose. I mean, if I'm lying on his couch thinking, say, about some client's testicles – Howard's, for example, whose right one hangs much lower than the left – I may actually start talking about a black cat I owned (or didn't own) called Persil, who was run over by a car, but never mention bollocks. I suppose I've always had an urge to break the rules, and this is one you can break and get away with, since John-Paul's none the wiser.

If I were following it now, I'd be talking about not following it (if you understand my meaning), but instead I keep my silence. The minutes tick-tick by: three separate whispered naggings. I'll strangle those damn clocks one day; smash their smug glass faces. Trust him to have three – and all exactly right, so I can't even steal a second's extra time. John-Paul's obsessed with time. First he splits his day up into different-shaped segments from other normal people's (which helps to make him richer, since you can cram in far more patients over twenty years or so, if you slice ten minutes off each hour, but still insist on calling it an hour, and still charge a hefty fee for it). Then he examines all our deep unconscious reasons for being early, late, or even merely punctual, and if we feel a mite aggrieved at being rationed or short-changed, he'll go groping back to infancy again and interpret that as grievance with our mother for depriving us of a satisfying breast.

'Bull!' I say to no one, as I outstare the largest clock. If you add his watch and mine and the church clock down the road, which chimes each and every quarter (and still often makes me jump), that's six separate time-machines, all fuelling his obsession, making me more tense. Suddenly it strikes, booming from the street outside, as if I've given it its cue. 'Ssh,' I tell it irritably, as its reverberations shudder through my skull. Quarter past. I've been lying here three minutes and it feels like two whole decades.

John-Paul doesn't speak. That's not his job; it's mine. I usually burst out with something, just through desperation – if not cats or testicles, then mortuaries or wives. Not today. I stare up at the ceiling – dingy white and cracked – then round at the dark walls which are hung with several pictures: tortured writhing abstracts which look as if they've been finger-painted by the most violent of his patients. There's not much in the room except the couch, his chair, three telephones, another chair (for patients who have hang-ups about lying down, or rape), and a sort of antique bureau thing with a bronze bust standing on it of a small man with a beard – maybe Freud, or even Christ. I asked him who it was, once, and he said I was avoiding the issue of my prenatal regression with inconsequential questions.

He hates me asking questions, rarely answers anyway, or only with another question like why am I asking such and such, and by the time I've tried to answer *that*, and he's both questioned my reply and revealed the contradictions

52

in the question and the answer, I'm so thoroughly confused I've forgotten where we started. You can see why analytic treatment takes so long. It's one step forward, four steps back, and instead of being satisfied with just the normal human problems like jobs and sex and money, or even infancy and childhood, he goes back further still, adds a whole lot more, like constriction in the womb because your mother wore tight corsets (which could give you headaches as an adult and a sense of claustrophobia), or even problems at conception. I suppose it secures him a good income, keeps his patients clocking in decade after decade, as they work slowly back from babyhood to their aggression as mere egg-cells or their sense of inferiority as unfertilised gametes.

I keep gazing round the room, which contains absolutely nothing you might describe as personal – no books except his textbooks and the medical *Who's Who*, no photographs of families (not even borrowed ones), no ornaments or trinkets, not even a small plant. I suppose he's scared a plant might die on him, like so many of his patients. He's got quite a reputation for successful suicides. Well, at least the poor sods showed resolve. John-Paul told me once it was better to make a decision, even an unwise one, than to keep dithering and fretting. I can hear a siren now, as an ambulance screams by – another of his patients being speeded to the stomach-pump too late.

I clear my throat, to prove I'm there. No answering cough or rustle. He may have nodded off, though it's difficult to sleep, in fact, with all the constant traffic noise roaring down below. The traffic makes me sad. More rivals, faceless strangers, potential suicides, filling in the void by driving fast from A to B, or back from B to A.

'A,' I whisper suddenly, which I suppose must be significant since it's the beginning of the alphabet, the highest grade in marking, the indefinite article, a note in music, a blood group and a bomb. All that rich material and he doesn't say a word. I'm not sure he even heard. Another siren started the second that I spoke, which seems significant itself. Analytic therapy is so damned complicated. Everything's significant, especially things you'd think were not, like non sequiturs or throat-clearings.

I daren't say 'B', in case he thinks I'm fooling, though 'B' is probably even more significant than 'A' ('To be or not to be . . .'), so I continue with the silence and even shut my eyes, to kid him I'm relaxed. It's really just a test of nerves. Will he crack first, or me? I can't hear a single sound from him, which really is unusual. I'm just beginning to wonder if he's actually left the room, backed away on tiptoe to down a double Scotch, when I catch a furtive rustle. The chocolates. He's unwrapping one. I knew he couldn't last that long without a puff or nibble. I listen to fat hazelnuts crunching in his teeth.

'Pig!' I say, though silently. The trouble with silence is that the longer it goes on the more unnerving it becomes. You know you're wasting money – at least a pound a minute – and that eventually he'll use words like 'resistance', or suggest you're quiet because you're angry with him. Everything goes back to *him*. He's the Centre of the Universe; likes nothing better than have you talk about him, dream about him, fixate on him or flatter him – then charge you for the privilege. The small-guy syndrome once again. I suppose they have to get power somehow. I dreamed about a woman once, who was ten foot tall with mammoth breasts, and he still claimed it was him; said the dream contained a reversal of the sexes, so that he was disguised in it as my all-powerful nurturing mother.

He's nurturing him*self* now; so busy with those fucking ritzy chocolates, he's forgotten I exist. I can hear the steady munching, which is deafening in my ear. Although I can't see him, he's sitting really close, his armchair almost touching the head-end of the couch, so that every sound is magnified (and hazelnuts are lethal).

'You didn't thank me,' I suddenly burst out.

'For what, Nial?' His voice is very gentle. That's just more provocation, a rotten subtle creepy sort.

'You never do, do you? If I bought you the whole sweet-shop, you still wouldn't say a word.'

'Why d'you think you need my thanks?'

I kick out at the leather couch, hope I've left a bruise on it. 'And how about offering *me* a chocolate? I'm real, you know, not just stuffed or bronze or something. I've got a mouth and stomach. And actually . . .' I swallow. 'I'm very fond of sweets.'

There's a sort of pregnant pause, then he speaks all soft and suave again. 'It seems your orality is such, you have rather a low tolerance of anyone enjoying oral gratification which you can't share yourself.'

'Oh, bugger off.'

More silence – which is broken by the spluttering of a match. I've obviously annoyed him. He's got to smoke, to calm himself, stop himself from shouting. He probably kicked the habit just last night, made a resolution that he'd never smoke again, threw away his lighter in some big symbolic gesture. I've spoilt his good intentions, maybe even killed him, indirectly. The risk of lung cancer for smokers is at least twenty times the rate of that for non-smokers. (I know – I stopped myself – and not that long ago. It wasn't lungs, but bowels. They suspected I had a tumour on the colon, and though I didn't mind the death bit, or even the two x-rays, I just couldn't bear the thought of dying from something so totally unromantic – John-Paul sitting in that hospice by my bedside, holding not my hand, but my colostomy bag.)

I begin to feel new terror as I switch roles in the hospice – John-Paul as the patient now, coughing up his lungs. His death would kill me outright. (So would just his anger.) I long to make atonement, to crouch down at his feet and feed him chocolates on my knees; masticate them first so he won't spoil his small sharp teeth, swap chocolate-flavoured kisses. No – kisses aren't atonement, kisses are sheer greed. He's telling me I'm greedy. I hate him, I detest him.

I can see his tiny wife, her tiny pretty shoes, her cloud of golden curls, her flirty cloudless eyes. He's pulling off her wrapper, biting into her. She's strawberry cream inside, or pink and white marshmallow, all soft and sweet and pastel. He wouldn't unwrap *me*, or he'd regret it if he did. I'd be hard unyielding nougat, or dark and gristly toffee. He's sucking out her cream, the last swirls and coils of mallow melting on his tongue, its tip probing her soft shell, lapping round and round it.

I leap up from the couch, pace up and down the room. Of *course* he didn't give up smoking – he hasn't got the willpower. He was smoking when I first came in. He probably smokes in bed, lights his wife, inhales her, sucks her right right in. I jab my foot against the skirting, speak to the brown wall. 'And why do you wear that fucking stupid ring, when you know damn well you haven't got a wife?'

'So a part of you would like to kill my wife.' His voice all corny low still; a crackle of gold paper.

'I've killed her, don't you worry. And it was a pretty nasty death.'

'That doesn't seem to accord too well with your repeated claims to be peaceable and gentle.'

'I'm only violent with your wife – wives.'

'But you say I haven't got a wife.'

'Well, *have* you?'

He dodges the question, as he's done a dozen times; asks me why I'm giving motility to my feelings, instead of verbalising. God – their language! All he means in plain no-nonsense English is why the hell I'm raving round his room instead of lying still and talking. I drag back to the

56

couch, flop down on the pillow. You're not allowed to work off your frustration on the carpet or the walls, but have to just lie quietly and yak about the breast, or womb, or last night's footling dream. I shake back all my hair, start twisting one long strand of it. 'My mother didn't *have* breasts, if you really want to know.'

Here we go again. It's so tedious, so boring, though maybe not for him. All his favourite subjects – maternal deprivation, ambivalence about the breast, dependence on it, rage at it, insatiability, orality. They're all his own problems, that's quite obvious. Why else all that sucking? (I can hear more rustles now, smell peppermints – those fierce ones.) It's just another subtle way of talking about himself, using me as his ventriloquist. But if I slam out now (as I did in fact last week), there'll be still more aching minutes to tot up, and I'll only have to face an inquisition at ten past two tomorrow. I close my eyes, swap my mother for his own, make her mean and scrawny, thin and stern and cold; make sure she looks like him – dark hairs on her thumbs, non-existent eyes.

'She just had nipples,' I explain, though he knows it all himself, must have bored his own analyst with the pathetic endless details. 'But even they were covered with these transparent Perspex shields, so you could see the teat, but never actually touch it with your mouth, let alone suck milk from it. There wasn't any milk, only water, or white vinegar, and her womb was made of scarlet steel, so every time you moved position or tried to kick or float, you bruised your tiny growing limbs or banged your still-soft head or . . .'

I smile. I'm in my stride now. He's sucking quite contentedly, the clocks are ticking slower, their three voices like a lullaby. I'm feeding him, I'm filling him, I've made him almost happy, and there hasn't even been a siren for five blessed peaceful minutes.

Dear Mummy,

I'd like to come back home. You could fetch me on Fryday when everyones at games. I don't play games. I hurt my leg. It bled a lot but your not allowed to cry here.

Thank you for the sweets. Fraser knocked me down and stole them. I saved two dirty ones.

Love, Jonathan.

# 5

'Have you considered, Mary, that your apparent concern about your son may be an identification with the child-part of yourself – that small shy child who was also sent away to boarding school at a very early age and missed its home and mother?'

Mary wiped her eyes. Friday was Weeping Day, as well as John-Paul Day. The two went hand in hand. She hadn't had a session yet in which she hadn't cried. She brought her own Kleenex now, a large box of the man-size. John-Paul had those small ones called 'Boutique', which were chic and very pretty, but tended to disintegrate.

'I *liked* my school,' she sobbed.

John-Paul stroked his chin, moved one foot a fraction. 'In insisting that you liked your school, you appear to be questioning what I've said.'

She frowned and chewed her Kleenex. Of course she questioned it – questioned most things now. John-Paul had made her thoroughly bewildered. Things she'd known for twenty years kept unravelling and crumbling – solid things like love or God or marriage. She tried to think about herself, instead of Jonathan. He'd gone down with tonsillitis and a temperature, yet still they wouldn't allow him to come home. She'd chosen a get-well card with a nice green frog on it, and packed him up some throat sweets and a new pair of pyjamas with a warm ribbed polo neck. She'd have liked to send his bear, as well, but . . .

'Since both your parents were abroad and therefore unavailable, it seems you invested your emotions in the only possible substitute – your school.'

She looked up swiftly, guiltily; had almost forgotten where she was. 'It wasn't their fault, honestly. They were posted to Dakar, Doctor, when I was only seven. And it was an extremely good school, anyway. They chose it very carefully.'

'Good?'

'Yes, very good. The nuns were a French Order who really . . . Well, you know the sort of thing – high standards and no slacking and a nice smart uniform.'

'But did that mean good for *you*, Mary?'

'I did very well at school, Doctor – not in my exams. I made a mess of those, but I was a Child of Mary and captain of lacrosse . . .'

'And cried every night in bed for two whole years.'

She blushed. 'I'm afraid I cry quite easily. I'm sorry.'

'Are you apologising to me, or to your mother?'

'My *mother*?' He made things so confusing. Her mother had been dead for fifteen years. Died in harness, people said. Charlotte Alice Delahaye had always been so busy, so devoted – devoted to the Africans, the natives – banishing illiteracy, disease. She often wished she had her mother's skills: her brain, her strength, her courage in adversity, the way she really lived her Catholic faith. John-Paul was right – she'd been a disappointment – a shy and clinging child who had kept crying to come home (though she wasn't sure where 'home' was, since her parents moved a lot, not just from house to house, but from continent to continent); then an awkward bashful teenager who'd been prone to eczema and flunked all her exams, and finally a tame suburban housewife. No degrees in anthropology, or doctorates in political science, no high ideals, no desire to save the world or serve her God. What had happened to her parents' genes, she often wondered, guiltily? Her mother had been a saint, a pioneer; her father a philanthropist, reformer.

Lionel Ernest Delahaye was still very much alive, though

60

she saw him only rarely. He was still too busy – yes, even in his eighties. Her parents had conceived her very late; had more important things to do in their brisk and tireless twenties, their zealous thrusting thirties, than simply making babies; had waited till their forties to produce their only child – though even then there hadn't been much time. She'd been born two months prematurely, as if her mother had lost patience with the passive tedious pregnancy, couldn't wait the whole nine months when there were vital projects piling up, life and death decisions hanging on her word. She – the wretched infant – had almost died, in fact, and been rushed to neonatal, a nuisance from day one. Her mother told her, some time later, that just one machine in intensive care, which helped to save a few small and puny babies, cost more than what was desperately required to feed a whole village in Nepal.

She'd mentioned it to John-Paul once – not Nepal, just neonatal. 'Do you recall anything at all of the experience?' he'd asked. He *did* have strange ideas. Remember things at only one day old! 'No,' she'd said. 'My memory's a total blank till nursery school at four. But my mother said the doctors were quite wonderful.'

She stared down at the carpet. It wasn't very clean. Did John-Paul have domestic help, someone to look after him? It couldn't be that easy lugging Hoovers up those stairs. He was definitely too thin, probably wasn't eating, just making do on snacks or sweets, with no proper nourishment. Though she liked men with that sort of build – not bluff and broad, as James was, but slender and refined-looking, a charming man of average height who didn't dwarf or swamp her, and with those lovely slim artistic hands, not James's carpet-beaters. His skin was rather sallow, though, which could mean liver trouble, or perhaps just a lack of God's fresh air. But how could he get out for daily exercise when it was patients, patients, patients, dawn to dusk? She knew he was too busy because

61

when she'd phoned to inquire about appointments, he'd said at first he couldn't fit her in, simply didn't have a space, but then he'd rung her back to say another patient who'd been due to start that week had suddenly been posted overseas, so he could offer her Fridays at five-ten. He also said he'd keep her on his waiting-list, since once a week was clearly not enough. It seemed an awful lot to her, and she was really quite astonished to hear many of his patients attended three or four times weekly. However did they do their jobs, or get dinner cooked in time, and the cost must be prohibitive?

She closed her eyes a moment, still aware of John-Paul watching her, his gaze piercing her closed lids. His own eyes were quite remarkable – dark and very lustrous, like the eyes men had in early silent movies when only eyes could speak – eloquent observant eyes, reacting to her every word, narrowing in sympathy, or clouding with her pain. He sometimes wore dark glasses, which she could completely understand. Too much pain must hurt, like too much light. Though he was sitting naked-eyed now – yes, even in the sun, which was flouncing through the window, beribboning his chest like some sash or badge of rank – and observing her so closely, she felt nervous, almost guilty. She'd had a dog like that once, who'd watched her while she ate, following every tiny movement of her fork or spoon or hand with dark reproachful eyes. In the end, she couldn't eat at all, or was forced to snatch a quick snack-lunch while he was gobbling down his Chum. *Pedigree* Chum. John-Paul was a pedigree – you could tell that by his suits, his large and stately car – a vintage Daimler, wasn't it, in simple tasteful black? – and also by his lean fastidious face, the way he'd pared his body to essentials, instead of lugging round a vulgar load of flesh. All the same, it wasn't wise to give up proper meals. Every time she cooked these days, she was tempted to make extra, bring it in a casserole, make sure he got his protein.

She shifted on her seat, wished he'd speak or even move; hated these stiff silences, which seemed rather impolite. She was sure it was his turn. She'd spoken last, hadn't she – though to tell the truth, she couldn't even remember what she'd said, had lost the thread completely. Perhaps John-Paul had lost it, too. He did look slightly strained, was probably tired from all his other patients, who were bound to ramble on a lot and have quite ferocious problems – lust and greed and murderous hate stalking through his room all day; tempests raging round him; perversions, vices, furies, detonating hour by frenzied hour.

It might be kinder, really, to let him have a breathing-space, just sit there very quietly and allow him to relax. In fact, that would suit her beautifully. She found it quite impossible to discuss the basic reason she was there – what James called . . . well, best leave all that alone. She'd done what James suggested – gone to see 'one of those trick cyclist chaps' – been absolutely terrified at first, ashamed and quite humiliated, but now a whole five weeks had passed and they hadn't even mentioned double beds. John-Paul seemed more concerned with absent mothers – if and when he talked at all. She felt almost a real pleasure now, writing 'John-Paul' in her diary every Friday, instead of 'Church Bazaar', or 'Plumber', or 'Collect James's suit from cleaner's'. She especially liked the way he invested her most trite remarks with such seriousness and import she could have been the Pope, speaking infallibly, ex cathedra, to and for the Church, instead of just a boring housewife who still didn't know the difference between a psychiatrist, a psychologist, and a psychoanalyst.

It was nice of him to listen so intently. People rarely did. Even at the hairdresser's, where she often talked quite happily about the children, or the price of beef, or their plans for next year's holiday, the girls weren't really interested; muddled up Jonathan with Simon, or the Azores with the Algarve, butted in with tales about their boyfriends, or kept shouting to each other against the racket of the hair driers, whereas John-Paul seemed to soak up every word, listen with his eyes as well as ears; listen with his body, even with his hands.

She glanced up at the wall. There was dust on all the picture frames – he really did need help. The pictures were those clever kind; not harvest scenes at sunset or Cornish fishing ports, like they had back home at Walton, but the sort of modern dangerous things they bought for the Tate Gallery, which had no right (or wrong) way up, and always made James angry because they wasted public money. But bar wasteful threatening pictures, she loved being in the tower. It was so unusual, so romantic, such a change from Sainsbury's. Towers belonged to fairy tales – which had been rationed in her childhood – princesses dangling braids from them, princes clambering up. She had fed her sons on fairy tales: Snow Queens with their Ricicles, fairy godmothers for tea. But they'd all preferred Space Invaders, and even Jon got restless now if she mentioned wicked stepmothers, or tried to explain the difference between an ogre and a troll.

She closed her eyes a second, imagined John-Paul in her nursery, reclining in the ayah's chair in the cool white house in Delhi, murmuring 'Once upon a time . . .' She was sitting on his lap, though the lap was rather bony, which forced her back to casseroles. They might give him indigestion if he had to eat them quickly, bolt them between patients who'd have no thought for his stomach and might pollute his digestive juices with their problems, like people dumping sewage in a river. Or he could be vegetarian, as artists often were. She supposed he was an artist – sculpting people, moulding them, writing happy endings. Fruit would be more practical, and probably better for him. There were no apples in the garden. James had been too busy to prune their moody fruit trees, and though she'd offered several times, he said she'd only ruin them. He didn't have much confidence in any of her skills. Before her marriage she'd been a West End secretary – well, almost a PA – with good speeds at shorthand typing and her own complex filing system. She'd suggested going back to work, now that Jon had left the nest, but James had put his foot down, said modern office methods would be totally beyond her.

She could buy fruit from the greengrocer, pretend they had a glut. 'Our garden's overflowing, so I wondered if you'd do us a good turn and relieve us of these apples. I've also brought some pears, John-Paul, and . . .'

'What are you thinking, Mary?'

She jumped. 'Er . . . pears,' she stammered out. You weren't allowed to lie – well, white lies about the contents of your garden, but no deliberate falsification of the contents of your mind.

'*Pairs?*'

She nodded.

John-Paul raised his voice a little, to compete with an articulated lorry. 'We were talking earlier about your parents, and of course they were a pair – a couple – and pairs can be a strong focus of resentment if you feel excluded from them. You probably experienced such feelings very early on, since your parents were away together and you here at school in England.'

Mary's mind was still on fruit – Comice pears, Conference pears. She took refuge in a Kleenex, not to cry, to blow. Her eyes were stinging anyway, always did in smoky rooms. She didn't like to tell him she was concerned about his diet, rather than her parents. It might sound far too personal, and maybe even critical. He'd been so kind himself, never criticised or taunted, or turned on her as James did, called her dead from the waist down, or Mrs Frigidaire, or just another bloody bolster in the bed. He hadn't even mentioned bed, must realise it embarrassed her and be keeping off it purposely.

The only problem was she wasn't making any progress, and James was getting tetchy, kept asking what the fancy chap was doing, when he paid him through the nose.

They'd had another argument, just this Wednesday night. She'd *truly* had a headache, often did at bedtime. It was probably an allergy to the foam they used in pillows now, instead of proper feathers. James was much more irritable since he'd stopped smoking in July. She wished John-Paul would stop. She'd rather have him irritable than her Fridays dead from cancer. He must be short of vitamins. Nicotine destroyed them, especially vitamin C. Was there C in pears and apples? She'd have to look it up, or maybe buy him blackcurrants which were the richest source of all.

John-Paul struck a match. It sounded more impatient than his normal purring matches, and his left foot had started twitching, as if in reprimand. It was probably her turn again and she'd forgotten where they were. He'd asked her something, hadn't he – when Jonathan came home.

'The thirteenth of December,' she replied.

John-Paul frowned a moment, as he inhaled his cigarette. 'The thirteenth of December? I wonder what that signifies to you, or why you should suddenly come out with it? Superstitious people might see it as unlucky.'

'Unlucky! I can hardly wait. It's the fifteenth for the other two, but they're far less a problem. I suppose it's my own fault. I've always babied Jonathan. He was small, you see, and premature and . . .'

'As *you* were.'

'He's got this tonsillitis. I can't help worrying. He's always had a weakness in his throat. The Matron there's quite callous. I mean, she wouldn't let me visit *or* allow him home. She'd never had children of her own. I'm sure that makes a difference – don't you think I'm right, Doctor?

66

And I'm not keen on the Head. I mean, I know James says he's sound, but . . .'

'I do understand you're feeling very vulnerable, so that you keep identifying with Jonathan, who is ill and weak at present, as you clearly see yourself.'

'I don't feel ill at all, Doctor. In fact, I'm never ill; haven't had a day in bed for years. But Jonathan is more like his poor Grandpa. They're both really far too sensitive, tend to . . .'

'Mary, if you lay down on the couch, you might feel more relaxed. Some patients find it easier to free-associate when no one's actually looking at them and their minds are free to wander.'

'Oh, no, Doctor, no really. I . . .'

'I notice you use the word "Doctor" nearly every time you speak to me. I wonder if you feel the need to maintain a barrier between us, or create a sense of distance?'

'But you *are* a doctor, aren't you? I mean, I thought James said . . .' Her voice had petered out. John-Paul's voice took over.

'I suspect you're using my professional title as a defensive manoeuvre because of your fear of informality, your need to avoid any sense of closeness or feeling of personalisation.'

Mary scrunched another Kleenex, mopped her sweaty hands. It was surely plain good manners to use a person's title. Jonathan's headmaster was very hot on it – 'Sir' for all the masters; 'My Lord' for the Bishop when he officiated at Prize Day. She hoped Jonathan would win a prize. He was doing very well, in fact, but if they neglected his bad throat, that could threaten his whole . . .

'Perhaps you'd like to experiment with lying on the couch – just try it for the last ten minutes, to find out how it feels, see how you react. It sometimes helps patients to come closer to their inner world, get in touch with their unconscious.'

Mary gripped both chair-arms. She hated the unconscious, saw it like a lavatory, somewhere strictly private where you always went alone and locked the door, then flushed away the evidence as quickly as you could, so it wouldn't smell, or embarrass the next occupant. Boarding schools and mothers she could cope with, more or less, but not sewers, cesspools, shameful private smells. Yet both John-Paul's feet were twitching now, and he was looking almost pained – the first time in five whole sessions. She stumbled to her feet, crossed the space from chair to couch, which seemed a mile, at least. She was trembling as she reached the brute black leather, could hardly force her buttons through the buttonholes or coax her skirt zip down.

'You don't have to undress; just remove your shoes.'

'I'm sorry, Doctor. I thought I . . .' She could hardly speak for sheer confusion. If she lay down at the surgery, it always meant clothes off. Though there was invariably a nurse there, a female chaperone, and some point to lying down – some pain or cyst or polyp which could be checked in just two minutes. If she lay down on this couch, she had a rather frightening feeling that she might never stagger up again till several years had passed. She'd avoided analysis on principle, as long-drawn-out, and foreign, and probably highly dangerous (not to mention 'ruinous' – James's word when he'd received the first month's bill). All she needed really was a little simple counselling, something short and basic, and strictly to please James, who'd first picked up the idea of sexual therapy from a new late-night series on Channel Four, which he watched avidly, voraciously, then condemned as porn.

She'd been astonished he'd suggested it all. It seemed so out of character – except he was clearly getting desperate about what he saw as her inadequacies in bed. He'd actually phoned the programme to request their 'fact-sheet' and 'resource guide', but when he'd finally made contact with some real-life sexual therapists, they all expected *him* to come, as well. One had even offered to act as surrogate partner for his wife, if he were having 'difficulties' himself. He'd been so scandalised, affronted, he'd reacted with extreme relief to the suggestion of a different sort of therapist, who would take a less intrusive line, approach the body via the mind – to start with, anyway – leave him safely out of it, and not expect to bed down with his wife. All the same, she herself had still felt most uneasy. *Any* sort of therapy suggested you were not 'all there', and if the neighbours ever twigged to it, they might label her a mental case and stop inviting her for coffee. There was also the pressing problem of the Church. Her parish priest would strongly disapprove of the shocking things they'd mentioned on that programme; the casual, even eager, way they'd tossed off words she'd never dared to whisper in her life – and broadcast to an audience of millions. But at least they'd all sat upright in nice no-nonsense chairs, whereas John-Paul was changing tack now, switching from the vertical to the threatening horizontal.

She still felt completely paralysed, had no idea how to lie down on a couch. Did one put a knee up, then swivel round and back, or just perch in the centre and swing one's legs up last? She couldn't see John-Paul now, but she could almost hear his feet tapping, his slim impatient fingers drumming on the chair-arm.

She half-fell onto the couch, clutching at her skirt so it wouldn't show her stocking tops, wincing as her fingers touched her burn scars. She'd hardly felt her wounds at all until this very moment, had totally forgotten her spiritual bouquet, despite the talk of convents, her excitement all the week. She'd forgotten the important things, the penances, the pain. But now she was all pain. The simple act of lying on a couch seemed to have plunged her back in time, cancelled out her entire thirty-five years of life, so she was a tiny naked infant weighing under forty ounces; tubes stuck through her body, lights dazzling her weak eyes. The doctor's voice was booming nearer, nearer – terrifying, thundering – six masked faces framing his each side. She could see his blinding long white coat, his gigantic hands swooping pouncing lower, until they were clamped against her limbs. Towers of steel and plastic reared up all around her, screens flickering, dials flashing, the pant and gulp of life-machines assaulting her dead body; her stomach pumped with fluids, her lungs jacked up with air. They couldn't know she'd died.

She was lying in a coffin, a coffin made of glass. Nobody could touch her, except that doctor for a moment, and even he had vanished. They had shut her in alone, left her corpse to putrefy. She tried to scream – impossible – too much in her mouth. It was crammed with tubes and rubber, foul with blood and slime. She couldn't even cry. She'd been born without tears, born without a lot of things, including skills and strength. She tried tugging at the wires, which were trailing from her stomach, hurting in her nose, but she could hardly close her fists around them, let alone dislodge them. She heard a tiny bone snap, somewhere in her body; a chilling wind gusting through her ribs. They had already cut her open, slipped odd bits and pieces in, taken things away. She was scarred and stitched and bruised now, purple mottlings livid on both legs, streaks of blood caked around the stitches, her small head bald and shaven. That's why no one wanted her – she was ugly and disfigured – a runt, an obvious reject they'd left naked and uncovered. She wasn't cold, just horribly ashamed; her private parts exposed, a pool of liquid excrement oozing from her bottom.

They had given her a teddy, a blue plush-velvet rabbit. She'd rather have had her mother, the pink plush-velvet mother whom she'd met for just a second before the Monsters in the Masks had snatched her up and trapped her in the cage, rammed her gag in, snapped her handcuffs shut. She hadn't seen her mother since, though she'd been calling her and calling her, through gags and tubes and muzzles, calling silently but desperately, for hours and days and weeks now. Had her mother died, as well, or rushed straight back to Delhi to feed her other babies, the black ones, the beloved ones, who deserved her love, were worthy of her presence?

She listened for a moment. Beyond the bleeps and boomings, she could hear someone clearly sobbing, a deep and desperate sobbing. Could it be her father, weeping for her death? Or someone else's father mourning someone else's death? People died a lot here – faces disappearing, doctors dashing in. She peered at her own hand. It was shrivelling already, heavy bands of sticking plaster pinioning both wrists. It was hard to move at all. She was lying on her back, her legs hunched up, her arms pinned back, eyes smarting from the glare.

Somebody was coming. Footsteps crashing closer, huge hands hot and heavy on her flesh. She must be still alive. They didn't touch the dead ones, just flung them into dustbin-bags, then burnt them in an oven. Life meant hope – she'd heard the midwife murmur that, the first second of her life, that thrilling searing second when she'd touched her mother's belly, groped wildly for the nipple – until the gloved hands hauled her back. Of course she must keep hoping, keep screaming for her mother till some tiny sound emerged, and her mother picked the sound up in Delhi or Dakar and came rushing home, arms open. She tried to spit the gag out, make the doctors understand. The tall one had returned now. She could smell his sweat, his powerful acrid male smell, hear his brutal cocksure voice drilling through her skull.

'No, we won't do a tracheotomy. She'll be dead within the hour.'

She made one last racking effort – thrashing, wrestling,

fighting cage and gag – her tiny muscles tearing as she summoned strengths she knew she didn't have. Another voice was thrumming now, right behind her head; another hateful doctor only waiting to destroy her.

'What's the matter, Mary? If the sun's too bright, you only have to say, you know, and I can simply draw that curtain.'

# SHOPPING LIST

olive oil
alarm clock
candles
cigarettes
feather pillows (real)
multi-vitamins (check C)
apples
pears
blackcurrants
peaches
nectarines
broom handle
rubber gloves
crucifix
strong chain

# 6

Bryan trailed along the corridor, shuffled back again. He really must go in now. If he left it any later, he'd have to squeeze past rows of legs to find an empty place, might tread on feet, knock knees. It was bad enough starting four weeks late. The others would all know each other, know about the subject. At least he'd got the reading-list, ploughed through over half of it, though actually it had made him feel far worse.

He glanced in through the door, almost turned and fled. Faces, faces, faces; closed and grim-lipped faces. They all looked brainy, highbrow – probably physicists, astronomers, who understood that tide of books he'd been struggling with all week. A few dreary Older Women in lace-up shoes and cardigans, with impressive-looking clipboards already open on their laps, and two terrifying punk girls – the sort who wore one earring and hated men on principle, especially men in suits. He should have brought his slacks and blazer into work, changed clothes in the gents. But there just hadn't been the time. The class began at six-fifteen and he'd been working till ten to. He'd dared not skive off early when he'd been away for eight whole days.

Asian 'flu, the sick-note said. It had started as a lie which he'd invented for John-Paul to explain his six missed sessions, though it was difficult explaining things to a suspicious answerphone.

'Hallo. This is 246 2321. John-Paul is not available at present, but . . .'

He'd been so panicky the first time, he'd simply put the phone down. The second time he'd only got as far as his colleague in the office who'd remarked how pale he was, and how that very afternoon he'd started feeling . . . when the machine just cut him off. The third time he spoke faster, stuttered out the symptoms he'd discovered in the *Reader's Digest Medical Companion* which belonged to his Mother and was full of slips of paper saying 'Ring Desmond' and 'Feed cat' (which unsettled him still further, since they didn't know a Desmond and had never owned a cat). The machine was not impressed. He could hear its heavy breathing in the background – its long accusing silence, sudden sneering click of disbelief. When, at last, John-Paul rang him back, he *had* developed 'flu, perhaps from guilt or desperation; now had every symptom in the *Medical Companion*, plus several more unlisted. Yet John-Paul still seemed suspicious, displayed no scrap of sympathy for his pounding head and weak-as-water legs. If you dared to miss a session, he accused you of 'resistance'. 'Resistance' was a broken leg, pneumonia, angina. It was also very expensive, since he still charged you for the time. Those six nonexistent sessions would figure all too solidly on his next steep monthly bill.

He'd finally slunk back, still weak and pale and aching and hardly able to climb the spiral stairs. John-Paul had quite alarmed him, made his 'flu so complicated he was amazed he had survived it. It was also clearly his own fault. Words like 'conversion hysteria', 'regression' and 'denial' left him feeling guilty and ashamed – even when he didn't understand them. He'd already had a grilling from his Mother, though of a rather different kind. Had he gone out in the wet without his raincoat, or been sitting next to people who had germs?

He wondered where to sit now. Germs were all invisible, so he might catch something else, however carefully he tried to choose his neighbours. Being ill had always been a worry – letting people down at work; being subject to his Mother and her 'nursing' (which included cod liver oil and senna pods, whatever his complaint); failing his next life-insurance medical – but since he'd been going to John-Paul it had become still more alarming. Sore throats, indigestion, even common toothache, were never simple ailments caused by germs or faulty diet, but deep-seated neuroses expressing (or repressing?) hostility, or fear of sex, or even parsimoniousness, in the case of constipation. He'd been constipated for years, but mainly because his Mother would stand outside the lavatory reminding him to wash his hands and not to splash the lino when he did so. John-Paul often mentioned potty-training, but he'd never had a potty. His Mother disapproved of them, had perched him on the toilet-seat from the age of eleven months; held him very stiffly with her face screwed up and her mouth a narrow line – or so he recalled her in his later vivid images.

Strange how bowels kept cropping up in therapy – bowels and breasts and wombs. Even this evening-class was connected with the womb. He hadn't fully followed John-Paul's line of reasoning (had felt too drained and shivery to listen with his usual mix of fear and concentration); just got the general message that he must stand up to his Mother and insist on one night out. That was doubly worrying, since John-Paul almost never gave advice; seemed to be acting out of character, as if he were becoming so frustrated with his patient's lack of progress, he was trying to force the pace, suggesting a new project and procedure – not reading-lists or science books, but an exercise in lessening his dependency, weaning him from the breast he loved to hate.

It had taken courage – worse, required decisions – a whole tangled snarl and pother of decisions: where he'd go and when; which class, which night, which institute? He'd lain awake at night comparing The English Country House with Industrial Archaeology or Karate for Beginners; the City Literary Institute with Ruxley Hill Community

Centre and Greycoat Lower School. And suppose the class were full? Enrolment had been weeks ago, with queues at all the centres. He'd barge in as a new boy, ignorant, superfluous; be turned away in public. Still, a disco would be worse, or amateur dramatics, or a ballroom-dancing class, all of which he had considered as alternatives. He shuddered at the thought of the slow foxtrot, or playing the vicar or the cuckold in some vulgar Brian Rix farce. At least night-school was anonymous, without your name in lights.

In the end, he'd chosen (chosen?) the Winston Churchill Centre, simply because it was the nearest to John-Paul's, which made him feel a little safer, slightly less alone. If the fears got unendurable, he could always sprint back to the shelter of the tower, stand outside it, leaning on the stone. (Old stone was strong and solid, which he'd never be himself.) And he'd finally plumped for Friday, though only after wrestling with the pros and cons of each and every evening, setting them out in different combinations on twenty separate lists. Friday was his worst night, since it was stitched to the weekend, so by arriving home at ten instead of seven, he could dock it (and his Mother) by three hours.

His Mother had been querulous when at last he'd dared to mention it, blackmailed him with tears, tales of rapist-burglars who were bound to strike on Friday – which was also late night at the supermarket where other (decent loving) sons helped their mothers push the trolley. She'd mentioned her bad leg, of course – that guilt-inducing swollen leg which had shadowed his whole childhood; always slowed her down and made her limp, embarrassed him acutely if other children sniggered, and which seemed to grow mysteriously worse if ever one dared oppose her, or was what she called obstreperous. Now he'd found an evening-class, her leg was twice its size, not to mention throbbing and inflamed. He had fetched her footstools, compresses; sworn he'd do the shopping the minute Tesco's opened on the Saturday – *and* go to the shoe-mender's, the cleaner's and the . . . She'd suddenly capitulated in the middle of his errand-list; said she'd solved the problem – she'd enrol as well and join him at the class.

'But it's science,' he'd explained, knowing he was safe. His Mother hated science, which meant atom bombs and bigger germs and the weather all messed up. He'd finally chosen 'Science and Society', since it was the only science on offer at the Winston Churchill Centre – a small and dingy institute which was nothing like its founder in either ambition or prestige. He'd always been attracted to the sciences, even as a boy – not bunsen burners or half-dissected frogs, which was all they'd had at school – but the thought of all those cosmic laws and measurements. He had hoped to go to college, do a course in Natural Order or First Causes, but his Mother had insisted that he find a job as soon as he left school; said three years with his nose in a book wouldn't help her pay the bills, and anyway, he didn't have the brains. He suspected she was right, tried to hack the longings out of him, like growths; though often in his fantasies he strode his vast laboratory, which was always dazzling white – white coats, white rats, white dwarfs, white heat, white hope.

Science meant ruled lines in the universe – lists tallying both sides – nice neat explanations, rules for things and proofs. Proofs seemed best of all. Sometimes, on his bad days, when he doubted who he was, he longed to have some proof of his identity, or even his existence – not just a footling credit card (or nametapes on his socks or cap, which had helped a bit at school) – but to become an 'x' or 'y' and form part of an equation, one which made some sense and added up.

But in just the last eight days, his whole view of science had come crashing to the ground. *Nothing* had identity

78

or sense. You couldn't even talk about 'the universe' –
not since reading all those books. One author was quite
certain that there was a whole vast array of what he called
'alternative universes' existing simultaneously with ours,
not tidy law-abiding worlds which knew what they were
doing – and, more important, *why* – but nightmare sorts of
places which plunged around and collided with each other,
and which the author said were probably quite pointless.
He hated that word 'pointless'; detested those black holes,
which weren't holes like in a pocket or even in the ozone
layer, but moody violent things again, which went roaring
around the place like mods and rockers, crashing into
anything they met. He just didn't understand it. How
could holes collide?

There was an awful lot of crashing altogether, an awful
lot of noise, far more black than white, and even space itself
wasn't quiet or simply empty, but kept seething, heaving,
bubbling, like a stew on a high gas. No – he'd got to learn
he mustn't say just 'space' – it had to be 'spacetime' now,
without so much as a hyphen in between, let alone an
explanation which made any sort of sense. There'd been
a separate book on Time, which sounded every bit as
perilous, since there *wasn't* any time – or so the author
said, though another book had insisted it ran backwards.
He was totally confused now, about space as well as time,
let alone the two of them together.

He peered in at the classroom once again. Why weren't
*they* all scared, when they'd been thrown into this
maelstrom, knew much more than he did, made to
face such terrifying concepts as 'failed worlds', 'ghost
worlds', infinite dimensions? They all looked rather bored
or supercilious, as if everything were solid still, and safe.
He dreaded that word 'infinite', couldn't tie it down. The
more he read, the worse he felt – dizzy, since he'd learnt that
the earth was careering round the sun at sixty-six thousand
miles an hour; bruised, when he discovered that millions of

neutrinos bombarded man each day; baffled and unsettled to hear scientists in Houston had come up with solutions, which had, as yet, no corresponding problems.

'E . . . Excuse me,' someone said. He jumped, dodged back, came face to face with a petite and blond-haired woman, who would have been attractive, except she'd obviously been crying and had red and swollen eyes. Her fine fair skin was puffy from the tears, and though her clothes looked stylish, they seemed rather creased and crumpled, as if she'd been to bed in them. She was obviously upset still, spine and shoulders drooping, voice tremulous, unsure. He felt instant sympathy, had some-times nursed a secret shaming wish to be a woman, just so he could cry. There was so much more to cry about in this new world of random chaos, where the only certainty was absolute uncertainty, and nothing stood still long enough for you to measure it or label it.

The woman rubbed her eyes, left a streak of mauve stuff down one cheek, which made it look as if she'd bruised herself. She already had burns on both her hands; was perhaps a careless cook who forgot the oven-gloves, or nervous in a kitchen (as *he* was with his Mother). His heart went out to her. She seemed so crushed, despondent, yet her face was soft and gentle, the sort of Ideal Mother he remembered from his children's books, who kissed your grazes better and stayed with you a whole ten minutes if you'd had a nasty dream, even sat down on the bed and held your hand. She was also small, as well as fair, which made him feel less threatened. His Mother was just five foot one, yet could dwarf a City tower-block.

He wished John-Paul were shorter. Tall men always shrank him; dark ones bleached him out. And John-Paul was so dramatic-dark, looked foreign, even Jewish, which seemed a double betrayal of his Mother, who blamed foreigners for everything from AIDS and germs and bus-queues to the weather, and refused to shop at M & S because it had been founded by a Jew-boy. The fact he never used his surname did seem a shade suspicious. It was probably long and unpronounceable, with a 'witz' or 'stein' or 'lasky' on the end, and the one he asked his patients to write out on their cheques was just a shortened version or a pseudonym. Even 'John-Paul' might be fake, an Anglicised alternative to some strange outlandish Christian name which his mysterious doctor had decided to disown. He found it near-impossible to use his Christian name at all. It sounded disrespectful, like calling his Mother 'Lena', or, worse, 'Mum'.

It was equally impossible ever to meet his eye – well, lying on the couch, he couldn't anyway – but even when he first arrived, he couldn't seem to look at him directly; just a brief glance at a hand or foot to make sure he *had* shown up, then back turned on the couch. Maybe John-Paul felt the same, since he often wore dark glasses, as if to put an extra barrier between them. (Or he could perhaps be shy and trying to camouflage himself? There'd been a survey in the *Daily Mail,* just a month or so ago, which revealed that seventy-five per cent of all adults of both sexes admitted being shy, and that included doctors, actors, publicans and prostitutes. It had made him feel much better – almost human.) But although he'd never seen his eyes, he knew they would be black – cold-black like his black-hole voice, crow-black like his hair. He always felt more mousy with his doctor – his own hair wispy, fading, compared with John-Paul's glossy crest; his skin pasty and anaemic beside that vibrant all-year tan.

He glanced back to the woman who was still faltering at the door, immediately gained a little colour as John-Paul's features faded; gained a little courage as he saw how shy she was herself. She took one nervous step into the room, looking bewildered and self-conscious as she scanned the crowded benches for a seat. He plunged in after her, her own bashfulness inspiring him; heard a voice which wasn't

81

his murmur almost casually: 'There's two here at the back.' Her relief was huge and matched his own astoundment. He'd spoken to a woman, spoken to a stranger, and she'd actually replied, not slapped his face or – worse still – failed to see him, but stuttered 'Thanks' and smiled. He wrapped the smile carefully in several layers of Kleenex, stored it in his pocket. Smiles were very rare, especially women's smiles.

He got out his green notebook, hoped it would impress her. He still hadn't dared the red, but green had seemed real progress. Green for life and youth and hope, and what he'd thought was science – before he'd read the books. He wished now he'd gone to nature study: Patterns of Migrating Birds or Badger Habitats. Nice to sit beside a mate and take notes on nests or burrows. A mate! He must be joking. He didn't even know her name, and she'd probably move seats anyway once they came back from the coffee-break. He racked his brain for something else to say. 'Do you come here often?' was obviously redundant, since she must come every week. (There was quite a strict paragraph at the front of the prospectus about regular attendance and no refunds if you just stopped turning up.) He could ask her where she lived, but it might sound rather nosy, and even a casual 'What's your name?' could well seem too familiar.

He sat in silence, which swelled the general silence in the room. No one else was talking, just a cough or two, a scrape of chairs, the faint rustle of a paperback, and one impatient tapping pen. The tutor must be late. Bryan checked his watch – almost half past six. He could have stayed at work, finished his report, even grabbed a cup of tea. He glanced up at his neighbour once again. Her hair looked soft, and real. His Mother's hair was steel and very tightly sprung, and she kept it in a hairnet which seemed to say 'Don't touch'. There'd been few things he could touch, especially in his childhood – not earth or sand or shop displays, not dogs or cats or feathers, not even sugar-lumps, without the tongs. He cleared his throat, edged his chair a tiny fraction closer. Perhaps a casual word about the tutor. He could ask his name, instead of hers, inquire if he were good, or often late?

There was a sudden ripple through the rows of chairs, people sitting straighter, thrillers whisked away. A small-ish, fairish, slimmish man with greyish hair and lightish hazel eyes had just shuffled into the room and was stumping up to the dais, loaded down with a Waitrose plastic carrier, a battered vinyl briefcase, and what appeared to be two raincoats, and murmuring 'Sorry sorry sorry!' in a boyish faintish voice. Boyish, no. He must be in his fifties. Bryan half-got up, reached forward, fighting shock. This was his dead Father – he knew it instantly. The same narrow shoulders, neatish nose, apologetic eyebrows, so faint they weren't quite there; the same smallish squarish face-shape and none-too-certain chin – even the same nervousness, as he flustered with his notes, dropped a dozen pages, banged his head as he stooped to pick them up.

But there was one overwhelming difference. This man was clever, brilliant, understood the infinite, felt quite at home with spacetime, never fell into Black Holes; wasn't bruised or even grazed when alien worlds kept crashing and he was in the driving seat. Bryan stared at him, kept staring. His Father – a scientist, a genuine intellectual with degrees from universities, a study full of books, a scholar's gown with ermine trim, like he'd seen on *Dreaming Spires*. (A shame he hadn't *worn* the gown, and was dressed in just old corduroys and a hairy sort of jacket with bulges in the pocket. But those bulges could be Knowledge – calculators, test tubes, even a miniature microscope.)

The man had started talking. He spoke in little bursts, the words eager, frisky, tumbling out, then drying up suddenly, as if they'd been too bold and breathless and had to skulk and blush a bit before bubbling up again.

Bryan could hardly concentrate. What were words when this was his own Father – the man he'd never seen, never thought to see, the half-god who'd half-created him, given him his genes? Of course his Father hadn't died, as his Mother always claimed. That was just her story, to save her face, invest herself with Tragedy, escape the blame for driving him away. He must have simply left, upped and gone in the middle of the night, or the middle of a mouthful, started a new life. Bryan admired him doubly, not just for his intellect, but for escaping from his Mother. That took heroism, a very special sort of valour he didn't have himself.

He gazed still more intently, trying to see inside the man, see his lungs and heart and liver, his bowels and his intestines, compare them with his own. He felt sure they'd match and tally – same brand, same size, same pattern, same noises and same smells. He kept jabbing at his thumb with his BRB free biro, wished it were a syringe so he could trap a drop of blood, then prick his Father's thumb as well, rush the still-warm samples to some waiting judge or doctor, their verdict like a chorale in his ears: 'Paternity proven'.

'If the area of the hole is used as a measure of disorder, then the black hole obeys the same relation between disorder and temperature as does . . .'

He fumbled for the prospectus, turned to page sixteen, so he could check the tutor's name. Disappointment seared the page like lava. Not Payne, but B.K. Skerwin. He glanced back at the dais. Could he be mistaken, *imagining* that resemblance? No. Even their four hands were so identical that if they each cut one off and swapped, the resulting pair would still match quite remarkably, give or take a few odd hairs or lines – broad, blunt-fingered, compact hands with knobbles at the wrists. Anyway, it wasn't just a matter of resemblance; it was a feeling deep inside him, a sense he *knew* this man, knew him

84

from his daily childhood fantasies when they'd shot the rapids, swum the Hellespont, won the Battle of Trafalgar, always hand in hand. Payne must be his Mother's name, her so-called maiden name, though the term 'maiden' seemed quite wrong for her. She had never been a maiden, never been a girl; been Mother from the start, Mother in her cradle, Mother as a foetus, Mother as an ovum. No wonder Skerwin left. She would have stifled him completely, flattened all his bulges, made him keep his gown in cellophane, with mothballs in the ermine. And in revenge, he'd removed himself *in toto*, snatched away his surname, as well as just the books, packed it with the microscope, left his Mother only Payne.

'The striking similarity between gases and black holes comes from the latter's compliance with an interesting new law which . . .'

Bryan let his biro drop. He should be taking notes, scribbling like the rest of them, but his fingers wouldn't work. He had lost all co-ordination, could only sit and gaze, trap a few rare words – macrocosm, analogue, anthropic, synchrotron. He remembered now – his Father had used words like that when he'd told him bedtime stories, those wondrous silent stories which ranged from Istanbul to Saturn, from Yentai to the Pole Star.

Skerwin. He sucked the name, rolled it round its mouth to try to get its flavour. Yes, he really liked it. It was bracing and unusual, ended on an upbeat with that triumphant clinching 'win'. He chewed at the B.K. 'B' could stand for Bryan. Perhaps his Father's last request had been that his son should bear his name – another bond between them. And that mysterious middle 'K'? Not Keith, he prayed, or Kevin, but something bold and regal like Kentigern or Kingsley. His Father deserved a more stirring second name than his own boring low-key Vernon.

'Even if the disorder-probability arguments have only

very approximate validity, the conclusion must be that we live in a world of . . .'

He glimpsed a young man yawning. How *dare* he yawn, insult his Father who was now in fullish flood. The woman beside him was quite a different story – obviously quite fascinated, and scrawling notes so fast her hand seemed battery-powered. He glanced sideways at her jotter. 'Tracheotomy,' she'd written. 'Unconglated hyperbilirubinaemia', 'Ventricular Peritoneal shunt'. He stared down at the words – long impressive words again, yet he couldn't remember hearing any one of them, and why had she jotted 'Neonatal' at the top? Had Skerwin been alluding to the birth-pangs of the universe, that violent cosmic havoc he'd read about with terror, when the new-born earth exploded out of madly crashing planets? He must have missed a good half of the lecture; been so deep inside his Father he'd been listening to the fanfare of his heart-beat, the sigh of his intestines, not his voice from the outside. He tried to burrow out, catch the shoals of words like flying fish, admire their gleaming scales, their writhing shining bodies.

'The exact mathematical relationship between disorder and probability is, in fact, a so-called exponential relationship, but we'll deal with that more fully after the break. So if you'd like to get your coffees now and be back at seven-thirty . . .'

Bryan checked his watch. Seven-twelve exactly. Almost a whole hour had passed – the swiftest of his life. It had seemed like just five minutes, five leaping singing minutes. He rose, half-dazed, locked chairs with his neighbour who was also getting up.

'I'm sorry.' 'I'm so sorry.'

Their voices locked as well now. Both blushed, both tried to speak again at exactly the same moment.

'Are you going for a . . .?' 'Where d'you go for . . .?'

Both stopped again, confused. 'Yes, *coffee*,' Bryan said clinchingly, drawing on new powers. 'Er . . . may I ask your name?'

She smiled shyly, picked her bag up. 'Mary Hampton.'

'Pleased to meet you, Mary.' Oh, how he wished John-Paul was here as witness! He'd never been so forward, so absolutely shameless.

'What's yours?'

'I beg your pardon?' Was she offering him a drink? He was so elated by his triumph he'd completely lost the thread.

'Your name?'

'Oh, I see. Er . . . Bryan. Yes, Bryan – Bryan Skerwin.'

'Skerwin?'

'Yes.' He felt a huge weight leave his shoulders – all his childhood sufferings: the asthma and the eczema, the hours locked in the coal-hole with the Devil peering in, the greenfly on the lettuce, the brown skin on the rice, the white socks he'd had to wear still when he was fourteen and a half – all gone, all someone else's.

'The same name as the tutor?' Mary clicked her bag open, dropped her jotter in.

'Yes.' He shrugged, made his voice more casual. 'He's my Father, actually.'

'Your *father*?'

'Yes.' 'Three yeses. He'd never felt so positive, even gestured with his hand to indicate that Mary should go first, that they were now definitely a twosome. She glanced up at the dais, where Skerwin was still sorting through his notes. One of his fawn raincoats had fallen on the floor and was lying like a skin he'd shed, a limp and dingy skin.

'Yes,' she said herself. 'I can see the resemblance now. It's actually quite striking.' She looked back at Bryan, her blue eyes narrowed slightly, as she appraised his form and features with what he felt was new respect. 'Gosh! He's frightfully brainy, isn't he?'

'Oh, yes.'

'I'm afraid I couldn't grasp quite all of it. I mean, it's very sort of technical and I'm not that . . .'

'Don't worry, you'll get the hang quite soon.' He nodded to the tutor, a collusive knowing nod, the sort that sons gave fathers, and which he knew Mary was observing. Skerwin blinked, seemed nervous, dared a smile, grabbed it back immediately, dropped his second raincoat and a pen.

'But I've been coming four whole weeks now. Do *you* come every week?'

'I shall be doing, yes. I had to miss the first month. I've been busy, very busy – business meetings, trips abroad, you know the sort of thing?'

'Oh, yes, I certainly do.'

She seemed worried suddenly, as if she'd slipped back to another world, one he couldn't enter. He mustn't let her go. 'Well, how about that coffee?' he said what he hoped was nonchalantly, aware the room was empty now and that they'd never get a drink at all if they didn't make a move. He held the door for her, even dared to pick her coat-belt up where it was trailing on the floor. This was Friday, the worst day of his week, and he was walking down a passage with a woman – a real woman – not just a fantasy, a dream or wish-fulfilment. Mary Hampton. He liked her name. Not quite the ring of Skerwin, but simple, honest, English, easy to pronounce. He also liked her clothes: a matching skirt and jacket in a flattering blue fabric which so exactly matched her eyes they looked as if they'd been run up from an offcut. And a pretty frilly blouse with tiny summer flowers on – summer in October. His Mother still wore mourning; had worn it thirty years.

He could smell the canteen long before they reached it. It smelt of disinfectant, not of food; must be almost closing, since despite the crowd queuing at the counter, two girls in nylon overalls were trying to scrub the floor, banging chairs on tables, knocking shins with mops. The walls were shiny eau-de-Nil, the floor curry-coloured, with darker khaki wet patches. 'Don't slip,' he warned, wishing they could escape from the long and jostling queue, those astronomers and physicists who now looked rather boring and were all in Mary's way. He might not find a seat for her, let alone a table to themselves. He frowned at the remaining food, a few dusty squares of fruitcake, where 'fruit' meant half a cherry or one lonely orphaned currant; a custard tart with a crater in its custard, and two stale and curling sandwiches labelled 'prawn' and 'ham' respectively, though he could see nothing much inside them save the same pink-tinged liquid putty. Nice to have offered Mary something chic: Black Forest gâteau, eaten with a fork, or an open sandwich garnished with a lemon slice and made from that expensive bread with the little nutty bits in.

She reached out for an Aero, put it on her tray.

'This is on me,' he said, gesturing grandly to the counter, as if to suggest his bank-account was limitless, and if she wished to eat the tea-urn or the hotplate, he'd gladly meet their cost.

'Oh, no – no, really.' Mary looked embarrassed, started fumbling for her purse.

'I insist.' He paid for the two cups of tea (polystyrene cups, no saucers, plastic spoons), her Aero and a Lion Bar. He liked the picture on its wrapper of powerful mane and strong white sharp incisors. His Father had lost neither mane nor teeth.

All the tables were now crowded with their classmates, though again the word was wrong. Few seemed really matey, most still sullen silent, communing with their currants or sorting through their notes. And not a soul had said hallo to Mary, despite her month's attendance. He was much relieved by that, steered her to the far end of the room, where he put the plastic tray down on a sort of jutting ledge thing which should have been a windowsill, except the canteen had no windows. (Perhaps they'd been a casualty in the recent swingeing cuts. Glass and china cut, as well as courses.)

'D'you live nearby?' asked Mary, as he passed her the sugar which was damp in patches like the floor, and streaked brown with coffee drips.

'No. Er . . . Woodford.' It sounded slightly more acceptable than Upminster, and definitely more rural. Upminster's only claim to fame was its position as last station on the District Line at its unfashionable east end. The last station on most tube lines seemed invariably down-market, except for Wimbledon and Richmond, and maybe Amersham.

'Ah, quite a long way out.'

'Yes.'

'Like me.'

*She* lived in Woodford? God, no! He'd never been there in his life, and now she'd ask him if he knew the Smiths or Joneses, or that marvellous little restaurant in the High Street which . . .

'We live in Walton – well, it's almost Weybridge, actually – a sort of no-man's-land between the two.'

'Oh, really?' He put his Lion Bar down, choking on that 'we'. He hadn't even thought to check her ring. He checked it now: a wide one – thick, expensive – yoking her to someone solid, wealthy. She could be widowed, though. 'We' needn't mean a husband. There were endless permutations, enough for several lists – a son, a dog, a daughter, a mother, father, sister, brother, aunt, a workmate or companion, or all of them together. Perhaps she was divorced, which might explain the tears. She'd come straight from her solicitor, or from a cruel and stormy meeting with her 'ex'. He must keep talking, mustn't lose her between the nisi and the absolute. She

90

was already glancing round, would be straying any second, joining that big tall man by the radiator, or the dark one with that daunting college scarf.

'Did you . . . um . . . find it hard to choose the class?' he asked.

'Hard?'

'Well, I mean, there's such an enormous choice. Not just all the sciences, but languages and arts and crafts and all the different histories and philosophy and music and keep-fit and archaeology . . .' He forced himself to stop. John-Paul had told him many times that his lists were counterproductive, since not only did they squander great reserves of time and energy, they also put his emotional life in a straitjacket.

'Well, my husband chose it, actually. I was rather keen on "Gâteaux and Patisseries", but he said I ought to stretch myself, and also try a London class, instead of always local ones, which he said aren't half as good.'

Husband! Bryan jabbed his plastic spoon against the ledge, watched it split in three, then snapped each third into splinters. Perhaps the husband had lost interest, and was insisting on the class so he could keep that evening free for someone else; had probably only suggested London so he could woo a local woman without Mary running into them. Silence loomed and jarred again, though it wasn't very silent in his head. He could hear the clash of sword blades as he and Mary's husband duelled in the Vienna Woods; could hear his rival's breathing, agonised and laboured, the harsh cry of a vulture, as steel clanged angry steel. Mary cleared her throat, kept glancing at him nervously, as if hoping he would speak. He couldn't speak and fight. At last, she spoke herself.

'I didn't realise there'd be so much of the science. I mean, I thought we'd have more of the "Society", but he hasn't even mentioned that, not in four whole weeks. I'm not criticising – please don't get me wrong. He's obviously quite brilliant and . . .' Her voice tailed off. Bryan didn't help her out. He had fallen to one knee to inspect his rival's wound, blood sticky on his fingers, the dawn mist closing in. She took a bite of Aero, brushed chocolate crumbs from lips and lap before spilling out a few more nervous words.

'I'm not that keen on London. It's so noisy, isn't it? But this centre was convenient, especially on a Friday. I . . . er . . . have to see a doctor every week. I'm having . . . treatment, actually, and the place I go to is only round the corner, so . . .'

Bryan streaked from the Vienna Woods back to the canteen. Mary's voice was breaking, one hand clenched, knuckles almost white as she fought to hold the tears back. So that's why she was crying earlier on. She must have something really serious – maybe even cancer. His aunt had died of cancer, *and* his boss's chauffeur's wife. No wonder she was stumbling on her words. Cancer was a word you couldn't say, nobody could say, just skirted round in terror or embarrassment. 'Treatment' would mean that ghastly radiation, or drugs which made your hair fall out, or even a major operation. They'd probably just informed her that the tumour wasn't shrinking, or they'd discovered secondaries. How brave she was to come on to the class, not to let his Father down when her life was in the balance.

She'd taken off her jacket now and he could see several small but livid marks blistered on her forearm. Was that part of her treatment, some tiny but malignant growths they'd cauterised this very afternoon? He knew nothing about cancer – save it killed. Those burn marks on her hands – they weren't to do with oven-gloves or cookers, but had been inflicted by some doctor in a bid to stave off death. He glanced down at her remaining stub of Aero, its texture of brown holes, peered at it in horror as he recognised the fabric of the universe. Spacetime was like that – he'd just read it in the books – a complex labyrinth of holes and tunnels, exploding bubbles, frothy foam-like structures collapsing on themselves. Chaos in a chocolate bar – and not just Aero. Wasn't Cadbury's Chocolate Flake every bit as threatening, paralleling the crumbling microworld where nothing was substantial, but all solidities and certainties flaked away to nothing?

He closed his eyes against the baneful images, tried to focus on the counter of the sweet-shop near his office. Why were all those chocolate bars called after the stars – Galaxy, and Milky Way, and even solid Mars Bars, named for a planet which was arid as a desert, dark and cold and barren, hostile to all life? Astronomy was even worse than physics – all those huge and dwarfing numbers where a million million was nothing but a sneeze. What had one book said – that the nearest – yes, the *nearest* star to the sun was a mere thirty thousand billion miles away? He couldn't grasp distances like that. He could judge a hundred yards (which was his front gate to the postbox, or his office to the sweet-shop), but light-years left him baffled – and horribly afraid.

He looked up apprehensively as nervous footsteps tap-tapped through the door. Skerwin – late again – tripping on a bucket and being refused a tea or coffee, as they'd just closed the till and turned off the hot water. He scuffed back to the door again, pausing at their table.

'You're a new student, aren't you? I don't think I've seen your face before. Nice to meet you, anyway. I'm Skerwin – Bertram Skerwin. They said someone new was joining, but I thought it was a lady. "Miss Pain", I've got down here. Oh, dear!' Skerwin jerked his coat away, retrieved its drooping sleeve, which had been dangling in Bryan's coffee and was now dripping down his neck. He threw a clutch of 'Sorrys' on the table, beat a swift retreat. Bryan leapt up to his feet, came face to face with Mary who had already kicked her chair back, and was staring at him, shaken, her face creased in sheer bewilderment.

'But I thought you said . . .'

'Look, he *is* my Father, honestly. He just doesn't realise yet. We've never met, you see. It's slightly complicated. Let me try to . . .'

No good, no good at all. Mary was already through the door, shrugging back her jacket with a mixture of distaste and almost fear. He picked up her Aero and its cast-off paper wrapper. Should he save them as a relic to remind himself he'd once had a real woman, sat next to her for forty-one whole minutes (and opposite for ten), exchanged names, addresses, shared a meal – well, two half-bars of chocolate? No. Best forget it, destroy all evidence. He crumpled up the wrapper, bit into the Aero, heard the crash of world on world colliding as he was punctured like a bubble, sucked down and down into the biggest of brown holes.

# 7

'Yes?' the buzzer purrs, sounding slightly more excitable than usual.

I swallow, find my own voice, press closer to the door, to shelter from the vicious grabbing rain. (I don't know why it always rains the days I see John-Paul. He'd probably try to analyse it, suggest that perhaps I *needed* rain, as I appear to need his anger or my illnesses, as just another variation of self-punishment. Nice to think my psyche can affect national annual rainfall.) 'It's Nial,' I say. 'Wet through.'

'Could you wait downstairs a moment, please.'

'*Wait?* But . . .' I've waited two eternities since three p.m. last Thursday. It's now Monday – two-eleven – a whole minute past my time.

'Come in and close the door, but just take a seat down there until I call you. Right?'

No, it *isn't* right, though my swearword is cut off as the intercom upstairs is disconnected. I slam the door behind me, spurn the three hard chairs, just slump against the wall of the dank and chilly lobby, where the stone is undisguised – no furnishings, no carpet, nothing much at all on the ground floor of the tower save the chairs themselves, an antique brass umbrella-stand, and a heavy wooden door which says 'TOILET, OUT OF ORDER'. That toilet's been dysfunctional (to use one of John-Paul's words) for at least a month or more. It makes me really mad. Patients *need* a toilet. Supposing they're caught short, or sick with nerves (as I am myself most sessions), or are suffering from a prolapse or cystitis? And anyway, it's not a good advertisement. If he can't

95

sort out a ball-cock or an S-bend, what hope of curing psyches?

I mooch towards the toilet door, realise with annoyance that a second notice has been added to the first – just 'SORRY!' in red capitals. Of course he isn't sorry, or he'd get a plumber in, and that jeering exclamation mark gives the game away. 'SORRY!'s just a new sadistic twist to make us feel he cares, when he's no intention whatsoever of providing any relief, either literal or metaphorical.

I mount the first two steps, strain my ears so I can try to hear what's going on upstairs. Impossible. I can't hear anything except the usual haunting sirens, the bad temper of the wind, and the stop and start of traffic which sounds uncertain of its course in life, plagued by indecision. Not a whisper from John-Paul. What in God's name is he *doing*? He's never late – ever – never keeps a patient waiting. It's all part of the treatment – to make you feel secure, provide order, regularity, in a treacherous shifting world. You're not even meant to see his previous patient, nor the one who comes straight after, so you won't suffer sibling rivalry, or feel you're not his sole concern. Each and every patient leaves precisely on the hour, and the next one doesn't enter till ten past. Those vital ten minutes prevent overlaps and jealousies, collusion, or vendettas (and probably give him time to have a pee. I imagine his own toilet is kept strictly operational, with only 'PRIVATE' on the door).

Actually, I must confess I've cheated several times, hung around the stairs till ten past three, so I could murder his next patient, or at least snatch a look at him – or her. They're mostly 'hers', in fact. I suppose he finds females more exciting, and can spend his breaks enjoying a quick wank after all that talk of vaginal orgasms or penis envy. I bet he's got some woman with him now – not a patient, a mistress or a wife – fair, of course; small, of course; and loathsomely attractive. They're screwing on the couch, have lost all track of time – *my* time – my overpriced (and precious) time which I'm wasting in this dungeon, where the stone smells almost fetid like some dead and rotting pond, and the walls are so thick-skinned they don't give a damn that I'm almost crying with frustration. He mustn't see me crying – never will, never has – not once in six months, two weeks, three days, which is how long I've been coming – except months and weeks mean nothing much when two minutes take so long to pass I'm just opening my royal telegram with gnarled arthritic fingers, peering at the words: 'Congratulations, Nial. A hundred today!' Actually, time for me is simply B.J-P. and A.J-P – before John-Paul and after. *Before* I had more money, fewer problems, and masses more free time. Now I have

John-Paul
John-Paul
John-Paul
John-Paul
John-Paul
John-Paul
John-Paul

I also get more coughs and colds from my eight long walks each week, six of which seem invariably to be wet. I'll probably get pneumonia this time, since it's not exactly healthy to sit around in dripping clothes in the stone bowels of a tower. I check my watch again, aware I'm over-reacting, yet still horribly upset. It just seems so unfair, when he never lets us patients have a single extra second. When your fifty minutes is up, it's up, and you're turfed out in the cold, even if you're sobbing and hysterical, or have just reached some vital breakthrough you've been struggling towards all year. A month or so ago, I worked myself into the most terrifying panic, but at three o'clock precisely I heard that cruel 'It's time, Nial', and was firmly shown the door, though I was shaking and near-vomiting, and in no state to leave at all.

The memory makes me shiver, and I start pacing round and round, not to warm me up, but because it's vital to keep active to stop myself from crying. The thought that he's forgotten me, or doesn't give a damn, makes me feel quite strange – sort of faint and blank and empty, as if he's rubbed me out or expunged me from his page with Tipp-Ex or blue pencil. I stop at the umbrella-stand, grasp its solid shoulder, envying its strength. There's just one umbrella in it, a pathetic broken thing, all skin and bone, with torn black flesh hanging from its ribs and a curved arthritic spine. I use it as a battering ram, poke its tip between the ancient stones, gore out a shower of debris from each join. Already I feel better. I've got a useful task now: I'll simply destroy the tower. The longer John-Paul screws that girl the more stones I'll dislodge. So if she's multi-orgasmic (like all those preening females in Masters and Johnson or *Cosmo* magazine, whom I always suspect of lying through their teeth), they'll both be simply rubble by climax eight or nine.

The dismantling doesn't work, only makes me wretched. I don't want John-Paul as rubble, only her. But I just can't seem to separate them. They're joined all along their bodies – mouth to mouth, breast to chest, groin to filthy groin. I sink down on a window-seat, ashamed at how I've injured the umbrella, which is scarred and scored and dirty now, as well as very sick. It looks like a dead crow, its black wings drooping, its beak split and sort of gaping. I've always loathed dead birds, dream about them sometimes – dead in cages, dead in butchers' shops.

Monday's dead as well – drooping, nothing left of it. The days just don't exist without John-Paul. I've got to see him – *now* – start toiling up the stairs towards his rooms, terrified of what (or who) I'll find. I can't bear to see the girl, or John-Paul naked, sweaty, yet if I stay down there without him then I die. There's a sudden yell of fury, a fusillade of footsteps. I dodge swiftly back to base again as a tall man with dark stubble but a haughty fine-boned face comes scorching down towards me, screaming out obscenities. He jumps the last three stairs, crashes towards the toilet, a taunt of naked flesh revealed between his shrunken purple sweater and his low-slung denim jeans.

'It's out of order,' I warn him, frightened he'll throw up where he is, from sheer rage or desperation.

'So is this whole fucking place!' he roars, as he slams out through the door, the wind and rain whirling in a moment, and a siren wailing, wailing, as if he's planned his whole wild exit with the appropriate sound effects, even bribed the elements to help him.

The silence seems more frightening when he's gone. Is John-Paul cold and dead upstairs, lying in his own congealing blood? Was the man some mad intruder, or just another of his patients, a psychotic dangerous one? I suddenly feel threatened. My rival siblings aren't mere virgin Marys, but violent psychopaths. I sag against the toilet door, wish I could creep in there, splash my face, dry my clothes, escape from all the blood and mess and mayhem. 'Nial,' says a voice – *his* voice – disembodied, but indisputably alive. 'Would you like to come upstairs now?'

'Would I like to . . .?' How can he be so *cool*? No explanations, sorrys, just that phlegmatic low-key drawl, as if it were normal ten past two, instead of monstrous two-nineteen. Nine whole minutes lost, which is the cost of a good meal, though forget the cash, it's the principle that hurts; the fact he's got this power to so disturb me. The stairs have never seemed so long before, and I'm shaking when I reach his room, in desperate need of comfort. He's *got* to touch me this time, meet me at the door, put a kind hand on my shoulder, apologise, make some restitution. Touch me, hell! He's just his usual chilly self, keeping

99

his safe distance a yard or two away – no overture, no word of reassurance. I stand my ground, refusing to speak either, still scared I might start snivelling. Stalemate. The wind frets round the tower, filling in the silence, and two drivers start a honking match somewhere far below, their double anger screwing up the tension. My legs are weak as sago. I've been on my feet since half past twelve; left ridiculously early, because my empty mocking bedsit seemed to close me in and in. At last, John-Paul decides to speak, his voice so low and passive, you'd think he'd been anaesthetised.

'Will you lie down on the couch now, please.'

'Okay,' I say. 'Why not? Though it's hardly worth it, is it? I mean, it's almost time to leave. Seems a waste of effort when I'll be getting up again in less than half an hour. Though of course you probably haven't realised what the time is. I know you wear a watch and there's a clock here on the bureau, and another one right opposite your chair and a third . . .' I pause for breath, bang down on the couch, leave my muddy shoes on. 'But when you're so busy with your lovers, or assassins – or whoever – it must be all too easy to lose track.'

'I see you're very angry with me.'

'Angry? I'm not angry. Why should I be angry? I'm just the patient, aren't I, so of course you can keep me waiting if it suits you? Make it longer next time. Yeah, go ahead. Take my whole damn session, if you want.'

'When you were waiting downstairs, you were identifying me with your absent father, who often wasn't there when you felt you really needed him – sometimes just walked out, or disappeared.'

'Oh, shit! That's just too easy. I wish I'd never told you, if all you do is use it as an excuse. You fuck up my whole session and then blame my rotten father.'

'*Rotten* father, Nial?'

I don't answer. What's the point? Nothing's ever his

fault. If you're a patient, then you're wrong. And you're wrong because your mother was inadequate and your father was a shit. What about *his* parents? Paragons, I suppose.

The church clock booms from down the street, chiming the half-hour, which seems to underline my point that we're wasting still more time. Though that clock is so hysterical, it needs an analyst itself. Every time it strikes it really suffers, shuddering and rumbling first, then exploding with great howls of 3-D pain. Since I leave dead on the hour, it seems to express my own despair that my time is up, and I'm banished for another half-millennium.

I lie in twitchy silence. My own voice sounds too feeble after the shell-burst of the clock. I wish I were a clock – all that attention – people checking you each moment, looking at you constantly, *needing* you, for God's sake, planning their whole life round what you say. I can hear John-Paul fumbling for his matches. God! I'd love a cigarette. It's still really hard to have to smell the smoke, hear the whole extended ritual – the rustle of the packet, the explosion of the match, the sudden sucking in-breath, the long slow exhalation – and not be able to join him. I'll just have to take it up again. What's a tiny tumour compared with sharing something intimate, like we did in my first month? I even switched to Chesterfields, our two identical packets mating on the table, our two smokes wreathing, fusing. (The *next* month was unspeakable – enemas and x-rays, endless hours in outpatients', withdrawal symptoms, cravings, and still not a word of sympathy from forty-five-a-day-at-least-John-Paul.)

That man was smoking, the one who crashed downstairs, his cigarette brandished like a death-ray as he stormed towards the door. I long to find out who he was, but somehow I daren't ask. If he's a patient, then he's special, since he's the only one who's ever beat the system and wangled extra time. I loathe the special patients, the psychotics and the Marys. Or he could be John-Paul's lover, which would ruin everything. If John-Paul's homosexual, then . . . I turn away. The thought is just too painful. I jab one shoe with the other, wishing for the billionth time that I wore size fives – or smaller. Perhaps he's John-Paul's son. They're both very dark, with the same aristocratic cheekbones, and though the man was taller by a good two heads or more, the *mother* could be tall. Like me. Nice to think John-Paul preferred tall women, got turned on by big feet.

I stare down at my hands, which are also big and clumsy; amazed to realise I'm still clutching the umbrella. I don't recall bringing it up here, let alone lying on the couch with it. And why did John-Paul say nothing? You'd think he'd have an interest in umbrellas, not just the obvious phallic thing, but the whole idea of shelter, keeping dry. Though he's so reticent at times, I could lie here with a rhinoceros on my lap and he probably wouldn't ask me where I'd got it, or inquire if we had problems in relating. I start stroking the umbrella, slowly, very gently. It's not quite dead, just wounded – like the bird I wept all Sunday for, when I was only five. My father burnt that bird. Its heart was still (just) beating, but he said a cat would get it and it was probably very germy, so he threw it on the fire. I heard its screams years after.

He was always burning things, my father. He burnt my passport once, when I'd booked a trip to Paris, and a photo of my boyfriend – a boy who really liked me, even liked my feet – and whom I rescued from the fire all scorched and charred and curling, and with both his own feet missing. Then he burnt a poem I'd written to a horse, which opened with a line about soft lips. I used to feed that horse with Smarties on my way to school and back, loved its hay-warm breath and velvet muzzle, the way it snorted through my fingers, kept nudging up against me. But my father just assumed that the soft lips were my boyfriend's, so the poem was cremated, like the boy. (I still write poems sometimes, but not about soft lips.)

Yet the bird hurt worst of all. It was the way he flung it, maybe, with a relish, almost pleasure, and the desperate way it tried to fight the fire, spluttering and struggling while the cruel flames licked and singed, then suddenly caved in, accepted death, broke up. I searched the cinders afterwards for a tiny bone, a feather, something I could keep, or maybe bury in the garden with a flower on top, a marker, but there was nothing, nothing – nothing but grey ash.

I suddenly rear up, seize the pillow from the couch and fling it at John-Paul. 'I *hate* you!' I scream out, as I watch it hit his shoulder, then thud against the bookcase. I hurtle after it, start lobbing all his books out, slamming each one down – stupid lying textbooks, pretending to have answers to fire and death and fathers. John-Paul doesn't speak, doesn't move at all, just sits and quietly watches, as I keep banging, mauling books. 'You don't care!' I shout. 'If I killed myself right here in your room, you wouldn't even notice, wouldn't try to stop me. You're just a block of stone – worse than stone, since you call yourself a human.'

Still he doesn't answer, doesn't say a word. Who *wants* his lousy answers? The last time I went wild and chucked my lighter at him, he told me I was attacking the Bad Breast. He's obviously got some hang-up about wanting to become a woman, envying their tits – worse than that – imagining he's *got* tits. Okay, so he needs help, but so do I.

· I glance at his (flat) chest, up further to his face. There's still a faint red mark where the lighter hit his forehead. So he isn't stone – he's flesh. My hands begin to falter as I dislodge a few more books. It must have hurt quite badly, and he didn't even whimper, didn't nag or threaten or refuse to go on seeing me. I drop one last small book, huddle in the corner. I'm horrible, disgusting; can feel my mind and body polluting his whole room. The patient who comes after me can probably smell my smell. Those four deodorants are absolutely pointless. The smell comes from inside me. I try to disappear, crouch right down on the floor; long to die and be reborn a completely different person – someone with ideals, who puts the world before their petty vicious self – a Mother Teresa, or Bob Geldof, or . . .

Slowly, I uncurl myself, crawl back to the bookcase, start picking up the books, handling them very gently, as if they're Mother Teresa's lepers, soothing each one back. I'm aware of John-Paul's eyes on me, but he doesn't break the silence. 'Pick me up!' I'm shouting. 'Put me back.' I'm begging him to move, to get up from his chair and scoop me off the floor, lay me on the couch again, smooth my crumpled pages. I'm also saying sorry to him, searching for the sorry-words which include some sense of contact, like 'opening one's arms', or 'kiss and make up'. And yet he simply doesn't hear. The silence just continues, though I'm screaming really loudly now, my voice so wild it's shattering the windowpanes, startling the whole street. 'Hold me, hold me, hold me, hold me, hold me.'

'Shit!' I say, out loud this time. He's not just deaf, he's stupid; doesn't understand even when I *act* the scene, show him how it's done. I retrieve the pillow, clutch it in my arms, hold it really fiercely, like a mother with her child – and all he does is light another cigarette, as if to prove his hands have more important things to do.

I stretch out on the floor. The carpet's very rough, scratchy and unkind, nags against my cheek. John-Paul clears his throat, which means he's probably going to venture some remark, at last. I'll kill him if it's all that stuff we had a month ago, about how he's holding me with his words, or with his presence in the room, although we can't be physically in contact. It's called 'therapeutic holding' in the books, and is the biggest of their cons, since they're actually so scared of any real involvement, they just use jargon-phrases to cover up their coldness and detachment. It's all so hypocritical. I mean, their constant talk of sex when they're obviously quite terrified of any kind of touching and even choose to sit where nobody can see them, let alone reach out to them. Yet first they lead you on, persuade you to lie down in a private dim-lit room, then try to strip you naked – at least metaphorically – penetrate you, break down your defences, use low and sexy tones; but just you try responding, try to make it real, and they're screaming 'Rape!' and rushing for the door. It's much the same with parents. All that stuff about breast-feeding, and bonding, and sharing the same genes, yet still they lock their laps up, double-glaze their hearts.

I can suddenly see my father once again. He's striding down the path and through the gate. Slam! He won't be back tonight. I crawl upstairs, slump against my mother's bedroom door. (They never slept together, not after I was born.) She used to nap all Sunday afternoons – napped through fire and death and shouting fathers. I stretch out on the carpet by her door. It's rough and very bristly, hurts my face, prickles my bare knees. I'm still crying for my bird, crying very softly. Mustn't wake her up, mustn't make her ill again, so she has to go away. Mustn't be a helpless, hopeless child.

'You're crying, Nial, because I'm a disappointing father, just like your original father.'

'I'm *not* crying.'

'So you wish to deny your tears?'

'Look, I've got to leave,' I say, half-getting up. I'm so humiliated I don't know where to look. I haven't got a handkerchief and John-Paul's box of Kleenex is just beyond my reach. I think he keeps it there on purpose, to screw us patients up.

His own voice is quite dispassionate. 'I wonder if you're confused about the time, or trying to retaliate, leaving early because I started late?'

We're back to where we started – me downstairs, alone; blanking into nothing, breaking into shards. 'S . . . So you admit you started late?'

'Of course.'

'And you don't care?'

'Just like your father didn't care.'

I grope back to the couch, try to hide my face, can't bear to have him see me all streaked and mussed and hideous. The silence only magnifies my snufflings, mocks those stupid little gasps which stab and hack my chest. At last, I hear him shift his chair, know he's coming out with something – a phrase, a krugerrand. He sees every word as gold – *his* words, not the patients'.

'Perhaps your tears are the most important contribution to the session. You haven't been in touch with your emotions up to now, or at least not able to express them here, with me. So we could view this as something of a breakthrough.'

A breakthrough! I roll over the right way, stare round the dark walls; my eyes still streaming, tears dripping into my mouth. The tears taste bitter, brackish, as if they've been kept inside so long they've turned rancid, even toxic. It's awful crying stranded on one's back. I feel totally exposed, like some rat in a laboratory being watched by the Experimenter, who remains outside my cage, observing grief, dissecting it, but declining to relieve it. I fight to gain control. Tears are far too truthful, say things too directly without the shift and snare of words.

I shut my eyes, keep clutching my dead bird. I'm crying for my bird, that's all, and you're allowed to cry for Death. No – it isn't dead, it *isn't*. I sprint towards the fire, snatch it from the flames, my scorched hands coaxing, soothing, imploring it to live. I can feel its feeble heartbeat stirring back to life, a faint flutter through my fingers, the grope of claw on palm. It's even ruffling up its feathers now, making tiny jabbing movements with its beak. Then suddenly I freeze. I can hear my father coming back; heavy footsteps punishing the stairs, harsh voice bellowing threats. The door bursts open. A tall man with dark stubble but a haughty high-boned face is crashing right towards me, cigarette waving like a firebrand.

'Go away!' I shout, as I press the bird close against my chest, try to shield it with both hands, my own panicked heartbeat thumping out of time. 'It's still alive – *alive*!'

# 8

'So what's your name?' I ask, still half-running to keep up with him, and screwing up my face against the rain.

'Seton.'

'What?'

'*Seton.*'

It's difficult to hear him. The traffic's very rackety and he slings his words like missiles, striding straight ahead and barely sparing me a glance. He's obviously still angry, though *I'm* the one who should be mad. He just barged into my session, broke it up completely, docked my time both ends – not only really threw me when I first arrived, caused me all that jealousy and terror, but to come storming back a second time . . . I mean, I could have been a corpse for all he cared. He totally ignored me, prowled round and round the room like some wild and maddened animal, snarling accusations at John-Paul, even snatching up a heavy metal ashtray, as if about to hurl that too.

I'm not quite sure what happened next, except John-Paul raised his voice and started bleating, sounded really vulnerable and shaky, so I just had to get away; felt more frightened by my All-Powerful Doctor's weakness than by Seton's threats and violence. I slipped down off the couch and through the door, hid in the small alcove at the bottom of the stairs, then when I heard them coming, I dashed into the street, ducked behind a van. John-Paul was trying to find me, calling out my name, but I simply couldn't answer. He'd somehow lost his power, seemed just an ordinary man, even a pathetic one, with a strand of limp and greasy hair falling over his forehead, rain-spots on his jacket, creases in his suit. He never creases, ever, and his voice is always deep and calm, not raised or querulous, and his hair's so clean and tidy, you'd think it was a wig. It was also most unsettling to see him outside in the street, competing with the traffic, dwarfed by ruthless buildings, heckled by the rain, instead of safe indoors and special, unchallenged on his plinth.

I just held my breath and crouched down where I was, till he turned back to the tower again, about to disappear. But no . . . The man suddenly lunged forward out of nowhere, and tried to force his way inside; cannoned back, cursing, as the heavy door slammed shut. I rushed up and clutched hold of him – yes, a total stranger, right there in the street. Oh, I realise it was dangerous and I should have gone straight home, waited for the phone-call John-Paul was bound to make, gulped down a few Valium, even put myself to bed. But I was just too overwrought. And anyway, I couldn't bear the thought of being on my own, with John-Paul somehow gelded and my bedsit closing round me, so I clung on to this man as a lifeline, a distraction, a new link with John-Paul – a fellow patient, a violent rival sibling.

'Look, I'm angry with him, *too*!' I yelled. 'We need to stick together. I mean, all us patients probably . . .'

'Patient? Are you joking? I'd no more pay to see that shyster than make an appointment with a cut-throat.' He sounded totally contemptuous, as if a patient was some lower form of life; but at least he didn't push me off – even let me follow him as he swooped across the road and started striding down the street. It took me all my effort to keep up, since he was untrammelled in old trainers while I hobbled in new shoes. Yet the exertion calmed me down, removed the sense of struggle from my psyche to my legs, and after another hundred yards or so, I even plucked up courage to speak to him again. And now I've got his name – the 'Seton' part, at least. I limp on a bit further, dodging a large puddle and a black kid with a Dobermann, then ask him for his surname.

'What?' I shout again. A motorcycle's revving past, colliding with his voice.

'Cusack.' He repeats it.

I'm not sure how you spell that, but it's Irish, isn't it? Which means we may have Gaelic blood in common, as well as just John-Paul. Not that he looks Irish, rather Middle-European, with sallow skin, dark untidy hair and eyes the sludgy colour of black olives. Seton Cusack. I try it on my tongue. The two names don't really harmonise, sound prickly and defiant.

I was wrong about his age. He's much older than I thought at first, and can't be John-Paul's son – looks nothing like him, actually, except for just their colouring. It was the clothes which fooled me – and the speed. He was acting young and dressed young, careering down the steps in skin-tight jeans, long hair. If you put him in a suit and sent him to the barber's, then arranged him very stiffly in a chair, he wouldn't look much younger than John-Paul. But why he's so attractive is, in fact, his energy. There's a dash and thrust about him – in his voice, his movements, body – as if he's fuelled by something different from normal low-key people who creep along the B-roads while he scorches up the autostrada. Also, he's so tall – six foot three, at least – which makes me feel more normal, an average sort of woman who doesn't dwarf her men friends. I can actually look up to him, which I do a moment, catch his eye, and suddenly he's laughing – a booming, crazy sort of laugh, as if the whole thing's been a joke. He even stops, as if to give the laughter time to breathe, or share it with the news-vendor who's screaming out 'Jumbo-jet disaster – ninety-seven dead!' I laugh myself, though mainly from sheer nerves. It's been a pretty jumpy day, so far, and if I've cried, I'd better laugh, even up the score.

'Want a drink?' he asks.

'What?' My laugh breaks off, sounds frightened now and forced.

'D'you say "what" to everything?'

'Er – no, I . . .'

'I said "Do you want a drink"?'

'Yeah. Okay. Why not?' I try to make it casual. My soggy skirt is clinging round my thighs. At least a drink would mean a roof.

'How much time've you got?'

It seems a funny question, but I calculate the minutes until two-ten the next day, feel a sudden terror at the thought of John-Paul creased and limp still. Will Tuesday have restored him? Will I dare go at all? 'Time's no problem,' I say rashly. What's another lie?

'Sure?'

'Mm.'

'Okay. Let's go to my place. If we stop off at a pub or something, I'll only run into the traffic and never get back home. It's a hell of a trek anyway, even out of rush hour.'

'Where d'you live?' I'm feeling really nervous now, especially when he doesn't answer, just zips around the corner to a side street. Are we about to drive to Brighton – or to Bradford? And why's he parked his car so far away? We must have walked a good half-mile, in dousing spoilsport rain.

It's not a car, but a battered Transit van, with no seats in the back, just a scrum of clutter – paint, rope, empty cans, an oil-stained duffel coat, two sleeping bags, some fishing rods, and a cardboard box marked 'JOHN WEST PILCHARDS. THIS WAY UP'. I fight a weird image of him fishing for canned pilchards as I climb into the front. His clothes and van and duffel coat don't match his voice and face, both of which are haughty and exclusive; sort of public school fused with Polish aristocrat. I'm also surprised by his driving, which isn't fast and slapdash (as somehow

I'd imagined), but courteous and careful, even cautious. He's apparently quite willing to pulverise John-Paul, yet he stops for two old ladies trying to cross the road, and waves on other drivers, even when it's not their right of way.

We're heading east, pass quite close to my place, though I decline to mention that; don't want to give too much away until I know who this guy is. The conversation isn't exactly flowing. I suspect we're both haunted by John-Paul. My own thoughts keep fretting back to him, and surely Seton must be brooding on those two violent confrontations, feeling guilty or resentful, or planning further onslaughts. John-Paul's a third person in the van, squeezed between the two of us, invisible but huge, silent but accusing. We're all three cold and wary, shivering in damp clothes. We carry on in silence to Deptford, Greenwich, dreary Woolwich, past used car lots and video shops, 'The Treasure Inn' (a sleazy Chinese restaurant), 'Hair Affair' ('Free blow-dry with restyling'), and rows of other small and squalid shops, some boarded up, some vandalised. At last, he turns towards me. 'D'you smoke?' he asks.

'Yes, *please*.'

He fumbles for his cigarettes, offers me a Capstan Full Strength, which must be higher in both tar and nicotine than any other brand I know. I grab it like a starving woman, seize the lighter from him, i–n–h–a–l–e. Christ! It's strong, or maybe six months' abstinence has just made me overreact. I'm coughing like a schoolgirl being seduced by her first fag, feel terribly embarrassed, especially when my eyes stream, but Seton barely notices – just one brief glance, then eyes back to the road, his own cigarette clamped between his teeth. Once I've recovered from the coughing, I inhale a second time, fight an instant wave of dizziness, a sudden queasy feeling. I'm amazed that just two puffs should affect me quite so strongly, yet, even so, I know it's right to start again. Mentally, I'm more relaxed already and my hands now have a function, whereas the last few months they've been totally superfluous, just dangling dead appurtenances with no real role in life. Who cares what I die of, when John-Paul won't be there? I don't even *want* him there – all weak and wet and bleating at his first sight of a tumour.

'So how d'you know John-Paul?' I ask, taking another slow deep drag to give me courage.

'I'm a friend of his ex-wife.'

'Ex-wife?' I'm riveted.

'Yeah. They split two years ago. Though it was a good three days before he even noticed she was gone. He's so involved with his own life – if you can call it a life.'

'Did he . . . ever . . .' (I plug my mouth with my cigarette, need another fix before I dare complete the sentence) '. . . marry again?'

'Who'd have him, for fuck's sake? He lives with these two huge wolfhounds, though it beats me how he finds the time to exercise them. Midnight walks, I suppose.'

I don't say a word – I can't. I'm trying to work out whether I'm more (or less) jealous of two wolfhounds than one wife. And why wolfhounds, in the first place, and not spaniels or Welsh corgis? Power again, presumably. Wolfhounds stand nearly fifty inches high. I know. A client had one once, talked about him constantly, even when we were both still horizontal.

I'm so bemused by dogs and wives, I hardly notice where we're going, until suddenly we're jolting down a rough and pitted track with what looks like country wilderness stretching to both sides. Last time I checked the road, it was belching factories, hatching dreary council flats; now it's breeding cows and sheep, a flock of cackling geese – yes, honestly – just twelve miles from the City and we're passing a real farm; straggling barns and outhouses with two mongrels nosing round; combed brown fields studded with white stones (which transform to wheeling gulls at our approach). The gulls keep soaring, soaring, seem to melt into the sky, which looks huge and sort of billowy, as if it's been shaken out and spread to dry, instead of crumpled up to nothing, as in London. London's disappeared. Noise and traffic, dirt and smoke, have simply been erased. Even the rain has stopped, at last; faint rays of wary sunlight flickering through grasses or rainbowing the puddles. There's a sudden stir of wings again, powerful ragged flapping wings, slate-grey against the curdled milk of cloud.

'Oh, look!' I shout. 'A heron.'

Seton shrugs. 'They're two a penny here.'

'Where's "here"?'

'Dartford marshes.'

I daren't say 'what' again, though I must admit I've never heard of them. Dartford to me is just a boring tunnel, a nothing sort of town. I hadn't realised there were marshes, least of all such lonely ones, no more farms or buildings, no sign of man at all.

I'm wrong. 'DANGER, PYROTECHNICS!' says a notice, and Seton stops a moment, points towards the high wood fence, emblazoned with barbed wire.

'See the fireworks factory? It's ancient, that old place, looks more like a relic, though it's still producing fire-works. In fact, it's buried in the wilds here because it also happens to make TNT for the Ministry of Defence.'

I peer up at a second notice, headed 'Explosives Act, 1875', feel a shudder of unease. We've already passed the Woolwich Royal Arsenal. Too much dynamite.

I'm relieved when he jolts on again, and we reach a sort of no-man's-land, overgrown with bushes, dead and tangled grass, and intercut with weed-embroidered creeks. The light is really beautiful – the last glints and shimmers gleaming on the rain-washed land, gilding the grey water. As I watch, it seems to slowly fade; sky and water melding, colours smudging, blurred. Greys and greens and browns and rusts all creep towards each other and embrace. The birds are dwindling too, now, larks skittering less wildly, piebald peewits flocking home to roost, one lonely kestrel hovering almost motionless. I can feel poems exploding out of me – winged and feathered poems, soaring high, migrating south, guided by the sun and constellations. I've always loved the country, feel calmer in it, grounded, as if I need a landscape to frame me, shelter me; need cleaner purer air to blast away the grit and fret of London. Yet this is London – unbelievably.

'There's the Thames,' says Seton, pointing not to water, but to the tops of distant boats – a mast, a sail, a chimney-stack – no hulls. 'See how low we are here – way below the river. And the land's still sinking, actually, subsiding just a fraction every day. That's why it's preserved, I suppose. No one dares to build on it. A solid house could land up in the bog.'

'So how about *your* house?'

'Who said I had a house?'

I recall his offer of a drink, see us gulping water from a creek, roosting with the birds. I don't mind at all. It seems simpler that way, safer. Possessions are so complicated, and walls make prisons, don't they?

Suddenly he stops, turns the engine off. I can hear the silence now; smell the marshes, a faint tang of mud and slime, overlaid with brine, as if they've been salted to prevent them putrefying. We both get out, walk towards the river, which means a lurch and pant uphill before we're standing by the wide grey brooding Thames – not the City river with its busy shipping, swarming wharfs, but a river almost empty, reflecting on itself as it ripples in towards us, weeds and bushes fringing it, instead of refineries and factories. It's cold, it's bitter cold; a savage wind blowing off the water and clawing at our faces. It's hard to light our cigarettes, so we turn back to the marsh again, following a winding creek which is edged with thick black mud. It's such perfect mud I long to take my clothes off and sink down down in it; feel it pressing close against my skin – rich, dark, oozy, slimy mud, soft and probably warm.

'Well, how about our drink?' says Seton, head bent against the wind.

I look at him, astonished. Is he about to conjure up a cocktail-bar from a waste of weed and water, pump draught Guinness from a creek? No. He strides on down the tangled path, turns a corner, stops beside a boat – well, half a boat – pulled up out of the water, so it seems to float on scummy grass, a flotsam of old debris lapping at its sides: gaping shoes without their soles, stained and tattered newspapers, a purple Crimplene dress looking solid like a corpse as it huddles on itself, even a rusty broken pram. The hull is battered, peeling, the deck stained with oil and paint, the brass around the portholes green with verdigris. Seton swarms up a rope-ladder until he's standing on the deck, motions me to follow. The rope is wet and treacherous, so I'm terrified of slipping. I reach the top (with difficulty), stare down at the amputated stern. It's hacked right through like those ladies in old travelling fairs who were sawn brutally in half. The surgery looks amateur, the severed edge encrusted now with scar tissue – weeds sprouting from the wound.

'Why half a boat?' I ask.

Seton doesn't answer, is already clambering down a second ladder into the main cabin below, which is strangely neat and tidy, as if the boat's inside and its outside are owned by different people. The two narrow bunks are spread with tartan rugs, the tiny kitchen clean and almost bare, though with a detritus of smells – Calor gas and paraffin, damp timber, cooking-oil. Seton has to stoop, is too tall for the cabin and especially for the kitchen which has a lower panelled roof. He's finding glasses, pouring drinks; doesn't ask me what I want, just hands me half a tumblerful of Kentucky bourbon – neat.

'Cheers!' I say, as we squat down on the bunks. Again, he doesn't speak, just gulps his whisky swiftly, as if it were mere water, then gets up to light the lamp. It's some ancient sort of gas lamp which makes a sullen hissing sound, as if resenting my intrusion. I begin to feel uncomfortable. Perhaps Seton doesn't want me there, is already regretting his rash offer of a drink. I glance uneasily around me, my gaze stopping at two pictures I vaguely recognise – wild explosive abstracts in savage blacks and browns. I get up to view them closer, touch the thick encrusted texture of the paint.

'They're a bit like John-Paul's pictures – you know, the ones all round his room.'

Seton nods. 'They *are* John-Paul's. I bought a couple from him. I suppose you know he paints?'

'Er . . . no, I didn't, actually.'

'Yeah, it's quite a passion. He's got hundreds more, just like these. He can't seem to move on. A lot of artists change their style, or at least the colours of their palette, but John-Paul still seems happiest smearing his own shit around.'

I take a swig of bourbon, feel really threatened now. 'But I . . . I thought he was a doctor, not an artist.'

'He's neither.'

'What d'you mean?'

'Well, he never went to art school, or studied art at all, though he does have shows occasionally. God knows why the galleries should bother with his stuff, except I guess he's pretty good at pulling strings. As for medicine, forget it. *I'm* more a medical man than he is, and that's not saying much. He never even trained as a lay analyst, or analytic therapist, or whatever he likes to call himself. The situation's crazy in this country. Anyone can set up as a psychotherapist or analyst, without even one day's training. The profession's always bleating for some sort of national register, with laws to make it bite, but nothing's come of it so far, so . . .' He shrugs. 'You get phoneys like John-Paul.'

'But surely . . .?' I'm too staggered to go on. I've always taken it for granted that John-Paul was not just trained, but so utterly professional he had every last word worked out for its significance, its pith; timed even every silence with hair's-breadth skill, precision. I slam back on the bunk. How dare he grab our money, tamper with our psyches, when he's nothing but a quack. Or waste time painting shitscapes when he's meant to put his patients first; always gives the impression that nothing else exists. I accept another cigarette, try to calm my churning mind while I inhale the smoke deep down. 'But he *is* a doctor, Seton. I've seen his name written out, several times, in fact – you know, Dr . . .'

'Yeah, Doctor of Philosophy, and from a second-rate foreign university, which probably means it's worthless. Oh, I grant you he's quite bright, probably knows Winnicott from Guntrip, or Wittgenstein from Heidegger, but he's still a con-man, pure and simple. And a jumped-up one, at that. His family are dirt.'

'Dirt?'

'Well, his father was a plumber. Whom I suppose we're meant to worship as the new aristocracy, judging by the cash they earn. But as far as breeding is concerned, or culture, or refinement . . .' Seton shrugs, refills his empty tumbler. 'More for you?' he asks.

I don't reply, just spring at him, start lashing out with fists and feet. How dare he decimate John-Paul, slander him, destroy him? It's obviously all lies. He's just a rotten snob, and with a grudge against John-Paul – I've seen that for myself. He grabs my wrists, holds them in a vice. I try to bite his hands, but he's far too strong for me, tips me on his bunk, then lies full length across me.

I thresh and squirm with fury, but I'm basically quite powerless.

'So you want to bite?' he asks, his face very close to mine, so I can see the pricks of stubble, the dark hairs in his nose.

'*No!*' My shout's aborted. His mouth is already clamped on mine and he's biting, kissing, hurting – biting lips and tongue. I can taste blood in my mouth, swallow it and struggle; realise I can't fight him, so I bite him back, instead – the most violent savage kiss I've ever given or received. I never kiss my clients or let them use their mouths; limit any contact to below the waist; remove my mind, my spirit, salvage what I can; outlaw words like intimacy or union. But the whole of me is rallied now, the whole of me involved, as teeth grind teeth, mouths lacerate. Oh yes, this kiss is intimate all right. I can taste his blood and my blood, taste his bourbon breath; feel the shape and pressure of his teeth, the rough, furred, cat-like darting of his tongue. I'm smoking his last cigarette, sucking out the relics of his lunch, the scraps of last night's dinner; I'm chewing on his past, his personality; scrunching up his cruelty, his rage.

My own mouth feels sore, misshapen, so I'm almost glad when he starts dragging off my blouse, turning his attention to my breasts. He doesn't know what button-holes are for, but he does know how to bite. I'm not wearing a bra – often leave it off the days I see John-Paul – so his teeth have found my nipples, can calculate exactly that fine red line between excitement and real pain. He oversteps the line, hears me draw my breath in, gasp with pain – bites harder. I'm almost powerless still, can only gnaw his shoulder through the tough wool of his sweater, claw my nails up and down his back. Everything feels rough and somehow angry – his stubble on my face, the prickly rug we're lying on, his coarse and curly hair, the texture of his hands – a labourer's hands, despite that

119

haughty face. He removes his mouth, but only for a moment while he fumbles with my skirt. It's wet still from the rain, tight and too confining, I fight him every inch, fight him harder still as he starts pulling down my tights. There isn't room to fight – the cabin's far too cramped. I've already knocked my head, banged my knees and elbows on the wall, yet there's some strange exhilaration in wrestling with this man, even knowing that I'll lose.

I'm naked. He looks at me, eyes tracking very slowly down my body. I don't know what he thinks – he doesn't say. He's still got all his clothes on, wet thick hurting clothes. The sweater smells of petrol; the jeans feel stiff and calloused beneath my naked legs. I've hardly seen his body, just glimpses of it, tastes of it – his bony wrists, his navel, the whorl of springy body-hair which plunges down his neck, the sourish gamy flavour of his skin. He won't let me touch his jeans, removes my hand, yanks down the zip himself. The jeans are cruelly tight and his prick springs out, impatient and inflamed, as if mad at being caged so long. It's tall and thin, like he is, with the same coarse and over-long black hair, and engorged blue veins running to the tip, which is moist and red and swollen like a plum. He isn't circumcised, and the foreskin is well back, looking slack and almost shrivelled against the taut vigour of the piston.

He forces in. I don't object, just use my teeth again. If he wants to fuck me, fine, but I shan't make it very pleasant for him. No submissive passive Nial slumped there like a dummy while her clients grunt and sweat, feeling nothing, doing less; refusing to yield so much as one small bead of sweat, or one stray pubic hair. I'll shed my blood for Seton, lose my life, if necessary, just so long as he experiences my anger, my contempt.

I buck and twist beneath him, trying to jerk him out. He apes my every movement, ramming in still deeper, following where I lead, as if we're locked together in some new and violent dance. He can scratch as well as bite and thrust, and all at the same time. But so can I – and harder. All I need are images to fuel me. I'm seeing him again in John-Paul's room, hurling insults, breaking up my session, breaking up my life. Okay, Seton, so you want to kill John-Paul, but I love the man, I need him, so I'm going to have to stop you – stop you killing, stop you bloody fucking me.

I use every last muscle in my body, call up every scrap and shred of strength, pummelling him, and threshing, lashing with my fists. He's furious himself now, furious with me for being in the tower when he wanted John-Paul on his own and to himself. Our two rages meet and kindle; our two breaths rasping, searing; our two rhythms syncopated. My hair is trapped beneath his arm. He's pulling it, and hurting – hurting everywhere, though I hardly feel the pain now. I'm too involved, too angry; taunting him with insults, the very ones he shouted at John-Paul. Once he leaves my mouth free and is snicking at my neck, I yell them out aloud. 'You stupid lying bastard! I'll . . .'

He *did* lie, didn't he? Called himself a doctor, pretended he was trained, charged me all that money for his expertise, his skills. And then pretending he's so busy when he's really painting pictures – no, not even painting, smearing shit around. I slump back for a moment as I try to take it in – John-Paul a fraud, a nothing. The hurt feels like a madness. All those endless minutes that I counted every day, totting up to pain and disillusion; all that infinite circling round a crumbling cardboard tower. I stare up at the porthole, see nothing but dull grey; no grass, no sky, no water, just a dead and blinded window. The lamp is hissing still, sounds weary, disillusioned. Nervous shadows fidget. I'm lying in a shadow, feel dark and half-extinguished.

Seton takes advantage of the pause, heaves me off the bunk and to my knees, rams in again the back way. I don't care. I've got more scope to move now, and I'm no longer slumped and passive, but mad with rage, rage against John-Paul, his cowardice, his treachery, his greed, his greasy lies. The cabin floor is wooden – old and splintered – tears my knees and hands. Seton's hurting, really hacking into me, yet we're bonded now, at last. His anger's changed, like mine, is directed at John-Paul, and not at me. We turn on him together – he's there in person, we brought him in the van – drag him to the floor.

'I know,' I shout. 'I understand. Of course you had to kill John-Paul. We'll kill him *now*, together. We'll . . .'

My shouting drives him wild. I can feel him gathering speed, his nails digging in my flesh as he grips my waist to steady him, slams in from behind.

'Don't come!' I shout. 'Don't come yet.' Too late – he's coming – a scorching maddened brutal come, as if he's pumping me with bullets, not with sperm. I pull away before he's even finished, feel him leaking out. He doesn't say a word, though his breathing's very rackety, shuddering and dangerous, as if something's loose or broken in his chest. He falls back on the bunk, shuts his eyes as if to snuff me out. I understand. Bodies aren't too pretty after sex. Mine is marked and reddened, filmed with sweat, knees grazed and bruised, top lip split and bloody. He still has all his clothes on, which saves him, in a way – just his grubby jeans unzipped. I watch his prick deflate. It looks wizened now and shrivelled, as if it's grown old in just a minute, can no longer stand up on its own, needs help, needs sympathy. I lean across and touch it, pity in my fingertips. Seton twitches irritably. '*Don't!*' he snaps, eyes shut still.

I sag back on the floor, watch his semen oozing down my thigh. It seems too thin, too pallid, too meagre altogether for our murderous double rage. Shouldn't it be scarlet, not that wan and sickly white; Niagara, not a dribble? I scoop it up, suck it from my fingers. It tastes slimy, slightly salty, like the marsh might taste, outside. Seton hasn't moved. I'm glad he isn't stroking me, or asking 'Did you come?'

I don't need to come. I'm sated.

# 9

'But you always said your mother was so tidy. "Neat to a fault" was the phrase you used, I think.'

'Yes, she *is*, of course she is.' Bryan felt a rush of shame. How could neatness be a fault, especially in a world where there was no order, regularity? John–Paul had simply failed to understand. He wasn't talking about chaos in his house or cupboard drawers, disorder in his Mother's fridge or larder, but chaos in the sub-atomic world. The problem was he didn't have the words for it. The books had made it hard enough, especially the huge new one he'd been working through all week, but there was still no avoiding its main theme: the universe was essentially chaotic, at least on the atomic level, and the total amount of chaos was going up and up. According to the author (and the second law of thermodynamics, which he remembered only vaguely from his schooldays), chaos was far easier to achieve than order and therefore far more likely. In fact, chaos was the norm. Mountains eroded, stars burnt out, buildings crumbled, people grew old, clocks ran down, the universe itself ran down.

Bryan closed his eyes a moment, listened to John–Paul's clocks. He could hear their ticking growing weaker, weaker; feel the tall and solid tower slowly tottering. He'd always loved the tower, had looked up its history in the library (a snug and cosy refuge until he'd found the science section) – amazed to find it dated from 1280, and had lost its nave and chancel only in the 1940 Blitz. The site had remained a ruin until the later 1960s, white with pigeon droppings, lush with tangled weeds. Then the bulldozers moved in, cleared the rubble for a block of monster office blocks. The tower was spared as an ancient monument, had been declared a listed building, its one remaining gravestone girdled with a preservation order. Ten years later, it had been legally deconsecrated, leased for secular use by the London Diocesan Fund, but still sacrosanct in one way, since there were extremely strict conditions about who could or couldn't lease it and exactly what they could or couldn't do there.

Sacrosanct! Bryan clenched his hands, shifted on the couch. What use were preservation orders when everything was doomed? You couldn't slap one on the universe, or tack one to each atom. As far as he could gather, atoms weren't quite there at all, weren't *things* with an identity which you could pin down or define. In fact, the author had concluded that matter was in a suspended state of almost-schizophrenia and suffering from an identity crisis. Which called for a psychiatrist – except how could one be found, when even John-Paul, with all his experience and training, hadn't seemed to grasp the point at all?

Bryan glanced up at the window. The morning light looked dirty and half-hearted. It would soon be dark at seven in the morning, clammy-cold as well. If he could only stop his therapy, he could stay in bed a whole hour longer three days every week, have time to chew his breakfast. (He could feel a piece of toast still whole, one sharp corner digging in his ribs.) How *could* he stop it, though? John-Paul had said he needed at least five or six more years (yes, on top of the first four), and now he'd discovered all these horrors in the subatomic world, it might well take even longer.

'I'm not talking about my Mother,' he said slowly. 'I'm talking about the cosmos.' He broke off instantly as he heard the faintest rustle from behind him – John-Paul lighting up. He hated the way they had to be positioned, so that John-Paul could see him, but not vice versa. It roused such painful memories. For many of his boyhood years his Mother had sat behind him, knitting coloured squares while he struggled with his homework. It had made him very tense, sapped his concentration as he'd listened to her breathing – the sighs or sudden in-breaths which meant she was displeased. She could see right through his back, knew when he was daydreaming or doodling in the margins. The knitted squares were something of a comfort, though – even if a mystery. She never joined them up to make scarves or shawls or blankets, just added to the ever-growing pile. Yet, nonetheless, they proved important in his life, endowed him with a sense of order, very early on: horizontals tallying with verticals, all angles ninety degrees. He wished John-Paul would knit. It might afford him some distraction, dilute his total concentration on his patient's feeble words.

'But don't you see, Bryan, you have allowed your mother to become so all-embracing, so central in your life and in your psyche, that she now appears to constitute your world? So in talking about the cosmos, as you put it, you are, I think, talking about your mother, though you may feel the need to deny it.'

Bryan said nothing. He didn't like to contradict a doctor. It sounded rude, ungrateful, and anyway, it would only be called 'denial'. The room seemed cold, unwelcoming, the couch hard beneath his back. He wished they could sit face to face, like friends. He hadn't any friends – well, a few acquaintances at work, and the woman in the paper-shop who always asked him how he was, but no one close or special. John-Paul was special, in a way, but so remote, so shadowy. He didn't even know his age. He was bad at people's ages. Both John-Paul and his Mother seemed old like rocks were old, or old like old cathedrals.

The silence felt unkind, yet he couldn't seem to fill it, despite the fact it cost so much – vintage-champagne-minutes simply pouring down the drain. Free association might sound fine in theory, but in practice it was difficult – nerve-racking, embarrassing, and probably very dangerous. He'd heard it called a sort of mental x-ray, and x-rays showed up frightening things like tumours, fractures, clots. Was his own mind cancerous, fractured or obstructed, ulcerated, haemorrhaging? And why did it remain a stubborn blank – even now, when his doctor/radiologist was impatient for a picture, waiting for a shadow on the screen?

A real x-ray would be infinitely preferable. At least he would be given his instructions, clear and firm instructions, like swallowing his barium-meal in a series of swift gulps, or holding his breath and counting up to ten. Whereas therapy was vague and quite amorphous, left him always muddled and confused, longing for more structure in the sessions, some goal or sense of purpose, some objective he could grasp, a methodical instruction-sheet setting out the guidelines. Even after four long years, he had a strange uneasy feeling that he'd somehow missed the point and been doing things all wrong, wasted all those costly baffling sessions. He didn't even understand the jargon – terms like 'splitting', 'super-ego', or 'cathexis', which remained nebulous but menacing, like the many mysterious concepts in his physics and astronomy books; a source of endless tribulation, yet impossible to pinpoint or define. Was it any wonder he lay awake most nights, when super-egos assaulted his frail psyche, and supernovae threatened further off?

He stared up at the ceiling, feeling quite demoralised, but still trying to find some topic he could broach. The ceiling offered nothing, so he examined all the in-trays in his head, all those pigeonholes and filing cabinets, which he always did his frantic best to organise and order, so that his anxieties were kept separate from his fears, his depressions from his phobias. Though even that was tricky. Most fears were depressing, so he often spent an hour or two nervously debating which section they should go in, or how large they had to loom before he refiled them under 'Panic'. And some items fitted every slot – chaos, for example, which induced panic, fear, depression *and* anxiety.

'Chaology,' he murmured, trying out the word aloud, which he'd never dared before.

'I beg your pardon?'

'It's a new word in the dictionary. I looked it up last week. It means the science of chaos. You can study chaos now, you see, like people study biology, or zoology, or all the other "ologies". Which proves it's *there* – and growing.'

'Bryan, it seems to me quite obvious that it's your *inner* world which is experiencing the chaos. We all tend to fear chaos when our own personal lives are threatened, so it may well be that since you've yielded all control to your mother, you feel you've returned to the powerless state of a child. I mean, it's surely not insignificant that you brought your toy snake with you today – a familiar object from your childhood, which once gave you comfort and security.'

Bryan glanced down at his side, still astonished by the fact that the snake was lying on the couch with him, its green head resting dumbly on the pillow, its red felt tongue lolling like a drunk's. However had it got here? He remembered sorting through his briefcase just last night, putting in his report on departmental stock control, his pakamac, his pilchard sandwiches, but not a green and yellow knitted snake. It had been knitted by his Auntie Anne, his mother's younger sister, when he was only four; had shared his life (and bedroom) ever since. It was now limp and rather lumpy, its stuffing semi-rotted from his constant childhood tears, one black button eye lost, its skin distinctly grubby. But he had to admit he was very much attached to it, couldn't simply chuck it out, or give it to a jumble sale. And anyway, he felt he owed it something, a refuge in its twilight years, when it had done so much for him when he was small. Even now, its one dim eye was fixed on him, imploring; its tail curled in towards itself, as if scared it might be docked. Yet if anyone at BRB should see it . . . He tensed in sudden horror. There was no privacy at work, not even in a briefcase, not even in a locker. He'd become an instant laughing stock – sniggers in the office, titters in the gents.

'John-Paul,' he stuttered out, almost gagging on the name, yet using it deliberately to stress the importance of his request. 'I . . . I wonder if I could leave it here, the snake? Oh, only for the day. I don't want to be a nuisance. I could pick it up this evening, if it wouldn't inconvenience you. It's just that . . .' The sentence petered out. How could he pick it up, when Friday was his class night? How could he brave the class at all, face Mary, face his Father? One hand groped blindly out, reaching for his snake, the comfort of its presence and its shape. He longed to pull the blankets over him, as he had done as a child, sob into its soft and yielding body.

He heard John-Paul shift his chair a fraction, do something with an ashtray. 'So you wish to leave your phallus with me?'

Bryan felt a blush suffusing his whole body, like a painter with a roller slapping scarlet on a wall. He hated that word 'phallus' which John-Paul would keep using and which made him feel inferior since he was sure he didn't have one. It sounded too important and definitely too large. *He* had something different – something English, insubstantial.

'Snakes have always been a symbol of sexuality, in many different cultures – the upsurging life-force which can move with neither wings nor legs. I find it very interesting, and perhaps significant, that *your* snake is not only multi-coloured, but knitted in a complicated stitch. Which makes me feel your genitality is complex, in some way – and probably confused. You appear to be drawing my attention to your phallus at this moment – in fact, wanting to "leave it here", which suggests you can't handle it yourself. Does your snake have any name, I wonder? What did you call it as a child?'

Bryan's blush had reached his ankles, now flooded down his feet. 'Anne.'

'*Anne?*'

Bryan nodded. He'd never been imaginative. Anne, to please his aunt.

'So you feel your snake is female?'

'No – well, yes. I mean . . .' He hadn't really thought about its gender. Everything was female in his home. It had seemed safer that way, natural.

'In designating your phallus as female, you're obviously seeking to deny your masculinity.'

'I haven't *got* a phallus,' Bryan said irritably, his eyes beginning to water as a new cloud of cigarette smoke drifted over his head. 'I've got a . . .' Abruptly, he broke off, couldn't get the word out. There *wasn't* any word for the footling thing he kept between his legs. His Mother had studiously avoided all the words, even childish ones like 'willie'; had always made him feel he shouldn't have that . . . that carbuncle, excrescence, cluttering up his underpants, when it was clearly very germy, probably highly dangerous, and certainly unnecessary. He'd never liked to touch it, even when relieving himself, felt he needed sugar-tongs as he stood above the toilet bowl, or perhaps extra-long chopsticks, specially sterilised.

'So now you wish to castrate yourself?' John-Paul exhaled more smoke. 'Isn't this the central issue? All your talk this week about sub-atomic particles is avoidance pure and simple.'

'It's *not*.' Bryan wiped his eyes. 'It's real. I mean, it *isn't* real. That's the point, the one I keep trying to explain. Nothing's real, not even basic matter.'

'Yes, I think I understand. You feel a sense of unreality located in your body, and especially in your phallus, because you doubt your own masculine identity. This may spring from basic guilt, of course, which brings us back to your snake. Serpents have always been a symbol of temptation. I expect you read your Bible as a child – the story of the Fall, in Genesis. The snake created chaos in the world, shattered the serenity of Eden, as *your* guilt about your phallus is causing chaos in your own world, or at least a fear of chaos. And even in the Babylonian creation myths, which Genesis derives from, there's a sea-monster called Tiamat, who . . .'

Bryan had lost the thread. John-Paul was far too clever for him. He'd never even heard of the Babylonian creation myths, yet John-Paul just flung them in as if they were as common as Red Riding Hood. No, he mustn't think of wolves. He'd been a lustful wolf himself as far as Mary was concerned, had spent thirty-seven seconds gazing at her breasts – well, only through her blouse of course, but he'd imagined them *without* the blouse, or brassière; seen himself alone with her while she undressed after the class – a hundred classes, actually, two hundred swelling breasts. John-Paul was right – he *did* feel sexual guilt, though he'd never laid a finger on her, not even in his fantasies, just gazed and gazed, and longed.

He could see her now, this instant, as the Winston Churchill Centre burgeoned into the Garden of Eden, an unchaotic sunny spot where Mary cavorted naked with her Adam. He cast himself as Adam, adding several inches to both his height and shoulder-width, and transforming his six chest-hairs to a dark and tangled pelt. Mary did resemble Eve, in fact, or at least the picture of her in his Children's Illustrated Bible – 'Eve Banished from the Garden'. Her breasts had been enormous in the picture – or had seemed so in his boyhood – full and soft and rounded, yet trussed up very high, as if supported by some supernatural pulley. But a snake had been coiled round them, a terrifying serpent with a long forked tongue and scales. His Anne was nothing like that. Anne was just a friend, and a very old and loyal one, not dangerous, not a symbol. But if John-Paul didn't understand, then it was probably his fault again. He just wasn't bright enough, didn't have symbols, only cuddly toys; didn't read creation myths, just the *Daily Mail*.

'What are you thinking, Bryan?'

He jumped. 'Er . . . nothing.'

'So you're still fixated on your sense of unreality?'

'No, I'm . . .' Bryan fished desperately in the shallows of his mind, came up with a mermaid in a blue flower-patterned blouse. 'I was . . . thinking about Mary.'

'The Mother of God?'

'Pardon?'

'I assumed you meant the Virgin Mary, since we were just talking about Eden. Eve's been called the precursor of the Virgin, and of course her name in Hebrew means . . .'

Bryan swallowed. Precursor. Hebrew names. This was worse than Skerwin. 'No, Mary's just a friend of mine.'

'You have a friend called Mary? You've never mentioned her before.'

He nodded, shook his head, drooped back on the couch. 'I don't know her, actually.'

'Yet you just called her your friend.'

'Well, she *might* have been a friend. We were getting on so well, you see. I think she really liked me. But then I saw my Father and . . .' Again, the words dried up. He could hardly bear to think that his Father hadn't recognised him. They were so physically alike – even Mary had remarked on it – but it wasn't only that. There was obviously a strong instinctual bond between all fathers and all sons.

He'd experienced it himself on some deep and almost sacred level the instant he'd glimpsed Skerwin; hoped, assumed the tutor would reciprocate. It could have been so different – Skerwin pulling up his chair in the warm womb of the canteen, while he introduced his Father to his girlfriend – no, fiancée – Mary; drinks all round, to celebrate. Or perhaps knickerbocker glories. He'd never had one, ever, but they had figured very frequently in his boyhood fantasies: he and his (vague) Father sharing one long spoon, one foot-high fancy glass; all shyness, strangeness, melting as fast as the ice cream.

'What d'you mean, you saw your father? You saw him in a dream?'

Bryan shook his head. He nearly always dreamed about his Mother – the Parcel Dream – where the postman's thunderous knocking on the door woke him with a start as he raced down the stairs to consciousness and found his squawking, crumpled, revenge-declaring Mother struggling from her wrappings on the door-mat. In the last few weeks, he hadn't dreamed at all, though he'd been trying really hard, jotting it on all his lists, the night ones and the day ones: 'Mow lawn, mend drawer, have dream.' John-Paul thrived on dreams, reacted like a dog might to a bone (especially sexual dreams, which seemed the equivalent of marrowbones). He also made them highly complicated, even brief and flimsy ones, which could fill the next day's session as they worked on them together, poking under the 'manifest content' to drag out the so-called 'latent content' (which he always pictured like a slug beneath a lettuce leaf). It seemed strange to call it 'work', but John-Paul always did, and indeed he often felt more tired and drained after fifty minutes on the couch than by nine hours at his desk.

'You imagined that you saw him, then?'

Bryan jumped back to his Father, exchanged his tortured

dream-life for the Winston Churchill Centre. 'No, I saw him really.'

'Bryan, you're projecting your fantasies into the external world. That's understandable, but all the same . . .'

'It wasn't a fantasy.' Bryan's voice was slowly rising, with the smoke. 'He was as real as you and me. I even saw him in the gents. I went in there to hide and . . .'

'You seem confused this morning, about the nature of reality. Nothing in your world today seems real, except your father, who died thirty years ago.'

. 'Thirty-one.'

'So you do agree he's dead?'

'Oh, no. I only meant they'd *said* he'd died thirty-one years ago. But he wasn't dead, in fact.'

'You appear to be hinting now at some idea of Resurrection. Are you confusing your father with God?'

'There isn't any God.' Bryan heard his own voice falter. He'd never been religious, despite that childhood Bible, but it still hurt to lose his God. None of the authors of those science books seemed to feel the need for Him – well, not the God he knew: the Managing Director who kept things organised, made the rules, hired and fired, could draw straight lines without a ruler, and did everything methodically – created night and day on Monday, sky and water Tuesday – even had a Mother and yet found time to rest on Sundays, which was impossible with *his* Mother.

'You're denying God because you've never had a father. It's the same principle again, you see – a very shaky sense of masculinity, whether in yourself, or in your father, or the idea of God Himself.'

'But I have got a Father. I keep telling you I found him just last Friday. I know I should have mentioned it before, informed you on the Monday or the Wednesday, but we talked about my Mother the whole time.'

'The two may well be linked. Your fixation on your

mother has created an overwhelming need to find your absent father, so as to reassert the idea of masculinity, and help you take a stand against your mother. This could well be a hopeful sign, the beginning of a change.'

Bryan sighed. John-Paul's skill was listening, but he sometimes felt he was listening to someone else – not B.V. Payne, but some other brighter patient, someone more important. That had probably been the trouble with his Father. Skerwin might have acknowledged him if he'd been brainier, more cultivated. He could always try again, though, approach him in a week or two when he'd completed the whole reading list and could reel off phrases like 'naked singularities' or 'extragalactic nebulae'.

He was aware again of silence, a hopeless dragging silence. If he didn't fill it quickly, John-Paul would ask 'What are you not saying?', which never failed to throw him. 'I'll be seeing him again tonight,' he murmured swiftly, wildly. 'Except how can I face Mary after last time? No, I think I'll have to miss the class . . .' He was talking to himself now, though John-Paul still swooped down.

'I know your mother's very hostile to your going, but didn't we come to the conclusion that you'd keep that one night free from her, not let her dominate?'

'It's nothing to do with Mother – not this time. It's Mary.'

'But you just agreed you didn't know a Mary.'

Bryan closed his eyes. He was feeling very tired. Maybe John-Paul was right (again) and Mary wasn't real. Perhaps the class was unreal, too, so that it wouldn't really matter if he missed it. He could go home and have an early night, go home *now* – immediately – take his snake and curl up tight in bed with it, tell his Mother he was sickening for a cold. If Friday wasn't real, nobody could caution him for missing a day's work.

He forced his eyes to open. It was rude to doze, as well

135

as being wasteful. Every minute cost. He glanced up at the pictures, which he'd always found intimidating. Only clever people had pictures with no people in, and these were really deep ones. He gazed with new intensity, a new sense of startled shock. There was Chaos on the walls – black and swirling Chaos, seething searing Void. Not one straight line in any of the paintings, not one familiar object, or single patch of colour. How could John-Paul dismiss chaos as just a disorder of a patient's inner world, when his very choice of paintings proved him wrong? That artist knew the facts – like the authors of those physics books – had expressed the inexpressible, depicted the grim truth that there *was* no truth, no certainty.

He gripped his snake, heart racing. Was John-Paul even real himself? If he turned his head to check, would he see an empty chair, or worse, no chair at all? Had he been talking to himself for four whole years? He touched his forehead, felt it burning hot, despite the chilly room. He wasn't sickening for a cold, but for something much more serious.

'I don't feel well,' he faltered, voice half-lost as the clock outside the tower began its strident chiming.

'It's time, Bryan. We must finish now.'

'But I'm feeling really rough.' He raised his voice to contradict the chimes. He welcomed them most mornings as his release from grim detention, but today he dared not face a crumbling world. 'I can't just leave like this. Everything's dissolving, breaking down.'

'We'll talk about it on Wednesday.' The clock spun out its seven, cadenced on a final braying eight.

'There won't be any Wednesday. Friday's gone already and . . .'

'It's time. In fact, half a minute over now.'

Bryan leapt up from the couch, snatched his shoes, his briefcase, the new and heavy physics book he took with him everywhere, so he could read it in the train, the lift, the gents. His place was marked with a strip of aluminium foil, stolen from his sandwich wrappings (which his Mother always washed and used again). He'd reached page four hundred and twenty-two – 'The Myth of Time'.

'You're wrong, John-Paul,' he shouted, as he staggered through the door, snake clutched to his chest. 'There *isn't* any time.'

# 10

'Beautiful chrysanthemums! Are they from the garden, dear?'

'Yes.'

'I love those bronzy ones, don't you?'

'Mm.'

'What's the matter, Mary? You don't seem quite yourself today. I noticed when you first came in. You looked a little flushed and . . .'

'No, I'm . . . fine. Absolutely fine.' Mary turned away, so Phyllis couldn't see her face. She *was* flushed. 'You don't seem quite yourself.' The words alarmed her, underlined her feeling of not knowing who she was. Would Phyllis believe she suffered murderous rages, fought secret battles with violent sexual urges, had even wished to kill her mother? Oh, they were all unconscious feelings, John-Paul had assured her, but even so, she couldn't come to terms with them, couldn't understand why outwardly she was still the placid, plodding Mary who never blew her fuse (either out of bed, or in it), when inwardly she was a seething mass of aggression and hot lust. She still *felt* the same, reacted much the same – rarely lost her temper or felt even mildly cross (except with Jonathan's headmaster who really was unreasonable, hadn't let her visit when she was passing just three miles away and only intended dropping in some underpants). And as for . . . bed, well, James was still complaining about useless shrinks who grabbed his money without delivering the goods.

It was as if John-Paul had eavesdropped on their night-time conversation and decided to change tack, since the last two sessions they'd actually discussed the subject, and full-frontally, so to speak. (Though she was still lying on that dreadful couch, with him out of sight behind her.) She'd blushed so much, perspired so profusely, she'd feared she might be suffering an early menopause and was experiencing her first hot flush. John-Paul's room was always hot, but those last two Fridays it had seemed like an inferno, especially when he'd talked about her powerful sexuality, which was apparently quite clear to him because of the equal strength and potency of something called her super-ego which opposed that sexual drive.

Sexual! Mary Hampton – who'd never really seen much point in all that grunting and grimacing which James preferred to a nice quiet read in bed, with a mugful of hot chocolate, and just a friendly cuddle before they put the lights off. Of course, she knew it was her duty to try to go along with him (and she meant that in all senses), but she sometimes wished he'd have a few more headaches, or a crisis in the office, or even a business trip (or two) abroad which didn't extend to wives. But that was not the *real* her, according to John-Paul. That was just her spoilsport super-ego, which was determined to suppress her naturally strong libido, deny her any pleasure or release. She still hadn't fully grasped the new (confusing) Blessed Trinity of Ego, Id and Super-ego, except that the latter seemed extremely sour and strict, rather like her first ayah in Calcutta combined with Reverend Mother. John-Paul said she had, in fact, internalised those figures of authority, who had now become a part of her, a punishing restrictive part which frowned on 'letting go'. Something like that, anyway. He'd used a lot of terms which had left her, frankly, baffled – terms like 'the pre-Oedipal phase' and 'parental introjects'. It all sounded most alarming and she had to confess she preferred the Catholic theory, which seemed simpler altogether: man composed of body and soul — body gross and sinful, soul vital and superior, rather like the cream in a profiterole or the battery in a torch.

'Mary! What *are* you doing, dear? You're meant to slit the stalks, not cut the heads off.'

Mary stared down at her flowers. She had decapitated six of the chrysanthemums, and without even noticing. Perhaps John-Paul was right in calling her aggressive – aggressive even as an infant, which had helped, apparently, to build that savage super-ego, which then turned on her, attacked. Violent as an infant seemed even more unlikely than sexual as a wife. The photos showed her plump – a docile, almost vacuous baby, staring into space or munching on her teddy. But Lesson One in therapy she *had* learned: nothing was what it seemed, least of all small babies, whom she'd always loved as innocent and sweet, but who were actually downright dissolute and vicious.

She scooped up an amputated flower-head. Could she salvage it perhaps, make a Chinese-style arrangement comprising one perfect stemless bloom floating on a saucer? No. She'd never find saucers in a church. They were restricted to brass vases which needed hours of polishing to make them worthy of the altar. She threw the heads away, hoping Father Fox wouldn't see them and accuse her of extravagance. She really ought to concentrate. It was a privilege to do the altar flowers, arrange them beautifully – for God – bring a part of her own garden to God's House. She and Phyllis had been doing them for years together. Phyllis was unmarried – well, married to the Church, perhaps, and very close to Father Fox, who shared her interest in . . . what was it, that name they gave to people who loved birds? Not loved them in the vague sense of saving crusts and bacon rinds, or buying robin Christmas cards, but studied all their Latin names and rushed around to breeding spots with binoculars and notebooks. Orni-something, wasn't it? She wasn't good at words today, could only remember shameful ones like clitoris, libido.

'Clitoris,' she whispered. She'd never said the word

before, never even heard it said, before John-Paul had brazened it. James wasn't one for words.

'What, dear?'

Mary wrenched her mind back, tried to fix her whole attention on Phyllis's brass vase. 'It's late for roses, isn't it?'

'Yes. Those were just the last few in the garden. I think we'll have to buy our flowers next week.'

'Orgasm,' she mouthed. The word felt strange – and shocking – especially that last syllable which rhymed with 'spasm', seemed to stretch her lips and jar her tongue. John-Paul had actually asked her if she had them – yes, just as casually, as chattily, as if he were asking whether she had oil-fired central heating, or cats, or fitted carpets. 'O-o-r-gasm.' She made the word much longer, spun it out; suddenly caught the eye of Ignatius of Loyola, who was frowning from his picture on the wall. She mustn't think of orgasms in church – well, they weren't quite in church, but in the sacristy, which was maybe even worse since it housed all the sacred vessels, the vestments and the altar linens, and had framed pictures of a dozen saints watching from three sides.

She stripped the lower leaves from a chrysanthemum, forced her mind to stay on flowers or birds. The leaves smelt strange – damp and slightly putrid; the dizzy scent of roses almost over- whelming the small and sober room which smelt usually of piety and mothballs. Smells were so important. John-Paul's room smelt dangerous – the clash of men's cologne with cigarette smoke, the faint tang of Mint Imperials cutting through the odour of old stone; the reek of sex, of rage. Then all those threatening noises – panting traffic, pouncing clocks, police cars squalling past. So different from this tranquil church where the silence was so thick you could bottle it and take it home – no confessions being heard, no organ practice, children's choir, no fussy Father Fox, just her and Phyllis alone with

141

God. She ought to feel serene; always had before, the days they did the flowers – until John-Paul had started joining them, unasked.

'Quick! Mary, turn that tap off. You're miles away today. Is it Jonathan again? I thought you said his ear infection cleared.'

'Yes, it did, thank God. He's still not really right, though.' Mary mopped her sodden skirt, swabbed water from the floor. 'I'm sorry, Phyllis, really. I think I'm simply tired. I'm not sleeping all that well.'

'You're not drinking coffee, are you? Late at night, I mean?'

'No, it's usually hot chocolate.' Too often, James would say. It seemed to be either sex or chocolate for some reason, never both.

'That's every bit as bad, dear. People just don't realise, but there's caffeine in hot chocolate, *and* in cocoa. I can't look at them myself. One sip and I'm jumping.'

Mary glanced across at Phyllis, tried to see her jumping, see her murderous. Could *she* be violent, too, exterminating mothers, fighting sexual urges? It didn't seem that likely. Her face looked pale and passionless behind the rimless glasses, the grey eyes weak but kindly, the prim mouth tightly closed, as if to prevent anything unpleasant either going in or out of it. Perhaps caffeine hyped her up, but without it she was dormant, like a small boat always tethered to its moorings, not risking the high seas, not risking any movement beyond a gentle lap and plash. She was dressed solidly and sensibly in lumpy tweeds with olive knitted knee-socks and men's brown leather sandals. Mary towelled a final damp spot from her own Berkertex two-piece, admired her new blue slingbacks which she'd bought in John-Paul's honour. She and frumpy Phyllis didn't really have that much in common, except the Church and lovely gardens. Strange how all her friends seemed wrong now, strangely superficial.

She'd never noticed it before – before John-Paul, that is. She longed to have a real best friend (the sort you had at boarding school and swore to giggly secrecy about periods or boys), so they could discuss vital things like super-egos or erotogenic zones, instead of the new Marks and Spencer range of frozen yogurts, or the price of football boots.

She sank back on the window-seat, crossed her legs, uncrossed them instantly, with a stab of guilt and shame. John-Paul had pointed out that when she'd been sitting in the chair in his consulting room (before she'd dared the couch), she had never once uncrossed her legs – no, not in all her sessions. He'd questioned her about it, asked if she were defending herself against something threatening, dangerous. She hadn't understood. She *always* crossed her legs, merely found it comfortable, that's all. Except it wasn't all. John-Paul went on probing, used the term 'reaction-formation', a word she'd never heard before, but which meant you did the opposite of what you really wanted, so that she could have actually been fighting an overpowering urge to *open* her legs, and open them for him. She had gasped in disbelief – open her legs, for a doctor and a stranger? Oh, she did find him attractive, there was no denying that, and there was something rather marvellous about him being still so young, yet so clever and experienced, but as for urges . . . Quite nonsensical.

'Did you enjoy your fireworks party, dear?'

'Oh, yes.' Mary leapfrogged back to Saturday – the drunken shouts, the bangs, the dangerous leaping flames. Today was Guy Fawkes day, in fact, but nobody had parties on a Monday. She hadn't liked the party. Guy Fawkes was for children, and hers were all away. She'd hardly dared to watch as the guy suddenly collapsed, was sucked down by the fire, consumed to ash. He'd looked so like John-Paul – dark, dramatic, dressed in James's old pinstripes – yes, and even with dark glasses.

She had found herself weeping, desperate shaming tears. 'No!' she'd shouted silently. 'Don't burn him.'

Phyllis was bulking out her roses with green fern, handling both with a mixture of affection and strict discipline, like a nanny with her charges. 'Dangerous things, those fireworks. You can lose an arm, you realise, or blast off half your face.'

Mary nodded, prayed her boys were safe indoors, not handling squibs or Catherine wheels, or out without their coats.

'It'll be Christmas next,' mused Phyllis, as she sucked a thorn from one pale and bony finger. 'Before we can turn round. Are you doing anything special, dear, this year?'

'Just the usual.' Mary sighed, tugged back a piece of laurel which had fallen out of line. 'The usual' meant cooking for a dozen – well, fifteen, actually, by the time she'd invited James's father (and Aunt Alice who looked after him), and his sister and her family, and those two poor chums of Simon whose parents lived abroad, and her own tetchy faddy father who always claimed to be too busy to stop work just for Christmas, then finally capitulated and stayed a good two weeks, insisting on quite different meals from everybody else's. 'What are *your* plans, Phyllis?' Perhaps she ought to invite her too. One more would hardly matter, and Christmas for unmarrieds couldn't be much fun.

'I'm going on a pilgrimage to Rome.'

'Oh, nice.' Phyllis always went on pilgrimages, if she went away at all, though it was usually to Lourdes and in the summer. 'Why Rome?'

Phyllis looked a little shocked. 'Well, it *is* the canonisation, dear – the first English saint for more than twenty years, *and* a local man.'

'Oh, yes, of course.' She'd quite forgotten the Blessed Edwin Mumford, born in Guildford in 1566 and martyred for his faith at the tender age of twenty-two, under

Elizabeth I. He was to be made a saint, in Rome, the first week of January, after a series of quite startling miracles, including casting out eight devils from a bishop. She found she took less interest in church affairs, or saints, since she'd been going to John-Paul; was now thrilling to *Your Dreams Explained* or *Psychology Today*, rather than idling through the *Catholic Universe*. She didn't envy Phyllis. Miracles or no, Christmas should be spent at home with a real coal fire and children. She had never been to Rome. James liked holidays which centred round a golf course, and since Father Fox had told her once that Rome had nine hundred and ninety churches, she doubted there'd be room for eighteen holes. She felt guilty about it, really. It was like supporting Spurs (as Simon did) and never having been to White Hart Lane. The boys should go, at least; see the birthplace of their Church, the centre of all Christendom. Perhaps next year, if James could be persuaded to . . .

'Right, I think that's it, dear. Let's put the roses on the altar and your chrysanthemums by the statue of Saint Joseph. I think he'd have liked chrysanthemums, don't you? Though it was desert, wasn't it, so I don't suppose they had them – probably only cactuses and things.'

Mary nodded vaguely, had never spared a thought for Saint Joseph's taste in flowers. There seemed more pressing problems. She let Phyllis take the vases to the altar; knew she loved to do it on her own, as if she were God's loyal and loving wife, organising His dinner party exactly as He wanted it, with no clumsy helpers messing up her table. She herself cleared the leaves and stalks away, cleaned the sink, closed the cupboard doors (Father Fox hated any mess), then picked up her coat and handbag and walked through to the church. She knelt a moment in a pew, praying for the boys, for James and his poor father, whose gout was getting worse; for that nice man in the evening class who'd only come the once and whose own father cut him dead, actually pretended not to know him; added one

145

last prayer – which cost her – for Jonathan's headmaster. She sat back on the bench, idly watching Phyllis as she moved one vase a fraction, then edged it back again, the myopic grey-blue eyes screwed up in concentration.

Her own eyes were almost closing. It wasn't caffeine in hot chocolate which was keeping her awake at night, it was rage at the breast – to use John-Paul's own phrase – or guilt about that rage. Could you really be so angry with a breast? John-Paul had said most definitely, especially as an infant who was denied oral satisfaction by an inadequate or absent mother. He didn't understand. Her mother was a saint, which made her anger all the more deplorable – if she'd really felt it (which she could hardly prove or disprove thirty-five years on). How did John-Paul *know* these things, and did it really help to dig so deeply? She'd felt such great confusion, such remorse about the matricide which she'd obviously been planning as a tot of just a month or so, that sleep had quite eluded her.

She fiddled with her handbag, took out a paper tissue, put it back again, stopped in horror as she recognised the movement. That was masturbation. She'd been doing much the same as she lay on John-Paul's couch, continually taking out her hankie from the pocket of her skirt, then stuffing it back in – out again, in again, out, in, out, in, out, in, like a finger in a . . . It was John-Paul who'd made the connection, first remarking fairly harmlessly that she appeared to be unusually preoccupied, and could she explain what she was doing with the hankie. She'd looked at him, surprised, hardly aware she was doing anything, then shrugging off her action as just a nervous habit. John-Paul disagreed, suggested that her 'habit' could possibly be interpreted as a masturbatory substitute, which would prove the force of her unconscious sexual drive, despite those strong repressions he'd mentioned earlier. She had almost *died* with shame, had never ever masturbated, never even used the word, yet there she was apparently doing it in public, and now – more heinous still - attempting it a second time, in church.

She clicked her handbag firmly shut, fell on to her knees again, begging God's forgiveness. It was all terribly bewildering. Masturbation was forbidden by the Church, yet encouraged by John-Paul, who was like another Church himself, with rules and dogmas, mysteries and ritual, articles of faith. John-Paul had actually instructed her to masturbate, set it like a sort of homework, to be practised every day, to help loosen her, relax her, make her more familiar with her vagina, more genitally aware. (The word 'vagina' had made her go all hot again. Her friends just didn't use such words, and she doubted Phyllis even *had* one – just a holy-water stoup between her veiny legs.) And of *course* she hadn't practised. There wasn't time, for one thing, what with the ironing and the shopping and her church work and the charities, and, anyway, supposing someone called – Father Fox himself, or Mrs Foster-Clarke, who ran the Surrey Women's Guild – found her flushed and naked with the curtains drawn?

She mopped her forehead, tried to smile at Phyllis, who, wifely duties finished, was tiptoeing down the aisle with her secateurs, her rosary and a laundry-bag of Father Fox's washing which she'd somehow mysteriously acquired. She stopped by Mary's pew, face wrinkled in concern, voice an anxious whisper.

'You *do* look flushed, my dear. I wouldn't be surprised if you'd caught some nasty virus. There's a lot of bugs around. I think you ought to go straight home and put yourself to bed.'

Mary nodded weakly. Everyone was ordering her to bed. Well – she shrugged, crumpled up her tissue – she'd better simply do as she was told.

147

Mary threw the blankets off, replaced her pants and tights. It hadn't worked – how could it? To put oneself to bed at five o'clock on a Monday afternoon with a husband expected home in just two hours, the dinner still to make, and that bit of urgent typing she'd promised to bang out for Emma Barnes, not to mention James's trousers, which all needed letting out . . . She'd better start the dinner straight away, and while the casserole was simmering she could do the other jobs. The phone shrilled in the kitchen as she was braising steak in oil.

'Is that you, Mary?'

'Yes, of course it's me, dear.' (James always asked if it was her, as if he were expecting someone else, or had failed to recognise her voice after thirteen years of marriage.) 'What's wrong? Oh, I see – that Crawshaw chap again. So you'll be a little late? A *lot* late. No, it's quite all right, don't worry. It's just a casserole, so it can't spoil, really, can it?'

She put the phone down, finished off the steak, turned the heat to 'simmer'. The vegetables were chopped and peeled already, the table laid, the lemon mousse chilling in the fridge. Horatio was snoring in his basket, replete after his own meal (and a chunk of best rump steak which he'd stolen from the table when she turned her back a second). She went to fetch the whisky, put it on a tray. James would need a double after two hours of Larry Crawshaw. She poured herself a sherry – just a modest one – took it to the typewriter, heart sinking as she saw the mound of pages. 'Bit of typing' had been Emma's phrase, not hers. It looked more like a saga and she really was so tired. Perhaps she ought to go to bed, not to do her 'homework', but to sleep – just a brief hour's doze to make her more alert for James when he finally came home. She could always do the typing in the morning, before her visit to the old folks' home and her cooking for the church bazaar.

She refilled her sherry – it would help her to relax –

drifted back upstairs. The double bed was rumpled and dishevelled, the way she'd left it earlier. She grimaced in distaste, smoothed the sheets and blankets, still reluctant to get in. That bed had such bad memories, seemed always to accuse her, hiss 'failure' at her, 'boring'. She sometimes wished secretly that James could be neutered as Horatio had been – just a whiff of anaesthetic, a tiny snip, and total transformation. No more mounting, rutting, coupling, sniffing round the females, leaping five-foot walls to reach a bitch on heat. It had also made him much more docile – placid, almost soppy, which would be nice in James as well.

She straightened the blue counterpane, backed out of the room. Perhaps she'd use the other bed, the spare-room bed, the one she always thought of as her daughter's – that non-existent daughter she chatted to in secret, had even named, bought clothes for. The shrine was still set up, the candles and the vases, though no fresh flowers, no recent smell of wax or burning flesh. John-Paul hadn't appreciated her spiritual bouquet. She sank down on the bed, disappointment struggling with new hope. Why not make him a different one, one he'd really relish? He had encouraged her to masturbate, to give herself an orgasm, so she could experience the feel of it, help herself to pleasure – which he seemed to see as duty, despite the fact such practices were forbidden by the Church. Now she saw a way of solving the dilemma, satisfying everyone, including even herself. If she made the masturbation really painful, she'd be obeying John-Paul's mandate (at least to the letter, if not exactly the spirit), offering him a new and quite unusual spiritual bouquet, while avoiding Father Fox's wrath and her own sense of guilt in indulging in what the Church condemned as 'solitary and sinful pleasure'.

She checked her watch. Nearly ten to seven. Nobody would call now. It was the suburban dinner hour, sacred to husbands and to families, when no bells rang except the oven-timer. She crept back to her bedroom, scrabbled through the bottom drawer where she kept her sanitary towels, drew out not a small soft pad, but an eight-inch hard vibrator. Well, she'd had to hide it somewhere, and James so hated periods he would no more touch her Kotex than approach a nuclear reactor with a leak.

She felt much the same about that plastic monster. Even James's was not as big or ugly, and did at least deflate at times, folded down quietly after use; wasn't labelled 'Super-Stud' around its rampant rim. 'Super-Stud' came complete with batteries, also labelled 'super'. In fact, everything was super – super-power, super-thrust, super-satisfaction. The catalogue had quite appalled her. Up till now, she had more or less ignored the existence of vibrators – known (vaguely) people used them, but only hardened people like prostitutes on clients, or perverts on themselves. She had regarded them as something rather shameful and obscene which went on far away, in another world from hers, like those brutish men who killed elephants for ivory, or turned tigers into hearth-rugs. But that catalogue had sold them like cereals or slippers – cosy everyday things which any normal woman needed. And even John-Paul seemed to champion them, saying with a little smile (which she couldn't see, but had picked up from his voice) that an artificial penis was often more obliging than the flesh-and-blood variety, since it wouldn't let you down. He'd told her a vibrator would be under her exclusive control and would go at her own pace: as long, as short, as fast, as slow, as she could cope with at each practice-session. It seemed incredible to her – to derive satisfaction, ecstasy, from something with no hands nor heart nor voice. James rarely talked himself, but he did at least make noises, or sometimes grunted 'Lovely tits' when she first removed her brassière.

She'd spent two whole mornings goggling at the pictures – yes, huge full-colour pictures with descriptions underneath, and such a wild variety – vibrators in soft latex, or gold, or rigid plastic; matt black ones, shiny silver; some with studs, or nobbles, or light-up tips, or 'thrill-frills'; or with several different screw-on heads which rotated or gyrated, or flexible extensions to reach something called a G-spot (which made them sound like carpet-cleaners); some shaped like little grinning men or even teddy bears. And those dreadful punning names: 'Wonderbar' and 'Joy stick', 'Bully Boy', 'Banana'. If she'd been cool before, that catalogue had frozen her completely, sent her sexual temperature plunging below zero. But penance was another thing entirely. The more you hated something, then the better as a penance, like their soft-boiled eggs at school, which were actually more raw than soft, and had little bloody specks in, which her best friend said were the beginnings of new chicks. From the age of seven to the age of seventeen, she'd swallowed every nascent chick she could, marked them on her spiritual bouquet. At least she'd learnt willpower, developed a strong stomach.

She got up from her knees, concealing the vibrator beneath the jacket of her suit, still vaguely anxious that someone might be watching – if not an actual neighbour prying with a telescope from the house across the street, then the Blessed Edwin Mumford, observing her from heaven, and distinctly disapproving. She lit the candles, removed her tights and pants again (left her other clothes on, which made her feel less blatant), then lay back on the bed. She wished she had some flowers, or even music. Ritual was important – she knew that from the Church. But at least the candles cast strong shadows, gave a certain atmosphere, and she'd set up a small photograph of John-Paul, like an icon. She had snipped it from the dust-jacket of his latest publication: *Eros and Thanatos: a Re-examination*. The book was very difficult – made *Psychology Today* seem as painless as the *TV Times* –

but she'd bought it for the photograph and the blurb about the author, which made him sound so busy and so brilliant she'd felt quite overcome to be allowed the privilege of paying for an hour each week of his time and genius.

She opened her legs a grudging inch, positioned the vibrator. You were meant to use a lubricant – some cherry-flavoured sticky stuff called 'Joy Jelly', which had arrived with the vibrator (and also with its 'supers' – 'super-rich, super-sexy, super-lubricating'). It would hurt more without the jelly, especially as her burns had not yet healed. Even using just one finger for five minutes, as she'd done at five o'clock, had made them twinge and shock. The vibrator had a setting like an oven – high for roasts, 'simmer' for just stewing. She turned it on to high, rammed it in, violently and suddenly. Her Pain Score soared to nine, jumped higher still as she directed it specifically against the largest of the burns. She closed her eyes to concentrate on pain, take it up to twelve, or even over.

'It's for *you*, John-Paul,' she whispered. 'All for you – the pain.' One burn had even festered, was throbbing, really griping, as she stabbed it with the rigid plastic shaft. Pleasure he had called it, but what were words so long as she obeyed him? 'As fast, as slow, as long, as short, as you can cope with at each practice-session.' She took it slower, turned the pressure down, let it almost idle – in and out, in and out, like a finger in a . . . It felt different from a finger, seemed to go in further, hurting still – oh, certainly – but a restrained and rhythmic pain now, which was soothing, almost kindly. The noise had changed, as well – no longer a harsh skirl, but a gentle droning purr, which seemed to calm her, reassure her. She had never known that pain could be relaxing; that she could want it to continue, not just for John-Paul's sake, but for her own. Maybe that was wrong, though, and she was being far too lax. Angrily, abruptly, she turned the power to highest, reeled back to her Pain Score, tried to tot it up again, as her burns cried out for pity. Thirteen, was it, fourteen? Still not high enough. She could hear the vibrator screaming now, as she reached twenty, twenty-one.

Perspiration was sliding down her breasts, sticking to her slip. She'd have to take it off, remove her skirt and jacket too, so she was less hampered, less restricted, could concentrate on pain. She put the vibrator down a moment, as she struggled with her clothes, tried to force the zip. The silence seemed unkind, and there was a strange ache between her legs – an ache for that lost rhythm, which had become part of her, had sprung from her, and which she felt she'd known from way back, known in dreams, or even in past lives. She drained her sherry first, dark sweet sherry, like John-Paul's rich brown voice. He was talking to her now, his voice very close and intimate from his seat behind the couch; his words warm amoroso dribbling down her body. 'You're doing very well, Mary. Just relax a little more – that's it. Now turn it on again and let it throb between your fingers, to try to get the feel of it, establish the best rhythm. That's good, that's very good. Now stroke it down your body – yes, slowly, very s-l-o-w-l-y, right across your breasts and down your belly and your thighs, until you reach your . . .'

'Genitals,' she said out loud. She had to practise all those words: forbidden words, exquisite words, words which made her hot and so ashamed. Her legs were opening wider, opening for John-Paul. Yes, of course she longed to open them – open them and please him, split apart and bleed for him. 'Vulva,' she said lingeringly. 'Clitoris.' 'Vagina.' Nobody could hear her. The vibrator was too loud. The noise was whirring out again, gasping, almost panicky, laboured like her breathing. Why should she be panting when she was just relaxing on a bed? Why drenched with sweat, why feverish? Had John-Paul switched her on, pulled some giant lever like the one in the

Steam Museum where they'd taken all three boys this last July – a lever which set flywheels into motion, started rods and pistons, mobilised huge pumping-engines, which had all begun to thwack and thrust, drowning conversation, dwarfing even James?

She'd felt threatened at the time, alarmed not just for the boys who might get trapped in all that dangerous machinery, but frightened on her own account. It was so masculine, so violent, that powerhouse of trapped steam, those bursting throbbing boilers and swollen cylinders; that overwhelming beam-engine rearing to the roof, its gigantic metal beam weighing fifteen tons at least, heaving up and down as it drove its frantic flywheel (which the man had told her would plunge straight through the solid wall if it ever broke off from its bearings). She had watched the pressure-gauges slowly rising, rising; the shiny oil-slicked piston-rods thrusting in and out; had felt some strange excitement suddenly curdling with the terror, longed to be connected to those wildly pulsing engines, part of that machinery – a feed-pipe or a blow-valve which could share its pounding rhythm. 'DANGER!' said the notice in huge red capitals. She'd deliberately ignored it, stepped closer to the piston-rods, even slipped inside the barrier.

She shut her eyes. She could feel the heat again, that stifling claustrophobic heat which reeked of oil and steam; could hear the steady rhythmic slam of the engines pumping pumping; see the scalding water-drops swelling on the glistening pipes, bursting, running down; could almost taste the clogging grease on the inflamed and sweating metal. Her own body was inflamed, running with hot oil, spurts of steam condensing into droplets, leaking down the insides of her thighs. She had forgotten pain completely. Did wheels feel pain? Or piston-rods? She just had to keep on thrusting, driven on, driven on – yes, right to danger-point.

She had reached that point – and passed it – could feel

her axle cracking up, wrenching from its bearings, her rev-counter so fast now it was spinning out of control. She was breaking off, flying free, plunging through a three-foot solid wall. She felt the crash, the impact, yet experienced no pain – only elation and amazement as she blasted into heat and light, heard John-Paul's shout behind her, a shout of triumph, sheer relief. He seemed to have arranged some celebration in her honour. She was aware of voices, noises, reverberating bangs; glimpsed a sudden hail of rockets snipering the sky, exploding in a shower of coloured sparks – laser-blue, throbbing-pink, strobing knife-blade silver.

She could hear another noise, coming from much nearer – footsteps on the stairs, an angry voice she knew too well.

'Are you deaf or something, Mary? I've been shouting for five minutes and you haven't heard a word. The dog's gone mad as well. It's those damn-fool bloody fireworks they're letting off next door.' The footsteps tramping closer, right up to the door; the handle slowly turning. 'Mary!' The voice lower now, and scandalised, almost disbelieving. 'What in God's name are you *doing*?'

# 11

'So how d'you like the pictures?' a young girl asks me, a so-called friend of Seton, and dressed rather like him in obscene-tight jeans and a skim-the-navel sweater (and with the sort of Ogen melon breasts John-Paul would want himself).

'They're shit,' I say. 'I mean literally. That's the new fashionable medium in art, I'm told – warm faeces.'

She stalks off in a huff. Who cares? There are at least thirty others like her – all gorgeous girls of seventeen or under; all what the ads call 'feminine', with huge blue eyes and tiny feet, morning-gathered dew-kissed skins, and eyelashes which double up as besom brooms. I assume they're John-Paul's patients, all those tiresome Marys who come at times I'm not around myself. They don't let on, of course, introduce themselves as Cressida or Amber, and a lot of other crappy names – all 'feminine', of course – some *doubly* feminine: hyphened names like Anne-Marie or Lisa-Beth, which probably means they're aping John-Paul's hyphen and are obviously hung up on him. I haven't got a chance. Oh, I may have waist-length hair ('Fantastic hair,' Seton actually called it just last night) and pretty decent teeth which are even reasonably white – though thanks mainly to Clinonym Smokers' Toothpaste – but why should John-Paul notice me with such dazzling competition?

He's not even here tonight. It's his private view, his evening, his so-called triumph as an artist, his biggest show to date, the culmination of five years' secret slog, yet he has to hide away, can't face the press (if any), can't face his fans, his groupies. Even his signature on the paintings looks shy and noncommittal – just a small black JPS at the bottom of each work, the initials almost swamped by swags of excrement. He's probably keeping a low profile because he's nervous of the medical establishment, scared they might protest, censure him for dealing with his *own* shit rather than his patients', or perhaps he's just embarrassed that the work is so inferior. Actually, no one's really looking at it, but that's standard at most private views. Don't tell me people come to see the pictures. They come to see each other, and guzzle the free wine (or bubbly, if it's Bond Street or environs). This is grotty Kilburn, so the wine is quite unspeakable – sub-Spanish plonk in plastic cups, with a few anorexic Twiglets to stop us getting pissed. No chance of that, alas. My cup's been empty a good half hour and no one's filled it except ever-thoughtful Seton who's used it as an ashtray.

I suppose I should be grateful he's still around at all, when he knows girls like Cressida who comes complete with baby (yes, fair; yes, cute; yes, female). Babies are the in-thing at the moment, especially when they dangle from those natty designer-slings with a bulging Filofax and/or portable computer balancing them the other side, to prove the woman is a loved and fertile Earth-Mother, yet also a whizz-kid Richard Branson clone, giving (Virgin) birth to airlines, record companies.

'Darling, *wonderful* to see you!'

I swing round gratefully, but it's not me they're thrilled to see; just another stunning female with an Adonis in tow. Kiss-kiss, yak-yak. 'Yes, we've just come back from Hamburg, and it's Singapore next week. I'm so frightfully busy I've hardly time to pee. This is Adam, by the way.'

I clutch at Seton's arm, to prove I'm a couple, too; long to tell the world he did actually invite me to move in and share his boat. We've been going out together fourteen days, which must be quite a record (for him, as well as me), though the term 'going out' is not exactly accurate, since we rarely budge from the confines of the cabin, except to change positions on the bunk or bench or floor. Well, *I* go out – he doesn't – except to drive me to the station for my appointments with John-Paul. I've refused to give them up, despite my disillusion, though Seton lours and threatens, says if I want to waste my money, there are more amusing ways of doing so than regaling some sex-obsessed shyster with the details of my latest love affair.

'Yeah, but you really have to do drugs first, to know how bad they are.'

'She's into healing trees now. They respond better than people.'

I edge away from trees and drugs, grab a last half-Twiglet. Actually, Seton doesn't know it, but I haven't breathed a word about our liaison. Oh, I know it's breaking the analytic rule, or whatever John-Paul calls it, but that hardly seems to matter now, when he's just a piddling amateur – and anyway I've been breaking it for months. I've even concealed the existence of my clients; just casually explained that I was paying for my therapy with a windfall I'd been left from my favourite (non-existent) Uncle Jack. It really bugs me sometimes that he doesn't see straight through me, use his basic nous if he hasn't any training, or operate some inbuilt shit-detector. I've sometimes tried to test him out, told him quite outrageous tales – like my mother was a despatch rider with a vintage Harley Davidson, and my father was a murderer – and he still appears to swallow them, or at least not call me 'Liar!'. Though maybe he's deceiving me, in turn; only pretending to believe me, and making jargon-loaded notes about my fibs or fantasies. What's truth, anyway? How can we know anything when everybody's lying, or at least acting or pretending? For all I know, my father might have murdered someone and concealed it in his turn. (He murdered *me*, in one sense, though that's another story.) And there's the added complication that the more you build up something, the more solid it becomes, like my Uncle Jack, for instance, whom I worship now and idolise; visit every Sunday in his converted Kentish oast house (or Spanish hacienda, or Manhattan penthouse with its view of Central Park).

'Actually, Jason of the Argonauts always struck me as an outsize wimp.'

'Who's he?'

'Hey, did you see that piece on gays in last week's *City Limits*?'

'No,' I say; faze the pouf who's asking, since he was addressing someone else – a guy in green-check trousers who looks a cross between a golf pro and a clown. The crowds are building up now, the air over-breathed and stale. We're stuck down in a basement with no windows and strip-lighting (which is hardly fair to any pictures, even ones as lousy as John-Paul's). I can't get away from basements. My own bedsit's subterranean, Seton's cabin's down a ladder, and of the eleven different pads I've had since I left home in my teens, eight were below street-level and two converted cellars. Perhaps that's the attraction of John-Paul – he's up a tower, not down a hole, though actually I just can't feel the same about him, since Seton put him in his context, so to speak. The whole point about analysts is that they're meant to remain a mystery, so you can fantasise about them, turn them into your father, mother, brother, sister (or favourite Uncle Jack). In that sense, they're not real, not intended to be real, but objects to be hated, worshipped, feared, so you can re-enact the way you felt in infancy towards your *real* father, mother, sister, brother or (unreal) Uncle Jack.

It drives you crazy sometimes, the way they never say a word about their own life or interests, relationships or politics, but I see now it's far preferable to knowing the grim facts. John-Paul divorced, with two great hulking dogs and a plumber for a father, isn't quite the stuff

159

of fantasy, and at first I was so furious, I vowed I'd never set eyes on him again. But then I got so anxious, so depressed and even desperate, I realised I was totally addicted to the man, and that in some ghastly way he'd become even more attractive because he *was* a fraud – an imposter and a charlatan who'd been smart enough to fool me. I've always been involved with swinish men – which according to John-Paul is an attempt to recreate my (swinish) father, try to change him, try to make him love me. It always fails, of course. I'm a glutton for (self) punishment, and now I've got a shrink who's every bit as bad as the bastards he's been slating. Though I suppose that proves him right, at least.

'Like the tan, Jean! Fake or real?'

'Fake. Sunorama's sun-beds. I've almost moved my office there.'

'They're meant to give you cancer.'

'What are?'

'Sun-beds.'

'Everything gives you cancer – or all the fun things, anyway – even men, apparently.'

'Too right,' I say to no one, as I maul my paper cup. Seton's strayed off somewhere and I suppose I should be 'circulating'; flinging more inane remarks into the pool of conversation. But I'm sick of all the small talk; can't seem to feel a part of it or tag on to some group; can't shift my mind and focus from John-Paul. Despite his absence, he seems more real and solid than all those prattling cut-outs, and I feel I'm here alone with him, carrying on a silent tête-à-tête. We've had some really hairy sessions this last fortnight. 'If your father's a plumber, why can't he mend your loo, John-Paul?' 'If you must have pedigree dogs to give you breeding, or huge ones as a power thing . . .' 'If you spent less time on art . . .' He pretended not to understand, turned everything back to me and my neuroses. Plumbers he associated with sewers, sewers with shit,

160

and shit of course with money (that's an analytic basic), so why was I so worried about paying his bills? I couldn't win with wolfhounds, either. He refused to discuss them as his own domestic pets, but interpreted them as symbols of my animal aggression which I was seeking to repress (and also linked with shit again – you know, dogs and excrement – which seems to me plain facile).

And then his phones kept ringing. They've always done, in fact, but I've never really realised how unprofessional it is. Three phones, like three clocks – he's probably got three mistresses, and three ex-wives, as well – all connected to the answerphone so that he doesn't have to pick them up in the middle of a session, but, nonetheless, horribly distracting, since they caterwaul at least six or seven seconds before the recording cuts them out. Before, I simply accepted it, but now I know he's just a quack, their shrilling sounds insulting, or seems to be expressing my own howls of pain, resentment. And the calls themselves are suspect – not the frantic patients I always took them for, desperate for his help or voice, clamouring to see him, but cantankerous ex-wives, or jumped-up plumber fathers, or maybe angry vets who have dosed or wormed his wolfhounds, but are still waiting to be paid.

'Hallo! Don't I know you?'

'No,' I say. 'You don't'; scuttle off from the creep in dove-grey suede whose eyes are on my breasts, but who'll probably feign an interest in my brain (as many so-called 'new men' appear to do these days). Several other people have tried to say hallo, or swap their names for mine, but I sense a wall between us; keep glancing round for Seton, who's completely disappeared. I'd really hate to lose him, need him as my anchor. He's become central in my life now, partly as a sort of counterirritant to John-Paul, but also for a host of other vital reasons, like his size-eleven feet, his lack of parents, wives or job, and his total disregard for things like dress or rules, tact or meals or mores. It's also great to have a guy who's not a client, and one who's head and shoulders above all the gaffers here, not just in his height and build, but in his sheer charisma. Okay, so he's aggressive, but he's also very generous, and surprisingly soft-hearted (not to mention skilful) when it's a matter of an injured tern or a stoat caught in a trap. There's a whole quite different side to him which he hides from other people, and which appeals to me especially because I tend to do the same.

I always feel I've got two separate selves, which makes life quite confusing since I don't know which one's me. My female self is vile – tough and sharp and bitchy and often pretty devious; but my male self's more poetic and compassionate, secretive, responsive, though also much more vulnerable. Sometimes, when it takes me over, I feel very strange and frail, and things lose their shape and boundaries, so the world becomes unreal. I've discussed it with John-Paul, and he used words like 'bipolarity' and 'split'; referred to my 'divided self', which made it sound like something in a textbook, rather than undefined and frightening. I sometimes swing from mood to mood so suddenly and totally, I confuse myself as well as him, feel I've changed identity, become a different person. But *Seton* understands – accepts me both ways round – the only one who ever has, which is why he's so important.

An explosive and defiant laugh suddenly rips across the room. I know that laugh – it's his. He very rarely laughs, in fact, but when he does, it startles. I trace it to its source; find him pawing Cressida, one over-friendly hand exploring the bare flesh between her child-bearing hips and her Page Three Playgirl tits. I turn abruptly on my heel, make for what I assume to be the exit, but it leads into another room – one I haven't seen – with huge black sculptures in it and crowds more giggly girls, many of them black themselves, as if they've been invited here to tone in with the works. I stare in horror at the hunks of painted metal which resemble the remains of all the worst accidents scooped up from the motorways in the last ten years or so, and set down here still wet with blood and gore. Are those John-Paul's as well? They seem far worse than the paintings. I don't mean worse artistically, which I suspect would be impossible, but worse in terms of size and sheer solidity, worse in terms of symptoms. If his patients are neurotics, then these are gross psychotics – schizophrenics, psychopaths, raving monomaniacs. How could any mere neurotic dare to take his time, when these awesome locked-ward cases must demand his full attention, must occupy his mind to the exclusion of all else?

I creep into a corner, try to make myself invisible, which may sound crazy when I'm five foot ten, but actually I'm shrinking all the time. Oh, I'm still the brazen Amazon outside, but inside I'm just an empty husk, shrivelling up to nothing. Seton's gone; I've lost John-Paul – or at least the one I thought I had – and I can rarely keep a man beyond two months. All around me people are in couples or happy chatting groups – relating, laughing, socialising. It's like a children's party where all the other lucky kids have been handed out their smiles, but the supply ran out just before my turn. The black girls seem especially wild and whoopy, sparkling with an inner oomph and verve; a powerful bottled tonic whose cork has just flown off, exploding in a shower of bubbly fizz. The noise sounds really threatening, surging up in waves, which seem to break across my head and half-submerge me. I can't even smoke to calm myself. Seton's got the cigarettes. That's a sign of coupledom – one pack between the two of you.

My hands are out of work. Even an empty cup was something to hold on to, but mine has got mislaid, probably trampled underfoot in all the crush. There's more wine on the carpet than in anybody's glass – a dirty threadbare carpet, to match the bare and dirty walls. I can't bear to think of John-Paul in this setting, or to accept those warped and twisted sculptures as his work. 'John-Paul,' I say, as if his name might bring him back. I need him desperately.

Someone else lolls up to me instead – a tall thin floppy-looking man who appears to have liquorice sticks or sash cords where most of us have bones. 'Hi!' he says, smiling, though his smile is sagging too, and his clothes are falling off him – folds of baggy trouser drooping round his hips, and a sweater so voluminous it could hide two football teams.

'D'you smoke?' I snap, nicotine addiction outlawing good manners. I should at least have parroted his 'Hi!'

'No, I do *not*!' He sounds as if I've asked him if he tortures Jews or buggers little boys. He's probably a member of that boring anti-smoking group which tries to lock up anyone who dares to take a puff. And it never stops with cigarettes – oh, no. They're all into saving seals, as well, and believe in things like ley lines; would probably stop us breathing if they could get the legislation through, reserve the air for some endangered species. (Actually, we smokers are now the most endangered species on the globe, with smoking bans in cinemas and tube trains, even offices and restaurants – need our own society to protect us from extinction.)

I sidle a bit closer, tighten my own smile. 'I suppose you know this show is subsidised by one of the biggest of the tobacco giants – yes, the ones who make Chesterfields, in fact. The artist's on their board, helps produce their advertising. So if you're drinking their wine,' I gesture to his near-empty paper cup, 'you're helping swell their profits.'

He crumples up completely, sags and droops away. Why can't I meet a macho man who's come hotfoot from the airport with two hundred king-size duty-free bulging out his sweater? All I get is a floss-haired Mae West-ette, half my height and at least a decade younger, who's intruding on my corner in little spurts and teeters. She stops to flirt with the largest of the sculptures, caressing all its angles, feeling up its knobs, running teasing fingertips down one long sloping side, as if it's John-Paul's naked back. 'Shit!' I say out loud.

'Sorry. Did you speak?' She swings round to check the voice, bestow a gracious smile on it. Another Mary, obviously – the usual misty cornflower eyes and double-cream complexion, and this one's wearing *bows*, for heaven's sake – yes, bows on her cute fringe like a pampered Yorkshire terrier.

'Hi!' I say. 'I'm Cressida.'

'Oh, h . . . hallo, Cwessida.'

Nervous, too. How *sweet*. And she can't quite say her r's, which is always a sure sign of being super-female. I ape her affectation. 'You're a good fwend of the artist, I presume?'

'Er . . . yes, I am – actually.'

I love that 'actually'. So casual, yet just a shade belligerent, as if to warn me not to challenge her position. I do, of course, immediately, spinning her some lurid tale of my own passionate liaison with the artist, then adding a wild threesome and an orgy. She hares off as if I've shot her, and I slouch back to the first room, even more depressed now. I don't like myself at all, or the way I treat the world. I was pretty decent as a kid, as far as I remember; the sort of eager generous child who'd weep for a dead fly, or send all her pocket-money to save lepers or black babies. I had more black babies by the age of twelve or so than most children have toys. I gave my coat away once to some poor thing in my class who only had a jacket and a father doing time. My own father beat me for it, but I think I meant it well.

I don't know quite what happened, but I grew up someone else, not the person I should have been – the hopeful happy adult who dared to trust the world,

165

but someone wary, brooding, who upsets other people, someone prickly and aggressive who's always on her own. The change was very gradual, like a blond kid turning dark, or a winsome little toddler growing big and ugly as a teen. I'm ugly now myself, inside as well as out, feel almost hideous sometimes, a sort of freakish monster normal people shun – yes, even my new lover. Seton's just ignoring me completely and has glued himself to Cressida (the real one), even managed to persuade her to part with both her baby and her briefcase, so both her hands are free – or would be, if he hadn't re-engaged them. I can hardly bear to look at him: that oil stain on his jeans which he got when we were kneeling on the deck, making almost-love in the windy rain and dark; those raised and purple bite-marks on his neck. We're both branded with each other's marks, which I thought meant we belonged, like people scratching their initials on precious pens or pocketknives.

'Seton!' I say sharply. He doesn't hear, doesn't even turn his head, has totally forgotten that we agreed we'd leave early so we could get back to the boat, incise some wild new marks. It's an air-sea rescue boat, used in the last war to scoop up drowning airmen from the Channel, and somehow seemed significant in the sense that *I* was also rescued, winched up from the deep. I suppose he'll rescue Cressida instead, now; fling her down a lifebelt, haul her into safety, let her recover on his bunk while he gives her mouth-to-mouth resuscitation. Then, once she's feeling stronger, he'll bite her nipples, say she's got fantastic hair, wind it round his prick, tie her up with it, then kiss and brush it better – all the things he did to me, as if no other girl existed. I know we said no jealousy, no ties, and how we'd each be free to see anyone else we fancied, but saying's so much easier than doing (which is why therapy fails so often, I suppose). Secretly, I've always longed for ties, while pretending to be liberated, footloose

– but no one else seemed keen to forge a bond – neither of my parents, and not even Uncle Jack who locked me out last time I tried to visit him.

I begin to feel quite sorry for the baby, who's been parked on Seton's coat and is whimpering pathetically, puckering up her face – abandoned, you might say. 'Join the club,' I whisper. I could pick her up and rock her, I suppose, but I'm so scared she's Seton's kid, I daren't get that involved, might even cry or something quite disastrous. The girl next to me is laughing, her boozy guffaws tightening like lassos around my neck. I expect she's got her offspring, too – three or four at home, maybe one *in utero*. Seton's probably sired babies on London's entire female population – all save me, that is. I've never managed to conceive, even when I tried for two whole years – and with anyone and everyone – though they didn't know, of course. I felt I'd be a better sort of person with a baby to look after, less self-obsessed and reckless. The fact I failed so miserably only goes to prove – again – that I'm just not wholly female. I tend to blame my father. He was so keen for me to be a boy, I guess I did my poor best to oblige him: achieved the height, the size-eight feet, the non-existent womb. (The doctors *say* I've got a womb, but then doctors will say anything to get you out of the surgery, so they can bark 'Next patient, please.') Actually, I feel I've lost a lot of things – not just my womb and ovaries, but my heart, my sense of hope, that skill which other people have of finding other-halves: saying 'we', instead of 'I', spending weekends joined and anchored, not separate, adrift.

I move off from the baby (and its still smugly nuzzling parents), find another corner, watch the hordes milling round a tray of paper cups, which has suddenly materi-alised from nowhere, along with some sickly-looking peanuts, dusted with a yellow film which could be jaun-dice or a curry-flavoured coating. No one's thinking art

– only food or booze or nicotine. I listen to the wisps of conversation which drift in my direction with the smoke – trivia, as usual.

'The third time I threw up was in the Russian Embassy . . .'

' . . . such a waste of caviare.'

'No, she only bought the bottom half. The top was . . .'

'I'm sorry, but I don't give a damn about my thighs.'

They no longer seem to form real words, just fractured broken syllables, limping strings of gibberish. 'Bah-bah-bah-bah-bah . . .' I've no heart to talk to myself, not even gibberish. Now I've seen this wretched show, I can't continue trying to kid myself that John-Paul's just a Sunday painter, dashing off a sketch or two, one afternoon a week, with all his prime-time energies still devoted to his patients. His priorities are obvious – art first and last, patients squeezed between. I kept hoping secretly that Seton was exaggerating (and also wrong about his claim that completely untrained people could set up as therapists. He's absolutely right, alas. I phoned several professional bodies to check he wasn't lying, and they all concurred: yes, regrettable but true.) I'm still fiercely disappointed not to see my bogus doctor. I spent hours this evening preparing in his honour, trying to out-Mary all the Marys in a baby-blue new dress with a Peter-Pan white collar, which I realise now must make me look grotesque. Actually, the other girls are not dressed up at all – just faded denim, shabby jeans, and two in men's grey suits and butch black clodhoppers. I suppose they're all so wildly confident of their looks and femininity, so naturally attractive, they just don't have to bother with dolling up or clothes. The coloured girls look even more inelegant, as far as gear's concerned; several in old boiler-suits and three in dungarees. Are they John-Paul's fans, as well, I wonder, a contrast to the Marys? I suppose he fancies blacks because they're noted for their passion, their unbridled sensuality.

I don't know why I bothered turning up at all. I not only squandered money buying this disaster-dress, I also wasted an hour or more inventing wild scenarios, imagining our meeting in a snazzy Mayfair gallery: how surprised he'd be to see me there – and flattered – how he'd take me on one side and explain that he was giving up his painting; that it demanded too much time, which he'd prefer to devote to patients, especially patients like myself, who were sensitive, discerning. (If we could only meet as equals, I do actually feel quite confident that we'd get on pretty well; share a lot of interests – not art, perhaps, but all those things I used to love before I became a 'case': poetry and the countryside, long walks, long thinks, even eating proper meals.)

'On your own?' a man asks, sidling up towards me with a dentist's sort of smile – 'This won't hurt, I promise.' He's not my type at all, looks less like a dentist than a failed and pensioned bank manager in a Burton suit and toecaps (and no hopeful-looking bulges which might suggest a lighter or a pack of Superkings).

'No,' I say. 'Meet Seton.' I gesture to the empty air beside me, which scares him off immediately. I've got one sharp eye on Seton, as it happens. He's at the far end of the room now, and mercifully free-standing; no longer joined in an embrace entitled 'Lovers' or 'The Kiss'. I try to keep my cool, not dash up and reclaim him like some unstable frantic wife, but pretend I'm happily absorbed in things artistic. Actually, it's time I gave the pictures some attention. I've only glanced at them quite cursorily so far, and with so much sheer resentment, there was no way I could be fair. I frown in concentration as I study the first three, try to be objective.

No, I'm really not impressed, and they honestly seem worse than the ones in his consulting room. Those I do admire in some ways, if only for their energy – though of course I'd no idea he'd painted them, which probably makes a quite substantial difference. And I'm also so damn used to them, lying on the couch four times every week, with them writhing all around me – tortured souls not unlike my own. They've got a sort of charge: a virulence, ferocity, which you can't ignore, even if you loathe it. The ones down here are basically the same, in the sense of dark and swirling shapes with no colour and no peace, but without the powerful thrust – looser and less organised, more 'shitty' altogether, the paint just smeared around with less control. Seton says he's never changed his style, but then Seton always disparages him on principle. I've still not discovered why he's so hostile to John-Paul, nor what was their relationship. I suspect it was a dispute about the wife, who was probably Seton's mistress before John-Paul divorced her. I've tended not to push the subject, aware that I'd be doubly hurt if I knew the steamy details – jealous both ways round.

Actually, if I'm honest with myself, I must confess I'm pretty damn ignorant when it comes to art or sculpture. I can't really judge these paintings, and if I called them 'shit' or 'lousy', I suppose it's more because they make me feel depressed – excluded, somehow threatened. All the same, I continue round the room, scanning every picture, trying not to damn them, even touching each a moment, so I can pick up John-Paul's vibes. Some Philistine is lolling back against one, leaning on it really hard, as if it's a back-rest or a bed head. I don't quite murder him – let's just say he gets the message. This may not be great art, but it has to be respected.

I'm back to where I started, the large and black-framed painting called 'Equinox 16'. (I don't know why '16', when there are no fifteen other Equinoxes, nor even why Equinox at all. They're mostly called Untitled 1, 2, 3.) I think I've paid due homage now and deserve a small reward.

I inch casually, so casually, towards the far end of the room, avoiding couples, Marys; rehearsing what I'll say to darling Seton (when not swearing at the crowds). No recriminations – just some amusing pert remark about the ambience, or a sensuous little grope to find his Capstans.

He's gone. Yes, honestly. And so has Cressida. I crash blindly up the stairs – no one at the top or in the toilet – hurtle down again, search the second room. The bank manager is there still, now talking to Mae West, the Whoopee Goldberg lookalikes, but no Cressida, no Seton, no puckered whimpering child. All the wine I haven't drunk seems to flood into my head, as if someone's spliced me to a fifteen-litre wine-box whose tap is pouring straight into my skull. I feel dizzy and disorientated, burning hot, yet shivery. 'Wimp!' I tell myself. Why *shouldn't* he walk off? I don't possess him, do I? Possession's very wrong. Even John-Paul talks disparagingly about my 'omnipotent' need to possess him and everyone.

Omnipotent? I laugh. I've no power left at all. Impotent, I'd call it – except that makes me sound a male. I slump against the wall, tug my stupid earrings off. That's exactly what I am – a not-quite male, a freak with breasts and earrings, but no sex-appeal, no womb.

I drag back up the stairs again, find my coat, slink out. There's a taxi cruising past. I flag it down, give it my address – the cellar, not the boat. My country idyll's over – the herons and the marshes, the huge swollen shining skies rippling upside down in ruffled water, the white herring-gulls leavening brown fields. I expect Seton's on his way there, switching on the night-sounds just for Cressida – the lap of waves on hull, the mournful scythe of wind through dying grasses, the hooting of a lonely boat winding its slow way towards the sea.

I force my attention back to dreary Kilburn, start counting my pound coins, alarmed how few they are. I can't afford taxis, let alone from this far-flung patch of London, which seems a foreign land. I haven't seen a client in three weeks, so funds are grimly low. But that's all got to change. I'll take every client I can get – yes, even the ones I've always avoided like the plague – the perverts and the maniacs, those leering casual kerb-crawlers whose pricks are loaded guns. Who cares if I get killed – or AIDS? I know it sounds dramatic or perverse, but I've actually *tried* to catch AIDS: slept with high-risk guys on purpose: bisexuals, drug-injectors. AIDS patients get hugged. I saw it on a TV documentary – nurses sitting up with them all night; heads on laps, kindly arms round shoulders. I suppose I also longed for the attention – not just loving nurses, but high-flown ritzy doctors with professorships and OBEs, and researchers from America, and television cameras focused on my deathbed, and John-Paul really moved this time, maybe moved to tears.

Though I'm not concerned with deathbeds at the moment. I'll come to those in time. I've got to live right now, so I can earn enough to buy up all those pictures – *and* the sculptures, if they're his – every last damn one of them. If other would-be purchasers object (and I didn't see one 'SOLD' sign at the show), I'll simply outbid them, offer the gallery so much it can't refuse. If I'm going to stop my sessions with John-Paul (and there seems no point continuing when he's not a proper doctor, and his chief concern is art), then at least I've got to own that art, not let a single rival get their hands on any work. All his life and spark is in those pictures, so by buying the collection I'll own *him*, in a sense, harness all his potency, hang the word 'omnipotent' all round my bedsit walls.

The taxi driver's trying to chat, or maybe chat me up. At first, I don't reply, simply haven't got the energy, find it hard to move out of my head. I'm thinking about faithfulness, a steady doggy sort of word I'd like to get to know. The trouble is it never seems reciprocal. No one's faithful back – not therapists, not fathers, not men who pick you up.

'Been to a party, have you?'

The poor chap's really trying, must have glimpsed my sick blue ruffles, my flimsy party shoes. 'Yes,' I say impassively, then realise he could help. Taxi drivers get to see the whole spectrum of humanity – including the stinking rich, so if I want to rustle up more clients, I could use him as an ally.

'Hey,' I say, in my most seductive voice. 'I'm . . . expanding my small business, and it might be worth your while to remember my address. I'll write it down, shall I, and perhaps we can work out some arrangement which could benefit us both.'

# 12

'Forty-two!' yelled Mary, as she dropped her gold vibrator in a final jerking spasm, clawed her still stiff nipples, shook back her tangled hair. Five within five minutes, and that last one really violent. She wiped the perspiration from her breasts (the sheets were damp already, damp with sweat, with juices); reached out for her score card, crossed out thirty-seven, wrote in forty-two. Not bad for just a week. Her Orgasm Chart was proving more a challenge than her Pain Score. She no longer chalked up just a list of numbers, but the colour, size and shape of the vibrator she had used, the intensity and duration of the feelings, and whether the climaxes were multiple or single. Five in a row had been her limit up to now, but weren't limits set to break?

She staggered out of bed, legs strangely weak and shaky, limped into her own room, the one she shared with James. The double bed accused her, not, as always previously, for being tense and frigid, but for being gross and greedy. Strange how James seemed to have gone off sex just recently (since *she*'d become more eager), or perhaps he'd not yet quite recovered from discovering her on Guy Fawkes night, lighting her own rocket. It could be just coincidence, of course. He'd had an extremely heavy week at work, with extra meetings, crises; his chief assistant rushed off to St Thomas's with sudden serious chest pains.

She crouched down by her bottom drawer, so full and heavy-laden now she could hardly tug it open; removed the giant-sized pack of Kotex which hid her new collection of vibrators. Which one should she choose to achieve that vital run of six? She didn't like the Teddy Bear – it seemed flippant, sacrilegious – and she was far too hot already for the light-up one called 'Beacon' whose tip had really scorched last time. She had never dared the black. It was the largest of them all, with ribbed gold bands around its shaft for extra stimulation and the name 'Black Stallion' stamped around its base.

She weighed it in her palm, felt its heaviness, its power, slipped back to the other room, dipped it in the lubricant. (She had graduated from 'Joy Jelly' to '*Vie-en-Rose* Xstasy Oil' which was pink and very slippery and smelt of candy-floss.) She paused a moment to gaze at her new icon which dominated the room. She'd had the tiny head and shoulders from the dust-jacket blown up by a photo-shop to very nearly life-size, so that John-Paul's eyes were black pools she could drown in, his open mouth a cavern she could fall down and down and down. The picture had gone fuzzy, but she didn't really mind. All her life seemed fuzzy now, her once-important jobs and chores strangely out of focus. There was no longer time for pressing James's trousers, or making jams and chutneys – not with so much else to do. She had to catch up with her reading, her whole missed education, including even Latin.

'Labia majora,' she said dutifully, out loud, as she explored them with a finger. 'Mons veneris. Labia minora.' She had discovered and identified all her different parts now, with the help of a small hand-mirror which the sex-books recommended, and the special pull-out diagram they'd printed for young girls. She was seventeen again, but a different seventeen – not Catholic, not a virgin, but a Lolita, a nymphet, just mounting her black stallion, her brutish bucking stallion. Already he was gathering speed, first off from the starter's gate, heading for the water-jump, rising up and over, as John-Paul in the commentary-box screamed out 'Forty-three!' She spurred her stallion on again – five more jumps to go – sweat sliding down her body as they galloped on together.

'Forty-four!' she shouted, voice whipped away by wind and sheer excitement, her breathing fast and dangerous as she cleared the brush, raced towards the five – no – six-barred gate. 'Forty-five, six, seven, eight – AAA-AAAAHHH . . .'

# 13

Bryan sat up in bed bolt upright, sweat soaking his pyjamas. He'd had a dream, a nightmare – not his usual Parcel Dream, but a serpent with the head of Eve curled up in the salad-drawer of his Mother's tidy fridge. Nothing else was tidy in the dream – terrifying fragments which made no sense or reason; amputated portions of his Father, B.K. Skerwin, skulking in a knickerbocker glory glass, and covered with whipped cream. He hated dreams, abhorred their lack of order, their random rambling muddle, the way they broke all rules. If it were a matter of an office desk, you could restrict paperclips to one drawer, staples to another, but dreams mixed and jumbled everything, lacked any proper structure, any beginning or firm end. The Parcel Dream was bad enough, but at least it wasn't sexual, whereas this particular nightmare was awash with sexual symbols – serpents, Eve, ice cream and glacé cherries – maybe even salad-drawers. John-Paul had never mentioned salads, not once in four whole years, but they were bound to be erotic – all those lush and damp green leaves, and things with *seeds* like peppers and tomatoes; and cucumbers and celery which went limp if they weren't used.

He reached out for the bedside light, hands fumbling in the gloom. The frog-shaped green glass night-light he'd had since early childhood and never quite grown out of, emitted only a faint and ghostly glow. He snapped the stronger light on, peered down at his watch. Four a.m. In just three hours he'd be lying on that couch again, trying to analyse a knickerbocker glory. Was the dream a ghastly warning? Was his Father in some danger that he'd landed up like chopped and pulped fruit salad beneath a white

177

shroud of ice cream? He must return to the class and check up on its tutor. Today was Friday – class night – or rather *Rambo* night. He'd spent the last three Fridays watching *Rambo*, instead of ogling Skerwin; been too terrified to face his Father, or a shocked contemptuous Mary who'd shun him as a liar. He hated violent films, but he'd misread the tiny entry in *What's On*, assumed the Piccadilly Plaza was showing *Dumbo*, the one film he'd really warmed to in twenty years or more. M60s and Kalashnikovs couldn't compare with baby elephants (and there were no doting weeping Mothers reunited with their sons), but at least it passed the time, saved him from the class – or his Mother's mocking triumph that he'd abandoned it so soon.

He'd sat through the bloody shoot-outs the following two Fridays, been forced to hide his eyes when Rambo wreaked revenge by circling in his chopper and destroying everything below him – men, women, children, dogs, howling from the carnage, charring in the flames. But at least it had spared him all the anguish of another grim decision, another three-hour grapple with *What's On*. And by the time he'd seen the film three times, it had set up a sort of pattern in his life, a blessed continuity, so that he was beginning to feel the need to watch it every Friday for the next thirty years or more; sit in the same seat (right-hand rear, no smoking), buy the same chocolate-nut King Kone. But now *Rambo*'s run had ended, disrupted his routine, and they were advertising *Heat and Lust* instead, which sounded most alarming, even worse than rocket-launchers or fragmentation grenades. He'd just have to make an effort and go back to the class – face his fears, his Father, the Chaos of the Universe – maybe get some courage from John-Paul.

Unlikely. John-Paul would favour serpents over tutors, spend all the session poking at the snake, or trying to scrape the bottom of the knickerbocker glory glass, so there'd be no time left for simple help, encouragement. It might be safer to stop sleeping altogether, to make sure he couldn't dream. Except he was so worn out already, he'd never do his work; had hardly had a good night's sleep since he'd been going to John-Paul. He fumbled for his own snake, found it at the bottom of the churned and tangled bed, a victim of his nightmare. 'Poor Anne,' he said, stroking its soft head. Nice if it could speak to him, say a word or two in comfort, listen to his dream with just a little basic sympathy, not John-Paul's sexual probings.

He could hardly wait for Christmas. He loathed it normally – a whole week trapped with Mother, who stirred guilt-soaked recrimination into her mince pies and laced her Christmas pudding with complaints and disapproval. But this particular Christmas John-Paul would be away not just for the Christmas break, but for the first two weeks of January as well. That spelled freedom of a different kind – if not from Mother and the whole Christmas sham itself, then at least from pre-dawn rising and the torments of the couch. John-Paul was going to Rome, as one of the main speakers at an International Congress of Psychiatry, and had warned his patients in advance, to prepare them for the trauma of his absence. Trauma! He could hardly wait. Mondays, Wednesdays, Fridays, would become normal working days again, with no need to go burrowing deep into his psyche, digging up old turds or phallic worms. A blessed month of sleeping in, ignoring any dreams, or merely emptying them like slops straight into the toilet bowl, flushing them away without a glance. He wished John-Paul would *stay* in Rome, permanently, indefinitely; turn his scholarly attention to all those ruined phallic-columns and Colosseum-wombs.

He couldn't even dislike the man in peace. His hostility was pounced upon, always probed and analysed; John-Paul claiming coolly that it was directed not at him at all, but really at his Mother – those dangerous murderous feelings he'd repressed since infancy and was now transferring to his therapist. If his Mother was a problem when he'd started therapy, she was now a can of worms. According to John-Paul, his longing to escape from her really masked a terror of abandonment, while his dreams of getting rid of her covered up a fear she'd murder *him*.

He frowned, smoothed out the blankets. Life was difficult enough without these complications. He'd started with one Mother, who'd been more than he could cope with – now he had a second – another all-intrusive figure of authority, criticising, larding him with guilt. He sat up against the pillows, tried to root John-Paul out from those compartments in his head which weren't labelled with his name. Strange how his slick therapist could sneak in everywhere; not just into drawers marked 'Science Class', or 'Mary', or even 'Strictly Private', but also into bedrooms, trains and (bolted) lavatories, as if he, too, were a snake and could slither into crevices barred to normal humans. He checked his watch again – still half an hour at least before he needed to get dressed. He daren't risk another nightmare, must use the time, distract himself, try to read, instead. He fumbled for his physics book, found his place, then let it slowly close again; could no more grapple with neutrinos than with flaccid celery.

He rifled through the bedside drawer, found *Amateur Photographer*, *Coin And Medal News*, and two old *Reader's Digests*. The *Digests* would be safest – no sex, no smut, and nothing too demanding, just cosy homespun stories, tales of courage, hints for self-improvement. ('It Pays To Increase Your Word Power', 'Teach Yourself Chinese'.) He turned first to the humour – 'Laughter Is The Best Medicine' – scanned the little anecdotes, the simple jolly jokes. It was difficult to laugh. He paused a moment, tried to remember when he'd last achieved it – four years or so ago, perhaps – before John-Paul, most definitely. He flicked on through the pages, found 'The Secret Life Of Cats And Dogs', span out the next ten minutes on feline scent-glands and how tail-wagging in dogs could indicate not pleasure, but conflict, indecision. So even dogs had problems. He fought a wave of sadness as he recalled the shaggy mongrel in the paper-shop, which wagged its tail so wildly when he went to buy his *Mail*. He'd assumed it really liked him, was pleased – no, thrilled – to see him; now he saw it was merely indecisive, like himself.

He shivered in his cramped and chilly bedroom, wished it had a fan-heater, a tiny silent one he could use without his Mother listening through the wall, and a bookcase for his science books which Mother called a 'Danger', not because she'd read them, but because they were piled up on the floor. And a picture would be nice, as well – perhaps a match-girl or a flower-seller; someone shy and sweet and female, to share his long dark nights.

He turned back to the magazine, hardly really concentrating until he found himself waist-deep in what had seemed a harmless article, entitled just 'Big Crunch'. He'd assumed it was a piece about the nation's eating habits: the switch from eggs and bacon to healthy breakfast cereals, or from things like Twix and Aero to those nutty oaty Crunch Bars – then realised to his horror that he was back with science, physics. The article reported that in just five billion years or so our own sun would collapse, followed (slightly later) by the universe itself – the Big Bang which had begun it all ending in an even Bigger Crunch. The author described this grim finale in terrifying detail: stars and galaxies plunging together at ever-increasing speeds, colliding in one single scorching fireball – the Apocalypse come true. Brian stared down at the print, imagining the noise, the total devastation, the turmoil and upheaval as everything broke up. The article assured him that man himself would have vanished long before, but that only made it worse, in fact. Who else would clear the mess up, untangle the confusion, sort out stars from planets, continents from seas?

He closed the magazine. He couldn't blame John-Paul for fifty laughless months. How could anybody laugh in such a world? He struggled out of bed, wincing as the chilly air nipped his wrists and ankles. He'd get dressed right away, just to beat the cold; could always use the extra time to let his morning tea cool down, instead of gulping it at scalding-point. He tiptoed to the bathroom, scared he'd wake his Mother, who rose at five-fifteen on John-Paul mornings, bitterly complaining about what she called the slave-drivers who whipped him off to work before first light. He loathed the dark himself, felt Chaos creeping up on him once the sun had set, all shapes and colours snuffed, all boundaries extinguished, his normal world eclipsed. He lifted the net curtain, gazed out into black. If only there were curtains he could hang up in his mind, kindly white frilled gauzes to stop Terror peering in.

He replaced the curtain, washed in melted ice, shaved with his old Remington, begging it to make less noise as it grumbled through his stubble. He crept back to the bedroom, put on his white shirt and grey-striped suit, which he'd laid out late last night, after hours of indecision about *which* grey suit, which shoes. The shoes were all plain black, of course, but there were still four separate pairs, which could drag out the whole process until one or two a.m. He was sometimes grateful to John-Paul for extracting all his money, so he couldn't buy new clothes. At least it cut the choices down – or some of them.

He pulled his socks up, eased on both his shoes, bent down to tie the laces, stopped half-paralysed. Which one should he tie first, the left shoe or the right? That was a decision he'd never really made before, never even thought about. How incredible, how casual, to have simply done them up, without working out the order, deciding on priorities, and for all those years and years. He stooped to tie the right, hands seizing up immediately. Why the right and not the left? He pounced towards the left instead, paused again, uncertain. He needed some fixed system, some principle or rule. There must be someone he could ask, use as guide or guru – John-Paul himself, perhaps?

No, he'd never get to John-Paul's in the first place with his shoelaces undone; might trip and break his neck, especially in the ill-lit streets, the gloomy blinkered tube. And his Mother would start nagging if he dared go down to breakfast what she'd call 'half-dressed'; would order him to do them up immediately. He wished she'd do it for him, as she had done as a child. He tried to recall her tying up his laces, buttoning his coat, but the small screen in his head remained obstinately blank. Had he ever been that tiny, or she ever had the patience to bother with a weak and helpless child? Wait! The screen was coming to life now – another woman stooping down to help him tie his laces – Mary, from the Winston Churchill Centre. He could smell her milky-mother smell as she bent towards his shoe, glimpse the plunging valley in her Eden-lily breasts. If he was going to the class tonight, he'd see her; could explain about his Father, confide in her, perhaps – except he was back to the same problem: how could he go anywhere until he'd tied his laces?

The left – he'd start with that one. His left foot was positioned just a fraction in front of the right, which was perhaps some sort of sign. He bent towards his left shoe, straightened up again. No, if everything was chancy in the universe, then the position of his feet was purely accidental. Sweat beaded on his forehead, despite the chilly room. Surely *someone* had laid down the Rules for Shoelaces, worked the whole thing out? He tracked back through his store of rules – office rules and school-rules, rules for witless children, rules for messy babies, rules for keeping neat and tidy in his Mother's cramping womb. Or how about cadet corps – that sweating red-faced drill sergeant who had always known the answers, had marched them round the drill hall yelling '*Left*, right, left, right, *left*', as if left had some priority. So he was back to left again. He stuck his left foot out once more, bent wearily towards it, only pausing as he examined his right hand. When it came to hands, the right one was superior (unless you were left-handed), so how could he be sure about the feet?

He shuffled in his unlaced shoes back towards the bed, sat down on the edge of it, cradling his poor snake. Not 'poor', for heaven's sake. Anne was extremely fortunate in having neither feet nor shoes. He checked his watch. It was getting very late. His Mother would be rising any moment, putting on the kettle, calling him to eat his Coco Pops. He could see himself taking his first mouthful, his own small scrunch completely lost in the Last Crunch of the universe as it came crashing down around them in the kitchen. Five billion years wasn't all that long. Just a few quite small decisions could take half that time on bad days. If the sun was going to shrivel, then shouldn't he be worrying, making some contingency plan, maybe increasing his insurance? There wasn't much time left.

'*Left*'. He started, frowned in concentration. Hadn't he just briefed himself by thinking of the word? Three times that word had come to him like a signal or a pointer. He'd better stop his dithering and follow where it led. His fingers made sweet contact with the lace of his left shoe, then fumbled to a standstill. If he was going to go by words, then 'right' had all the edge; meant 'correct' and 'fitting', 'proper', even 'orderly', in the sense of putting things to rights. He slid his right foot forward, stared at it unseeingly. His thoughts were higher up. He'd just read in that *Digest* that the left side of the brain was meant to be superior, so maybe he was wrong about the right.

'Right, wrong, right, wrong, right, *wrong*!' He could hear that sergeant's voice – furious, contemptuous, as he drilled them faster, faster, up and down the asphalt in the sticky mocking sun. 'You don't know right from wrong,

Payne. It's probably in the family. Did your mother know your father?'

He sank down on the bed again, kicked both his shoes off violently, heard his Mother's warning cough as they crashed against the wall. *Had* she known his Father – ever, once, at all? He wormed beneath the covers, still in suit and socks, slumped face down on the pillow and wept into his snake.

# 14

Must stop, must stop. Things to do – lunch to cook, shirts to wash, typing to return to Emma Barnes. Oh, Blessed Edwin Mumford, help me and forgive me – I *can't* stop, just can't stop. A hundred and eight. Oh, wonderful! It's out of this world. If only I'd started earlier, years ago, decades ago, I'd have reached the million mark by now. A hundred and nine. Terrific! That's *enough*, that's it. I really must switch off now, go down and light the oven. Phyllis coming round for lunch, to discuss the church bazaar – mustn't find me naked on my bed. Fricassee of veal and apple pie. I've made the pie already, and the veal won't take that long. Okay, just one more small one, before I braise the meat; one teeny tiny one. A hundred and . . . No, take it nice and slowly, really spin it out this time if it's going to be the last. Why small, in any case? Why not a quite colossal one, a naughty big outrageous one? A hundred and what? Lost count now. Who cares about the count? Harder, faster, *harder* – turn it to top speed. Two million and . . . Oh, God! It's broken – *broken*.

# 15

'Drawers go in and out, Bryan, so any drawer can be seen, of course, as phallic, but in this particular case, it would appear to me that the salad-drawer represents your mother's genitals. The serpent is your father's threatening phallus, coiled inside your mother's "box" or hole – a fertile place, as depicted by the salads. You dare not go in there yourself, or you may be bitten by a snake.'

Bryan reached out for his own snake, traced the outline of its mouth, the contours of its lumpy red felt tongue. He was glad it had no teeth, not even woolly ones. He murmured something indistinct and anodyne, tried to blank out the statistics he'd just read on passive smoking. John-Paul was on his fourth already.

'The whole dream seems to me to reveal an obvious obsession with genitals – or what could be described as a "displacement outwards" from genitals to knickers.' John-Paul tapped his cigarette, removed a phallic worm of ash. 'I've already mentioned the meaning of drawers as undergarments – an old-fashioned word, but nonetheless emotive – and the "knickerbocker glory" re-emphasises this. Once again, your father seeks the glory in the knickers, though he seems injured by his attempt this time, which I suggest is a manifestation of your own castration fears . . .'

'No,' said Bryan, to no one. No one heard.

'It could also be Oedipal, of course: your wish to harm your hated father, as a rival to your mother's favours – the one who is allowed inside her drawers or knickers, whereas you yourself are banned.'

'I didn't hate my Father,' Bryan objected.

'I beg your pardon? You're speaking extremely indistinctly. I wonder if that indicates some reluctance to participate, perhaps reluctance to be here at all, today?'

'Yes,' mouthed Bryan, to Anne. 'No,' he said, much louder. 'It's just that I think I'd like to talk about the class now. I should have told you earlier, but I . . . I went back just last Friday and my Father *was* quite badly injured.' He took a deep breath in, inhaling John-Paul's smoke, eyes watering and smarting. '*And*,' he added, voice a keening wail, both hands clutching Anne, as if for comfort, 'Mary's died of cancer.'

# 16

I'm swamped in black and brown, swirling lines crisscross-
ing in my head, whorls of sticky still-wet paint churning
in my stomach and my bowel. It's difficult to breathe.
Someone's slapped gouache right across my face, dammed
up my nose and mouth. There's no air in the room. The
pictures need it all. I can hear them panting in and out,
breathing far too fast. They're all squashed and jammed
together – some not even hung, but stacked around the
skirting, balanced across chairs. 'I'm sorry,' I keep telling
them. 'I need a bigger place, but . . .'

I didn't buy the sculptures. There wasn't room – or
cash. I can't take any more clients, not with pictures on
the bed. I'm too tired, in any case, too raw and sore and
smarting, all my different orifices screaming out in pain. I
can't really blame the blokes. They paid for what they got,
didn't overstay their time; were mostly lonely misfits, not
sadistic dangerous maniacs. One even said he loved me,
bought me twelve red roses. The thorns were bigger than
the blooms, which died within the day.

I weave around the room, avoiding pictures, furniture.
I've got to get more cash. I haven't seen John-Paul for
three weeks, two days and fifty-seven minutes. I kept
praying that he'd ring. Even with my clients there, I
was listening for the phone, all psyched up to answer
it, naked, wet or shagged. I rarely left the bedsit, so I
wouldn't miss his call, even contacted British Telecom
to check the phone was working. Surely he was worried,
wondering where I was? After seven endless days, he wrote
me two brief lines, enquiring – curtly – was I ill, since I'd
stopped attending sessions? I responded with two words:

'No, fine' – scrawled in blood-red biro on a huge white sheet of paper. Last week he wrote again: if I wasn't indisposed, then my absence could suggest that I'd found the last few sessions quite disturbing, and that itself seemed an obvious indication against any thought of termination at this stage. It hurt, that letter, actually – its chilly tone, its coldly formal phrases – especially 'termination', which is the word they use for pregnancies, and a euphemism for murder. Oh, I know he said I shouldn't even think of it, but the fact he used the word at all must mean it's on his mind; means he probably *hopes* I'll terminate, while urging that I shouldn't. There's a word for that as well – a jargon word: projection. He's guilty of the very things he accuses all us patients of – reversal and denial.

He even sent his bill, enclosed it with the letter, charged me for missed sessions when I was bleeding here at home. I was dying on account of him and all he was concerned about was whether he'd be paid. I was so upset I decided that I'd gratify him: do what he was angling for and quit therapy for ever; not stay where I'm unwelcome and resented. I kept repeating that word 'terminate', like a sort of evil mantra. 'Yes,' I said. 'I'll terminate, if that's what you're suggesting. Do murder me – feel free.' I even considered changing my whole lifestyle, leaving London and moving back to Shropshire; digging up the corpse of my old home, unearthing my dead parents, my dead and rotting childhood; living as a ghost there. I tried to pack a suitcase, check rooms to rent, and train times, but I felt too ill to travel, too weak to deal with house agents; just flaked out on the sofa and lay there several days, shivering and feverish and hardly knowing where I was. Yet John-Paul assumes I'm 'fine'; accepted my scrawled note – the most flagrant lie I've ever told, and he took it at face value.

'Fine,' I say, repeating it, as I light a cigarette. 'I'm absolutely fine.' People hate it if you're ill. Sympathy's like money – you need it for yourself. I'd better call on Wilhelm, suggest a new arrangement: not fellatio for dreams, but fellatio for cash. Dreams are quite superfluous if I'm not going to John-Paul, and my own are more dramatic now, in any case. Last night I dreamed John-Paul was a monster who lived in the Dead Sea, and had sucked me in as food, along with weeds and snails and debris and tiny writhing eels. I was living in his stomach which was lined with scarlet snot; swimming round and round it, battening off his food supply, excreting through his bowel.

I fetch my coat and handbag, lock my door so the pictures can't get out, climb the steep iron stairs to street-level. It's dark outside – dark at four p.m. The year is dying with me: brief days, bleak nights, decay and damp heavy on the streets. Though winter in the country is always more oppressive than winter in the town. I keep thinking back to Shropshire, where all life seems suspended by the last week of November – the sun a pallid blur in a waste of homeless cloud; sap falling, leaves abandoned, bracken beaten flat; no green except the ivy strangling dying stone. How quiet it must be there now, with all life folding down, all helpless creatures hibernating – toads shrouded under tree roots in their coffins of dead leaves; bats huddled in old churches, wings folded round their bodies like thin black ragged duvets.

London shrugs off winter. Red buses pant and sweat, and traffic noise masks the sound of death-knells. There are no leaves here to fall, just shrill-green plastic Christmas trees sprouting in small sweet-shops, wreaths of ersatz holly. 'Only twenty-four shopping days till Christmas. Order your turkey NOW!' Only a million billion shopping days till I pluck and truss John-Paul. I stop a moment, fight to get my breath. It's not good for me to think of him, especially not outside. I might faint, or fall, or get those crimson pains again, the ones I had all yesterday.

The butcher's isn't crowded, but I still dither for ten minutes before I dare to enter. I haven't eaten for two days, so my stomach starts objecting to those palely naked chickens with their puckered goose-fleshed skin, those pink and hairless rabbits lanced on metal hooks, those blood-smeared surgeons' overalls. The back room's always worse, of course – furred but eyeless calves' heads watching while I kneel, mounds of shining ox livers seeping blood into the sawdust along with Wilhelm's sperm.

'Don't cry,' he says. '*Mein Herzensschatz*. I make you happy, no?'

'No,' I say, then, 'yes'. It's vital that I please him. I let him dry my eyes on a dirty off-white handkerchief which smells of sausagemeat – the gamey sort, with herbs. Did he dry the eyes of all those Auschwitz victims, before he gouged them out, flung their Jewish giblets in a pail?

'I'm all right now,' I tell him, still waiting for my payment. I don't get cash at all, but a huge great flank of beef, ice-cold from the freezer. He bestows it with such triumph, such a sense of liberality, it numbs all my objections, though my landlady's away, and her own freezer isn't large enough to hold it anyway. It's almost too big to carry, and I keep stopping, shivering, as it drips melted ice (and blood) down both my legs. I'm wet through as it is. It's raining, always raining, though this is different rain – spiteful callous winter rain slashing in my face. In fact, it's hard to see the wolfhounds when they first start following me, though I turn round once or twice to check their stealthy padding. I dismiss them as vague shadows, or just the moaning of the wind, until they actually brush against me with their rough and hairy coats, noses jabbing me at waist-level, tails whipping me both sides. They're the biggest dogs I've ever seen, with deep and powerful chests, long muscly legs, and substantial brawny hind-quarters which suggest Olympic power. They're both slavering at the meat, intense dark eyes focused on the carcass, tongues lolling from their mouths.

It's obvious why they've come: John-Paul must have sent them to relieve me of my burden – which shows he cares, remembers who I am, isn't trying to oust me, as I feared. I turn into an alleyway, ease the side of beef onto the ground. They fling themselves upon it, tear it with their fangs, eating with a voraciousness I recognise. If John-Paul were a joint of beef and I a simple dog, I'd fall on him with just that same abandonment, devouring him, consuming him, gulping down every smallest morsel. I've never taken Communion (or even attended a Communion service), but I assume that's how believers must eat God – desperate to ingest Him, get Him down inside them, not let a cell or corpuscle go to waste.

Once the dogs have finished, licked their lips, licked and sniffed the gutter, hoovered all around for any last remaining blood-trails, they start fawning on me, mobbing me, tails thwacking at my coat, dark moist noses sniffing at my cunt. I'm feeling a lot better just to be appreciated. They're so warm and so alive, and I'm bonded to John-Paul again by annexing his pets; his cruel letters cancelled now, his wounding words erased. I pick their trailing leads up, turn right instead of left as I leave the narrow alley, take a puddly detour to the recreation ground. I let them bound and gallop past the dark and dripping slides, watch them barking at the shadows, loping through the mud. I climb on to a child's swing, which feels wet beneath my skirt, swing to and fro, to and fro, thinking of John-Paul. I'm no longer even cross with him. Anger needs great energy and mine's all leaked away. Or perhaps I really love him and what I classed as fury was something else entirely.

I wish I were his dog, so I could lick his face and eat his scraps and smell his human smell; brush against his trousers, fetch endless sticks for him. Perhaps I'd be his lap-dog, his pouting poncy Pekinese, so I could lay my fancy head against his waistcoat buttons and have him feed me humbugs. Or his fierce and ravening guard-dog, who'd maul and claw all those rival patients, savage them to bone. Or his loyal and trusty guide-dog, so when he's groping-old, he'd never dare let go of me, and, joined at last, I could lead him up to God. Or, best of all, his sick dog, so he'd stroke my head, suggest I sleep on *his* bed rather than my basket, coax my tablets down me with scraps of chicken breast. My pills are all at home. I'd better go and get them, put myself to bed. I'm feeling very strange.

I call the dogs to heel, wish they wouldn't pull so hard as I limp and struggle back. Both my hands are reddened as I finally unleash them in my room.

*'Down!'* I shout, as the larger darker-coated male bolts towards the door, knocks a picture flat. The slightly smaller female is prowling up and down, restless and suspicious, only stopping for a moment to claw the chair, rip a piece of fabric from its seat. If my room was cramped before, it's now completely overwhelmed – the pungent smell of crude damp dog choking the scant air; a wild tangle of wet paw-prints patterning the carpet. They keep shaking themselves, so that showers of dirty droplets spray against the pictures, stain my pale cream shirt. The paintings shift and tremble. They're frightened of the dark, have never liked my bedsit with its mean and grudging light. I need to let them out – not just the dogs – the canvases.

The male dog springs towards me, starts pawing at my shoulders, almost knocks me over. I fight it off, escape into a corner, try out commands like 'Sit!' and 'Stay!', but they're totally ignored. Both of them are barking now, a hoarse and hacking sound, as if their throats are cracked, inflamed. I'm worried other tenants will complain. Pets are not allowed, not even quiet and harmless ones like cats.

I reach up to the cupboard where I keep my tranquillisers, make a bread and Valium sandwich, feed half to each dog. They devour it with such passion I can hardly believe they guzzled that huge flank of beef just an hour ago. I'm beginning to feel frightened. How will I keep up with them – their energy, their appetites? They're killer-dogs, this breed; were used to hunt fierce wolves before the invention of the gun; can still annihilate a deer, or rip a sheep to pieces, even turn on smaller dogs and tear them limb from limb.

I swallow my own pills, try – and fail – to eat an old half-pizza which has been around a week or so, light a fag instead. I wish all food could be inhaled, not masticated, and came ready-flavoured with tar and nicotine. Four eyes are watching me, dark distrustful wary eyes, tracking every smallest movement of my hand or foot or head. I approach the smaller dog, inching very cautiously towards her, and holding out my hand for her to sniff. She's brindled brown and grey, with lighter paws and muzzle, and protruding whiskery eyebrows. 'Good girl,' I murmur softly, as I stroke her wiry coat. (Strange how we tell animals they're 'good'. No one tells us humans.) She still seems very fidgety, her long tail tense, her body rigid, braced, but I keep stroking very rhythmically, and soon the rhythm and the Valium begin to do their work, and in less than fifteen minutes both dogs are slumped and quiet. I sprawl beside them on the carpet, too tired to clear the chairs or move the pictures from the bed – close my eyes, sink back.

It's wonderful to sleep alone – or at least with dogs, not clients. These last three weeks I've been sharing bed and bath. I let some jokers stay the night, because despite the squash and horror of it, I was charging them an hourly rate, so it made financial sense. Actually, it all seems rather pointless now. Okay, I bought the pictures, but I couldn't buy John-Paul.

I say his name aloud and very slowly, repeat it like a lullaby or mantra, but it doesn't resurrect him, nor help me get to sleep. He feels very faint and far away, even with his dogs here. I wonder what their names are, try out several likely ones, then realise they're the names of my new clients – Barry, Richard, Warren, Spencer, Mike.

They weren't much cock, those blokes, and I mean that literally. If I confiscated all limp pricks, my cupboards would be full. I'm not that keen on penises. They aren't exactly beautiful, never smell or taste that good; are always strictly limited in the sense of skills and repertoire, yet still persist in seeing themselves as VIPs, big guns. Perhaps I'm simply jealous, a basic case of John-Paul's penis-envy, but I honestly don't think so. I suspect Freud dreamed the phrase up to distract attention from men's own obvious envy of the womb. It's women who give birth and life and suck – normal women, anyway. To produce an eight-pound baby with intellect and brains, maybe even genius, from one tiny pinhead egg-cell seems to me miraculous. I envy that myself, far more than penises. If there is a God, then He made men very badly. If they ejaculated Grand Marnier in decent double measures instead of dribs of sperm, far more women would be rushing to fellate them.

The only prick I envy is John-Paul's, but then I envy *all* his organs – his liver, spleen and kidneys, his lungs and heart and brain – just because they're close to him. I can see his liver clearly, its shape, its size, its texture; imagine his appendix, his tonsils or his pancreas, but somehow not his prick. It must be some taboo thing. (Though I did once have a fantasy where he died and was cremated, and I stuffed his still-warm ashes in a dildo and thrust it up my cunt. I suppose it was the only way of having him inside me.)

I try to shift my mind from sex; think of God instead, but I can only see His genitals, His womb. I allow Him to make love to me, slowly, very slowly, with all my favourite (non-existent) words: tenderness, devotion, mercy, loving kindness. It doesn't last that long. Seton barges in instead, rams me from behind. Or perhaps it's just his brutish boat and he's too busy to be bothered. Its prow feels very hard and stiff, splitting me apart. I lie in muddy water while it judders back and forth; climaxes, at last, in a spume of dirty jetsam.

Then the clients trickle back again – Warren, Mike and Spencer (whose name is really Joe); Richard in his shirt-tails, Barry with his doll. Amazing how I'm wanted, how everyone desires me; grown men queuing, jostling, fighting for an opening, even hirsute Wilhelm challenging a rival. 'Wait your turn,' I tell them, but nobody can hear. There's too much noise – the crash of waves, of tempers, a shrill and strident barking. Yes, the dogs are joining in now, the male erect and mounting me, as I crouch down on all fours, like his trembling bitch on heat. I *am* on heat – feverish and sweating, all the pulses in my body throbbing far too fast. The dog's coarse pelt is prickling my bare back, his wild claws clutching, tearing. 'Stop!' I shout. 'Lie *down*.' I wish I knew his name. It would make it less impersonal. I can only think of saints' names, the four Evangelists.

> Matthew, Mark, Luke and John,
> Bless this bed I lie upon.

Someone used to croon that, long ago, long ago, when I was in my cot. Or perhaps they didn't croon it, but I just hoped or wished they had; invented it myself, called it Truth, like Uncle Jack. I try to coax them back, those four Evangelists – Uncle Matthew, Uncle Mark, Uncles Luke and John – to bless my dirty-carpet-bed, send the mortal men away, leave me pure and solitary.

197

Four white angels round my bed,
Two at the foot and two at the head,
One to watch and one to pray
And two to bear my soul away.

Oh, yes, I beg – yes, that.

# 17

Bryan lounged back on the scarlet vinyl banquette, a pint of Carling Black Label in one triumphant hand. He was not just in the King's Arms, but in Mary's arms – or nearly. He felt a king himself. The pub was spacious, tasteful, with pillars, mirrors, framed paintings of the British monarchs from Ethelred the Unready to Edward VII – who looked more than ready and was brandishing a sceptre-cigar which John-Paul would call a phallus. The carpet was imperial-purple, patterned with impressive gold medallions (and several spills of beer). The tables looked antique, with lion-claw legs and crinkled pie-crust rims. He'd bagged the most secluded one, in an alcove on its own, though with a stately potted palm rearing up behind them like a chaperone. He wished the fire was real, or even warm, but then you couldn't have everything, and those pretend coal fires looked really quite convincing from a distance.

He glanced across at Mary, still couldn't quite believe it: she was not only alive (and back in both science and society), but she had actually suggested a drink after the class – not coffee in a paper cup in that shabby old canteen, but a private drink in a royal tavern where he had her to himself. He hardly knew how he'd stuttered out his 'Yes', tried to make it casual, as if drinks in bars with blonde attractive women were simply part of his routine – perhaps followed by a nightclub, and then a midnight saunter along the romantic River Thames, even a lingering embrace beside the throbbing star-kissed water.

'Same again?' he murmured, pointing to her empty

glass, its damply swollen cherry looking so inviting, its lemon slice smiling with wide lips.

'D'you really think we should, Bryan?'

'Oh, yes,' he said. 'I *do*.' He needed courage, Dutch or otherwise, to quash the image of his Mother limping up and down in hairnet and beige dressing gown, ticking like a clock herself as she watched the minute-hand's slow circling and realised her cruelly selfish son had missed the twenty-four and was probably going to miss the fifty-two. Her leg would be much worse of course – always was the evening he was out. He cursed that damaged leg, which crippled him as well, made him swell and fester with a curdled mix of pity, guilt, resentment.

He hobbled to the bar, casting anxious looks behind him, to make sure Mary wasn't kidnapped, raped, abducted, the minute that his back was turned. He'd been trying to keep a check on every male aged seventeen to seventy who came into the pub, or dared to pass their table, especially all the handsome hunky ones. He didn't trust the barman, a brashly jovial type with a roving eye (and an eye more darkly blatant than his own wishy-washy hazel ones), who might inveigle himself dangerously close to Mary, or even proposition her, by simply using the expedient of wiping down their table or collecting up the empties. How mean the fellow seemed as he measured her Dubonnet – two grudging paltry inches, when she deserved at least a firkinful, a hundredweight of cherries, a whole lemon grove in sunny Taormina.

He wheeled round again, quite suddenly, to catch out any rivals. Mary was alone still, but some brazen blue-jeaned upstart was just swaggering slowly up to her, enquiring if the seat were free. He tossed a fiver on the counter, streaked back to the alcove so fast he spilled his beer. He rarely drank Black Label – rarely drank at all, in fact – but last night's TV commercial had showed a macho man with a hearth-rug chest and shoulders like the

Admiralty Arch crumpling up a car with one bare hand, after imbibing just half a bottle of Carling. *He* was on his fourth bottle – already felt much stronger, even dared ask Mary why she'd missed the last two classes.

'But you missed three yourself,' she parried, smiling quite disarmingly. 'Before that. I was looking out for you, even saved you a seat.'

He gulped down froth and ecstasy together. He must find that seat, rip it from the row, heave it home and preserve it as a monument, inscribe it in gold letters: 'SAVED FOR BRYAN BY MARY', with the date in Roman numerals. 'I was . . . er . . . abroad again,' he said, gesturing so nervously his fingers caught the foliage of the watching potted palm. It was plastic, like the chandeliers, he noted with a twinge of disappointment. 'Busy month, November.' He tried to put jet-lag in his voice; appointments, meetings, conferences, product-launches, working-lunches, frantic daily phone calls to check the progress of his shares. 'D'you know, I sometimes barely find the time to clean my teeth?' He cleaned them four times daily, twice at home and twice at work, a full five minutes by the clock, and following a formula which included every surface, angle, crevice, plane and cutting-edge.

'Gosh! It must be awful.' Mary shook her head. '*I* was busy too, in fact, but nothing on that scale. Just . . . domestic matters. I seem to have so much to do – just recently, I mean. The chores keep piling up the way they never did before, and I haven't got the energy, not now, not since . . .'

He wondered why she'd broken off so suddenly, why she was blushing, looking down, fiddling with her hand-bag. Cancer, obviously. She must still be having treatment, but be too distressed to spell it out by name. That would explain her lack of zest, her feeling of fatigue. He laid his hand down on the table between their two stained beer-mats, as if to say: 'It's there if you require it – a helping hand, a steady hand. I care. I understand.' He longed to touch her own hand, to demonstrate that care, but dared not risk repulse, or, worse still, laughter.

'I know you've not been well, Mary. You told me so the first time that we met. I must admit I have been rather anxious. In fact, when I didn't see you at the last two classes, I actually thought you'd . . .' He took a long draught of Black Label to help him get the word out. It still hurt extremely badly, had cost him two weeks' sleep. 'Died,' he said, half-choking on the lager.

'*Died?*'

'Well, the treatment isn't always that successful. I mean, my aunt was in and out for six whole months, but still they couldn't save her.'

'What treatment? What d'you mean?'

'The . . . er . . .' He couldn't spell it out himself, tried a more circuitous route. 'You said you were going to a place right near our class.'

'Oh, I see – oh, *that*.' Mary seemed confused again, embarrassed, then suddenly broke into a giggle, took a slow bite of her cherry, relishing the mouthful almost blatantly, as if she, too, had been watching those commercials, copying the models who sold lipsticks or ice cream. Bryan kept glancing up at her, relieved, yet somehow jealous. She must be better, surely, if she could laugh like that, flirt with shameless cherries. A month ago, she'd been so very different, tense and almost tragic. And those burn marks on her hands were fully healed – he'd noticed that the instant he first saw her, noticed she looked sparkling, very nearly smug.

'The treatment worked then, Mary?'

'Yes, it did – extremely well, in fact – better than I dared to hope.' She was giggling still, quite girlish. 'I'm completely cured, you could say. My . . . doctor's very pleased with me.'

'*Wonderful!*' Bryan offered thanks to any God who'd

managed to survive the quantum revolution, or co-exist with Chaos. 'Let's have another drink.'

'No, really, Bryan, I . . .'

'This calls for a celebration. And anyway, we ought to drink to Skerwin, since he's recovered, too.'

'*Who?*'

'Our tutor.' He didn't say 'my Father'. He'd get to that eventually; maybe over dinner in what people called an 'intimate' little bistro, with softly flickering candles, sweet seductive music. The pub was getting noisy – a muffled roar of overlapping voices rising all around them, the slap and clink of glasses, even a tactless jukebox churning out a song called 'When You Left'. Dare he risk a meal? Even if they gobbled it, or ordered just one course, it would still mean missing five or six more trains. His Mother left his dinner out on Fridays – cold Reproach on Toast, or a shop-bought Cornish pasty, all air and cold potato. Could he force a pasty down after fillet steak with Mary – or afford fillet steak at all? ( John-Paul had warned him of his annual rise in fees, only a month or so away now.) Perhaps Mary liked Chinese, and he could toy with a few bean sprouts and still leave room for his Mother's guilt-and-penance salad or how-could-you-leave-me sandwich.

'Has Mr Skerwin been unwell, then?' Mary looked concerned, pushed her empty glass away, still refusing to accept another drink.

'No. He had an accident – fell down a step which wasn't there. He told the class two weeks ago, limped up to the lectern all swathed in bandages and with his right hand in a sling.'

'How brave of him to come at all. Most tutors would have cancelled.'

Bryan said nothing. It wasn't done to boast, but of course his Father was exceptionally courageous. Clumsy, too, alas, but then geniuses were often absent-minded. He'd been half-horrified, half-worshipping, as he'd watched the doughty figure struggling to his desk, still loaded down with shopping, textbooks, outerwear, despite his *hors de combat* arm and all too obvious bruises. It had ruined his weekend – that and Mary's absence. He'd hoped to get some help on Monday, at the session, but John-Paul had made things worse, in fact; insisted it was Oedipal – again – an unconscious but quite clear desire to lame and cripple his hated Father-rival.

'But it wasn't me who did it,' he'd complained. 'He went crashing down a step.'

'Which wasn't there,' John-Paul said, lighting up. (Eight kingsize in thirty-seven minutes.)

'No, but he thought it was there.'

'Just as you thought *he* was there – your father at the class.'

'He *was* there.'

'Bryan, you appear to have a need today not to understand.'

'Blast!' he said out loud.

'What's the matter?'

Not John-Paul, but Mary, sounding worried. He'd lose her if he wasn't careful, allowed John-Paul to bedevil him again. He marched his doctor to the door, shooed him from the pub. He had quite enough rivals there already – not just the gold-framed monarchs who were all squinting at her breasts, Edward VII leering almost pruriently, but the two men sitting opposite who'd actually inched forward to get a better view. He moved his chair to form a screen, glared at any other male in view, then tried to force his mind back, resume their conversation. 'Such a shame you couldn't make last Friday. It was really fascinating – we did antiparticles.'

'Anti-what?'

'Particles. For every particle, there's apparently an antiparticle, so Skerwin said there could in fact be whole antiworlds and antipeoples. He warned us not to shake hands with our antiself, told us we'd both vanish in a huge great flash of light.' He tried to laugh, to prove it was a joke, though he hadn't felt like laughing that particular Friday night; had kept fretting about antitrains as he rushed to catch the thirty-two, or imagined slaying antiMothers as his all too solid present Mother regaled him with the story of her almost-heart-attack. (She had heart attacks each Friday, when she wasn't being burgled, raped or mugged.)

'Gosh!' said Mary. 'Antiselves. I wish I hadn't missed it, but last Friday was my youngest son's eighth birthday. He's away at school in Sussex, but they let us go and see him – well, just from two to four. James took the afternoon off, which is a rare event itself. I was terribly excited, but it turned out rather badly, I'm afraid. He didn't have a party or any proper celebration, just the cake I'd brought him, and we were on our way back home again by shortly after three. He seemed – you know – on *edge*, as if he didn't want us there. It's that headmaster's fault, I'm sure. He seems to hate all parents, probably tells the boys we're . . .'

Bryan stared down at the carpet, loathed it when she used that 'we', talked about her sons, or worse still, James. He could just imagine James – a combination of John-Paul in the brain department, and last night's Carling commercial hulk, as far as looks and prowess were concerned. *He* was Mary's husband – not James, but Bryan Payne-Hampton – her youngest son, as well; the one she dandled on her lap, so his head was resting right against those breasts. She was wearing several layers today, so her curves were rather blurred, alas, despite the tempting cleavage. If he took her to a really stifling restaurant, she'd be forced to take her jacket off, and perhaps that woolly white thing, and he might even glimpse her brassière through the flimsy floral blouse. But would he ever find a restaurant cheap enough and hot enough, yet also intimate, romantic, and with really speedy service, and close to Fenchurch Street, so he could dash there for his train – oh, and also totally empty so that nobody would see them?

'Well, I *offered* him a party as soon as he broke up, said we'd make it up to him, invite all his local Walton friends and maybe hire a conjuror and . . .'

'I'm hot,' said Bryan. 'Aren't you?'

'No, I'm rather chilly, actually. Though compared with Jonathan's dormitory, this place is like a greenhouse. It's arctic, that whole school. No wonder they get colds and things. Jon looked really peaky when . . .'

'Yes, there *is* a draught, isn't there, with all these people barging in and out? Look, why don't we make a move, find ourselves a cosy little . . .?'

'In fact, I think he must have been sickening for a virus. It's the only way I can account for how he was. D'you realise, Bryan, he didn't *want* a party, said he was far too old for conjurors, and party-games were just for weeds and wets. I cried, you know, I really did, once we'd left him at the gates. I know it may sound stupid, but he is my baby – too old, at eight, for games.'

Bryan heard a voice screaming in his head: '*I'm* your baby, I'm your baby – and not too old for games.' If Jonathan were sickening, he should be dispatched straight up to Scotland, the northernmost remotest part, with no trains, or even roads; left alone in quarantine until the bracing air had cured him – or better, killed him off. He hated to be cruel, but if the boy upset his mother so, absorbed all her attention, then wiser to remove him altogether. 'It's *my* birthday,' he said casually. 'Next Friday, actually, and I wouldn't mind a conjuror myself.'

She laughed. 'Oh, Bryan!'

'No, I'm serious. I've never had a party in my life.'

'What, not even as a child?'

'No, my Mother was too busy. She had to earn our

living, hadn't time for parties.' The beer had made him reckless. He was plunging wildly on, telling her the story of his deprived and desperate childhood. 'I never knew my Father. He walked out on my Mother before she'd even had me.' It sounded rather flat, the sort of standard sob-stuff on any social worker's course. He added some embellishments, Carlingesque hyperbole. 'She kept dragging me to see him, used to lie down on the pavement right outside his house and refuse to move all day. He lived in this huge mansion with two new wives and . . .'

'*Two*?'

'Oh, more than two, quite often. And a whole horde of other children. Of course he didn't want to acknowledge us, refused to let us in. We'd often stay out there all night, huddled in the rain or snow, shunned by other people . . .' Bryan glanced at Mary's shocked and stricken face. Had he gone too far? Her voice was harrowed, faltering, not that far from tears.

'B . . . But he doesn't seem that type at all. He looks so sensitive and gentle, and you said yourself how he only lived for science and . . .'

Bryan shut his eyes, saw Skerwin in his mind again, not the Skerwin of the harem, but the Skerwin of the class, whom he'd been admiring just an hour ago – a kindly and unworldly soul, who did, indeed, live for books and learning. Could John-Paul actually be right and he was blackening a blameless man through unconscious fear and jealousy? 'He reformed,' he muttered tersely, compressing half a century's struggle into one dramatic gesture. 'Divorced his wives and betrothed himself to science.'

'Gosh!'

He knew he was impressing Mary, was impressing even himself. He had never been so imaginative, so voluble. He must drink Carling regularly, find an empty syrup-of-figs bottle and decant it through a funnel, so he could keep it in his bedroom. He could see his Mother now, rifling through his cupboards in a wild attempt to discover where he was, turning out his pockets, spying in his drawers; maybe removing all his science books as 'unhealthy' and 'pernicious'; certainly clearing off his supper, so he would go hungry (and penalised) to bed. He shrugged. He didn't care.

The phrase startled him, appalled him. He'd never said that in his life, never even thought it, never dared to think it. 'I don't care,' he said aloud, rising from his seat. He wanted everyone to hear it – the two men opposite, the wild crowd at the bar, that obese and henna-ed woman with her scarlet nails and purple skirt guffawing on a bar-stool as she sprayed foam from her Guinness; the young couple with their feet entwined on the banquette in the corner; the three barmen in their blue bow ties; the old boy by the pseudo-fire with his slipping china teeth. 'I don't care,' he said again, hoped John-Paul could hear him from his high room in the tower, and every last employee in the whole of BRB, its twenty storeys reeling in surprise, and all those strait-laced semis in spiteful Ivy Close, scandalised, recoiling, as they repeated the three words. He didn't care, he didn't care – let them taunt and gossip, let his Mother nag. He didn't even *want* her rotten pasties, planned to share a T-bone steak with Mary.

'I don't care,' he said, a fifth time, still marvelling at the phrase. He must be better, cured. Just two pints of Carling Black Label had won him independence, where fifty months of therapy had failed. 'Cured.' He tried the word, relished it, pinned it on his chest like a medal, decoration, as he swilled the last gold liquor from his glass. He could hear the fifty-two whistling out of Fenchurch Street, followed by the seventeen, the twenty-two, the forty. He didn't care, he didn't care. 'Cured,' the wheels were thundering, as they plunged past Limehouse, hurtled on to Barking, juddered into Upminster with B.V. Payne not there. He only had to prove it now, translate it into action.

He sank back on the bench again, stretched a clammy trembling hand towards Mary's steady cool one; raised his voice to compete with rattling carriages, the hoot and bray as train passed whooping train. 'Mary?' He wished she looked less tense, less apprehensive, but it was probably only hunger. They'd both relax once they were settled in the restaurant, with violins, an ice bucket. 'I was wondering if you'd join me for a meal? There's this little Chinese bistro just around the corner . . .'

'Oh, no, Bryan, thank you, honestly. I really must get home. James is waiting for his own meal. In fact, it's fearfully late already. I'd better phone him from the station or he'll . . . Where's my scarf? Ah, good. I thought I must have dropped it. Did you have a coat, Bryan? No? Gosh! You're hardy, aren't you? Look, why don't you come and *meet* James, one evening after work, pop down and have a meal with us? It's not far on the train, and I'm sure you two would have a lot in common, with all your trips abroad and conferences and everything. His life is just the same as yours – busy, busy, busy. What's wrong? What's the matter? You're looking almost . . . Was it something that I said? Oh, Bryan, don't *cry*, please don't. Look, here's a nice clean hankie. There – blow your nose and I'll put you on your train.'

# 18

It's three a.m., the worst hour of the night. Things which seem too tragic for the daytime or the evening, come true at three o'clock. I've worked through suicide, bereavement, fatal accident, and am now considering all the 'loss' words – loss of bearings, loss of purpose, loss of face and nerve and love. It's impossible to sleep. The dogs make too much noise, continually fretting, scratching, shifting, or prowling round and round. Their smell is overpowering. I've dared not let them out since they killed a cat on Thursday, ravaged every shrub and flowerbed in the park. I bought some sawdust, laid it thick on newspapers, so they could do their business in one restricted corner, but they didn't seem to understand, or perhaps preferred to punish me by shitting where they sat.

The bitch stinks in a different way. She came on heat just yesterday, and all last night the male kept mounting her and mounting her, in a sort of angry rutting greed. I'm terrified of puppies, could never manage half a dozen more dogs when just these two have done such frightening damage. The breed have huge and powerful mouths, made for ripping wolves; extremely sharp strong claws. There are no wolves in my bedsit, so they've ripped the chairs instead, clawed and chewed the furniture, attacked the walls and floor. They're so tall and strong and curious they can reach nearly every surface in my room; have stripped the shelves, knocked things to the floor, tried to eat my poetry books, my clothes. They've destroyed all my collections – those small and precious things which were like a private diary in that they marked the seasons, told the years, recorded my slow progress from child to case to crone – all trampled now, dismantled.

I can't satisfy their appetites, not in any way. They need more food, more space, more exercise, more scope for all that energy and leg-power. Wilhelm dropped round pounds of meat, ready boned and chopped, but the whole lot was demolished in two days. He also left a carcass, still frozen and quite stiff, but though it's thawed I haven't cut it up yet. I can hardly eat at all myself, but every time I try, they snatch the crust or morsel from my hand. I was attempting a banana, just a very small and soft one, which I hoped I might mush down, but the male just bounded over, devoured it in one gulp. I tend to live on sweets now, sweets and cigarettes, which makes me like John-Paul.

I split his name in two last week and gave it to the dogs – John for the female (so that like her sad new mistress she's saddled with a boy's name), and Paul for the real male. They haven't learnt the names yet, but I keep teaching them, repeating them, and occasionally they listen. In some ways, they're quite friendly, seem to crave attention, even seem to need me, the female more especially. She'll push her nose right into me, to try to make me fondle her; attempt to share my bed (or chair), follow me around. I suppose she's missing her Master, which creates a second bond between us. Every time the phone rings, we all three go berserk, the dogs howling, barking, me snatching the receiver, praying for his voice. It's never him, in fact, though we keep on hoping, hurtling. That's another disadvantage of the early hours – no one phones at all, except crackpots or wrong numbers.

I struggle out of bed, switch the main light on. I've been sleeping in my clothes, and they and all the blankets are covered with coarse hairs, so I'm 'coated' with the dogs. I try to brush them off, but they cling and stick as if to prove that John and Paul will never go away. I can't shift the pictures, either. I tried to persuade the gallery to buy them back, or even take them back for nothing, but the girl in charge was very rude and strange. I've moved them from the bed, stacked a few behind the headboard, but they're mostly still surrounding me, jeering from the walls, pressing in, complaining. I'm a prisoner in my room, can't go out and leave the dogs, yet dare not take them with me. I stare up through the bars of my small window. It's black outside, like the black of John-Paul's bowel. I keep dreaming I'm inside him – squashed in his intestines, or snug inside his bladder. His bowel is best of all – dark and hot and pulsing and very intimate.

I plunge towards the door, feel I must escape, if only for ten seconds, just to breathe clean air, just to prove there's something real beyond my prison-room. I lock the door behind me, shamble up the steps. The night feels raw, as if someone's ripped its skin off; smells of blood and dustbins. The lampposts cast harsh shadows, light up strips of pavement, but leave the rest dangerous and blurred. The stars seem blurred as well, and very far away, as if they've withdrawn from earth, lost interest.

Everybody's gone. The entire street's been evacuated, windows blank and black, front doors barred or padlocked. A car zooms past, but I think it's driverless. A cat sneaks through the railings, a thin and homeless tabby mewing for its master. We're all searching for our Master, searching pretty hopelessly. There'll be nothing left at all soon, now John-Paul has gone. He was the centre of the universe, the Atlas who held up the world, the pole and fulcrum of the globe, its linchpin and its bedrock. He was also gravity and oxygen, $H_2O$ and light. All things die without him; fade, or fall apart.

I return indoors, half-frozen, walk straight into the dogs who fight me to get out. They've been waiting by the door, quivering with excitement, frantic for some exercise, or slaughter. '*No!*' I shout. 'It's dangerous out there. Get back! Lie still. It's sleep-time.'

Sleep? I'll never sleep. I need John-Paul to sleep, need to count the minutes like insomniacs count sheep; need the goal and purpose of my next appointment with him. Those appointments were like bones, giving me a structure, holding me together, helping me keep upright. Without them, I'm just pulp; a trail of thin grey blood oozing from a smashed and broken world. Twenty-six days since I last saw him.

I find my watch, though time means nothing much now. Sometimes I forget both time and date. Yesterday was Saturday – I think – which means we're three hours, twenty minutes into Sunday. I suppose I ought to change, put on my Sunday best. I drag my dirty clothes off, fetch my last clean dress: the one with the white collar I bought specially for John-Paul. Funny how everything leads back to him – collars, stars, wolfhounds, even sheep.

I wonder what I'll do today – besides feed the dogs, feed the dogs, pace around my room with them, brush off hairs, count stains. Sundays always seem a cheat – all those names which don't apply: the Lord's Day or the Day of Rest, when there isn't any Lord or rest, or the Sabbath, which it isn't. I'd love to celebrate a Sunday – just one, just once, just now – go to church, eat a Sunday lunch with real apple pie, real parents; read the Sunday papers, toast muffins by the fire, know it's only fifteen hundred minutes till my next session with John-Paul.

I ought to take his dogs back, but he's always refused to tell me where he lives, and even Seton seems unsure, said he thought he'd moved. If I wait until tomorrow and return them to the tower, he'll only say I stole them in that cold and hostile voice of his. I feel very faint when I think about his anger. It would probably kill me outright in my present weakened state. I don't mind dying, but I'd rather die another way, not killed by John-Paul's voice.

213

I slump back in a corner. My dress is spoiled already, stained with urine, dog shit. I couldn't go tomorrow – or ever, in this state. I haven't washed my hair or brushed my teeth; can't seem to find the energy, the will.

Paul is mounting John again. It's always brief and silent, but then he'll repeat it and repeat it, as if he's never sated, never had enough. It's like the food again – insufficient for all that mass and muscle. I sit and watch, reach out for my matches, strike one, two, three, six, eight. My Capstan gasps and fidgets, but still it fails to light. I try three more – no use. The whole box seems damp and neutered, or perhaps it doesn't like me. Paul mounts once more, though he's only half-erect, does his thing, withdraws. It's so basic with most animals – simple, public, matter-of-fact, whereas we humans make it complicated, secretive and shameful.

I'll have to borrow matches. I had two lighters once, but Seton snaffled one and the other disappeared – as most things do, in time. I slip out of the other door, the one that leads upstairs into the house, rather than out into the street; bolt it top and bottom to prevent the dogs from following. I stop to listen. Silence. Sasha's still away and the man in number five. I knock at number three's door, know he never sleeps. 'Hallo?' I call. No answer.

I'd like to knock on John-Paul's door, but I don't know where he's sleeping. I don't know much about him. I may think about him all the time, but thoughts aren't facts or postcodes. He's just a trembling shadow now, like the shadows of the banisters which grope my feet as I climb two flights of stairs. There are seven people in the house, not counting lovers staying nights, or hangers-on, or stowaways. Two away leaves five. Except there's no one here at all. All decamped, departed.

I tried to go away myself, have a sort of holiday, or at least a change of air. I was still thinking of the country – Gloucestershire or Shropshire, but knew I'd never get that

214

far, so I took the dogs to Rickmansworth last Tuesday afternoon. It was awful on the tube. The dogs were really terrified and the passengers quite spiteful, especially when I came back in the rush hour – all that crush of people panicking or grousing, which only made things worse. One small boy got hurt, in fact, and the dogs were near-hysterical and kept trying to slip their leads and dash away. In the end, I got off at the Embankment, walked the rest – or tried; was tugged and dragged the last few miles, both hands raw and bleeding.

I trail back to my room again. The dogs are really hungry now, edgy and bad-tempered. I've just that one last carcass left – a quarter of a bony pig, whose gamey almost rancid smell pounces on my stomach as I remove it from its wrappings. Wilhelm left a butcher's knife as well as all the meat, an extremely sharp efficient knife with an expensive-looking handle and a blade so fierce I haven't dared to touch it. I force myself to pick it up, hack some chunks of pig off. The dogs can barely wait. I'm scared I'll cut myself – or them – the way they nose and jostle me, jump up at the table, keep pestering and cadging.

At last, they're fed, and quieter, and I stretch myself between them on a pile of dirty bedding, stroke them both in turn: John, then Paul; Paul then John, murmuring their names – 'John, Paul, John, Paul, John, Paul.' Soon the names are joined and hyphened: 'John-Paul, John-Paul, John-Paul, John-Paul.' They seem to like the stroking, nuzzle me quite lovingly, thump their heavy tails. I think I could get fond of them if we had more room, and time. I know they're big, but so am I. They're also greedy, randy, violent and ungrateful, but I'm all those things myself – or was once, anyway.

I can hear their breathing slowing, as they begin to sleep, at last. I doze as well, fitfully, dream of John-Paul's pineal gland which is coated in gold leaf; and then about his navel, which is smooth and very deep, so I can thrust right down inside it, like a finger in a glove.

'Wake up,' I say. 'It's morning.' I haven't checked my watch, but I'm good at judging shades of dark, and the thick serge blackout of the night, tacked up behind my window-bars, has been taken down, replaced with flimsy grey. It's Sunday proper now – still silent, still deserted. The day should be all glossy like a colour supplement, full of pictures, promises – cars and boats, food and wine, good friends, good fun, good taste. Children should be scampering off to funfairs, fathers cleaning cars or building shelves, mothers making treacle tarts, lovers sipping orange juice from each other's cunts or navels.

'Breakfast time,' I tell the dogs, though there isn't any orange juice, only pig and water. They're on their feet immediately, once they hear my voice. I struggle up myself, go and fetch the knife. I didn't bother washing it and it's smeared with dried-on blood. Paul is mounting John again. I wait until he's finished, then dawdle over, plunge it in his chest. He dies as quietly as he fucks – no gasps, no fuss, no anguished howls or panting. The female's less courageous – shudders, whimpers, tries to fight the knife, but soon she's quiet as well. I lug the two great bodies to the corner, lay them on the sawdust (which I hope will absorb the blood), cover them with blankets and my coat.

I'm tired. I'm very tired now, but I have to kill the paintings next, kill all John-Paul's things. I clean the knife, spear it through a canvas, watch it groan and writhe. I think that was a Mary. The next one is a black girl, very dark and wild. I ease the knife in slowly, aiming for her heart; continue slowly round the room, working anticlockwise and slashing each in turn. My arm is really aching and there's blood all down my dress – dark and sticky blood which smells of oil

216

paint. He's got too many patients, far too many fans, scores of faithful Marys, swarms of mistresses. Every one must go, though – all the black girls and the groupies, all his wives and ex-wives, all the unborn babies, all the growing gangling children – everyone but me.

My room is full of bodies. I killed the puppies, too, the ones they hadn't had yet; couldn't cope with more dogs. The smell is really terrible, blood as well as faeces. At last, I lay the knife down. My hand feels limp and useless, dangling from my side now, with nothing more to do. I fumble for a cigarette, remember I've no lighter; keep it in my mouth, unlit, as I go to fill the kettle. I don't want tea; just need to wash the blood off.

I'm not feeling any better. I imagined I'd revive once I'd disposed of all my rivals, but nothing's really changed. I hobble to the mirror, examine my reflection. My eyes are only sockets, and I should have washed my hair. 'Fantastic hair,' Seton said. 'It reaches almost to your bum.' I glance around for Seton, know I had him close once. Perhaps I killed him, too. There's a body in the corner, bleeding under blankets, which could be his, judging by its size. I wash my hair every day – when I'm feeling well, that is. Seton said it paid; said he liked its glossy sheen, its smell of lime conditioner. It looks awful now, unkempt and limp and tangled; smells of dog, not limes. I tilt my head, so it's hanging down in one greasy yard-long cascade, hold it very steady with my left hand, while I use the right to reach out for the knife. Two hacks and it's off. It slithers to the carpet with all the other corpses, coils across a painting – dark on dark.

I limp back to the mirror. Yes, a real improvement. It's very short and ragged, makes me fit my name. I know I'll find John-Paul now. He only went away because he was

217

hoping for a boy-child, praying for a son, and I turned out a freak, a female.

'I'm better now,' I tell him, as I sit down by the phone, relieved and almost happy as I wait for him to ring and say he loves me.

# 19

Mary sat back in the carriage, smiling at the young girl sitting opposite (and the chubby baby dribbling on her lap); beaming at the old man in the corner, who looked a babe himself with his woolly pompommed hat and missing teeth. She could feel smiles popping out of her, as if she'd swallowed a whole cartonful and they were escaping through her mouth, settling on her coat lapels like pink enamelled brooches. Smiles seemed only natural when she was en route to John-Paul's. It wasn't even Friday, but boring washday Monday, yet there she was in her best Windsmoor navy suit, with a package of still-warm mince pies she'd made specially for the Doctor, stowed into her bag – a tiny humble offering to thank him for the privilege of a second session every week, which he himself had suggested.

Actually, she was getting on so frightfully well, she'd have thought he might have cut the sessions down instead of doubling them, but he'd told her that although he was very gratified by what he called her 'symptomatic relief', they had hardly even touched on the underlying problems. She'd lived half her life without *knowing* she had problems – certainly not the serious ones John-Paul had specified – separation anxiety, pre-genital ambivalence, and several others she couldn't quite remember, or hadn't really grasped or understood. (She didn't always like to ask him to explain things. It made her seem so ignorant, and he was so fearfully clever himself, he probably didn't realise she'd panicked at exam time and so failed her GCEs.) Still, if it meant more time lying on his couch, then she was almost pleased to be 'arrested at the genital stage', or 'prone to projective identification of a self-undermining kind'.

In fact, it had increased her basic confidence to feel she had such complex layers and depths to her that even a doctor as brilliant as John-Paul required months – no, years – to plumb them. Her once-tame restricted daily round was now totally transformed by a knowledge of her inner life; that seething hotbed of passions and emotions she didn't know she felt. Even her childhood had been a succession of explosive stages, each one with a formal name, and each involving conflict and high drama – the oral stage, when she'd attacked the breast, swallowed everything in sight, even gulping down her mother whole; the anal stage, when she'd held on to her faeces, or refused to use her potty and done her business in a corner like a dog; and finally the genital stage, when she'd poked sticks up her knickers to give herself a thrill, or stuffed cushions between her legs. She couldn't quite imagine doing *any* of those things; felt sure her angry mother (or disapproving ayah) would have intervened in no uncertain terms, but John-Paul had assured her she was merely suppressing all that early rage and turmoil.

And all those other terms he used had added to her feeling of importance. She might not have her A-levels, but she had ego-instincts, libidinal cathexes, something called 'affects' (with the stress on the first syllable); obsessions, sublimations and repressions. She'd always seen herself as rather boring, a dabbler with a shallow mind, whom even Jonathan dismissed as 'dumb' when she couldn't understand his prep-school maths. John-Paul thought otherwise, reached deep inside her psyche and pulled out plums – maybe mouldy ones, in some cases, but still with curves and colour, ripe flesh surrounding deep-embedded stones, themselves a promise of new fruit.

James had been a little less delighted about the extra weekly session – in fact, really quite unpleasant, if she was honest with herself, but it was probably less John-Paul than Larry Crawshaw who was making him so crotchety, plus all the other hassles at his work. She'd have to make it up to him, maybe go to Austin Reed and buy him some new shirts (which would prove a boon for her, as well, since she hadn't ironed his old ones in a fortnight). She'd already tried to mollify him by reporting John-Paul's four-week break, which the doctor planned to take from the seventeenth of December to the fourteenth of January, and which would therefore mean a reduction in his bill. Of course she wouldn't dream of saying so, but she'd have gladly paid the bill in full, even paid it twice, if she could only stop him going in the first place. Two more footling weeks and he'd be off to Rome for Christmas and the Congress, leaving her bereft – well, extremely busy with all the cooking and the shopping and the boys home, but still reduced to a mere housewife and a dimwit, instead of a complex *femme fatale*.

She leaned forward to retrieve her *Woman's Journal* which had slipped down off her lap. The baby reached a hand out, grabbed a fistful of her hair, kept tugging really hard. 'Lovely girl,' she murmured to its mother, while trying to unclasp the tiny fingers.

'*Boy*.'

'Oh, I'm sorry. He's got such pretty curls, I thought . . . What's his name?'

'Brian.'

'Oh, Brian.' She subsided in her seat, returned to *Woman's Journal* – how to make Christmas decorations from silver foil and pastry-cutters. She hadn't wanted to think of Bryan – not till Friday, anyway, when she'd be forced to see him at the class – again. She'd spent all last Friday's train journey worrying about him, after that quite extraordinary session in the pub. She'd only suggested a drink at all because James was out till late that night, and anyway she'd been skimping on her charities, neglecting her lame ducks, and Bryan was clearly crying out for help. Of course, she'd never realised the poor soul was homosexual, had never really met one in her life before, or known anything much at all about what the media called 'gays', until she'd started ploughing through her new dictionary of psychology which she'd bought just last weekend. There'd been a whole long article on homosexuality (under D for Deviance, though you weren't meant to call it that), which had helped her understand poor Bryan, explain his eccentricities.

She'd been suspicious at the time, in fact, when they were sitting in the pub and he'd kept ogling other men, whipping round to leer or gawp every time a male passed near their table, especially big and brawny ones, or young lads in skin-tight jeans. And then that whole sad and sorry business with his father. The article had emphasised the very frequent problems gays had with their fathers, especially if those fathers were insecure themselves about their masculinity and felt threatened by a weak effeminate son. Things were obviously extremely bad between Bryan and Skerwin senior. To pretend not to even know his son did seem especially heartless, but if Bryan often cried in public, broke down in pubs or evening-classes, his father probably couldn't handle the shame and sheer embarrassment. She'd been a little thrown herself, with everybody looking and him shouting 'I don't care' like that (which was presumably an attempt to 'come out of the closet', to use another phrase she'd learned). James had never cried in the fifteen years she'd known him, not even when his mother died of a combined stroke and heart attack, and they'd found her, cold already, at the bottom of the stairs.

And talking of mothers, Bryan was obviously devoted to his own, could hardly bear to tear himself away from her, either literally or conversationally; had spent a good half of the coffee-break embroidering on her endearing little ways, explaining all her fads and fancies, and always circling back to her, every time she'd tried to change the subject. That, too, was a symptom. According to the article, gays were often hung up on their mothers, stayed close to them emotionally when normal men had married or moved on. And his obsession with illness was also most suspicious, probably springing from a basic fear of AIDS. He'd told her he was frightened she had died, simply because she'd missed a couple of classes, but he was clearly harping on his *own* death, and only disguising it as hers. That was called 'projection', a term John-Paul had taught her (in another context, actually, but the point was still the same). The poor soul's voice had broken as he stuttered the word 'death'. Could he be infected, what they called HIV positive, with only months to live?

It really was quite tragic, a man as young as he was, and all that pathetic business about his childhood and no parties. Even walking to the station, he'd brought it up again; how he'd never kept his birthday, never had a party or any treats at all. She'd seen through him straight away. He was angling for an invitation to meet her own three sons, to attend Jon's little junket and indulge his lust for soft-skinned eight-year-olds. Well, that she *couldn't* have; wouldn't dream of letting any child within an arm's length of a deviant, let alone her pure and precious sons.

'Mama!' screeched the baby, lunging out at her again and pulling not her hair, but her blue Venetian beads. She tried to save her necklace, an expensive one from James, whilst hoping the poor infant wasn't suffering from an identity crisis at quite so young an age. 'I'm not your Mummy, darling. There's Mummy over there.'

'I'm *not* his Mum – no fear!' The girl tugged the squirming child back, slapped his sticky hand. 'Sit still, you little monster!'

The baby's howls rose to fill the carriage, seemed trapped in it, circling round and round. The woolly-hatted pensioner had got out at Surbiton, but two younger men had slammed in shortly afterwards, and were now casting surly glances round their *Daily Telegraphs*. Mary scrutinised them shyly – one tall, with long and powerful legs; the other almost pudgy, but with thick fair hair, a sensuous wide-lipped mouth. She had never really noticed men before, except as rather alien beings who were usually bad-tempered and always in a hurry, and needed lots of other people like wives or maids or secretaries to keep them functioning at all (and even then, were forced to recuperate in golf clubs or join expensive health clubs to help them bear the tension of their lives — lives far more meaningful, momentous, than any poor mere woman's). But she was becoming more aware of men, recently, excitingly; not just their jobs or needs or shirts, but the bodies underneath the shirts, the hands which held the briefcases (which she sometimes wickedly imagined straying down her tautly naked breasts). She had even found herself glancing at the space between their legs – or rather *not* the space . . .

Ashamed, she dragged her eyes away. Neither man looked exactly wild with passion. Both were clearly irritable, fidgeting and muttering as the baby's screams crescendoed. She longed to hold the frantic child, soothe his desperate wailing. All he needed was a cuddle, not a slap – and an instant change of nappy, judging by the damp patch on his rompers. Where *was* his mother, she wondered almost angrily? Doctors like John-Paul were invariably so busy just because of mothers who gave up on their role, entrusted their own flesh and blood to callous substitutes.

And yet it worried her, the theory that all crime and mental illness was a result of faulty parenting. Did it mean you couldn't blame even hardened vicious criminals, but excused, say Adolf Hitler, because his mother fed him Cow and Gate instead of offering him the breast, or felt sorry for the Yorkshire Ripper because he'd been potty-trained too early? Or suppose a man like Bryan did something most unpleasant to her darling Jonathan, would it be wrong to want to murder him, instead of sympathising? She'd tried to bring the matter up with James, who sometimes helped unsnarl her muddled views, but when she'd mentioned Hitler, he'd gone off at a tangent and said that bloody Larry Crawshaw was a little Hitler in himself and if someone didn't take a stand, it would be gas chambers for his firm.

She unbuttoned her thick jacket and the top button of her blouse. It was stifling in the carriage, and probably full of germs. One of the *Daily Telegraphs* had a really nasty cold, kept trying to find a clean spot on his stained and soggy handkerchief, which she wished she could take home to wash and iron. If she'd been sitting by the window, she could have opened it a crack, let in some fresh air; watched the streets and houses flashing past the pane, glimpsed dreary Monday housewives hanging out their washing or making shepherd's pies. That had been her own life just a month or so ago – a worthy round of cooking, ironing, church work, which ignored the wild exotic realms she'd discovered only recently: New Worlds between her open legs, undiscovered territories between her marvelling skull-bones.

She closed her eyes a moment, thought back to Friday's session with John-Paul. She'd been telling him quite shyly (though slowly gaining confidence as she sensed his quiet approval) about her so-called 'Thrill-Kit' – her new vibrator-plus which came complete with a dozen separate snap-on heads described as 'Happy Endings', and a clitoris-excitor with seven different speeds. She ran it in her mind again, revved the switch from purr to roar, added the rattling of the wheels, the juddering of the train, watched the signal rise, the lights change from red to green, as the 125 went racing up the incline and down the other side, finally thwacked against the buffers exhausted but triumphant.

'Two hundred and five,' she whispered, as she dabbed her sweaty forehead with her glove, gave a secret gloating smile to the Minister of Health who was facing her on page three of the *Telegraph*. 'Housewife Snatched From Death-Trap', she read, several columns down. So Bryan had thought she'd died. Well, she had died, in a sense – died of pleasure, anyway. A climax *was* a sort of death, or so the sex books said, and one tome had even mentioned that seventeenth-century poets used the word 'die' or 'death' as a sort of pun or *double entendre* meaning orgasm. They'd never taught her *that* at school, nor words like *soixante-neuf* or detumescence. She was learning such a lot these days – forget 'Science and Society' – she only went to that to keep James happy, prove she wasn't quite the bird-brain he assumed, though, if she were truthful with herself, she could hardly grasp a word that Skerwin said; sometimes suspected he was teaching a quite different class from the one described in the prospectus, or was so involved in his own high-powered research, he'd totally forgotten that his students weren't all physics graduates with doctorates from Oxbridge. But once she moved from science to psychology, then she had surely earned her doctorate by now, if not a few gold stars.

She unfastened the next button of her blouse, imagined John-Paul leaning over to pin the gold star on her chest (breast); his strong male hand making contact with the nipple, lingering a moment before creeping down her cleavage . . .

'*Stop* that!'

She jumped, removed the hand, swiftly did up both her buttons, looking round for angry Nanny who would slap her any moment, send her to her room. She heard the slap resound, but it was the baby who'd received it, right across his buttocks. 'Shut up, you noisy bastard, or you'll get a harder one.' The girl shook the child quite callously, as if he were a kitchen mat or pillowcase and not a fragile psyche. She knew she shouldn't interfere, but if someone didn't take a stand, then in another twenty years or less he'd be lying on the couch.

'Could I hold him for a moment? I've got three boys myself, so . . .'

'By my guest,' the girl said, as she dumped the howling infant on Mary's ample lap, retuned her Walkman, lit a cigarette, ignoring the 'No Smoking' signs.

'Hush now, precious. What's the trouble? Teething, are we? Let me look. Oh, dear, it *is* sore, isn't it? Poor pet, poor wee mite.' Mary rocked the red-faced infant to and fro, let him bite her finger, stroked his fuzz of hair. The wild yells slowly quietened, changed to shuddering gasps, one final choking hiccup, then silence, blessed silence. Mary could feel the tension dropping in the carriage. The two men settled back, both turning over pages of their newspapers, as if to prove they could concentrate once more on the rise in the inflation rate or the car bomb in Beirut. The girl blew lazy smoke rings, one foot gently tapping to the private rhythm of her Walkman. Even the train itself seemed to decrease its feckless speed, stopped lurching quite so violently, as it rattled over points. Mary longed to rock and soothe them all: blow that poor man's nose for him, rub some Vaseline on his swollen reddened nostrils; remove the young girl's cigarette and replace it with a dummy; gently chide the train for making too much noise, distract it with a picture-book or jigsaw.

'Shall we kiss it better, then? There, that's it – all gone now.' The baby closed his eyes, at last, pressed his tear-wet face against her bosom. 'Good boy, good little sausage. You sleep now, Brian, all better.' She settled back herself, smiling round the carriage. That's all the other poor Bryan needed – a little basic comfort, a little understanding. If it was his birthday this next Friday, then why didn't she invite him for a birthday tea on Saturday? James would be away the whole weekend at a conference in Scarborough, and all she'd planned to fill the gap was some help with teas (and washing-up) at the Union of Catholic Mothers' jumble sale. Tea for an AIDS victim was surely more important. Catholic mothers had quite enough already – families, security, free coffee mornings every week, Father Fox on call – whereas infected homosexuals had nothing in their lives save the prospect of the grave.

If Bryan's poor mother had never found the time to arrange a children's party, then she must lay one on herself – a little late in life, perhaps, but some therapies she'd read about did actually encourage a return to early childhood as part of growth and healing. She'd even discovered one amazing case of a sixty-year-old male patient who'd gone back into nappies and been fed three-hourly from a bottle, snuggled on his (female) doctor's lap. She wouldn't go that far with Bryan, but was there any reason why he shouldn't have a birthday cake, and even a few games and things to help pass the afternoon? Of course she couldn't ask the boys he craved – it just wouldn't be responsible – but the two of them together could have quite a jolly time, and it would provide a chance for him to talk to her, open up, confide. She had so much help herself these days – John-Paul twice a week must be the equivalent of a whole *life* of children's parties, with cakes from Harrods' bakery and the best conjurors in London – the least she could do was help others in her turn.

She glanced up at the window as they jolted past Vauxhall. Only two more minutes and they'd be into Waterloo. Had James found a seat, she wondered, when he'd tackled the same journey a whole three hours ago, or been forced to stand on a jam-packed rush-hour train? Poor James. She ought to help him, too, if he were kind enough to keep paying John-Paul's fees, which would be going up from January, and were pretty high already – that she did admit. But if only he could understand how exceptional the doctor was; how not just wise, distinguished, but sensitive, artistic, and with that really rather thrilling voice, which appeared to issue from somewhere deep inside him, to bypass throat and larynx and well up from his groin.

She held the baby closer, ran a gentle finger around his open mouth, heard him mew with pleasure. Babies were much easier than husbands. How could she soothe James, make him mew with equal satisfaction, kick his feet ecstatically? Invite Pam and Larry Crawshaw for a really special dinner, which might defuse the tension; or buy him a new putter (except the only money she could use was what he gave her anyway, so it would hardly be a present)? Or how about *The Joy of Sex*, Volumes One and Two, compressed into a single night, to stagger and astound him, prove the sessions with John-Paul were triumphantly successful; worth double what he charged?

The problem was would James respond? He'd been so strange these last few weeks, wary and defensive, as if the more she lost her hang-ups, the more his own increased. She couldn't understand men, especially not the real ones, as compared with those in sex-books. The husband-kind seemed only to desire you when you put up some resistance, offered them a challenge, or a fortress to be scaled. She'd dismantled her defences after a dozen years of barricades and ramparts, and what had happened? James had stopped besieging her, curtailed his nightly forays, appeared even to have lost his own libido (to use John-Paul's second favourite word). She'd tried at first to blame it on his work, the constant mounting pressure at Holdsworth, Pierce and Hampton – but it could well be her own fault. No good her making overtures unless she got them right. According to the experts, sexual skills took practice, were a bit like GCEs, demanded study and commitment, total concentration. And you had to go all out – yes, even with a husband – woo him like a lover, use every ruse and wile. She could pick one night next week, make it really special, discard the role of boring wife and play geisha girl or vamp, do everything those sex-books recommended: douse herself with perfume, buy a skimpy nightie and a black suspender belt, dim the lights, feed her man oysters and champagne, ignore the bed and spread-eagle on the hearth-rug, or even the kitchen table, as one enthusiastic book advised.

She checked the baby – sleeping now – then gently closed her own eyes so she could see the kitchen table in her mind. It was a little cluttered for a night of throbbing passion, but if she cleared the toaster off, removed the bread-bin and the ironing, swept up all the toast crumbs so they wouldn't tickle her bare skin, then it would probably serve the purpose. She leant back against the grainy wood, trying to smell *L'Aimant*, and not Clean-O-Pine and onions; reached out a sultry hand to James, coaxed him down towards her. 'I love you, darling,' he whispered in his vintage-brandy voice, already mollified and melting as his open mouth met and startled hers.

'I love you, too, John-Paul.'

# SHOPPING LIST

champagne
oysters
*L'Aimant* (scent and bath oil)
suspender belt (black lace?)
negligée or nightie (Check Ann Summers catalogue)
KY Jelly
Vaseline
shirts for J. (Still slim-fit? Check his waist.)
flour/eggs/butter/sugar/icing sugar
jellies (lime and raspberry)
birthday candles (blue)
sandwich loaf (check fillings)
batteries (high-power)

# 20

It's freezing on the step, the wind cutting round the corner and slashing my bare face before it hurtles on across the road and up north to the Arctic. The step is stone and damp. I'll move off in a moment, once I've found the strength to face a bus or tube train. I've no more cash for taxis, used every cent I had, first to check out Seton's boat, then to drag up here to Kilburn. I hoped someone at the gallery might know where Seton was – he seemed so much at home there, knew so many people – but the door is locked and bolted. I arrived here just too late, at five-thirteen, when the damn place shuts at five. Actually, somebody's inside still, but they wouldn't let me in, ignored the bell completely.

It's cold without my hair. I never realised all these years how I've used it as a sort of extra muffler. The wind sneaks into places now it never did before, and I'm more conscious of my ears. They're too big, of course, and ugly, but no one ever saw them through my mane. I don't think my hair will grow again. I'm too old for any blossoming, regrowth. I try to work out days and times, conclude it must be Thursday, which means it's four days since I scalped myself. It feels more like four years, and, anyway, Thursdays seem quite different without John-Paul embedded in them. All my days are empty now, or crippled – frames without their pictures, boats without their engine-rooms.

It was awful at the boat. The taxi driver got more and more sarcastic about the stony unmade track, and in the end I walked the last half-mile, listening to the silence, the heavy winter pall of dusk and damp and loneliness which had been laid across the marshes. I could smell not just swamp, but sickness – the sickness of the Isolation Hospital, which Seton said was founded there a hundred years ago, its bleak windows looking out at the ancient smallpox cemetery, stiff with pock-marked corpses. The boat was dead itself – no lights, no fire, no movement, just a hulk adrift in mud. I kept shouting Seton's name, in case he might be fishing further down the creek, or out collecting driftwood. No one answered, save a few screeching gulls echoing my voice. An old salt told me years ago that seagulls are the restless souls of sailors wrecked and drowned at sea, still searching for their bodies and their ships. Perhaps Seton's died at sea and is circling far away now, soaring past the lonely Arctic Circle.

'Seton!' One last cry, though my throat hurts from the shouting and my whole face is stiff with cold.

'Hi, there!'

I swing round, see not Seton, but a fleshy, grey-haired man wearing immaculate cream trousers and a rather poncy-looking jacket in a designer shade of dung. He's standing on the top step and locking up the gallery, this time from the outside. 'It's Nial, isn't it?'

I nod, surprised he knows me. I bought all the pictures long-distance, as it were, spoke to women mostly, when I was negotiating prices, or arranging for delivery.

'I met you at the private view.'

'Oh, yes?' I don't remember, but then my memory's not good these days.

'Though you've had your hair cut, haven't you?'

I don't reply. It seems a stupid comment, obvious, even cruel. His own hair is thick, luxuriant, longer than my own; layer-cut by a clearly skilful barber, then lacquered into place – not hacked off with a butcher's knife and left *au naturel*. The grey is quite deceptive. He can't be more than thirty-eight or nine, and his face is tanned, unlined. He looks the sort who jets off to the sun most weekends

233

from October through to March, or spends his lunch-hours
reclining on a sun-bed.

'Were you looking for Amanda?' he asks, pausing on
my step.

'Who?'

'She said you phoned, weren't happy with the pictures.'

'It's okay,' I say. 'They're dead.'

'They're *what*?'

I'm too weary to explain, sink back on the stone again.
He hovers, walks a circle, even puts his bag down,
one of those sporty leather holdalls with loads of zips
and straps.

'Are you all right, Nial? You don't look frightfully
well.'

'I'm fine.'

'Well, can I offer you a lift? I'm heading north to
Brondesbury Park.'

'I live south.'

He seems a touch offended, frisks across the road to a
low-slung car the colour of sour cream – this year's registration. 'Hey, wait!' I yell, as he fumbles for his keys.
'You could take me to the tube.'

'Which one?'

'Any one,' I shrug. It hardly matters really where I go
tonight – home, or somewhere else. Or I could spend the
whole night sitting in the underground. At least it would
be warm.

We never make the tube. After less than half a mile,
things start sort of fading, and though I can hear his voice
still stabbing through my head (even hear my own voice
trying to reply), I'm no longer really there, no longer in
my body. I'm aware we're stopping somewhere, but I can't
see any details, only trembling shapes and shadows, which
keep rippling, blanking out. I can feel my feet on stairs,
unsure how to climb them; someone's arm heavy round

my waist, trying to heave me up. Then a block of time goes by, which could be only seconds – or a year – and I'm floating somewhere else, somewhere high and thin and frightening I've never been before. When I force my eyes to open, I'm not up at all, but down – lying on a sofa in some large and ritzy pad, with an expensive sheepskin jacket draped across my body. I check my clothes – they're on – and judging by my pounding head I am genuinely ill, yet I somehow feel suspicious. Did my mysterious new companion bash me on the head, lure me here for some unsavoury purpose? My eyes aren't properly focused yet, but I can hear him talking at the far end of the room, sounding slightly frantic. Once I've worked the words out, I realise he's trying to phone a doctor, not plotting rape or murder. 'It's okay,' I call. 'I'm better.'

'You *fainted*,' he accuses, fussing to the sofa, the cordless phone still in one plump hand. He makes it sound a crime, as if I've nicked his silver, or peed on his best carpet. We argue for a while about the advantages or otherwise of calling in a doctor, and I eventually convince him that I faint quite often nowadays and it's really nothing serious. I close my eyes as another wave of dizziness interrupts my words, and once things have straightened out again, he's crouching down in front of me, holding out a floral cup and saucer, which I presume is tea until I see the soggy skin on top.

'I'm sorry, but I loathe hot milk.'

'Drink it up.'

I'm too weak to disobey him, so I take a grudging sip; realise with relief it's adult milk, not kids' stuff, strongly laced with brandy; more booze than cow, in fact. He even holds the cup for me, stops me spilling half of it down my clothes or neck. I'm still a bit distrustful, not used to what seems kindness. What's in this for him, I wonder, as he offers me his own crisp linen handkerchief to wipe my milky lips? It might also help if I knew his name, knew who the heck he was.

'Are you sure I'm meant to know you?' I ask, at last, after a slightly awkward silence, which feels worse because the milk's all gone, so we've lost our little ritual. It *is* a bit unusual to land up horizontal being babied by a stranger in a house you've never seen. I'm also feeling slightly fuzzy still, so that everything is blurred around its edges, including names and faces. My stomach feels much better with something comforting inside it, but my head is still a war-zone.

'Zack Ridley.' He makes a deprecating gesture as he introduces himself, half-grimace, half-mock bow. Both name and gesture seem bogus, unconvincing. I can't imagine any mother christening her son Zachary when he's a mite of two days old. It sounds an ad-man's name, probably adopted in mid-life to replace boring Mike or John, and then fashionably shortened to suggest zip or matiness. The Ridley's also suspect, doesn't go with Zachary.

He removes my empty cup, sits down on my feet. 'I run the gallery. I met you twice, in fact – once at the private view and once on Seton's boat.'

I suddenly remember – not the name, the guy himself – though I only met him for a sum total of ten minutes, and when he came to visit Seton on the boat I was naked (and resentful at being interrupted), so I hardly said a word. I was also somewhat jealous of his being friends with Seton; in fact close enough for Seton to stop screwing me and start chatting with some interloper who looked dressed for cocktails rather than a boat. I realise now why he's proffering booze and sympathy. He's wooing me as the wealthy git who bought up his whole show, hopes I'll buy more pictures, sign a second whacking cheque. I glance up at his face, try to take it in this time, so I won't forget again and cut him dead. It worries me, my vagueness. I fear I'm losing brain cells.

His eyes are rather boring blue, that washed-out faded-denim shade, which makes them look as if they've been dumped in a launderette on far too high a programme and left there several days. I suspect he'd dye them if he could, sear them on his sun-bed to a deeper vibrant sapphire. They're narrowed now and frowning as he checks his watch, an ostentatious black one with a butch and spiky strap.

'Look, I'm in a bit of a spot, Nial. I don't like to leave you here alone, but I promised Seton I'd drop in for half an hour.'

'*Seton?*' I fling the sheepskin off, no longer cold, no longer even dizzy. So Seton's well, alive – and near.

'Yup. I'm late already. I said half past five or six.'

'Let's go, then.' I'm already standing up. Okay, my legs are paper, but I'd run a mile for Seton.

'You're in no state to go out, my love. I suggest you stay put on that sofa and . . .'

'No fear! I've got to see him. That's just where I was going.'

'Come off it, Nial. You weren't going anywhere, just sitting on my step.'

'Yes – gathering strength to see him.'

'But I thought he said . . .'

I don't hear the rest too clearly. I *do* feel pretty rough, but I've got to somehow get downstairs and back into the car. I don't want to talk – well, dare not – need every ounce of concentration just to keep myself upright in one piece. I pretend there's a programme I'm keen to hear on LBC, so that the radio can help me through the journey, do the talking for me, as it were. A hundred questions are churning up my mind, like a tractor in a flinty field gagging on sharp stones – where's Seton living now, and will he want to see me, or be furious with me for barging in? Why did he go off like that, quit the boat, move house? I suppose it was too cold to spend winter on the marshes, but he could at least have told me. Is he on his own still, or shacked up with Cressida, playing father to her baby?

Something tears inside me when I think of babies, mistresses; a so-called mental pain this time, but still stabbing wrenching sharp. I feel Zachary must notice, but his eyes are on the road. The traffic's pretty clotted, but he drives extremely fast in tiny violent bursts between traffic lights and snarl-ups, as if he can't bear to let his zippy car idle at a tame and tedious thirty. He keeps braking very suddenly, which is bad news for my stomach and surely for his tyres. It seems strange for him and Seton to be friends. They seem so entirely different, not just in type and build and dress (and style of cars and driving), but in their basic aura. Zack's a Persian cat, fed on cream and chicken breast, which have made him soft and slithery; Seton's a wild beast. I suppose it's the old business of opposites attracting (which I've never quite believed. If I met my own opposite, I suspect I'd really hate her, just through jealousy).

Zack brakes again, alarmingly, joins a fretting tailback of impatient rush-hour traffic; pats his hair to make sure it's still in place. 'When did you last see him, by the way?'

'Ssh,' I say. 'I'm listening to this programme.' I'm not sure how much Zack knows, but I'm not keen to tell the world – or him – that I've been discarded and supplanted. The radio interviewer is talking to a girl who's crossed the Gobi Desert on a camel, then spent six months on her own in another smaller desert, with no human company except the passing nomads. She's exactly my own age, but the similarity ends there. She wouldn't pine for Seton after just four endless weeks, nor feel incomplete without a man, a lover. I can see Cressida in my mind again, attached to Seton, skin to skin, like Siamese twins who've been not surgically divided, but sutured even closer, spliced together the whole length of their bodies. I feel so nervous, so rejected, my milk-and-brandy cocktail starts sloshing round my stomach. I only hope I don't throw up before we reach Seton's flat – or crèche. God knows where we're going. North London is another (alien) continent as far as I'm concerned, and I'm beginning to feel uprooted as we pass dreary council houses sulking in the dark, or graffitied rain-stained tower blocks. This isn't Seton country. I connect him now with water and wide skies.

'Nearly there,' says Zack, as if he's read my thoughts, and flashing me a salesman's smile, which displays his white and well-crowned teeth, but fails to reach his eyes. 'Amanda told me you don't drive. I suppose you get a taxi when you go to see him, do you?'

'Yes,' I lie, still queasy. The guy must think I'm loaded if he imagines I take taxis from my own south London pad to Seton's foreign north one. I'm cramped up really close to him in his sporty sprat-sized car, breathing the same ounce of gasping air, yet we're still complete and utter strangers to each other. He knows nothing about me except lies – I'm Seton's current girlfriend, I'm rich, I'm into art.

'And how about your camel?' the interviewer asks. 'Did you develop a real bond with him?'

'*Her*,' the girl says, in her strident sun-parched voice.

I try to keep my thoughts on camels' gender. I suppose they all seem female in a way, with those great humps sticking up from them. Perhaps Seton left me because he didn't like my breasts. Cressida's are larger – impressive camel-breasts.

Zack signals left, draws up in a waste of concrete, flanked by Portakabins. Has Seton moved to half a Portakabin, instead of half a boat? No, we're walking the other way, towards a huge and faceless building which seems to scream 'Keep Out'. I wish I could obey it, race back to my bedsit. I don't like what I see; not just the brute stone walls and rows of glaring windows, but all the bossy notices, the waiting panting ambulance. One wing is lost in scaffolding and a stretch of roof is covered with tarpaulin, as if the building's had an accident and is still convalescent, shaky. They've cut out any frills or softening touches – no curtains at the window or welcome at the door. This is not a home; it's a Dickensian institution where you expect the smell of poverty and soup. It smells of nothing, actually – just heat. The fug slaps us in the face as we enter the grim foyer with its stern and scowling portraits of sadistic-looking benefactors. The ancient parquet floor has been overlaid with squiggle-patterned lino, which doesn't fit the corners, reveals odd-shaped strips of polished wood, like fossils from a former (gracious) age. The lino seems to tremble as we tread it – I have to hug the wall to keep from falling.

'Are you all right, Nial?'

'Fine.'

'You don't look fine to me.' The salesman's smile again. I suppose he hopes I won't peg out until I've bought up his next show.

I keep grinning twinkling cheerful as we drag on down a corridor with a different patterned lino and shiny turquoise walls. Of *course* I'm fine, and not at all surprised that Seton's in a hospital. Of course he told me he was ill. Sudden, was it? Serious? Appendicitis? Heart attack? Yes, sure I know the way. I've been visiting each evening, sitting by his bed with grapes and Lucozade. I'm his girlfriend, aren't I, his mistress and his shipmate? 'Sorry, darling, I forgot the grapes this evening; had a little accident en route – no, nothing serious, just a bit of trouble with my head. Yes, it *is* still rather painful, spreading to my chest now, difficult to breathe, fierce pain in my ribs . . .' My steps are faltering. Can I face a ward the way I feel – tubes and drips and bedpans, the smell of disinfectant, Seton scarred or cut about, Seton in pyjamas when he always wore his clothes to bed? I pause a moment, pretend to ease my shoe. You're not allowed to flag here. Everyone looks busy: nurses striding past us with trays or notes or folders; harsh fluorescent striplights glaring overhead; a porter disturbing the whole corridor with his rattling clanking trolley.

'Okay?' Zack asks again.

I nod, brace myself as we turn a corner, enter a green door, not the green of living things – grass or leaves or glossy Granny Smiths, but the green of mould and verdigris. I stare. It's not a ward at all, and no one's in pyjamas. The dozen odd bods in the room don't have a scar between them; shabby men and women in jeans or baggy skirts, slumped on a variety of scuffed and ill-matched chairs; some jabbering, some knitting, most staring into space; at least three-quarters smoking. Two radios are playing two rival brands of music, one soppy, one hard rock, and a woman in fur boots and a floral summer frock is making her own music, thumping on a sweet-tin with her fist.

I light a cigarette myself, need courage, instant calm. Seton can't be here. He's a loner, an outsider, a maverick, a nomad; would never fit this tasteless room with its balding haircord carpet, its dreary khaki walls; nor spare a word for these gormless shambling people – that wide-hipped coarse-faced woman leering with her legs apart, that straggle-haired old gaffer playing Ludo with himself, moving first his own red counters, then the yellow, then the green, chiding his two invisible opponents. Perhaps we're visiting someone *else* – Zack's assistant or his tea-girl – or perhaps his girlfriend is a nurse here.

He's certainly talking to a nurse, though I didn't twig she was one when he first went up to her. He called her simply 'Sally', and she isn't wearing uniform, just a shapeless denim dress with a beige cardigan on top, and greasy hair dripping down her neck – no hygienic chignon or starched white frilly cap. Once I hear her mention Seton, I duck out of the way. I'm probably meant to know her, know all Seton's history, if I've been visiting each night and I'm the Girlfriend with a capital. In fact, I'm totally bewildered. Did Seton get ill suddenly, receive some dreadful news or shock which dragged him to this place? Or was he always sick?

I feel sick myself as I scrutinise the notice board. This is not just any hospital — it's a lunatic asylum — or a psychiatric hospital if you want to be polite, yet he never said a word, not even when I admitted my own symptoms, or discussed John-Paul with him; always played the tough guy who despised the whole soft business of running to a doctor with one's illnesses or problems; loathed the word 'patient' with all its connotations of suffering and passivity. Yet now he's labelled 'in-patient', which is surely much more serious, means he suffers full time and is locked into their system of programming and rules. I scan the loonies' timetable — an exciting daily round of table tennis, basket weaving, slide shows ('Dutch Elm Disease', 'Big Cats' and 'Adventure In The Holy Land' — tea and biscuits afterwards), and a whole variety of therapies, including group therapy, dance therapy, art therapy, music therapy, and something called just 'Therapy. Dr B. Patel'. I try to imagine Seton dancing (Scottish? Ballroom? Jive?), singing *Ten Green Bottles*, or perhaps telling Dr B. Patel about his preference for buggery, or the way he bites both mouths and cunts instead of merely kissing them.

I jerk my head violently, shift the vivid image of Seton's mouth clamped against my cunt. I loved him because he wasn't like most people, didn't need jobs and games and hobbies to fill his day, make him feel important. Sex was his main sport and he took it very seriously, gave it an intensity which more selfish and conventional men reserve for their careers. He's far too wild and headstrong to be confined and tethered down, far too tall to fit this narrow cage. All the other patients look drugged and somehow shrunken, as if they're subjects in some medical

242

experiment which is slowly leeching life out of their cells, lopping inches off their height. Even the woman with the sweet-tin has slipped sideways in her chair, eyes closed, toffees scattered, once-thrustful arm now trailing like a dead branch from a tree.

'Hey, Seton!' Zack calls. 'Over here.' I glance up at the door, can hardly bear to look at the sluggish apathetic man shuffling slowly through it. That can't be Seton, surely, not the one I knew, who stampeded through his life, picked up the world and shook it, if it didn't go his way, kicked and thrashed his problems like he bit and thrashed my body. He's faltered to a swaying halt and is just standing, looking dazed. He was always rather sallow, but his face is dingy-pale now, as if the skin from a dead body has been wrapped around a living one, left slack and loosely fitting. *Is* he living, though, I wonder, as he slumps against the wall, saying doing nothing as Zack goes brightly up to him with a gesture and a smile. He's gesturing to *me*, in fact, so I walk slowly slowly over, trying out absurdly normal greetings like 'How are you?' or 'Hallo, darling', as I traverse the endless carpet.

'Hallo,' I say, at last – real thing. No 'darling'. I never said it anyway, just imagined Seton murmuring it to me: 'I love you, darling,' 'I'll never leave you, darling,' 'Darling, you're quite beautiful.' No one's ever called me beautiful, or darling – except clients, who don't count. My father called me 'dear' when he was angry.

Seton doesn't answer, doesn't seem to see me, let alone know who I am. His eyes are looking through me, absorbed in something else, something terrifying, unspeakable, which no one else can see. I clear my throat. Perhaps it's just the hair. It was my only decent feature, so I'm probably quite anonymous without it.

'Nial,' I say. 'Remember? The one with the fantastic hair?' He doesn't laugh. I try to, though it comes out like a howl. He suddenly beckons Zack into a corner, elbows him into a chair, drags his own chair right up close, so their heads are almost touching. I follow, feeling spare, pull a third chair up, make a few inane remarks about the weather and the traffic while conducting a different conversation in my head. 'Yes, it's great to see you, too, Seton. Of course I've missed you – terribly. I always loved the way we shared things, shared illnesses and breakdowns, told each other everything, swapped doctors, symptoms, lives.' I never knew him, did I, never even helped him? If only he'd confided, trusted me enough, I could at least have sympathised, offered some support.

'It's the Pope,' he whispers suddenly. His eyes are looking through me still, as if there's something just beyond my body he has to keep a check on, something unpredictable and dangerous. But he's addressing Zack, not me. I'm not really there for Seton, except as just a window. 'The Pope,' he says again.

'Yes,' says Zack. 'You said.'

'Have you got him yet?'

Zack shakes his head, looks painfully embarrassed. A few patients have come up to us and are staring with that unselfconscious deadpan curiosity you see in cows or children. Seton totally ignores them, grabs Zack's wrist, keeps gripping.

'You know he killed my mother?'

'Yes – you told me.'

'He was here last night.'

'Really?'

'They weren't supposed to say, but I found out.'

At this point, I escape, though Seton doesn't notice. I find a gents' toilet, which I use because I'm desperate, and there isn't any ladies'; sick up half my milk. A patient barges in, a tall man with protruding eyes which look as if they're bolting from their sockets, perhaps keen to move to more congenial ones. He's wearing a navy nylon anorak over stripey blue pyjamas, the old-fashioned

244

sort which do up with a cord. 'You here again?' he asks me.

'*Again?*' I'm beginning to feel disorientated. Am I the mental patient and only imagined Seton? Or am I sitting on that step still, back outside the gallery, hallucinating quietly?

'They all come back,' he says, and proceeds to pee in front of me, in a sort of shallow metal trough thing, flanked by cracked white tiles. I suppose he assumes I'm a fellow male, broad-shouldered and crop-haired.

I hide in a cubicle, remain there half an hour or so, head resting on my knees; listen to excretions, bits of conversations, try not to remember the toilet in the College of Technology where I always spent the final minutes before my appointments with John-Paul. Everything seems 'final' at the moment. 'Final,' I say softly. It's not that far from 'fine' – just a matter of a consonant, a vowel. Last time I saw John-Paul (which seems months ago, millennia), I took him a pink rabbit made of marzipan, with chocolate buttons down its front and a pink-striped chocolate muffler. He gave it back – yes, honestly – said he rarely accepted gifts from any patient and he'd only taken all my previous ones because he felt they were part of *me*, a good and generous part which I needed him to share. But now he feared they were becoming just a substitute for any real progress in my therapy, and he'd rather be presented with some dynamic change or breakthrough, instead of sweets or biscuits as a 'payment' for resistance, or even as 'reparation' for the harm I felt I'd done him. What about the harm to *me*, for heaven's sake? I felt totally rejected, rushed blindly down the steps and flung the rabbit in the road, watched a lorry squash it into pulp.

The memory makes me retch again, so I stay put where I am, read all the graffiti scribbled on the walls – all those hopeless hoping strangers lusting in a lavatory, entrusting their hot fantasies to cold white sterile tiles. At last, I'm well enough to venture out and try to find that room again, which according to the notice was apparently the Day Room. After two wrong turnings, I locate it by its sick-green door, but it's empty now, abandoned – no Zack, no tragic Seton, no Sally and her patients; only fag ends, crumpled cushions and the smell of smoke and feet. I suppose they've gone to supper, or the slide show on dead elms, or been tucked up in the Night Room – at seven twenty-five. I trail up and down the corridors, glancing into wards, proper ones with bed and chairs, and relatives with flowers (those expensive ones in cellophane which are really floral guilt: 'I loathe this place, didn't want to see you, can't wait to get back home – yes, beautiful chrysanthemums, to prove how much I care.')

Zack and I eventually collide. He's also stalking corridors, searching not for Seton, but for me. I'm beginning to wonder (guiltily) if I've judged the man too harshly. Why should he visit Seton in a depressing dump like this, if he's only out for his own ends? Seton's skint, can't do any favours, can't even talk coherently. And why should he keep bothering with *me*? Okay, he thinks I'm rich, but he must have loads of other clients far wealthier than I am, and I'm sure he doesn't steer them all to hospital canteens because they're feeling weak and faint again and can't quite make the exit without a cup of tea.

'You sit over there, Nial. I'll get the tea. Anything to eat?'

I don't think he hears my 'No'. The canteen is very noisy, with another strident radio, this one playing reggae, which sounds tragic and bouncy both at once. Various machines explode or buzz or hum behind the counter, and the serving girls shout above the racket. All the colours fight – orange nylon overalls, scarlet plastic chairs, walls the colour of dead celandines, floor blue and yellow squiggles. Hospitals are very rarely quiet. I suppose they keep them brash and bright to try to deny tragedy or sickness, insist the world is in the pink, and whooping.

Zack looks out of place, as if he's strayed on to the film set of a kitchen-sink drama, when he actually belongs in a drawing-room comedy, the slick and stylish kind. No one else is smart or coiffed or lacquered, or wears calfskin shoes and a Mondrian-style tie. It's mostly jeans and trainers, with a few droopy Oxfam dresses under army surplus coats. Does he visit Seton often, brave that frightful Day Room several times a week? He seems to know his way around; knew Sally, knew the porter. I suppose nice guys *can* be rich and plump and have rotten taste in ties. I don't exactly like the man, but I can't deny he does seem quite concerned; says I look so pale he's worried, and will I promise to see my doctor in the morning? I haven't got a doctor. I lost John-Paul with Seton, blame one loss for the other.

I somehow force my tea down, and even two dry biscuits (the ones they call 'Rich Tea', which are anything but rich, and prove – again – how often most words lie). I have to keep pretending I knew all about my lover being ill, and am not shocked or stunned or shaken to find him drugged and crazy and shut up in this madhouse; nor bitter and resentful that he totally ignored me as if I don't exist. I limit my inquiries to the Pope, ask why the hell Seton should have mentioned him and what he meant by . . .

'You mean he hasn't *told* you, Nial?'

Zack sounds quite incredulous, as if I didn't know the world was round, or the earth went round the sun; simply can't believe I haven't heard about Seton's chief obsession; says the crazy fellow brings it up continually, talks of nothing else.

I shake my head. He's talked of other things to me – marshes, herons, art, a trip he made five years ago to the source of the Euphrates; all sane substantial things.

Zack shakes his head as well, though more in incredulity, I suspect. 'You must know he was brought up ultra-Catholic, with a really devout religious mother, the sort who buys her kid a crucifix rather than a teddy?'

'Oh, yes,' I say convincingly, fumbling for my Capstans. I know absolutely nothing about Seton's mother or his background, and we never talked religion. I know him in a deeper way, know another side to him, which I suspect Zack's never seen; a private, hidden, secret side, which he entrusted only to me.

'Well, she almost died having him. I'll spare you the grim details, but she refused to risk another child, and being a rigid Holy Roman, that meant no more sex. His father wasn't all that thrilled, but he was Catholic too, so instead of pushing off, as most men would, I suppose, he stuck around, but really took it out of them.'

'How d'you mean?'

'Well, he was violent, to begin with, what they call a batterer.'

'He battered *Seton*?'

'Yup – and the wife. It was pretty horrendous, as far as I can gather. Seton never said a lot about it, until he was in hospital last time. Then he started turning on the Church, blaming its whole system, rather than his father. You know what this present Pope's like – completely sold on the strict, old-fashioned line – no divorce, no contraception, Catholic couples tied together till death do them part, even if the marriage is a domestic Armageddon. Well, Seton seemed to hold him personally responsible for all his own neuroses, his father's violence, his mother's three-day labour . . .' Zack breaks off to drink his tea, sipping it disdainfully, as if plastic cups demean him and he expected rose-sprigged Meissen in a hospital canteen. 'Then, in 1981, that young Turkish revolutionary tried to shoot the Pope, and poor Seton went quite potty – thought the Turk was *him* and . . .' Zack holds his head, breaks

248

off. 'Christ! The whole thing was so complicated. You see, Seton was in therapy with a doctor called John-Paul – the same name as the Pope – so . . .'

'John-Paul?' I almost shout.

'Yeah. Weird name, isn't it? Though that's why Seton chose him in the first place. It seemed so odd to me, I mean totally incredible. I was scared he'd found some screwball who'd only make him worse. It wasn't pure unselfishness on my part. Seton was working as my framer and a bloody good one too, so I didn't want to lose him, or see him more fucked up, or even . . .'

'Working?' I've interrupted twice, repeated Zack's words twice, but I'm astonished by those words – first John-Paul, then a job. Seton continually assured me that all paid work was beneath him; said he lived on some (vague) legacy from an (even vaguer) relative. And he always let me rant about my shrink, even drove me to the station for my sessions in the tower, yet never once admitted he'd been consulting him as well.

'Oh, yes.' Zack drains his cup. 'He's been my framer for a good twelve years or more – on and off, of course, depending on his mental state. But when he works, he really works – all day, all night, all out – doesn't seem to bother with things like meals or sleep. I suppose it's an obsession, but quite a useful one this time – damn good for his employer, anyway.' Zack laughs cynically, wipes his fingers on his handkerchief as if the cup has somehow soiled them.

'And John-Paul?' I ask, obsessed myself.

'Which one?'

'The doctor.' (Fuck the Pope.)

'Well, I thought I'd better check the fellow out, which wasn't easy, actually, since these trick-cyclist chaps seem to keep the lowest of low profiles. But I'm a pretty good detective, and surprisingly (since I was expecting Woody Allen crossed with Shylock), he turned out to be quite

249

sound – in fact, one guy I consulted said he'd rate him among the ten best shrinks in London.'

I choke on my last biscuit crumbs. '*What?*' I say, jumping to my feet.

Zack looks startled. Why am I so vehement? What is it to me? I suddenly decide to tell him the whole story – well, not quite 'whole' – I always censor everything, even with John-Paul, withhold a few key facts. But things are getting so involved, if I don't come clean and tell more or less the truth for once, I'll just tie myself in circles even further, never solve the mysteries: discover why Seton is in hospital at all, and what makes Zack describe an untrained pseudo-artist as one of the ten best shrinks in London.

'*Artist?*' Zack exclaims, once I've galloped through my history as fast as all the complications and my still aching head allow.

'Yes, artist, artist, artist! The one whose bloody pictures I've just bought.' I'm shouting now, waving both my arms around, my anger surging back. Several people stare, though the serving girls just shrug, continue filling cups or clearing tables. I suppose they're used to scenes here.

'But you bought Jane Steiner's pictures.'

'*Who?*'

'Nial, you're crazy! No one else in my entire career as gallery-owner has ever bought every single painting in a show, and then not known the artist's name.'

I subside on my red chair again – red for danger. Zack just called me crazy and I suspect he's probably right. Am I dreaming this whole evening and things will only make some sense once I've woken from the nightmare, or am I totally deranged? 'But they were signed JPS,' I mutter.

'Yes, why not? Jane Priscilla Steiner. She hates the Priscilla, actually. I call her that when I want to needle her.' He grins, sounds sort of fond.

'Is she your bloody girlfriend, Zack?' I'm on my feet again. I'll murder her, as well, find out her address

250

and march round there straight away, pay her out for buggering me up, wasting all my money.

'Good God, no! She doesn't even *like* men.'

'What d'you mean?'

'She's a lesbian, the butch kind – a rather lively girl, in fact, though it's a pity she can't paint.'

'Can't paint?' I kick my chair-rung. I'm totting up the price of all those pictures; that precious hard-earned money I've chucked straight down the drain. And not just cash – emotion – all the energy and fury it took to slash the canvases; all the love and hate I felt for them, when they weren't John-Paul's at all. I shudder at the memory, recalling their dark spell; the way they undermined me, tainted me, infected me, so that I became a different person, a shadow-person, suffocating, cut off from the world. I turn on Zack again, try to hide my bitterness with a brief sarcastic shrug. 'So why waste your valuable wall-space on an artist who can't paint?'

'Well, she's got energy, at least, and loads of sort of guts, and the Council were behind her – gave her a year as artist-in-residence at the local Arts Centre, where she churned out all that stuff. This is Brent, remember, so she was probably subsidised not so much for her huge artistic talent as for the fact she was a radical lesbian feminist. Anyway, Brent were quite impressed and agreed to arrange a show for her. But just when all the plans were made, the Arts Centre closed down – the usual problem: lack of cash – so they got on to me instead. It wasn't easy to say no when my lease was running out, and I needed their goodwill not only to renew it, but to save my precious gallery. They own the whole damn block, you see, and there was talk of redevelopment.'

Zack crumples up his plastic cup as if the memory appals him, rocks back in his chair. 'Well, of *course* I held the show, even included their second little protégée, the sculptress Lovena Ross – another lousy artist, but a Marxist activist, this time, *and* a single-parent disadvantaged black. I've never known Brent sponsor any right-of-centre hetero-sexual whites, but . . .' He grins down at the wreckage of his cup. 'Who cares who the heck they are, so long as I'm in business still. Actually, I was really rather chuffed when you bought up the whole show. I'd resigned myself to selling one or two, at most, and had already written off my losses, then you popped up out of nowhere and did wonders for my bank balance, not to mention Jane's.'

'I *loathe* the bloody woman!'

'You don't know her, Nial. You thought she was John-Paul. I still can't understand that. Didn't you see her name on the invitation card?'

'I didn't *get* an invitation card.'

'Well, the receipt, then?'

'It wasn't on the receipt.'

'Okay, the price-list at the show itself. No, it wasn't on there either, come to think of it – just the titles and the prices. God! This is quite ridiculous. What I just can't understand is why you should connect John-Paul with the pictures in the first place – apart from just the initials which prove absolutely nothing. I mean, there must be thousands of JPSs in Brent alone, and if you include the rest of London . . .'

'Seton,' I say grimly. '*He* told me it was John-Paul's show.'

Zack lets out a noise which is half a yelp of disbelief, half a bitter laugh. 'Christ! He must be bad – I mean totally obsessed. For years and years I heard nothing but John-Paul – what he said, why he . . .'

'How long did Seton go, then?'

'Oh, a good ten years, at least.'

'*Ten?*' I'm aghast. 'If John-Paul's so bloody marvellous, then why isn't Seton cured?'

'Actually, I reckon he was brave to take him on at all. He's pretty batty sometimes, and a lot of shrinks won't touch psychotic patients, run a mile from anything which smacks of schizophrenia. It means too much damn hard work, and it's seldom that rewarding. They can slave for years, apparently, and then just one brief crisis can undo any progress, dump the wretched patient back in hospital again.'

'You seem to know a lot about it.'

'I've had to, haven't I – with Seton round my neck for twenty years? We met at art school, actually, when he was pretty bloody talented, but still a basic nutcase. And anyway . . .'

'I'm sorry, but we're closing. I've let you sit here far longer than I should have, but if I don't lock up now, I'll catch it.'

A woman with a dishcloth is swabbing us away. She's got her coat on over her apron, and a look which says 'No argument'. I've been so absorbed in Zack, I haven't even noticed that the canteen is almost empty, the counter stripped and shrouded, machines and music dumb. I struggle up reluctantly, clinging on to Zack, though it's not support I need now, just more information. I don't want this guy to vanish before I've checked out certain facts, so when he offers to drive me home I accept enthusiastically. It's a pretty lengthy drive, in fact, so we should tie up some loose ends before we reach my pad.

As we tramp back down the corridor, I suddenly start laughing quite hysterically, have to stop a moment while I clutch my sides, the wall.

'Nial, you're mad! What now?'

I'm *not* mad – that's the joy of it. I've lost a score of rivals – all those black girls at the show were Lovena Ross's groupies, not John-Paul's ex-mistresses. And the Amandas and the Cressidas weren't his rotten Marys, but radical lesbian feminists who'd come to flirt with Jane. I now understand the boiler-suits, the dungarees, the sheer preponderance of females. And were they really all that

253

gorgeous? They seemed so at the time, of course, but only because every girl connected with John-Paul is immediately given a face-lift in my mind (followed by a boob-lift and all-over body sculpture); transformed into an amalgam of Aphrodite, Helen of Troy and the latest 38-22-36 Miss World. But they *weren't* connected – not at all. John-Paul's far too busy struggling near-heroically with schizophrenic cases to bother with mere art. I'm so relieved I haven't harmed him, haven't slashed his paintings or murdered all his women, I go swooping up the corridor, can't wait for Zack to catch me up, skitter back, still hooting.

'Hey! Let's go out to dinner. *My* treat.' (I haven't any money, but I can always pay by credit card.)

'But you're ill, Nial.'

'No, I'm not.' I feel completely better, a different person, actually – and I mean that literally. All the sickness, faintness, madness, seem just a ploy, a nightmare; something I invented to win myself attention, or destroy myself, or hurt myself, or all the other things I do which John-Paul calls self-punitive. No more need for punishment or pain. I'll go the other way, in fact – indulge. 'Listen, Zack, I'm starving, I mean absolutely ravenous. I haven't eaten for a week, which is probably why I fainted. Let's go and find a restaurant and pig our way through the biggest, richest, most disgustingly outrageous meal we've had in both our lives, with waiters prancing round us and at least a dozen different courses and one of those huge menus with tooled red leather covers like the collected works of Shakespeare and . . . Oh, don't refuse, Zack, *please*.'

I hug him – yes, right there in the passage – fling my arms around him and squeeze him tight, to stifle his objections. A passing nurse looks daggers, but she doesn't understand. I'm hugging not a fat-cat super-salesman, who looks comically embarrassed and is worried for his hair, but one of the ten best shrinks in London.

# 21

'More salad?' asks the waiter.

I shake my head. I've hardly eaten anything. Forget the dozen courses – even one has proved too much. Actually, we never made the restaurant and Zack's the only waiter, tripping in his shirt sleeves from his ultra-modern kitchen to his ultra-stylish sitting-room. I hardly even noticed it the first time I was here – barely noticed anything except my thumping head. But now I'm *compos mentis* I can take in my surroundings. Carpet, walls and sofa are all the same rich shade of cream, like his car is cream, his trousers, and the cheesy-eggy-soufflé thing he served up on the coffee table (which is darker cream-streaked marble and looks frighteningly expensive). If you could buy cream lettuce, I'm sure he would have done so, but he's settled for that crinkly reddish stuff which fashion-cooks prefer to flat green cos, and added trendy extras like pine nuts and capsicums and some suspicious-looking fungoids which I offload to my handbag once he's safely in the kitchen.

I'm meant to eat just plain food – he told me so himself, when he made his worthy little speech about the dangers of a heavy meal after a period of fasting, and how if we went back to his own place and avoided 'risky' restaurants, he could rustle up something light and nourishing. I didn't believe a word of it – I've known too many men – but I was so keen to talk about John-Paul, I said 'Fine. Why not? You're on.' I still haven't quite decided whether he's an unprincipled self-seeker out for the main chance, or a closet do-gooder trying to disguise his softish centre in a hard shell of outward cynicism. It hardly matters, really, since he's not my type at all, either in looks or basic style. His appeal is strictly limited to his connection with my lover and his knowledge of John-Paul. Still, I must confess I'm flattered that he appears to fancy *me* – enough to lure me home and take this trouble – especially now I'm pollarded (though if he mixes with butch feminists, then perhaps my ragged haircut may not seem extreme). I also wonder if he minds my being taller – only by an inch or so, but all the same, guys like him usually prefer to look down on their females.

Perhaps that's why he wouldn't let me help, just arranged me on the sofa, strictly horizontally, while he launched into his chef's act just off-stage. At last, he's come to join me and is wolfing down his salad, while I push mine round the plate – yes, floral and bone china. Although my stomach won't co-operate, I've been swamping him with compliments: what a fantastic cook he is, and how I've never had potatoes so fluffy-light and buttery. That's true, in fact, and the soufflé was quite perfect (kept its erection, so to speak, and ejaculated cream). The compliments are genuine, but like most men's flattery to females, they're double-edged, and I'm using them for barter. I've traded three 'Fantastic!'s for more of Seton's history (especially his last fortnight, which appears to have transformed him from a tiger to a zombie), and I'm now starting on John-Paul's. I've got an easy entrée. When I went to use Zack's loo (also rose-sprigged Meissen – or something pretty close to it), I passed through a sort of hall place which was hung with scores of paintings, including two or three like the ones in Seton's boat and John-Paul's tower. Those damn pictures seem to haunt me. I just can't get away from them. If I moved to Timbuktu or Torremolinos, would I still find them on the walls?

Anyway, I question Zack about them, once we reach the cheese and fruit, and he confirms they're rather special and then reveals (astonishingly) that he himself sold them to John-Paul, to hang in his consulting-room. He knew the worthy doctor wasn't exactly short of cash, and his detective work disclosed that he was also a bit of a collector, so ever-prudent Zachary puts him on the mailing list. It seems once he'd done his probing for the sake of wretched Seton, he then decided to exploit it for himself. Though he never breathed a word, of course, about his connection with a patient, just kept sending invitation cards, until, two or three years later, John-Paul actually turned up at the private view of an artist called Phil Dyer, who'd become the toast of fashionable London, partly because of extremely good publicity in a whole rash of magazines, and partly because he was confined to a wheelchair and painted with the brush strapped to his hand.

'*Another* lousy artist,' I say, a mite sarcastically, removing an outsize pip from an outsize grape with a fantastic purple bloom.

Zack bridles. 'No, a brilliant one. I may hang rubbish at the gallery, if the Council twists my arm, but never in my own place, Nial.'

'But they're just the same as – what d'you call her? – Jane's.'

'Like Jane's? You must be joking! Phil's are in another league entirely. Okay, they're both abstract, both muted in their colours and pretty free with the brush, but there the resemblance ends.'

I say nothing for a moment. I'm not only humiliated by my obvious shaming ignorance, but also I feel nervous at how misleading most things are. Those pictures *looked* the same, quite apart from Seton's leg-pull, or lie, or fit of madness (or however one describes it), which confused me even more. How can we trust anything: our eyes, our minds, our lovers? Can I even trust Zack himself on anything he's said so far, yet here I am still hanging on his words? He's explaining why John-Paul was drawn to Dyer in the first place – because he spent half his early life in a mental institution, when he was actually a genius – a case of wrong diagnosis, as it were.

'Look, is John-Paul *married*?' I suddenly blurt out.

Zack looks a little nonplussed, but I'm sick of pictures actually. There are far more vital things to check – John-Paul's wives or ex-wives, the whole issue of his expertise and training.

'No, he lives alone.'

'But *was* he married?'

'What is this, Nial, an inquisition?'

'No – yes, if you like. There's this . . . er . . . girl I know who fancies him and she asked me to . . .'

'Tell her not to waste her time. The man lives entirely for his work. Apart from his collecting, which is extremely sporadic anyway – he's ignored every invitation I've sent since Dyer's show – there's zilch else but patients in his life.'

'And *dogs*?' I ask.

'Dogs?' Zack peels a grape, which looks more like an eyeball as he transfers it to his mouth.

'Wolfhounds?'

Zack stops chewing in surprise. 'I shouldn't think so, no. The only time we met he admitted he was a cat-man, and wolfhounds *eat* cats, don't they?'

'Yes,' I say with feeling, then suddenly relax, push my plate away, sink down on the cushions. There *were* no dogs, no wolfhounds. Of course I didn't kill them. They were never there to kill. It was my shadow-self which killed them in its mind – shadow-dogs, mere hallucinations. I'm so relieved I loll right back, let out a great laugh. Zack swoops on me immediately, abandons grapes and Camembert, tries to plug my open mouth with his. He misses, tries again. I let him have his wet and slobbery kiss. I never kiss my clients, but he's not a client, is he, and I'm actually not there. He can have my mouth and body – my soul and self and essence are back on John-Paul's couch.

258

'You're beautiful,' he says. 'D'you know, I couldn't take my eyes off you at the private view? You were the most attractive woman there.'

He's mocking now – he must be. I wrench my mouth away. 'Seton didn't think so,' I say acerbically.

'Seton's no real judge.'

I realise what he's doing now. I've met his type before. It's not me he wants, but the chance to do his friend down, steal his buddy's girl. I've known men sleep with frights and frumps just because they belong to someone else and they can't stand being told 'Don't touch'; have to prove they're grown-ups who are allowed to break the rules. I suppose if I wore a wedding ring, he'd find me still more irresistible.

'You're so *exciting*,' he says softly. He's not drunk, just good at lying. My face is Gruyère-pale, I probably smell of vomit, and my size-eight feet are displayed in all their gracelessness, since I've kicked off my tight shoes.

'So you like the hair?' I ask him. 'Vidal Sassoon spent *hours* on it. It's called the natural look.'

'Well, it was a sort of . . . shock at first – that I must admit, but now I've got more used to it, I find it rather striking. It's dramatic, isn't it? And you've got such fantastic cheekbones, it really shows them off.'

I bet he's good at writing blurbs – all his lousy artists billed as 'exciting' and 'dramatic'. He's already described that Steiner girl as 'lively', and no doubt black Lovena has amazing Marxist bones. I've never trusted men who talk about a woman's bones when they're really after flesh.

'How about my ears?' I ask.

'Your ears?'

'Are they exciting, too?'

'You're exciting all over, Nial.'

He assumes that deserves a second kiss and a hand inside my blouse. He's not a brilliant kisser, dribbles saliva down my chin. I wipe it off with my serviette (which is cream, of course, and damask); take advantage of the pause to return to his chief rival. 'Hey, Zack . . .' I make it teasing to put him off his guard. 'Did your detective work extend to John-Paul's family?'

'What?'

I've thrown him. Men can never do two things at once. Most normal women (the sort with homes and kids) often manage five or six at least. 'Seton told me John-Paul's father was a . . .'

'Darling, let's not talk about John-Paul – not now.'

God, a 'darling'! I spent naked weeks with Seton trying to coax just one – and failing – yet Zack's obliged before we've got our clothes off. Actually, he's unbuttoning my blouse, trying to slide the buttons through the holes in such a suavely sneaky way he thinks I'm unaware. Seton did it better by just tugging.

'I mean, you didn't happen to hear his father was a plumber?' I don't remove his hands. I'll swap a stretch of naked cleavage for a few more solid facts.

'Christ! Your tits are . . .' He kneads one like a pastry-cook, seems lost for adjectives.

'Too small,' I murmur softly, trying to help him out. One favour for another. 'I mean, did anyone you speak to know about his family or background?'

'They're perfect, Nial. The big ones always droop.'

I let him suck a nipple before I return to John-Paul's father, smile at him coquettishly. 'No one mentioned plumbers, for example?'

He sits up rather crossly, one hand on my breast still. 'Plumbers?'

'Yes – you know – geysers, boilers, stopcocks, all that sort of thing. Seton said . . .'

'Let's leave Seton out of this. All right?'

I nod. I'll kid him if he wants that, but I can't say I admire him. He doesn't seem to realise he's doing Seton down, nor blush for his hypocrisy in claiming to be shattered by his friend's recent sad relapse, then touching up his mistress a cool twenty minutes later. I admit I did encourage him by hugging him so wildly, which must have seemed the most outrageous come-on, especially when I offered him a twelve-course slap-up dinner. But even so, I backed off pretty quickly once he'd got me in his car, refused to let him stroke my thigh, told him almost primly he needed both his hands for driving. Now he's backing off from *me*, and I haven't got my answer yet, so I pop a grape between his lips (which is what they do in porn movies, and always with results). 'Just tell me if the plumber bit was true, Zack?'

'What plumber bit?' He crunches up a grape-pip with more venom than it needs.

God! He's not just hypocritical, he's thick. I've repeated it at least three times. I try again, a fourth time, but he still looks mystified.

'John-Paul's father is a *doctor*, Nial – a rather eminent neurologist. Half the family are doctors – brothers, cousins, nephews. That was easy to find out. His surname's so unusual and the clan are fairly thickly clustered around Harley Street and . . .'

'But is *he* a doctor?' I interrupt. 'I mean a proper medical one? Seton said he'd only got a doctorate in philosophy from some foreign university.'

Zack grabs the cheese-knife, hacks off a chunk of Brie, masticates it angrily, as if he's chewing up a whole Harley Street of eminent neurologists; devouring John-Paul in a gulp, then wolfing down his brothers, cousins, nephews. He's still talking as he chews, so that tiny flecks of Brie-and-spittle spray into the air. 'Well, I suppose Seton had to deny him as a doctor, just to give himself an excuse to quit his therapy and blame someone else for his failure to improve.'

I look at Zack with new respect. That's really rather subtle, even worthy of John-Paul, though again disloyal to

Seton. Maybe they're not good friends at all, just employee and employer, which still doesn't quite explain why Zack should waste his evenings visiting a mental case. I decide to give him the benefit of the doubt – he's genuinely kind (if a shit in other ways) – concerned for Seton as a suffering human being, and not just as a framer who works eighteen hours a day and probably charges well below the market rate. I offer him my breasts again – a reward not just for kindness, but for saving John-Paul's family. An eminent neurologist's far safer than a plumber. I'm feeling safer altogether – no dogs, no lousy paintings, no jumped-up Cockney father. In fact, I'm so thoroughly elated, I let Zack remove my skirt, admire my black net stockings. My own mind's still on doctors, and prickles with unease again as I realise Zack didn't actually answer my last question. I don't repeat it yet – timing's crucial in these matters – but pretend to moan with lust as he inserts his podgy hand inside my stocking-top.

He's so encouraged he starts tackling my suspenders, which affords me a remission, since he's obviously more artistic than mere practical and seems baffled by their simple snap-on fastenings. I use the breathless pause to ask a question. 'You mean, he's got all his degrees and things, and went to proper medical school and did his . . .?'

'Christ! They're so exciting, stockings. Whoever invented tights deserves to burn in hell.' He outmanoeuvres one, at last, rolls it down in a sort of panting ecstasy, strokes my naked leg from thigh to toe, and back to inner thigh.

'If you could just fill me in on the basic facts – I mean, which particular medical school or analytic training, the year he qualified – all that sort of thing.'

Zack's not concentrating, doesn't even seem to hear me. It's probably my own fault. I'm speaking very huskily, in that sexy throaty sort of voice which is meant to drive men wild, so that they obey your every whim. *This* man's blithely unaware there's anything I want – except his hot hand travelling back towards my groin. I clamp my legs together, pretend I need the loo again. He's thrilled – assumes I only need it to insert my diaphragm, so we can go full steam ahead. I pout him a long-distance kiss as I glide towards the bathroom. 'Don't go away,' I purr.

He doesn't vanish – just his clothes – which is definitely a mistake. Zack undressed is not a pretty sight. His clothes were his best feature and without them he's a slug, one of those pale fat ones which (sensibly) stay hidden under stones. His body's bald, except for two small greyish tufts sprouting from his underarms and a sort of mangy ruff around his prick. His prick's another slug: erect, but small and squashy. It always rather fazes me that men make such a thing about their pricks, comparing them to Martello towers or howitzers, when they're really more like fungi or invertebrates. John-Paul's the worst of all; wrote this book called *Penile Greed* (though I'd have called it *Phallacies*), in which he associated phalluses with anything and everything which is long, tall, pointed, powerful, extendible or sharp, or which thrusts, probes, inflates, explodes, turns on and off, spurts, squirts, slogs, strikes and batters. His list went on for ever; included trees, spears, cars, cocaine, whips, taps, thunder, lightning, pistols, tigers, sharks, swords, Zeppelins, Cape Kennedy, Mount Olympus, and even God the Father.

I shift my gaze from Zack's Ferrari/oak tree; glance around the room. It seems also full of phalluses – John-Paul's kind, at least – knives, pens, lamps, plants, and a still unopened wine bottle. Neither Zack nor I have drunk much. We're still on our first Chardonnay, haven't touched the hock. I stroke the cool green glass, embrace it like a lover, so my hands are safely occupied. 'Hell! I'm thirsty, darling. Can we open this, d'you think?'

He doesn't look too pleased, despite the 'darling'. I suppose it isn't very flattering to prefer a phallic symbol to the genuine McCoy. Mind you, he's made it very difficult.

I'd planned a little respite, a spot more gentle questioning before we returned to heavy petting, but it's not easy to conduct an inquisition when the respondent is stark naked and wondering what to do with his erection. Actually, it punctures quite dramatically once he struggles with the cork, so I quickly get my word in.

'So Seton was mistaken, then, about John-Paul's doctorate in philosophy?'

'Nial, I'm just slightly sick of Seton – right? I've had him up to here these last two weeks.' He gestures to his neck, which looks both fatter and more slack without the arty tie to hold it in.

'We're not talking about Seton, we're talking about John-Paul.'

'Well, I've even less interest in John-Paul. I realise you're obsessed with him, as Seton was himself, but frankly, Nial, I . . .'

I gulp my wine, upset by this new peevishness, and by a sudden shaming insight that I'm betraying Seton just as much as he is, could share that label 'hypocrite'. Seton's in a hospital, not in a clinch with Cressida, so what exactly am I doing lolling on a sofa with his friend/employer/confidant? I grab some weird exotic fruit, which looks a cross between a mango and a small Belisha beacon, remove its pips and peel, then stuff my mouth with it, which provides me with a good excuse not to talk, or kiss – a chance to think a moment. Am I really such a cow? After all, Seton said 'No ties', and he ditched me at that private view, never phoned me to apologise or find out how I was – *and* lied to me quite flagrantly on almost every subject. Okay, he's schizophrenic, which I suppose excuses him, but it excuses me as well. If my (ex?) lover doesn't know me, treats me like a chair or stretch of carpet, then it's high time I moved on.

The fruit tastes almost bitter, or perhaps it's just my mood – a sudden sad sharp longing to have Seton back in bed – yes, even drugged and crazy. I miss him terribly: his size eleven feet which made mine small and feminine, his whorls of wild black body hair which seemed alive in their own right – rough and hot and springy; even the smell of nicotine which lingered in his mouth. Zack's mouth smells of Roquefort, fighting with mint mouthwash. The fact Zack doesn't smoke seems another missing bond. We're just two aching strangers. Even our two bodies look completely wrong together – his legs too short and plumpish for my longer leaner ones; his pallid doughy skin-tone making mine look sallow. (He's two-tone, actually – face and hands well-bronzed, the rest like uncooked pastry.)

I drain my glass. Better a mild hangover than self-pity and regrets. And anyway, aren't I more concerned with John-Paul than with Seton? John-Paul's my whole future, Seton just my past. I could even keep my next two-ten appointment, if I could get the final evidence that my therapist's a fully trained professional – turn up on the Monday as if I've never been away. If I agonise much longer, I'll lose scowling Zack as well as vacant Seton. I try a few soft words, but they fail to change his mood. (Men never quite forgive you if you ignore their full-blown pricks. It's like ignoring the Pyramids of Egypt, or the Colossus of Rhodes, or the other Seven Wonders of the World.) I'll have to try much harder, divert him with some party trick. I kick Seton from my mind, edge up close to Zack, fill my mouth with chilled white wine, transfer it to his own mouth (spending some time on the process); then wow his limp Colossus with my lips, my hands, an ice cube and a few peeled grapes, though not in quite that order. He's so ecstatic, he not only rears up instantly, but disgorges facts like semen, and by the time we're both stretched naked on the sofa, ready for the final lap, I'm chanting in my head, 'BSc, MD, FRCPsych, editor of the new *International Journal of Psychoanalytic Psychotherapy*, member and ex-president of . . .'

'Happy?' Zack whispers, as he lumbers up on top of me, plays that game which babies play of fitting round pegs in round holes.

'Oh, *yes.*'

I hardly notice what he's doing. I'm mulling over John-Paul's long career, seeing him at Cambridge where he did his BSc, then going on to Barts to train, remaining there a decade for a gruelling spell of National Health drug-and-shocks psychiatry (and even a foray into sex therapy – *real* phalluses, for once); then his second (analytic) training, and his move to private practice; his phase as brilliant author, writing books on . . .

'All right, darling?'

I wish he wouldn't interrupt. I'm busy counting minutes now and he's made me lose all track. I twist my neck, so I can peer down at my watch – the only thing I left on, very fortunately. It's a pity that it's Thursday, which is the longest gap of all between my sessions – four thousand aching minutes till two-ten on the Monday. No, I think I've got that wrong. It can't be quite as . . .

Zack lets out a sudden gasping moan, slumps inert on top of me. I only realise he's been thrusting when he stops, though it was so extremely brief and feeble, the word thrusting seems hyperbole. A trickle of saliva oozes from his open mouth and dribbles down my neck. 'Was it all right for you, darling?'

I fight a laugh. I thought people only said that in bad novels or worse jokes. 'Mm,' I whisper softly, as I recount my triumphs one by one: no wives, no dogs, no plumbers, no murders, no slashed paintings – best of all, just three thousand, eight hundred and ninety-seven minutes until I see my fully-trained, totally professional, indeed almost over-qualified John-Paul.

'Yes, absolutely wonderful,' I tell him, truthfully.

# 22

Bryan slipped behind a tree, wished it had its leaves still, so it could hide him more effectively. The woman working in the garden of number thirty-three had been watching him suspiciously for the last half hour or so. He'd walked up and down Thurlston Grove twenty-seven times so far, passing her each time. He might be less conspicuous if he weren't carrying such a huge bouquet, wrapped in rustling cellophane and fastened with a showy yellow bow. It had already proved a hassle on the crowded tetchy tube trains, the jam-packed lifts and escalators, and finally on British Rail, where a child had cannoned into it, snapping off at least three precious flower-heads. He had almost retaliated by breaking off the child's head. He wasn't often violent, but those flowers had cost nearly half a session with John-Paul – not that he begrudged the cash. Wasn't Mary worth it, worth an arm or leg? He limped on down the road again, imagining he had lost a leg, proud to sacrifice any limb she specified.

The houses all looked closed and almost hostile – no children in the driveways, or friendly garden gnomes; just a rash of officious notices saying 'Beware of the dog' or 'No hawkers, no circulars' (or even 'No charities') – suburban euphemisms for 'GET OUT!' 'GO AWAY!' Burglar alarms bristled everywhere, and many of the houses had not just dogs, but lions – the fierce stone sort rearing up on pedestals, threatening him with bared teeth and fearsome manes. He hoped Mary's road would look a little friendlier. She lived in Sylvan Gardens, which was the street exactly parallel, though he hadn't dared approach it yet. She might see him from her window, realise he'd arrived a good sixty minutes early and was already semi-dead with cold and fear.

He'd left off his vest and sweater, so he'd look leaner and more elegant, more the city gentleman, but the bitter wind was cutting through his favourite lightweight suit. It had taken hours to choose his clothes. What *did* one wear to a birthday tea in Walton? Grey shorts and his Cub tie was his first immediate thought. He'd told his Mother he was going to a seminar. She hadn't known the word, been immediately suspicious, especially as he'd never left her on her own before on a Saturday afternoon. Saturday was Mother's Day – well, every day was Mother's Day – but weekends most especially. He could hear her voice still squalling in his head – all those guilt-inducing words which ruined his own pleasure: 'selfish', 'thoughtless', 'giddy', 'irresponsible'.

He repositioned his bouquet. The wet stalk-end was oozing through its cellophane, and it would give quite the wrong impression to turn up with a damp patch on his groin. He checked his watch again: nine minutes to four. Only eight and three-quarter minutes and he could knock on Mary's door. The thought so terrified him, he broke into a run – *away* from Sylvan Gardens and back towards the station. He sweated, stumbled, shilly-shallied; finally forced himself to change direction, recite the eight-times-table to calm his jangling nerves, as he turned the corner into Mary's road. 'Eight threes are twenty-four, eight fours are thirty-two, eight fives are . . .'

'Forty.' He could see it spelt out on a plaque attached to Mary's gate – more classy than mere '40', and befitting the smug house itself, which was Queen Anne period style with two white columns flanking the front porch, ornamental shutters on all the latticed windows, a double garage (panelled), and coloured gravel on the drive in tasteful shades of pink and green. He felt ashamed for his own hencoop in vulgar Ivy Close, with its plain and basic semis, which had neither appealing house-names, nor what the estate agents called 'character'. Mary's home wasn't simply 'Forty', it was also gracious 'Wych Elm'. He admired the second carved wood plaque, the name itself with its stylish sloping 'y'; felt he shared a bond with it. Bryan with a 'y' and wych with a 'y' was surely a good omen. He couldn't see an elm – either wych or otherwise, but it was probably round the back, and he was still dithering in the street. He took a deep breath in, checked his tie and smile were both in place, then opened the front gate, plunged up to the rustic oak front door, heard the tinkling door-chimes echo down the hall as he pressed the bell with one damp and trembling finger.

A fierce barking from inside made him back away immediately, ready for full flight. Perhaps he'd got the day wrong, or even dreamed the whole idea. Why should Mary bother with a . . .?

'Hallo, Bryan. You found us, then?'

'Look, I can go away if it's not convenient, or if I've muddled up the date . . .' His words were petering out. Mary looked so lovely, so womanly, so *perfect*. She was wearing blue – the colour of high summer: blue sea, blue cloudless sky, blue gentians, blue heaven.

'Muddled up the date? But we confirmed it only yesterday. Come in. Are those for me? How gorgeous! You shouldn't, Bryan, really. It's your birthday, so you should have the presents. Down, Horatio! I hope you don't mind dogs.'

'No, I love them.' Bryan fondled the old labrador, which was the colour of rich honey, its sagging pregnant belly contrasting with its well-developed testicles. He'd love an orang-utan or a man-eating piranha, so long as it were Mary's. He'd never had a dog. His Mother had dismissed the entire canine population as dangerous, germy, expensive and a tie. He'd invented an imaginary dog when he was eight or nine – a small mongrel called

Rover (he'd never been imaginative), who was faithful and devoted and quite flatteringly affectionate. Horatio seemed the same, was licking both his hands, sitting on his foot, trying to reach his face so he could cover it with kisses.

'You've really made a hit, Bryan. He usually growls at strangers. That's enough now, Horatio. Let Bryan take his coat off.'

He wished she'd take her own off, or at least that jacket thing which was concealing her full breasts and surely quite unnecessary in the warm fug of the house. He looked around appreciatively – fitted carpets everywhere, even in the hall, and those big broad-shouldered armchairs in the sitting room (with what looked like large blue dandelions blooming on their comfy cushioned seats), and a piano and a hi-fi and a proper cocktail cabinet with cut-glass decanters labelled 'Port' and 'Sherry' respectively, and nice safe cosy pictures of the countryside and coast, and china spaniels on the bureau and a clock which seemed to smile, and best of all, a real coal fire which purred with noisy pleasure as he sat down on the sofa, stretched his legs towards it.

The only thing which spoiled the room was the preponderance of photographs – all of other men – an overweight and scowling chap whom he assumed must be the husband, and several smugly smiling boys in various stages of undress; starting with a semi-naked baby and proceeding to a gangly lad in swim trunks, sucking an ice cream. He dragged his eyes away from them, rehearsed his opening line of conversation. He'd decided to impress her by talking about *Superspace*, a new and very complex book he'd borrowed from the library (and which his Father had commended at last week's science class). He'd spent the whole night reading it by torchlight, so he could drop it sort of casually into the birthday conversation. The book had said that total chaos in the universe was averted only because matter was undisciplined and lazy. He'd been called the same himself – since infancy, in fact, but for *matter* to be lazy sounded downright dangerous, yet according to the author, it was feckless and plain indolent – lolled about, ran down.

He cleared his throat, prepared his opening lines. He must avoid all boring jargon, while sounding deep, intriguing; perhaps crack a little joke, as Skerwin did so often, to dilute his frightening braininess.

'It's . . . er . . . cold for early December.'

'Mm.'

'The fire's nice, though.'

'Yes, isn't it?'

'My Mother doesn't like coal fires.'

'Oh, really?'

'No. She says they make a lot of extra work.'

'Well, I suppose they do, but it's worth it, don't you think?'

'Oh, *yes*.'

Silence. Except for Horatio's heavy snuffling breathing. He was lying on Bryan's foot. Bryan stroked the silky head, rubbed the smooth gold tummy. He had pins and needles in his leg, but he didn't like to shift the dog. It was miraculous he'd 'made a hit', as Mary had expressed it; gave him hope he might succeed not just with a labrador, but – later – with his mistress. Could he stroke her silky head, rub her smooth gold tummy? He rifled through his mind (and books) for something to astound her: muons, tauons, leptons, the Grand Unifying Theory, the Anthropic Principle. 'I . . . um . . . like the silver cups.'

'They're James's – for his golf. *They* make extra work, as well, but he's so frightfully proud of them, I like to keep them nice and bright and shiny.'

Bryan wished he'd never mentioned them. He'd imagined they were Mary's – cups for schoolgirl hockey, or cookery, or mothering, or just for being the most desirable woman in all Walton, Weybridge, the whole of southern England, and probably . . .

'What are you doing for Christmas, Bryan? Will you be abroad?'

He stared at her, unspeaking. He'd been bragging once again of his non-existent foreign trips just last night at the class. She must assume he spent most holidays lolling on the beaches of sun-kissed Acapulco, or exploring the high Andes. The longest trip he'd ever made was a Brontë Country coach tour, which had been ruined by his Mother catching shingles. 'It . . . er . . . depends on Mother,' he answered enigmatically. That was true, at least. Everything depended on his Mother. 'How about you?' he inquired of Mary, smiling. Best to shift attention from himself.

'We'll be at home. We always are for Christmas. It's funny, I've always rather liked it other years, but I'm feeling a bit restless this December, wondering if we ought to book a holiday – you know, go abroad straight after Christmas Day, break the pattern, so to speak.'

'Had you anywhere in mind?' Bryan tried to disguise the anguish in his voice. Bad enough Mary living down in Walton, cruel miles away from Upminster, but if she was going to put a continent between them . . .

. 'Rome,' she said, smiling now herself, a smug and secret smile he didn't like at all.

'Rome? Why Rome?' He tried to work the mileage out – Ivy Close to the Forum.

'Well, Oliver's doing classics, so it would help him with his school work, and I've never been there in my life, which is shameful for a Catholic, and there's a local Surrey saint being canonised just twelve days after Christmas, and . . . and . . .'

Bryan wiped Horatio's slobber off his trouser leg. Why was Mary blushing, lost for words? Perhaps the mention of religion. He'd heard a programme on the radio just a week ago which said many modern people found it more embarrassing to mention God than sex. He tried to help her out, fill the awkward silence, but his sheer unadulterated misery at the thought of her and James cavorting in the Colosseum made all speech impossible. He'd throw James to the ravening lions *and* his rotten golf cups.

'Are you thirsty, Bryan?'

He jumped. He'd been watching a huge leo devour James's last pale limb, its blood-stained fangs still slavering as it crunched up bone and silver. His eye caught the decanter label – 'Sherry'. Was she offering him a drink at only five past four? A litre of Black Label would help to calm his anger, give him instant courage, but she might suspect he was a secret alcoholic. 'Er . . . no, not at all.'

'I was going to suggest we started tea, but if you'd rather wait a while . . .'

'No, please, I'm very thirsty, absolutely parched, in fact.' He jumped up to his feet, alarming the fat labrador who started barking at imaginary intruders, and upsetting an arrangement of dried grasses and silk flowers. He almost wept with shame. He had obviously inherited his Father's clumsiness.

Mary rushed to save them. 'It's quite all right, don't worry. They needed dusting anyway. Those dried ones get so dirty and I never seem to find the time these days.' Her flush deepened, stained her cheekbones, rippled down her neck. He watched it hungrily, longed to strip her clothes off to check how far it spread.

'The kettle's boiled already, so I'll go and make the tea. Come into the dining-room. I'll only be a second.'

He followed with Horatio, stopped in rapt amazement as he stared down at the table. It was covered with a crimson cloth, though the cloth was barely visible beneath the vast array of plates – sandwiches and vol-au-vents, iced biscuits and meringues, every sort of cake from feathery ones in tiny paper cases to a magnificent iced birthday cake with 'HAPPY BIRTHDAY, BRYAN' written in blue capitals – and *candles*

*candles* – yes, eight candles, arranged in a triumphant circle on the top.

Mary's eyes were also on the cake, anxious eyes which swivelled back to his. 'I'm afraid I didn't know how old you were, and it seemed rather rude to ask, so I decided to put eight on, as I would have done for Jon. I hope you don't object?'

He sank down on the chair she offered. *Object?* This was a near-miracle, the most awesome and amazing thing that had ever happened in his life. All those cakes and biscuits were home-made, and exquisitely home-made, oozing jam or butter-cream, and decorated variously with coconut or almonds, cherries, glacé fruits. His busy work-worn Mother had spent hours and hours slaving in the kitchen just for him; had gone to all that trouble and expense. All his favourite goodies: éclairs and strawberry tartlets, cream-filled brandy snaps – treats he was forbidden as too rich or too extravagant, or bad for his digestion (or liver or complexion). And – oh! – a rabbit jelly, a wobbly gleaming scarlet one, eyes and whiskers piped in white whipped cream, and sitting on a bed of chopped green-jelly grass. Never in his thirty-two long years had he ever (*ever*) had a rabbit jelly, let alone one made in his honour.

His eyes tracked back to the birthday cake. She'd even spelt the Bryan right – with a 'y', and piped fantastic fragile spiral things all around the edge and sides, and put it on a silver board with a ribbon round its middle. And there were crackers piled at each end of the table, not Christmas ones in red and green, but blue to match the cake, and special paper servi-ettes with 'Happy Birthday' on, and balloons above the sideboard, hung in glowing clusters, and a second real coal fire, lit specifically to warm him, when his own Mother would have groused and grudged. 'Money doesn't grow on trees, Bryan, and if you did a bit more round the house, instead of idling with your nose stuck in a book, I might not have this backache from lugging coal all week'.

Mary was still out in the kitchen, making tea. He checked the door – all clear – leaned across and touched the food, to make sure it was real, not just a dream, a mirage. 'Don't touch!' his Mother snapped. No, she wasn't there – only his other angel Mother, who wouldn't mind if he stroked a marvelling finger against the soft breast of a sponge, scooped a flake of chocolate from a plumply moist éclair, inserted a bold finger into the hollow of a brandy snap, eyes closed in total ecstasy as he tongued cream off his fingertip.

'Bryan, are you all *right*?'

'Er . . . yes. Er . . . fine. Just feeling a bit . . . faintish.'

'Gosh, I'm sorry. It's probably the heat. D'you think you ought to lie down for a moment?'

'*Yes*,' he screamed, ripping off his shirt. 'Lie down all day, all night, all week, so long as you are with me, stretched out on our double bed, naked and embracing.'

'No,' he said, straightening his straight tie. 'It's nothing. I sometimes get these dizzy turns, but they never last that long.'

'Well, perhaps a cup of tea will help. Milk and sugar, Bryan?'

'Just a drop of milk, please.' His Mother had insisted he give up sugar in his tea, after reading the headline 'PURE, WHITE AND DEADLY!' and the article which followed it in last week's *Daily Mail*, which claimed sugar was an extremely dangerous food. So many foods were dangerous, at least in Ivy Close. Cheese clogged up his arteries, bacon killed him outright, coffee gave him heart attacks, and most common fruits and vegetables were sprayed with poisonous pesticides and grown in toxic soil. Mary's house and garden seemed safer altogether.

She passed his cup and a brimming plate of sandwiches.

He stared at them in awe. Not only were the crusts cut off, but they had been stamped into artistic shapes – triangles and circles, even hearts – and stuck with tiny labels written in her own neat hand: 'Egg and cress', 'Smoked salmon', 'Cheese and Marmite'. He chose a heart, a jam one, which looked as if it were bleeding, pretended to be chewing it, so he wouldn't have to talk. He was so touched by her trouble his voice had disappeared. He put the sandwich down again. He could no more eat than speak. It would be sacrilege and outrage to chew up Mary's heart.

His hand crept back to the plate again, withdrew a perfect circle with a pink filling of smoked salmon. He'd never had smoked salmon in his life – only Shippams Salmon Paste spread thinly on his Mother's doorstep sandwiches. He moved it to his mouth, stopped half-paralysed. He couldn't eat that either. He wanted to preserve this tea, take every item home with him, not casually devour it. Even when the cakes went stale and the sandwiches turned mouldy, he'd still have the solid evidence of his Mother's selfless love. He reached out for a pink meringue, a jam-glazed strawberry tartlet, two fairy cakes, a flapjack; piled them on his plate, eating nothing, tasting nothing, just gloating and admiring.

'Leave room for the hot things, Bryan.'

'Hot things?'

'Yes, I've got them in the oven – mince pies and sausage rolls. Oh, I know I've made far too much, especially for just two of us, but I got quite carried away, and once I'd started I couldn't seem to stop. Cooking's my main hobby and I don't get much chance to cook these days, especially not cakes and pastries. James has to watch his weight, you see, and the boys are all at school and . . .' She bit into a cheese and Marmite triangle, dabbed a thread of Marmite from her lip. 'I really enjoyed this morning. I got up at the crack of dawn and went through all my recipe books and tried to choose the things I thought you'd like.'

'The things you thought I'd . . . *like?*'

'Of course. You're the guest, the birthday boy, the VIP today.'

'Oh, *Mary* . . .' He gulped his tea to hide his burning face. The VIP! Someone so important that she'd sacrificed all Saturday to cook for him, and had actually enjoyed it, poured out thought and care on his preferences, his tastes. His Mother hated cooking, saw it as a thankless chore; always seemed to intimate that *she* could live quite happily on plain water and thin air, and it was only his gross appetites that forced her to keep slaving over dirty dangerous stoves. *This* tea was made with love. Ingredients like flour or sugar were purely insignificant. Love had made the cakes rise, puffed up the meringues, filled the tarts and sandwiches, iced the birthday cake. He leaned back in his chair, gratitude and sheer dazed incredulity fighting in his breast.

'You're not eating, Bryan. What's wrong?'

He shook his head, didn't trust his voice.

'Are you feeling a bit faint again? The fire *is* very hot.'

'No, no, it's . . .' He wanted to say 'wonderful' – *two* coal fires as birthday presents – what luxury, what spoiling! Could he take those home, as well, their golden flames leaping from his carrier-bag, their crackling logs warming his chill bedroom?

'Well, I'll fetch the sausage rolls. If you're not that keen on sandwiches, then . . .'

'I *love* the sandwiches.'

Too late. She was already through the door, reappeared with a plate in either hand: tiny tiny sausage rolls made of tissue paper, and light-as-angels mince pies dusted with fine sugar – not white and deadly, but white and magical. She passed him both at once. He shook his head again. He could no more eat them than eat the Holy Grail, devour Aladdin's lamp or chew up the crown jewels.

'Oh, don't refuse, Bryan, please.'

He was astonished by the tremor in her voice, watched her face begin to crumple up. Whatever could be wrong?

'It's stupid, Bryan, I know it is, but I'm just a little sensitive about my m . . . mince pies. You see, I made some just last week for . . . for . . . Well, he's not a friend exactly, but . . .'

'An acquaintance?' Bryan suggested, aghast that she was so upset, as lost for words as he had been himself.

'No, not really an acquaintance. Let's just say somebody I know, somebody important. Anyway, he refused to take them, wouldn't even *try* one, just gave them back to me. I was terribly upset, Bryan. I mean, I was going shopping for James's shirts and socks, and I had to carry them all round those huge department stores in the heat and crowds and everything, but it wasn't really that. I felt – well – so *rejected*, and sort of stupid and put down. I know I shouldn't be telling you this when it's your birthday and a happy day, but you haven't touched a thing yourself, you see, so I'm beginning to feel that perhaps I've lost my cooking skills and no one wants to eat the things I make.'

He leaned across, seized two mince pies, tried to eat them both at once, only burnt his tongue. He crammed a third one in, heard his Mother's voice reproving: 'Manners, Bryan. *Manners!*', wiped his mouth in deference to her, before reaching for a fourth. He must finish every last pie on the plate, and any others still heating in the oven – two dozen, twenty dozen – never mind the numbers. How dare some odd acquaintance spurn Mary's perfect pastry – except he *wasn't* an acquaintance, but 'somebody important'. Could she mean a lover, some cruel and mocking sadist who wanted only to upset her, destroy her self-esteem? He'd kill the cad, throw him to the lions with James, burn him in hot oil. His own mouth was scorched and throbbing from the still fiercely hot mince pies, but he continued to devour them, one following the other with hardly time to chew. He'd show his puny rival how lovers should behave – with devotion, dedication, and shrugging off mere pain.

He paused a moment to express his appreciation – how light they were, delicious; how he loved the touch of lemon peel, the pretty scalloped edges. Mary still looked worried, her face creased in concern.

'Don't you think you ought to stop, Bryan?'

'Stop?'

'Well, you . . . you must leave room for the birthday cake. Look, why don't we light the candles now?'

He threw a last pie down his throat. The plate was almost empty, so he could afford to call a halt. His heart was pounding wildly as Mary drew the curtains, switched off the main light. How intimate, romantic, to see the dancing candle-flames reflected in her eyes. He wanted to preserve not just the birthday tea, but this magic sacred moment; never have it end, never have to face the thought of some hated heartless rival who was 'important' in her life.

'Aren't you going to blow them out?'

'No,' he whispered. '*Never.*'

'But they'll melt the icing, or set the house on fire.' She was giggling almost nervously. Still he shook his head. Better that the house burnt down and they died together, clasped in one another's arms, their ashes fused at last, than destroy this perfect moment, this sense of reeling intimacy.

'But you get a birthday wish, Bryan. And if you blow out every candle with just one puff of breath, your wish comes true.'

Bryan edged his chair up closer, still gazing into her eyes. 'Are you certain of that, Mary, absolutely sure?'

'Oh, yes. Last year Jon wished for a guinea pig, and his aunt turned up with two of them that very afternoon – *and* a lovely cage.'

279

Bryan stood up, leaned closer to the cake. Forget guinea pigs or cages. His wish was only Mary – her body and her breasts, her breath, her heart, her love. He took a deep breath in, the deepest of his life, eyes bulging with the effort, chest hurting as it swelled, then – PUFF! – he let it out. Seven candles died. One flickered, panicked, dithered, flared back to mocking life.

'Oh! What a shame,' smiled Mary. 'You were very nearly there.'

He kicked his chair back, hurtled from the room and up the stairs, searching for the bathroom. He found it, locked the door, realised too late it was literally the bathroom, and didn't have a toilet. Tears were streaming down his face now, so he dared not venture out again, just sank down on the cold edge of the bath. He'd lost his wish, his love.

'Oh, Mary,' he kept murmuring. 'I want you, how I want you. I've been waiting, hoping, all my life for a woman just like you. I wanted you when I was only two or three. I didn't know your name then, or know I'd ever meet you, but the longing was still there.'

He mopped his face on a fluffy-soft blue towel, the initial 'M' embroidered on one corner. It must have touched her skin, that towel, touched her breasts, her . . . He draped it round his shoulders like a vestment. He felt so tired and drained; had lain awake for four whole nights fretting over Mary; been tense and jumpy all the week, preparing for this tea; tense especially yesterday when he'd tried – and failed – to tell John-Paul that he'd been invited down to Walton for a party. He'd spent the entire oppressive session in grim silence, searching for the words, until at nearly ten to eight, John-Paul had asked if there was anything he wished to say, since they had just ten minutes left – or was his silence an expression of hostility? He'd said 'no' to both, and then 'Oh, God!' – four words in fifty minutes.

And he'd been so on edge at last night's class, he hadn't heard a word of Skerwin's lecture. He'd kept hearing

Mary's voice instead, saying 'I'm fearfully sorry, Bryan, but I shall have to put you off tomorrow. Something else has just cropped up. I know you'll understand.'

He'd felt sick and dizzy at the words, even though she'd never actually spoken them, and there he was sitting in her bathroom. Perhaps he ought to rest, as she'd suggested in the first place, have a little lie-down. He dared not risk a bed, climbed into the bath, instead, stretched out fully-dressed, neat black polished shoes against the gold swan taps. He closed his eyes, leaned back. All he needed was a moment's peace, a respite, a chance to calm and quiet himself before returning to the dining-room. He reached out for the plastic duck quacking on the bath-rim, hugged it to his chest. He was eight again, like Jonathan, needed his sweet Mother to wash his neck and ears, reach down and soap his tiny bud-like penis. It didn't matter now that it was small. He was just her little boy, and little boys had little ones. He could feel her gentle careful hands soaping it and swelling it.

'What a big big boy you are, Bryan!'

He flushed with pride, felt better now already, couldn't understand the almost frantic knocking at the door. Mothers never knocked.

'Bryan, what's wrong, what's happened? Can you hear me in there?'

'Yes,' he whispered. 'I can hear. I can always hear you, Mary, your soft sweet voice murmuring in my head.'

'Let me in, Bryan, *please*.'

Of course she could come in. She'd come to soap his tummy, rub a hot rough flannel down his chest. He struggled up and out, unlocked the door. Mary stood there, flustered, her jacket off at last, her blouse straining over superbly swelling breasts.

'Look, Bryan, I understand. There's no need to hide the truth. I know you think I might be shocked, but honestly I'm not.'

'You're *not*?' He let her take his arm as she led him to her bedroom, sat him on a turquoise wicker chair.

'No. Not at all. I admit I might have been, some months ago, but I've changed a lot since then.'

'Oh, Mary . . .' He was actually in the sanctuary of her boudoir, the double bed stretching like a high road, inviting him to drive; her arm around his shoulder, her smell of summer roses reviving bare December. So she knew, she understood.

'I just want to try to help you, Bryan. I can't do much myself, I realise that, but . . .'

'You can, you *can*! You can save my life.'

'No, Bryan, I'm afraid I can't. We've got to face the facts, however tragic.'

'But it isn't tragic, Mary, not now you understand.'

'Bryan, calm yourself. You need to save your strength. I know you must feel great relief at being able to discuss it openly for once, instead of having to live a lie, terrified that everyone will judge you, or shrink away in horror, or . . .'

'And *you* don't shrink away?'

'No, I don't, Bryan, truly. It's just that I feel so . . . well – inadequate. I've not had much experience of . . .'

'But nor have I. We'll learn. So long as we're together.'

Mary wasn't listening, but pacing round the room, picking up small ornaments, fiddling with them, frowning. He loved the fact she was just as shy as he was, every bit as nervous; was enchanted by her modesty, her obvious coy embarrassment. He bobbed up from his chair. This was his big moment, nervousness or no. If he didn't touch her now, unbutton that blue blouse, slip a hand between the Monts Blancs of her breasts, he might never have the chance again – the two of them together and alone. He lurched towards her just at the same moment as she sprang towards the door, alerted by the telephone which was shrilling in the hall. They collided in the bottleneck between the wardrobe and the bed, Bryan trying to restrain her, handcuffing her wrists.

'Don't answer that!' he shouted.

'Why not?'

'It's James!'

'No. James is up in Scarborough.'

'I know.' Ringing from the conference hall in a fit of murderous rage, to say he'd had the house bugged and was on his way to wreak revenge, hack his hated rival into pieces. Or – worse! – not James at all, but a frantic phone-call from his local general hospital, Emergency Department: his Mother had collapsed and was on a life-support machine, weeping for her absent son, as the pulses from her stricken heart grew fainter, fainter, fainter, on the screen.

'I'll only be a moment, Bryan. You sit here and . . .'

'No, don't! I'll leave. I'm sorry. I never meant to . . .'

She'd gone – tripping down the stairs without a trace of fear. He crept out to the landing, sweat sticking shirt to skin; hardly dared to listen as she picked up the receiver in the hall.

'Hallo, Phyllis. No, I'm fine. And you? Oh, I'm sorry, dear. Have you tried fresh garlic? They say it helps catarrh. Or you can get it in those capsule things – you know, without the smell. Yes, I know I said I'd help to clean the presbytery, but . . .'

He collapsed back to the bedroom, straightening his wild tie, almost fell towards the photograph of Mary in what looked like her nightdress, but worn with pearls and high-heeled shoes. He kissed her naked cleavage, stroked his trembling finger down the outline of her thigh, traced one shapely ankle. Could he take a high heel home with him, some memento of her, trophy, which he could sleep with every night? He swung round the other way, pulled the wardrobe open, came face to face with a battalion of grey business suits, all stern, all smart, all James's. He slammed it shut again. A shoe was quite impractical, would bulge his pocket out, be impossible to hide. What about a brassière? That would slip into his pocket like a hankie. But supposing he got careless, pulled it out to blow his nose, once they resumed their tea downstairs? An earring might be safer, or a lipstick, something really tiny, and not too intimate.

He started opening all the drawers, found a cache of panties, tiny flimsy lacy things which almost stopped his heart with sheer excitement. He stuffed six or seven pairs inside his shirt-front, tugged them out again. '*Thief!*' his outraged Mother was accusing, her face a mask of horror and disgust. 'Fornicator, pervert.' He hurled them back, then tried to fold them neatly, so nobody would guess he'd even touched them; tried the drawer beneath; found James's baggy underpants, which looked torpid, somehow, dead. He unrolled a pair of off-white woollen long-johns, fastened with small press-studs at the crotch. Torpid – no! Those lustful smirking press-studs were popping wildly open as James's organ rose, swelled wider, longer, stiffer, climaxed at near-vertical. He throttled the coarse wool between his hands, twisted, wrenched and mangled, gave a final lethal squeeze, dashed back to the landing as he heard a noise below.

'No, I'm sorry, Phyllis, honestly, but I simply can't do Monday. I'm busy every Monday now. Yes, I know I always used to, but . . .'

He shut the door again. The coast was clear still, mercifully; Mary perching on the table in the hall, displaying her sweet knees, and apparently quite happy to keep talking. He fell onto his own knees, pulled out the bottom drawer, the only one he hadn't yet investigated. He gazed in horror at the large and lumpy packet squashed in on the top. 'Kotex super-towels for maximum absorption. Soft, secure and flushable.' He shuddered, looked away, could never quite believe that women *bled*. It seemed so messy and unhealthy, not to mention dangerous. He liked to think of Mary as pure and clean all over, even her insides; not oozing blood or babies, but filled with fresh whipped cream like those moist éclairs downstairs.

He removed the offending package, reeled back in shock as he saw what it concealed; rubbed his eyes for fear he was hallucinating. No. All real, too real – that solid flaunting plastic and obscenely rigid rubber – stallion-sized, the lot of it, tireless and unflagging, like James before his throttling. Was Mary a Loose Woman, the type his Mother had warned against in words of execration when he was still too young to know such words at all? Had she lured him into her bedroom as just one more casual conquest, another stud to pleasure her? Or was it *James* who was the pervert, using all this . . . this hardware on his appalled defenceless wife? Or perhaps they'd bought the stuff together, these lewd and shameful sex toys, to boost their mutual ecstasy, bond them in some crudely lecherous rite?

He crawled on hands and knees towards the bed, crouched down on the carpet, laid his face against the silky counterpane. He couldn't bear these new and cruel uncertainties, this increase in his jealousy, which was already like a precipice, looming stark and dangerous in his mind. He held his pounding head, let out a howl of pain.

'Bryan! What *is* it? Shall I call a doctor?'

He turned swiftly round, still on his knees, shook his head in misery as he saw Mary's perfect form stooping down towards him, but with those monstrous plastic dildoes now jammed between her legs – eight or nine or ten of them, all throbbing and vibrating. He hid his eyes, groaned softly.

'You're so *brave*, Bryan, honestly. I can see what pain you're in, yet you try to struggle on, refuse to just give in, or hide away at home. But you really do need help – professional help, from someone properly trained.' She took a step towards him, sat down on the bed. 'Look, there's this . . . this . . . man I know whom I'm sure would understand. He's really wise and . . .'

'*Man?*'

'Yes, a doctor, actually. His name's John–Paul, and though he's quite expensive, he . . .'

'What?' said Bryan, leaping to his feet. 'What name did you say?'

'John–Paul. I know it's rather unusual and the same name as the Pope's, but that's just sheer coincidence. He's not religious, honestly, won't try to convert you or tell you you're in sin or . . .'

'Where's my coat?' Bryan gasped.

'What's the matter? What ever have I said? If I've upset you, Bryan, I'm sorry, honestly I am. Please don't go. Don't leave. I know how dreadful it must be, with the shame and guilt and everything and all those ghastly symptoms, but if you'd only let me help – or *someone* help. Look, I'll write down John–Paul's name for you on this empty Kleenex box, then you won't forget it, and if you ever find you need him, then . . .'

Bryan brushed aside the Kleenex box, dashed headlong down the stairs and out through the front door. 'I won't forget it – *ever*,' he called hysterically to no one. '*Or* your bottom drawer.' He slammed the gate behind him, was swallowed up in darkness.

# 23

It's one-eighteen exactly. Just fifty-two minutes left – no, fifty-one, if I arrive a minute early, which John-Paul can't object to, when I haven't seen him for over a whole month now, missed seventeen separate sessions, which add up to a total of eight hundred and fifty minutes. It's Monday, perfect Monday, and I'm sitting in the College of Technology, not in my usual cramped and smelly toilet, but in their new and bright canteen. I've actually eaten lunch, the first time ever before an appointment with John-Paul. The lunch was celebratory. I even bought some wine, which they sell in miniature bottles like the ones you get on airlines. My bags are piled all around me – supermarket carriers full of groceries and polishes, disinfectants, cleaners. This is my new start. I spent the whole weekend blanked out – sleeping, sleeping, sleeping, as if to compensate for all my midnight pacing the week or two before, or perhaps to make the minutes pass more quickly, let go that aching count.

I woke refreshed and healthy, as if I'd slept through the whole winter into spring; intend to *make* it spring – to eat, and even cook, again; scour my filthy room, purify it, purge it; remove the stink and scars. I bought all the soaps and scourers on my long walk to the tower, so I can start this afternoon, as soon as I get home from my appointment – also bought a clutch of presents for John-Paul. If he tells me they're a recompense, he's right. I bought them to apologise for doubting him; for believing he had dogs and wives and mistresses; labelling him a con-man and a fraud. I chose him really special things, not mere sweets and biscuits, but precious books, silk ties. I had to pay by credit card, since I haven't any cash. Money is a problem. I really need to give up all my clients, so I'm pure for him, and celibate, as now he is himself. I'm wearing white, as a promise of that purity – new white pristine clothes.

I drain my glass of wine, scoop out the last half-spoonful of matching white iced sorbet, gather up my parcels, dawdle down the stairs. No one stops me, or asks me what I'm doing, what right I have to eat in their canteen. Today I have rights everywhere, nowhere locked or banned. It isn't even raining, but a perfect winter's day; the sun weak but convalescent, the December sky the colour of a puffin's egg. I pass my last half-hour walking slowly, very slowly, down the road beside the tower, the words of Luke, 15, chiming in my head – the story of the Prodigal Son. I know those words almost off by heart; used to read the Gospels in my teens – secretly and shamefully, since my father viewed the Bible as a salacious dangerous book. It always meant so much to me, the emotion of that Father, his obvious love, compassion, the way he could forgive. My own father would have left me grovelling with the pigs, feeding off their husks. (One trendy modern version calls them 'bean-pods', but 'husks' is so much better, suggests their utter worthlessness, their empty barren dryness.)

'And he would fain have filled his belly with the husks that the swine did eat.' I repeat that quaint archaic 'fain', roll it round my tongue like one of John-Paul's toffees; continue with the story. 'But when he was yet a great way off, his Father saw him and had compassion, and ran and fell on his neck and kissed him. And the son said unto him, "Father, I have sinned against heaven, and in thy sight, and am no more worthy to be called thy son."'

I've forgotten the next line, except I know the Father summoned all his servants, urged them to dress his son in finery, put a ring on his finger and shoes on his feet, kill the fatted calf for him. 'For this my son was dead, and is alive again; he was lost, and is found.' There was never a

Prodigal Daughter – no girls at all, or even wife, or none that I remember.

I pause a moment, put my shopping down, run my hands across my short cropped hair. John-Paul will know me as his son, run to meet me, kill the fatted calf for me. The husks are over, finished; the cold nights with the swine. I cross the street, jog towards the tower, bags and parcels banging at my knees. It's still only 2.06, but he'll give me those four minutes – a present like the fatted calf, the ring.

I stop in queasy shock. Someone else is encroaching on the tower, not just a casual passer-by, but someone striding right up to the door, about to press the buzzer. No – 'someone else' is wrong, far too vague and flat a word for the slim and striking female who's trespassing on my own square foot of pavement, one hand reaching up still, while she pauses, checks her watch. She looks roughly my own age, though there the resemblance ends. She's the sort of girl you have to turn and stare at – not a pale-blue Mary, submissive and demure, but confident and coltish, with long athletic legs and a tiny show-off waist. Her clothes make mine look cheap. She's wearing daring purple, which clashes quite superbly with her shout of auburn hair, outglares my pallid white. I lunge towards her, grab her hand before it courts the bell-push. She pivots round, astonished, and I meet her crafty eyes, that subtle greenish-greyish shade which elude all definitions save 'special' and 'enchanting'.

'What the hell?' she snaps.

Aggressive, too, I see. I stand my ground, inform her very coldly that ten past two on Monday is *my* appointment, actually – has been for eight months.

'I'm sorry, but it's mine now. John-Paul is expecting me. I was told to come at ten past two today.'

I can't bear to hear her speak, her husky Sloane-ish voice, the way she says 'John-Paul' with that air of gloating certainty, that hint of pure possession. She shakes my hand off roughly, reaches for the buzzer. I hear it answer 'Yes'; hear her give her name: Beata. I *loathe* the name – arty and pretentious – press the bell myself, push up right against her, as I yell my own name: 'NIAL!' Then I spring at her, tug her coil of hair, claw her face, pinion both her arms. She's crying. So am I. The only difference is she looks gorgeous when she cries, her huge eyes brimming, melting.

The door suddenly bursts open, and I half-fall against John-Paul. It's a double shock to see him. First, he looks quite different from the John-Paul I remember – taller and more tetchy – and second, he's at ground-level, instead of high up in his room. He never ventures down to greet a patient, always summons us to him. I cling on to him desperately, terrified he'll vanish. 'It's *my* appointment – mine. You can't give it away.'

He fends me off immediately, tries to reassure Beata, who's still standing on the step. 'Come in please, Beata. Would you go upstairs and wait for me.'

'*No!*' I shout. His words are like a blow. He's hit me in the stomach, injured me internally. The world goes black a moment as I sway against the wall; hear his voice so steady and impassive I'm tempted to attack it, claw it open, find out if it's human.

'Sit down,' he says to me, gesturing to the small hard chair in the cold and grudging foyer. No 'please', no name at all. He said 'please' to Beata, used her name caressingly, with affection, almost intimacy. I'm just a lump of nothing, a scrap of dirty paper which blew in at his door. I don't sit down – I can't – but dash towards the staircase to watch Beata groping slowly up, her auburn hair trembling down her back, her tight immodest skirt hampering her progress. I start calling up the stairs, begging her to give me her appointment, insisting that I'll pay for it – double, triple, anything she asks. I'm pleading with her, grovelling, shaking with cold fear. If John-Paul turns me out, I'm not sure I can . . .

'Nial!' he raps, more sharply now; propels me from the staircase towards the nearest chair, seats me forcibly, pressing on my shoulders, so I can't get up again. He's stronger than he looks, and his grip is really hurting, but I don't resist at all. His hands are on my body. He's touching me, in contact, his warm breath meeting mine. I've craved that touch for naked starving months, longed to be this close to him. Tears splash on my hands. I'm only close as a prisoner would be close – a prisoner to her gaoler, a convict to her guard. He'll touch Beata in quite a different way, not hold her down, restrain her, but stretch out on the couch with her, lap her in his arms. I scrub my eyes, try to speak through hurting racking sobs.

'She . . . She's no right to go up there. She's stolen my appointment. This time's *mine* on Monday.'

'Nial, you know quite well you told me in your letter that you wished to terminate your therapy, refused even to discuss it with me. And you appear to have forgotten that when I wrote to say we should meet at least once more, and that I'd keep your appointments free for you, in case you changed your mind, you replied quite categorically that you were leaving London and going back to Shropshire, had already found a cottage there, and were departing on the third. In fact, I'm most surprised to see you here at all.'

'I *never* wrote! You're lying.'

'You wrote three separate times, Nial, three letters in a row.'

'Well, the letters were just lies then – stupid crazy lies.'

'I'm afraid I'm not a mind-reader.'

'But that's your job – you ought to be. It was obvious they were lies.'

'What seems to me more obvious is that you're unaware

at present of the difference between reality and its opposite.'

He sounds so cold, sarcastic, and he's no longer even touching me; has shifted back a pace or two, as if my body somehow taints him. I long to be Beata, so I could make him press back close; own her velvet voice, which matches his. My own voice comes out spiteful – hessian, rough sacking.

'You're dying to get rid of me, that's all. You know I couldn't leave you, and that I'd fall apart if you ever moved away. I suppose that's what you want, though – to have me just crack up. You gave away my session to that . . . that woman, so you can fondle her and stroke her and tell her she's your favourite. And I notice she came early, which you've never let *me* do. A whole four minutes early, so you'll have more time to . . .'

'I realise you're extremely overwrought, Nial. I'm also genuinely sorry that you've made this journey for no purpose, especially if you've come all the way from Shropshire. You're welcome to sit down here until you've calmed yourself, but I just have to start my session now.'

'Start your *screwing*, don't you mean?'

He doesn't answer, just turns abruptly on his heel, and starts striding up the stairs. I dash after him, still shouting, try to block his way. I hate myself, hate the things I'm yelling; want to say I'm sorry, want to just be quiet, but all the gentle harmless words are squashed and almost smothered, dying like myself.

'Nial, if you continue in this fashion, I shall have to call an ambulance, which I don't think you would like.'

I sink down on the steps, silent now, defeated. The stone is hard and chilly, like his voice; seems to shrink from any contact with my flesh. So he'd allow me to be carted off by a gang of total strangers, abandoned in some heartless institution. It's happened once already, so he knows how cruel his words are, knows just what he's threatening. My head slumps on my knees. No point fighting any more, no point even pleading. I fix all my concentration on his footsteps, listen to them fade; strain to hear the whinny of the door, which always creaks on opening, steel myself for its curt and hurtful slam. Then I hear the catch turn – the final shaming insult. He never locks his door. He's not only excluding me, he's insisting on his privacy, so he can strip that girl and enter her. He probably sleeps with half his patients – the little ones, the loved ones; invites them to his home, cradles and caresses them. They're good, you see, and beautiful; never made their mothers ill or drove their fathers out; weren't a disappointment from the womb.

I limp downstairs, one step, one step, one step, like a child. My carrier bags are lying on their sides, retching half their contents. They look lonely and abandoned, very sick. I pick them up and nurse them, sort them into piles, smooth the crumpled ties out, swathe things back in tissue. John-Paul told me I could stay here until I'd calmed myself. I'm feeling calm already, sorting out my shopping, rearranging bags.

'The ties are yours, John-Paul,' I say. 'And this book of Sanskrit love poetry, and the ones on modern art. And please do take the food – share it with Beata. I chose some quite exotic things, so you can have a proper love-feast. No, don't refuse – I'd like you to, and anyway, I shan't be eating myself, not now, not any more. All I need is just these soaps and cleaners. I know my clothes are white, John-Paul, but underneath I'm dirty, really filthy black. Which is why you didn't want me in your room. It's okay, I understand. I don't blame you at all. Stay there with Beata. She's clean and very good; Daddy's little good girl. Hold her really close to you, dry her pretty eyes.'

My own eyes are dry, and dirty, as I push the heavy door, pick up just one carrier, step out into brilliant mocking sunshine.

# 24

'Mary? Are you all right? What's happened? Why didn't you ring for an electrician if the lights fused?'

'They . . . didn't.'

'What are you doing groping in the dark, then?'

'I thought candles would be more romantic, darling.'

'Romantic! For Christ's sake, put the lights on and pour me a stiff Scotch. I've had the devil of a day and a bloody awful journey home on top of it – a signals failure at Wimbledon, or so the moron said who calls himself a guard. More likely a go-slow. They never do a stroke of work, those layabouts. Down, Horatio!' James pushed the dog away, fumbled for the light-switch in the hall.

Mary blinked in the harsh glare, pressed herself against him, one naked leg seeking out his trousered one. James removed the leg, and then his coat and scarf.

'Mary, what's got into you? You'll catch your death wandering round half-undressed when they've just forecast a sharp frost. What *is* that thing you're wearing?'

Mary nuzzled his right shoulder, tried out the sexy throaty voice she'd been practising all day. 'It's a playsuit, darling.'

'Playsuit? I thought Tuesday was your Old Folks' Day.'

She nodded.

'So did they have a fancy dress or something?'

'No, bingo.'

'Two fat ladies – eighty-eight.'

'James, I'm *not* fat.'

'Well, you look it in that romper thing. It's made for someone Jon's age, judging by its length. Go and put a

294

sweater on. You sound as if you've caught a cold already. Your throat's quite hoarse, you realise.'

Mary trailed into the kitchen. It wasn't going right at all. According to the books, James was meant to respond to her with passion and abandon, fling off all his own clothes, not suggest she put hers on. She draped the kitchen towel around her shoulders. It *was* a little chilly. She'd built up such a fug at first she feared James would get a headache, so she'd opened all the windows, gone too far the other way. Typical of her these days. Her moods were like a roller-coaster. John-Paul seemed delighted, said she was more in touch with parts of herself often inaccessible – the raging infant, fractious child, rebellious adolescent. But she must forget all that tonight. This evening she was not John-Paul's, but James's – his floozie and his sex kitten, his Playgirl of the Month.

She went to open the champagne. You were meant to do it with your 'partner' (which sounded more exciting than mere husband); snuggled close and naked on the kitchen table or bathroom floor, or under the grand piano on an exotic tigerskin rug, or among the phallic orchids in the greenhouse. They had only an old upright, and no greenhouse at all, so she'd settled for the kitchen, but her 'partner' should be with her all the same. The exploding cork, the foaming whoosh of bubbles were a foretaste of the man's ejaculation – or so one book explained – helped build up the erotic tension, set the mood of intimacy, excitement. She could hear James in the hall still, banging things about, shouting at Horatio, grousing to himself (or her?) that the idiot roof-repair man had never returned about the leak. She removed the kitchen towel, shimmied out to join him.

'I'm sorry, darling, I'll ring him in the morning. But let's not think of roofs now.' (She had dreamt about their leaky roof just a week ago, and John-Paul had interpreted it as fear about conceiving – the roof symbolising a condom

295

which was intended as a barrier against the rain – or sperm; meant to keep the wet out. It didn't sound convincing. James had never used a condom in his life, and, secretly, she *wanted* to conceive.) She pressed a brimming glass into her husband's restless hands, its golden bubbles sparkling in the light. She had glazed the rim with egg-white, frosted it with sugar.

'What's this? Champagne? I can't touch the stuff – not now. I've got frightful indigestion, so the last thing I want is any more damned bubbles exploding in my gut.'

'Oh, *James*.'

'What d'you mean "Oh, James"? What *is* all this, for God's sake?' He grimaced at himself in the mirror on the wall, arranged a strand of limp grey hair across his thinning patch. Mary steered him into the sitting room, which she had prepared with scented candles, piles of scatter cushions, bowls of exotic fruit. She tugged his favourite chair back into its place, patted it encouragingly. She couldn't see him perching on a cushion, or stretched out on the carpet. The husbands in the sex-books were a different breed entirely, followed droolingly and slavishly if their naked-breasted 'partners' suggested bathing in champagne. James refused even to drink his, had totally ignored the fact her nipples were on show. He was making for the sideboard, poured himself a triple Glenmorangie, the soda syphon hissing his annoyance. She followed, dared an arm around his waist.

'Don't you know what day it is?'

'Yes, I do – settlement day. I'm not likely to forget it, Mary. It's been chaos in the office from eight o'clock this morning till I dragged myself away, half-dead. Apart from having to square all the accounts, I've had three really bloody meetings and . . .'

'It's our wedding anniversary.'

James collapsed back in his chair, started counting on his fingers. 'Christ! You're right – the eleventh of December.

Forgive me, darling. It completely slipped my mind. I'm sorry, Mary, really. I've been sounding off, and it's hardly your fault, is it? I'm just absolutely knackered. I had a rotten night last night, worrying about the accounts, and by the time I've sweated twelve hours in the hot seat, I'm more or less at screaming pitch. Look, let's go out to dinner. If I phone Pierre's immediately, we'll probably get a table. Or we could try that little Greek place in . . .'

Mary squeezed his hand. 'I've . . . er . . . bought food, actually. If you come into the kitchen, darling, everything's laid out.'

'Let's not slum it in the kitchen, Mary. What's wrong with the dining-room?'

'It's cold.'

'Well, light the fire – and can't you get your clothes on? You're making me feel cold as well, displaying all that flesh. Okay, I'll come, I'll come.'

Mary watched the whisky spill as James jerked up from his seat. He'd apologised for shouting, yet was cross again a scant two seconds later. He was drinking far too much these days, splurging money on twelve-year-old malt whiskies, then worrying about the bills. The bills *were* huge – she knew that – not just three sets of school fees, but now John-Paul as well. She longed to make it up to him, get closer in all ways, break down that shell of worry and bad temper which had crusted over the softer more romantic James she'd known once, long ago. Perhaps things would be better once he'd had a bite to eat. What he described as indigestion was often only hunger-pains, or tension. She led the way into the kitchen, her husband stumbling after her, tripping on the dog's bowl as he entered the dim room.

'More candles? Has Father Fox been turning out his stocks? Sorry, darling, just my little joke. It *is* a bit depressing, though, sitting in this gloom. Reminds me

297

of the power-cuts we had two years ago. And what's the funny smell?'

'Incense.'

'So you *have* been round to Father Fox. It feels like church in here. It's taking things a bit damn far to re-create the wedding service. Can't we settle for a simple anniversary?'

'Kiss me, James.'

The kiss was disappointing. She'd been learning how to kiss – at least the theory of it – the eyelash kiss, the tongue-bath, the kiss *à la cannibale*, which the books said left a bruise, and something called *maraichignage* which was definitely advanced. All she needed was some practice, not that brief peck on the cheek.

'There! Now, when do I get my supper? My stomach's sort of grinding on itself. I missed out on lunch completely. That wretched Crawshaw turned up at half past ten and was still jawing four hours later – and on settlement day of all days, would you believe? I had another meeting at two-thirty, so there wasn't even time for a sandwich.'

James was groping in the gloom to find a kitchen stool. Mary set a second one beside his. (Cushions were obviously advanced, like *maraichignage*, would have to wait till later.) It *was* extremely dim. Half the candles had gone out when she'd opened all the windows, and she'd forgotten to relight them. The food had been another problem – where to lay it out. The table was strictly out of bounds, transformed into a love-nest, and anyway, Horatio could reach it. The dog could reach most surfaces, so she'd arranged it on two trays and placed them high up on the freezer. She went to get them down again, Horatio in hot pursuit, sniffing rudely at her groin, as well as just the food. James was still complaining about his lack of lunchtime sustenance.

'Couldn't you have asked your secretary to send you up a snack?'

'I could, if she'd been there. She's off with what she calls a "virus" – which probably means a hangover.'

'Or oysters?' Mary crouched by James's stool, one naked arm reaching back behind her to the tray.

'*Oysters?*'

'Yes. Open your mouth.'

James opened it, half-swallowed, choked the oyster back again, plugged the void with whisky. 'I'm sorry, Mary, but if there's one thing I can't face, and especially not tonight, it's oysters. The last time I had oysters was at that damn-fool pricey restaurant the Crawshaws took us to, and I went down with salmonella. You can't have forgotten, surely? I was ill for two whole weeks.'

'No, I . . .' Mary's voice was faltering. Of course she hadn't forgotten. She'd bought the tinned ones specially, as far less of a health risk, and also easier to serve. James was an impatient man, hated anything in shells, or with fiddly bones or skins, or even things like artichokes or grapefruit, which required a lot of effort for rather mean returns. At least four different sex-books had recommended oysters. They were not only aphrodisiac, but apparently symbolic of the womb, represented the creative force of female sexuality. Yet James had spat his out, flung it to the dog. Even Horatio had spurned it, just sniffed and walked away. But then Horatio was replete with Beef and Rabbit Chum, whereas James was clearly ravenous. Yet all the books had warned against a heavy meal, or even a conventional one. 'Feed your lover titbits from your hand, or even mouth. Slice and peel a passion fruit, pass it from your lips to his.' The passion fruit was ready in the fridge, dipped in wine, and chilling, to provide a double thrill. It was James himself who clearly wasn't ready – or only for his normal solid supper.

'Look, if you don't feel up to cooking, Mary, I'll scramble us some eggs, but I'll have to have some light. It's like the Black Hole of Calcutta.' James plunged towards the light-switch, gazed around the kitchen, now lit by ruthless strip lights. A tiger-print travel rug was draped across the lilo they'd bought in Tenerife, and laid between the cooker and the fridge. The saucepan rack had disappeared – in its place a vase of scarlet ostrich feathers and an ornate incense-burner. 'What *have* you done in here, Mary? How can I cook eggs when I can't even find a saucepan? And where's the toaster gone?' He swung round the other way, stared in disbelief. 'What in God's name is our bedding doing on the kitchen table? Has that leak got worse upstairs?' He blew out the last candles, snuffed the incense wick, returned the kettle to its socket on the work-top. 'Mary, we're going out – *now*. I'll phone and book a table while you go and put your clothes on.'

'The steak for you, Mary?'

'No, I think I'll have the scallops.'

'But you're having prawns to start with.'

'Yes, I know.' Mary shook her napkin out, sipped her sparkling wine. She couldn't seem to move away from shellfish. They symbolised fertility, the life-force, and scallops in particular were a sign of sexual passion, the two half-shells bonded close like lovers. She doubted they'd get round to love tonight. James still seemed tense and harassed, still fixated on the crises at his firm. When he'd come upstairs to change his shirt, she'd tried to hold him close, say she understood, whisper to him teasingly that if only he'd allow her, she could distract him from his problems, help him to relax. He'd seemed actually embarrassed, had backed away, suspicious, even hostile. Men were so perverse. All her married life he'd complained that she was tepid. Yet now she was on heat, his own flame had blown right out, as if he somehow needed her reluctance to fuel him, turn him on. It seemed totally irrational him spending all that money on her sessions with John-Paul, so she'd respond to him with passion, yet once he got

300

that passion, rushing to defuse it. He'd left her in the bedroom as if she were dangerous high-explosive, sought refuge in his study. She had changed, alone and mortified, into boring woolly tights, a high-necked 'wifely' dress, and they'd driven to Pierre's in silence, both of them resentful that they were going out at all.

She loved the restaurant normally – its soft pink lights, pink napkins, the grave and formal waiters who made dinner like a sacrament, the mingled heady smells of garlic, sizzling butter and cigars. But tonight she felt restless and on edge, slighted, almost cheated, found it hard to concentrate on James's monologue.

'Well, I agreed to use their new integrated software package for all our commission accounts, though I must admit I had my doubts, right from the beginning. And I was absolutely right, Mary. They've buggered up the printers, and all our invoices are coming out as statements.'

'Gosh! How awful, James.' Mary tried to keep her mind on integrated software, but it had somehow moved to Bryan. She had still not quite recovered from Saturday's débâcle. It had been the feast of the Immaculate Conception and she'd gone to Mass that morning, begged Our Lady's help for him, tried explaining to the Blessed Virgin that she was giving up her church work for the more vital task of providing tea and sympathy for AIDS victims. In the middle of her prayers, she had found herself thinking of what Bryan did in bed – yes, with other men – all the shameful 3-D details while she was actually kneeling in St Anthony's about to listen to a sermon on virginity and sinlessness.

Then, later on, when he turned up at her house all sluiced and starched and scrubbed, yet still looking rather vulgar in a cheapo chainstore suit and see-through nylon shirt which James would have given to a jumble sale, she'd imagined him stark naked – heaving on the floor with another man, his 'partner' – a shadowy figure, with the body of Frank

Bruno and the face of her own precious Jon. She'd been so appalled, her normal conversation had totally dried up and she'd sat there mouthing platitudes, while poor Bryan himself seemed equally self-conscious, the pair of them tongue-tied with embarrassment. She had tried to pray, right there in the sitting-room, plead for instant help, but how could she beg succour from the Immaculate Heart of Mary when her own mind was like a sewer?

James was attacking his bread roll, tearing at the fragments as if they were his enemies at work. 'And then we had more trouble with Morton Cardigan. They can't agree the balances, and they're blaming *me*, of course.'

'James, your soup is getting cold, dear.'

James stared down at his bowl, jabbed it with his spoon, removed the parsley garnish to the safety of his side-plate.

Mary smiled encouragement. 'It looks lovely, doesn't it?'

'What's that white stuff on the top?'

'Just a swirl of cream.'

'I'm not meant to look at cream – not with my cholesterol levels.'

'Just once won't hurt you, darling. It *is* our anniversary.' Mary bit into a prawn, imagined it a penis, a tiny tiny penis – the sort you chose to learn things on, advanced skills like fellatio which still frightened her to death. That's what homosexuals did – she'd read it in the books – did with little boys. The minute Bryan walked in he'd been gawping at her sons, lustful eyes tracking to their photographs, lingering on their young and naked flesh. Pity and revulsion wrestled in her breast. His AIDS must be quite frighteningly advanced, what with the dizzy spells and the fact he couldn't eat at first, then couldn't seem to stop, and him begging her to save his life and letting out that frightful scream when the pain got too intense, and finally rushing off into the night because she'd mentioned

302

John-Paul's name. John or Paul must be his lover's name, the one who had infected him, repaid his love with death. Or maybe even both of them. If Bryan were the promiscuous type, he might have a John as well as Paul. Both were common names (except when they were hyphened, which made them rare and special).

'I tried to get a temp from personnel. At three p.m. some bloody useless girl shows up who doesn't know our system from a wheelbarrow. *And* she smoked, made all the . . .'

Mary glanced up at the handsome man sitting on her right. He was smoking, too, drawing on his cigarette very deeply and intensely, the way John-Paul often did. The tables in the restaurant were crammed so close together she could smell his aftershave, see the dark haze of almost-stubble shadowing his chin. He was the foreign-looking type with a tough and virile beard, unlike James, whose facial hair appeared to be dwindling with his scalp hair, as if both had lost their youthful thrust and vigour.

'Oh, *yes*,' the man said softly, smiling at his girlfriend – a fat and rather vulgar blonde, whose daring yard of cleavage displayed a rhinestone pendant which spelt 'Love'. She was doing all the talking, he answering with yeses, but such assured and ardent yeses, they seemed far more than monosyllables, seemed charged with passion, import. Mary dragged her eyes away, returned her mind to James.

'Some wine for you now, darling?'

'No, thanks. I'll stick with whisky.'

'What, with soup?'

'I don't like the soup. It's fishy.'

'It's watercress and leek, James. It said so on the menu, underneath the French.'

'Well, either their translator's duff, or their chef doesn't know a dogfish from a leek.'

'Dogfish?' Mary had a sudden startling vision of Horatio with fins. Strange the dog had fawned on Bryan like that.

Could dogs be gay as well? 'Would you like some prawns instead, dear? There's more than I can eat here.'

'Yes, *please.*'

Mary jumped. The man next door had spoken, but to his companion, not to her. She glanced at him again, drawn by his resemblance to John-Paul – not just the darkly foreign looks and the sensual way he smoked, but the same dramatic bone structure, and long-lashed deep-set eyes. He was younger than John-Paul, in fact, with a thicker broader body, but that was mostly hidden by the table. 'Yes,' he said. 'Yes, yes.' The yeses were staccato now, emphatic, almost solemn, the voice itself powerful but low-keyed. He suddenly turned his head towards her, distracted by her scrutiny, caught her eye and held it. She feared he was annoyed. She'd been rudely staring, eavesdropping, deserved to be reproved. Instead, he smiled – a lazy and indulgent smile, which started with his mouth and spread up to his eyes, eyes which narrowed slightly, challenging and teasing, daring her to meet his gaze, not falter, look away.

He looked away himself, at last, turned back to his pudding with a self-deprecating shrug. She took refuge in her wine. She had drunk too much already, but she found this man disturbing – the way he courted his *crème brûlée*, piercing through the brittle crust of sugar on the top, then toying, almost playing with the cream. Would John-Paul eat like that, with such teasing sensuous zest? She knew he liked his food (despite the rebuff of the mince pies), had once watched him eat a tiny square of fudge, astonished by the fervour with which he bit into the cube, devouring it with relish and solemnity, as if it were the Host. She presumed he'd only turned to sweets to cut down on his smoking, provide him with some substitute (as James had done himself, chomping on mint humbugs while still craving nicotine). But all the same, it had seemed extraordinarily intimate, him eating right in front of her, as if he had allowed her to participate in some private, almost dangerous ritual, withheld from other patients. She had found herself licking her own lips, tasting sweetness on her tongue, sucking out stray flecks of fudge from the secret slavering crannies of her mouth.

She shifted both her body and the angle of her chair, so that the man was less distractingly in view. 'So what did Crawshaw finally decide, then?' she asked James dutifully, tried to listen to his answer, and not the seductive 'yes' throbbing from her right. She took another gulp of wine, felt strangely hot and tingling, as if all the chafing-dishes in the restaurant had been lit beneath her body, their gases turned up high. The room was trembling slightly, its colours smudged and running, the crimson velvet curtains blushing into tablecloths, the still-lifes on the crowded walls not still at all, but bulging from their frames.

'Yes,' the man laughed. 'You bet!' She just had to move her chair back, watch him touch the woman's cheek, his slim artistic fingers haloed with gold nicotine. She drained her glass, could feel those burning fingers on her own cheek, hear the fervent yeses in her ear. They weren't wasted on that prattling freckled fatty, but addressed to *her* – in bed – wearing nothing but her perfume and diamonds in both nipples, and whispered by John-Paul himself, also wildly naked. 'Yes,' he said, impassionedly, as he traced the diamonds' carats with his tongue. *He* hadn't spurned her oysters and champagne, had been enchanted by the candles, enraptured by her playsuit, had gladly snuggled down with her on the transformed kitchen table, lips meeting vibrant lips . . .

'I finally lost patience, Mary, marched up to R.B. and said, "Roland, either you change that cretin of a programmer, or I'll go up there myself and throttle him bare-handed." And d'you know what Roland said . . .?'

'Yes,' she breathed, John-Paul breathed. She stuffed a prawn whole into her mouth, practising her tongue-bath, allowing her own tongue to lick and lap the tepid trembling mollusc, turn it into John-Paul's tongue, make it move and writhe. She licked her lips, scooped a swirl of sauce from his mouth into hers. 'Yes,' he kept on saying, approvingly, insistently, as she sucked the three last naked prawns slowly in and down.

'Mary, I thought you said you had more than you could eat there? If you don't stop soon, you'll be scraping the pattern off the plate.'

She blushed, glanced up at James, surprised to see blue eyes and greying hair, though neither was in focus, quite. 'Sorry, darling. I *am* feeling rather hungry.'

'Well, if you'd only put your fork down, they might bring us our main course. We've been here a whole hour now and I'm still waiting for my steak. I need something safe and solid they can't ruin.'

She leant back in her chair while the waiters fussed with plates, brought steak and scallops, vegetables and salads, three mustards and the pepper mill, a different wine, fresh glasses. At last, they were alone again – John-Paul and her alone – relaxing on the silvered grass just beyond the greenhouse. They were so close now they were two scallops in a shell, face to face, chest to chest, thigh to . . .

'Would you believe it, Mary, this steak tastes fishy, too. And they've hardly even cooked it. I said rare, not raw and cold. The place is really going downhill. Give any restaurant a Michelin star and it just lies down and dies.'

She was lying down herself, her body open, naked, the whole sky wild with Michelin stars, the moon a golden scallop-shell, smiling in the darkness – Aphrodite's emblem, or so all the books had said. '*Yes*,' John-Paul agreed, in his thrilling potent voice. 'Aphrodite, goddess of love.' 'Yes,' he said again, as she forked in her first mouthful, eager tongue exploring the pink folds. The taste was strange, exciting, the texture soft yet firm. She crammed in several more, almost retching as her throat was stretched.

'Mary, *really*! What's got into you? You're eating like a pig.'

She hardly heard her husband, filled her mouth still more, let the juices dribble down her throat, allowed her lips to squeeze and suck, then used her teeth, gently, very gently – remembered what she'd read.

'*Yes!*' A near-crescendo as the white sauce hit her taste buds, an unusual and exotic taste, slightly salty, even brackish. Mustn't spit it out – all the books agreed on that. She swallowed, wiped her mouth, eyes half-closed to savour it, relish the last drop.

'More!' she clamoured, glancing up, reaching for the vegetables, the tiny heads of sweetcorn, the mangetout, cooked *al dente*.

'*More?*' James laid his own fork down, swilled out his mouth with whisky. 'You can't still be hungry, surely?'

'Yes,' she thrilled. 'Oh, yes.'

# 25

I was born again yesterday, at lunch-time. The birth was very easy. I just slipped from John-Paul's uterus into the womb of his consulting-room, felt very little difference – the same dark warmth, the same safe and rounded walls, the same rhythmic tick-tick of his heartbeat. I think he named me Lazarus. 'For this my son was dead, and is alive.'

I was dead three days, in fact; three dark days when he was lying with Beata. Then he summoned me to life again, gave me new appointments – not two-ten, but lunch-time. Lunch-time's very special, the only hour he's free from seven in the morning to ten o'clock at night; the only hour he doesn't see his patients. It's his time for food and resting, his one and only chance to phone family or friends. Yet he's given all that up, made me his own family, given me his breathing-space, his Sabbath. He said it was just temporary, a way out of a crisis until he could arrange some different sessions, but maybe he'll continue it, perhaps even come to need me. He also said he had to go away, talked about some Christmas break, a month he'd be in Rome. He must have meant next year. He wouldn't leave his new-born son, not so soon, so cruelly.

The lunch-times were a present, like the love-feast. Yes, he killed the fatted calf for me, did it very quietly without knives or blood or fuss. He didn't overwhelm me with recriminations, questions, didn't even mention my docked hair – just understood I had to be a son. I felt loved and very honoured. No one else was fêted – the ring eased on their finger, the silk robe round their body, the seat of honour reclining on the couch. The elder son was griping that it simply wasn't just; he'd never shirked his duty or wasted money on loose living, yet no one killed the fatted calf for *him*. His voice was deep and throaty like Beata's, but John-Paul took no notice, had ears for me alone.

He's listening now, with that careful rapt attention which makes my every word seem precious – even all my silent words, or just my sighs and shiftings. I prefer to lie in silence, need all my concentration to focus on his name. Everyone and everything is thrumming it, repeating it – pipes beneath the pavements, dark and secret sewers, twanging power-lines, live electric cables. Police cars blare it as they siren past the tower; distant jet-planes throb it as they arc above the clouds, writing it in vapour-trails across the churning sky. Whole oceans thrash and pound it as they slam in on the strand. Lions roar it across Africa, and it catches fire immediately, scorches half the continent. It's engraved into the hard face of the moon.

'John-Paul?' I say myself.

'Yes, Nial?'

I settle back, say nothing, don't need to talk at all. It's enough to know he's there and real and listening. I like the tiny noises from his body, which prove he's still alive – a rumble from his stomach, the slow sucking of a sweet. I wish I were a sweet myself, so he could suck me very slowly. Or a ship, so he would put me in his bottle. Or his half-a-boat, so he would lie down on my deck. I cut out every John and Paul I could find in all the magazines and newspapers, joined them all with hyphens, hung them over road-signs, stuck them on to street-names. Every road now leads to him, every house contains him. He's living in my basement, and in all the rooms above it, one to five.

I couldn't eat the fatted calf. My stomach wasn't right, wasn't quite developed. I was still inside his womb, still feeding from his blood-supply, still waiting to be born – born a proper son. I felt very safe and snug, floating in warm fluid, continually tugged back to him by the umbilical cord, the steady clock-beat of his heart ticking very rhythmically, recording my nine months.

The clocks are ticking now. I don't mind them any more, don't object to anything, now he's made me special, now he's had me back. I listen to him swallow the last sliver of his sweet, know he's going to speak. I can nearly always tell. He sometimes moves his chair a fraction, or breathes just slightly differently.

'Nial,' he says, in his patient kindly mother's voice. 'It's five minutes to time now. I've written down those dates for you, so you can put them in your diary and be absolutely clear about the time I'll be away.'

I close my ears immediately. He tried explaining earlier, but I didn't hear then, either; just untethered my tired mind and let it graze in another field entirely. He wouldn't go away, never takes a holiday, has nothing in his life beyond his patients – not even lunch hours now. He can't eat lunch, or sleep; just hasn't got the time. I don't eat or sleep myself; want to be the same as him – male like him, and thin like him; very quiet and calm like him.

He tries to say goodbye, wish me happy Christmas, but I don't say either back. It's not Christmas – it's still spring – and anyway he's not meant to say goodbye. No greetings or 'How are you?'s, no hallo, goodbye. That's the way they heal you, saying almost nothing. I think I'm almost healed now.

I ease up from the couch, and he gets up as well, hands me a small sheet of stiff white paper. I glance at it perfunctorily, thrust it in my pocket, then as soon as I'm downstairs and through the door I screw it up to nothing, toss it in the gutter. All the same, it makes me feel uneasy, slows me to a crawl. I don't think I'll go home. It's safer to stay close to him, so he can't slip away or vanish when he thinks I'm off my guard. I lost Seton by not watching; lost John-Paul himself; have only just recovered from those winter weeks without him.

It worked all right last night. I camped out near the tower, to make sure he couldn't leave, and when I pressed the buzzer at exactly ten past one, he was still safely in his room, answered me immediately. I tried to sleep in the College of Technology, but they shooed me out at ten. I was quite upset at first, but then I found another niche, still closer to the tower; felt less lonely sleeping in the open than caged up in my bed-sit.

I cross the wide and busy road which leads down to the river. It's not time to think of sleeping – still broad sunny daylight, another perfect day – air crisp, sky nervy blue, bandages of sunlight soothing raw grey stone. The plane trees are twice dappled, once by nature, once by sun and shadow. My own shadow blends with theirs, so I become half a tree, a bare tree, but with leaves and spring throbbing in my finger-twigs. The water's also throbbing, restless, never still – quivering and rippling, as reflections of reflections drown themselves, resurface. River Lazarus.

I find a bench and dream there. I forgot to bring my coat or scarf, but I'm not uncomfortable at all, hardly feel the cold; even when the hours slip by and the sun sinks slowly down. It lacquers the whole sky, stains me gold inside. My thoughts are on John-Paul still, rarely leave him now. I try to write him poems in my head, but they all seem very thin – just bony ribs and skeletons. I toss them in the water and two mallards lunge and flurry, imagining they're bread. Everything seems hungry – poems, ducks, the river – everything save me. For me it's always lunch-time, and I'm always feeding, feeding – feeding off John-Paul. I wonder if he's lonely without a wife, or dogs; imagine him beside me, the bright points of our cigarettes weaving their own language in the air. The light is dimming, fading, the gold darkening into red, the wounded sky bleeding into swirling scarlet water.

A police launch cuts the red with black, skimming down

the river. The policeman-skipper smiles at me, and waves. He must have seen my own smile, know how well I'm feeling. I watch him dwindle into dusk, listen to the silence. Police mean blaring sirens, and there wasn't any siren.

No sirens means I'm healed.

# 26

'Mother?'

'Yes, Bryan.'

'I've . . . er . . . got a little surprise for you.'

'Surprise? Well, I hope it's not flowers again. The last ones dropped all over the place and I'm sure they over-charged you for all that fancy fern. We've got better in the garden.'

Bryan said nothing. There was little in their garden except gloomy laurel bushes and a small square of mangy grass which had never earned the distinction of being called a lawn.

'Chocolates, is it, Bryan? I'm not keen on those great nutty ones you bought for me last month. They kept sticking to my teeth.'

'No, Mother, it's not chocolates.'

'Anything to eat?'

'No.'

'I try to cook you decent meals. If you're complaining that you're hungry, I'd say you've got a tapeworm. It's not natural being hungry when you've just wolfed down shepherd's pie and semolina – and all made with milk.'

'I'm not hungry, Mother. I didn't even mention food.'

'You did. You said you . . .'

'I didn't, Mother. All I . . .'

'Are you lying to me, Bryan, again?'

'No, Mother.'

'Good boy. Now turn up the television. I've missed at least five minutes, and that insolent little hussy was just telling her poor mother she was in the family way – at fifteen and a half. I know what I'd do if . . .'

Bryan fiddled with the volume knob, then sagged back in his chair. He'd been trying all weekend to break his news. Saturday had vanished in a drag and clog of shopping, jostling in the sleety rain from a tinsel-wreathed Co-op to a crowded glaring Woolworth's, buying Christmas goodies in a mood of distinctly unChristian hostility and spleen. He had loathed his fellow shoppers who impaled him on their Christmas trees or gloated over their expensive loot from hi-fi shops or male boutiques. Why couldn't *he* buy Italian silk striped smoking jackets, or liquid-cooled speaker systems, instead of deodorised foam insoles, sugar-free baked beans, and three cut-price pork pies which were past their 'sell-by' date?

They'd eaten the pork pies later on that evening, with Branston's pickled beetroot, which had made him think of car crashes as he forked in blood-stained pastry, gobbets of raw flesh. He'd tried again to broach the vital subject, but his Mother was entrenched in *The Two Ronnies* and refused to let him speak. She professed never to watch television, complained about it constantly – the vulgarity, the violence – yet never had it off. It made reading very difficult. He sometimes found dramatic lines from *Neighbours* or *EastEnders* were clashing with his close-packed prose on chaology or superspace, resulting in more chaos and a sense of constant crises, since neither matter nor the universe nor the players in the soaps seemed to know what they were doing, nor have any great control over their fate or their existence.

A night had passed, a day had passed, and they were still staring at the screen; the words he'd practised all week long, unspoken, rusting up. He watched dispassionately as the sobbing pregnant schoolgirl downed half a pint of gin, quickly got a word in as she disappeared to run a scalding bath. 'Don't you want to hear about the surprise?'

'What surprise?'

'Look, may I turn this off, Mother? I need to . . . talk to you.'

'What d'you mean, "talk to me"? We've been talking all the evening. Which is why I'm in the dark about the father of that baby. Do *you* know who he is?'

'No.'

'It's probably her teacher. I disliked him from the start. They let anybody teach these days – perverts, social-ists . . .'

'Mother, this is *urgent*.'

'Bryan, I've never known you like this. What's got into you?' Lena dropped her knitting suddenly, stared at him in horror. 'You're not trying to tell me you've got a girl into trouble?'

He blushed, saw Mary in his head again, her stomach swelling with their child, her breasts engorged with milk. '*No!*' he almost shouted, hands gripping both the chair-arms as he forced the fateful sentence out before it mouldered and turned rancid, poisoned him inside. 'Mother, I've . . . I've booked us on a holiday.'

'A holiday – what for?'

He hesitated, lost for words. He couldn't think what holidays were for. It was so long since he'd had one.

'Well, I hope it isn't Margate. It's a very common place is Margate. It had class before the war, but now they've . . .'

'No, it's Rome.'

'*Rome?*'

He nodded, a surge of wild elation flooding his whole being. He'd not only got the word out, he'd booked a glorious fortnight there, paid for it in full, had the blessed confirmation smiling in his wallet. Fourteen days with Mary among the ancient ruins, the romantic sparkling fountains. There was still the minor problem of disposing of her husband, shaking off his Mother, but love would find a way. He had to rescue Mary – it was a duty, a necessity, to save her from that bestial James who cheapened and abused her with those disgusting sexual implements. All last week his mind had kept returning to Mary's home and bedroom, her sudden startling mention of John-Paul. Whatever could it mean, the fact she knew his doctor, and knew him well enough to recommend him? He'd agonised for hours about it, lost sleep, lost vital working time, upset his boss at work. Totally impossible to imagine her in therapy herself – a woman so serene, so calmly sanely normal. He'd finally concluded it was James who was the patient – James and his perversions – not just the vibrators, but other vile debaucheries he couldn't even think about without blind and jealous rage.

He glanced up at his Mother, whose own anger seemed diluted with amazement. Her knitting needles were frozen in mid-row, the screen abortion totally forgotten. 'But Rome's *abroad*,' she faltered.

'Yes.' He gloated to himself. He'd be getting his first passport, flying in his first jet plane, tasting foreign food – real Italian pasta, not Heinz spaghetti hoops.

'You know I hate abroad, Bryan.'

'You've never been abroad.'

'Well, I wouldn't want to, would I? Rome's a very dangerous country. It's full of Communists. I saw it on the news.'

'It's full of Catholics, Mother.'

'They're just as bad. I've never trusted Catholics, not since Bridget O'Riley used to underweigh the bacon.'

Bryan bit his lip, subsided in his chair. How could he explain that they were going on a pilgrimage in the company of at least two hundred Catholics, the fervent and committed kind, with a six o'clock alarm call for Holy Mass each morning, their own Spiritual Director, and a ticket to some shindig which involved a brand-new English saint? It was the only way they could get to Rome at all. He'd left it far too late. Every other package-tour was completely full by now, and to fly out independently and book his own hotel would be prohibitively expensive. The pilgrimage had worked out very cheap, in fact, but only because they'd be sleeping in a dormitory in a disused Roman seminary which the brochure described as 'quaint'. All the brochure's language was alarming. Homely, modest, simple, unpretentious, were all alternative words for poor and bare, and 'friendly' probably meant they were squashed so close together in the dormitory, it would be impossible not to strike up an acquaintance – or even come to blows.

He had dithered hours and hours before he finally made the booking, had rung a score of other agents, even other pilgrimages, but the reply was always 'Sorry, Sir, nothing left at all. You should have booked up in September.' How could he explain to them that he'd been someone else entirely in September, hadn't had a Mary in his life; would never have found the courage to stand up to his Mother, break the pattern of thirty-two past Christmases? Lena was still fretful, her steady drone of protest providing a soft descant to the shrill sobbing of the half-aborted teen. She had snatched her knitting up again, a mishmash of odd balls of wool, which grew longer every week, yet, like the universe itself, seemed to have no ultimate point or purpose, no consoling shape or pattern which could pin it down, define it with some name. The neat squares of his childhood had long since disappeared, as if to prove that life became increasingly chaotic as adulthood took over and each baffling year lurched by.

'Rome hasn't got a government, you realise – just the Mafia. And it's very old and dirty.'

'It's *ancient*, Mother. That's the reason people go there, to see the ancient ruins.'

'We've got ruins enough here. You should have seen London in the war. And anyway, coaches make me sick.'

317

'We're not going on a coach. We're flying.'

'Flying?'

'Yes.' He closed his eyes. It was the only way to go to Mary, soaring through the sky, leaping earthly obstacles, leaving jams and scrums behind.

'Bryan, do you *want* to camp for five days in an airport with nowhere to sit down and the toilets all bunged up?'

'That was just a strike, Mother. And Spain, not Italy. The Spanish air controllers had . . .'

'Spain? Rome? What's the difference? It's all abroad, isn't it? And you still get all the terrorists.'

'What terrorists?'

'At airports. You can hardly move for terrorists. And bombs on all the planes. I suppose you've forgotten Lockerbie, my lad.'

'No,' he said. 'I haven't.' He tried to fight the sudden stab of black and scarlet fear, replaced it with a golden thought of Mary. How could he be panicky when winging to his Love?

'Mrs Fenton in the paper-shop was stopped by those security men and had to unpack all her bags. She was terribly embarrassed. They were full of . . . well, I'd rather not say, not in male company. And then they did a body-search – the cheek! Well, no one's going to search *my* body, terrorists or no.'

Bryan glanced at Lena's body, which went neither in nor out at chest or waist or hip, but continued in one bony line from narrow scrawny shoulder to swollen veiny leg. It was shrouded in grey Crimplene, a life-denying shade, which reminded him of ashes or mouldy pigeon droppings. Her slippers, fawn, with fake-fur trim, had been purchased via mail order and tended to slip off, so that he could always hear her coming – nag and flap, nag and flap.

He turned back to the screen, watched the credits rolling, the sun-kissed suave commercials for other people's holi-days, other people's mothers; always sugar-coated, always silver-lined. The next programme was a game-show, its ageing host, Les Dunkley (saved by toupee and fake tan), already cracking his first joke.

'I tried Lady Grecian on my hair. The grey's still there, but my dandruff all went black.'

Hurricanes of laughter, hailstorms of applause. Bryan scanned the cache of prizes dazzling into view – a microwave, a video recorder, a portable TV, a bulging Christmas hamper complete with turkey, Christmas pudding, and what Les called 'all the trimmings'. He tried a different tack with Lena, as a jar of cranberry sauce loomed into crimson close-up.

'I thought you'd like the change, Mother. You always say how tired you are of cooking Christmas dinner. Well, this year someone else can cook it and you can put your feet up.'

'Bryan!' Lena cheetahed from her seat, knitting lashing like a tail. 'You're not telling me we'll be away for . . . for Christmas?'

'Yes, Mother.'

'But that's impossible.'

'Impossible?'

'We're always home at Christmas.'

'That's why you need a change, Mother.'

'Don't tell me what I need, boy. You don't imagine foreigners can cook a Christmas dinner?'

'Yes, they can. It said so in the brochure. "A traditional Christmas dinner with turkey and mince pies." ' He didn't add that the seminary had no restaurant of its own, so they were being 'bused' for all their meals to a small 'family-run' hotel, where they would have to eat in several different sittings, due to the smallness of the premises. He prayed they'd get first sitting in the evenings. The latest one was past his Mother's bedtime.

'But I've already bought the mincemeat, *and* the brandy

butter. In fact, I've stocked up for a month, at least. You saw the bill at Tesco's.'

'It'll keep.'

'Keep? You think a turkey keeps? Or Brussels sprouts?'

'But you haven't bought the turkey, Mother, or the . . .'

'I've ordered it, haven't I, went to all that trouble asking for a fresh one, just for Mr Fusspot here. Frozen would have done for me – *and* half the price, I'll have you know. And d'you think I'd spend those hours and hours stirring Christmas puddings till my arm was dropping off, just to feed my own face?'

'You only made the one, Mother.'

'So one pudding's not enough now. You want half a dozen, do you?'

'We can take it *with* us, Mother. And the brandy butter, eat them in our room.'

'And encourage rats? Or cockroaches?' Lena subsided in her chair, rubbed her swollen fingers. Bryan looked the other way. His own hands always itched and throbbed if he watched her scratch her chilblains. He'd never seen chilblains on another single person in his life, let alone such bad ones. His Mother's circulation was obviously defective, her health poor generally. It wasn't just her leg, which was bad enough, for heaven's sake, with its constant dragging pain (and which was probably half the reason why she was so often tense and irritable), but all her other ailments. He felt a pang of conscience. The house was cold and damp, needed proper central heating, complete rewiring, a new effective damp-course. If he didn't have John-Paul's bills to pay, he could afford all the repairs, relieve his Mother's inflamed misshapen fingers, her bouts of sinusitis, her frequent chesty coughs. He buttoned up his jacket. He was feeling cold himself now, the feeble one-bar fire failing in its efforts to beat the frost and fog outside. The temperature was rising on the screen, though; Les cracking out his questions as two new contestants, all teeth and grins and glasses, giggled from their gold and purple stands.

'Can ducks sink?'

'No, Les.'

'Sorry, Babs, you're wrong. Ducks sink if they're moulting.' Les tugged his coal-black toupee. 'I'd better keep tight hold of this or I'll end up in the drink. Ready, Tony? Your turn now. When did car ignition keys first come into use?'

'Er . . . 1921.'

'No, they were still driving Roman chariots in 1921. The answer's 1949. It made wife-swapping parties much more civilised. It was murder throwing your starter-handle on the table.'

'And what d'you suppose you're going to use as money?'

Bryan jumped, swung back to Lena. 'Pardon?'

'Well, I don't expect it's cheap abroad, especially not at Christmas. How can we afford to go gadding off to Rome, when you told me just last month you'd had another pay cut?'

Bryan searched the screen for answers, longed to fold down like a camping spoon, to avoid this line of questioning. He'd spent four long years explaining to his Mother that there was never any money left for luxuries or extras. In fact, he was using all the cash he'd save on four weeks of John-Paul, but his Mother didn't know John-Paul existed. He was beginning to wish he didn't. That avaricious doctor had made everything far worse – four years of debt and lies. Even the lies themselves seemed every bit as difficult as they had been at the start, despite his constant daily practice over fifty-one long months. He still found it most distressing to have to kick the truth aside, blast it into bits, when he actually revered Truth, sought it in the universe. He fiddled with the cover on the chair-arm (placed there by his Mother to prevent his dirty – twice-washed – hands from fouling up the furniture); tried to sound ingenuous as he prepared his next deceit.

'Er . . . you know that chap at work, the one who stole my wallet?'

'Stole it *twice*, you mean.'

'Well, he's feeling very guilty now and he's offered us this holiday as a sort of restitution.'

'Tell him I'd rather have the cash, please. The cooker's playing up again and I doubt if it will last till . . .'

'He can't give us the cash, Mother. He's already spent the lot.'

'So how can he afford holidays in Rome?'

'He . . . he . . .' Bryan blew his nose, to gain himself some time. John-Paul had once remarked that the easiest and safest course was to aim to tell the truth. Just let his doctor try! Tell the truth to Lena and he'd land up in his bedroom with his bottom smacked and his pocket-money docked for half the year. He'd like to dock John-Paul's fees, lock him in his bedroom and never let him out. He didn't make things easy. He'd faced much the same hazards trying to tell his therapist that he'd booked a trip to Rome as he was experiencing with his Mother – had nowhere near succeeded after two relentless sessions. Every time he'd mentioned the word 'pilgrimage', John-Paul had tried to relate it to his therapy, made deep but futile comments about ungratified religious needs he was seeking to fulfil, no longer as a patient but a pilgrim. He'd also linked it to his so-called 'negative transference', suggesting that his patient was now reacting to him not just as hostile parent, but as inadequate spiritual mentor, who must be replaced by an Almighty Omnipotent Father. In the end, he'd just lain there saying nothing, trying to think up some diversion (or even kidnap-plan), which would dispose of James, John-Paul, his Mother, in one dramatic daring coup, freeing Rome for him and glorious Mary.

322

'*Well?*' his Mother urged.

'He . . . works for a travel agent.'

'So they employ common thieves now, do they? No wonder this country's in the state it is. Teachers fathering babies on their pupils, travel agents picking people's pockets. Well, tell him straight your Mother doesn't like abroad, and could he please arrange something nearer home. Bournemouth's nice in winter. I saw an advert in the *TV Times* for Christmas at the Seaview. They've got a conjuror on Christmas Eve and a Mystery Tour on Boxing Day. And if you want a proper English turkey instead of some scrawny foreign bird . . .'

'It's *booked*, Mother. We're not allowed to change it. Everything's arranged.'

'You've no right to arrange my Christmas, Bryan, without consulting me.'

'But I wanted it to be a surprise.'

'Well, you've got what you wanted, then. I *am* surprised – shocked, in fact – deeply shocked that my only son doesn't value Christmas in the comfort of his home, but has to drag his poor old Mother to a dirty dangerous country, then call it a surprise.'

'I'll . . . I'll go and make some tea, Mother.'

'You've *had* tea, Bryan – three cups. And that's another thing – you won't get tea in Rome. That woman in the ironmonger's went to France last year and she said they'd never *heard* of teapots. And then they expect us to join the Common Market.'

Bryan faltered in the doorway, eyes back on the screen, where Les was being fondled by a sixteen-stone pensioner in a purple lurex catsuit and lilac hair to match. The disembodied audience kept braying, whooping, shrieking, every time Les cracked a joke or a contestant got an answer right. Dramatic chords and fanfares screwed the tension tighter, the music near-hysterical when Anthea from Ipswich won a thirty-piece dinner service in a pattern called 'Argave'.

323

The revolving silver stairway and spangled turquoise back-drop made their own small sitting-room look shabby and low-key – the chairs fawn and hard and bony like his Mother, the drooping curtains skimpy and unlined.

'Bryan, while you're up, go and get the brochure, dear.'

'What brochure?'

'The brochure for the holiday. I'd like to have a look at it.'

'I . . . er . . . left it in the office.'

'Silly boy.'

Bryan glanced at her, surprised. She sounded almost affectionate, had even called him 'dear', was obviously relenting. Perhaps now she had recovered from the double shock of 'abroad' and no home turkey, she was touched her son had thought of her and was acting like the loving boy she always seemed to crave, booking her a holiday, so she'd be spared the usual chores. His guilt screwed up three notches. He *hadn't* thought of her . . . only of himself. She'd hate a crowded dormitory in some old and draughty seminary; would never cope with the Spanish Steps or the narrow cobbled alleyways of Rome, when her leg played up so cruelly even in their wide and level High Street. Whatever happened, she mustn't read the brochure – all those pious references to Mass and Benediction, and the 'cradle of our Roman Catholic Faith'; the daily expeditions to catacombs, basilicas, churches, churches, churches; the conducted tours of Christian Rome, the papal audience. He'd just have to go and check on it, hide it somewhere safer in his room.

'Just . . . popping to the bathroom, Mother.'

'Well, don't be long, and don't leave all the lights on, and be sure you . . .'

He bypassed the chill bathroom, sneaked into his own room, extracted the brochure from deep inside the mattress-cover, which meant dismantling half his bedding. He smoothed the blankets straight again, sat down on the bed, re-read the opening paragraphs which introduced the pilgrimages – not just to Rome, but to other Catholic centres. He liked the word 'pilgrim', the idea of suffering hardship, heat or cold or hunger, in travelling to an object of devotion – in his case holy Mary. The brochure mentioned Mary constantly – as Blessed Virgin, loving Mother, Queen of Angels, Queen of Peace, Comfort of the Afflicted, Gate of Heaven. Mary was all those things and more – his Virgin and his Mother, his own private grace and comfort, the source of future bliss.

He read on a bit further, admiring the two pictures of Mary with a gentle smile, Mary with superb though well-draped breasts. 'We have every confidence that you will return from your pilgrimage with a renewal of both faith and hope, and spiritually and physically refreshed. No one leaves Our Lady empty-handed. Mary's precious gifts include the gift of healing, the gift of strength, the gift of perfect love.'

Perfect love. Bryan prayed it would be his – and strength, as well – he needed that most specially; not just mental strength to outwit James and stand up to his Mother, but the physique of Tarzan, the shoulders of King Kong. Even more miraculous to return with Mary on his arm, Mary to himself; a Mary humbly grateful to escape from James's lewdness and find real and lasting happiness with . . .

'*Bryan!*'

He catapulted to his feet, stuffed the brochure down inside his underpants, turned to face the door. Not his Mother, just her querulous voice, resounding through the landing and the hall.

'What are you doing up there? You know it's not your bath night. We'll have to ration water even more now, if we're going to spend our Christmases abroad.'

He limped downstairs, the crumpled brochure rustling

in his groin. The game-show was just finishing, an elated couple exclaiming with delight as their Mystery Prize was revealed in vibrant colour on the screen – a holiday for two on a sun-drenched island paradise. He watched them kissing, hugging in excitement, as palm trees and gold beaches passed before their marvelling gaze. He closed his eyes a moment, saw himself and Mary on their own island paradise, the palm trees whispering in the breeze, the lazy surf frothing round their ankles, mangoes and bananas plopping off the trees. She drew him close, pushed up her grass skirt and the heavy perfumed flower-wreath which encircled her sweet neck. 'The Mystery Prize,' she murmured as she pointed to her naked breasts, the honey-filled moist valley which . . .

'What's that rustling, Bryan?'

'Banana trees – grass skirts.'

'You're mumbling, dear, as usual. I can't hear a word you say.'

'Er . . . mice.'

'*Mice?*' Lena dived into the kitchen to find a trap, daub poison on the cheese. He watched her go, withdrew the guilty brochure from his groin. Worse than guilty – shameless. The pages were quite damp, sticky, glued together. He shut his eyes again as he mopped himself, recovered. 'Thank you, Mary,' he whispered very softly. 'Gate of Heaven, Comfort of the Afflicted.'

'Hallo. This is 246 2321. John-Paul is not available at present, but if you leave your name, address, phone number and a short message, after you hear the tone, he will get back to you as soon as possible.'

'This is Nial, your son. I need you.'

'Hallo. This is 246 2321. John-Paul is not available at present, but if you leave your name, address, phone number and a short message, after you hear the tone, he will get back to you as soon as possible.'

'This is Nial. Remember Nial? The great big strapping clumsy one, with hulking hands and feet. I used to come on Mondays, Tuesdays, Wednesdays, Thursdays, always at two-ten. Then you made it lunchtime, made me very special. I came today, at lunchtime, but you wouldn't let me in. Please ring me. Soon. I'm hungry – getting very small.'

'Hallo. This is 246 2321. John-Paul is not available at present, but if you leave your name, address and . . .'

'This is bloody Nial. I *hate* you! You're doing this to punish me. I know you're there – listening, but not answering. Jeering, aren't you, mocking, getting a real kick because you've made me cry again? You always tried to do that, tried to make me weak. Well, I'm *not* weak, not at all. I'm coming round, this minute. I know it's not my session-time, but I'll just break your stupid door down. You're with Beata, aren't you; gave her all my lunchtimes, span them out to nights? I'll kill her, I'll destroy her, I'll hack her into . . .'

'Hallo. This is 246 2321. John-Paul is not available at present, but if . . .'
· 'I'm sorry. Honestly. Just say you forgive me. Just say one short word. Anything at all. I've got to hear your voice – your real voice, not the answerphone – so I know you're still alive. Just one word can save me. Please save me. Please say "Nial".'

'Hallo. This is 246 2321. John-Paul is not . . .'

'Okay. You want to kill me. No sweat. I'll kill myself. You'll be sorry then, won't you, ashamed you didn't answer, wouldn't say one footling word, didn't care a fig? I'm going to do it now – swallow all my sleeping pills, fifty of them – more. I've got the bottles here, and I'm shaking all the pills out on the table. Can you hear them rolling, some falling on the floor? They're so pretty, all the colours: red and blue and purple, happy singing yellow, cosy friendly pink.

'I'm cramming in a handful – gulp and down – like sweeties. I've always loved sweet things. We're alike in that respect. If we'd only met as friends, we could have had so much in common. I'm eating sweets like you do – suck and swallow, suck and swallow – another handful gone.

'No. Why should I take pills, let you off so lightly? They're far too quiet and peaceful, and I want you to be sickened when you see my mangled body. I'll hack myself to pieces, like I did with all the paintings, send you limbs and organs through the post – blood weeping through the wrappings onto your breakfast eggs and bacon; my cold heart like a kidney on your toast.

'Don't imagine I'm just threatening. I mean every word I say. I know exactly how to die. I've studied it for years, like other people study art or music. It's an art itself, in one way, and I've always been artistic. Fuck! Your damn machine's just clicked and . . .'

'Hallo. This is 246 23 . . .'

'I'm scared. I'm really scared. If you're dead, I die as well, and I don't want to die, not really. Please come back. Please live. I'll do anything you say. I'll lick your shoes, I'll lick your bowel – the inside – I'll hang head-down from your steeple, like a murdered drooping weather-vane, naked in the wind. I'll climb the tower ten times a day, on my knees and weeping. I'll crush myself to mincemeat and let your wolfhounds eat me, then when you stroke and fondle them, you're really stroking me.

'John-Paul, I'm dying – *answer*.'

'Hallo. This is . . .'

'Will you bloody fucking speak to me and turn that cruel machine off, or . . .'

'Hallo. This is 246 2321. John-Paul is not available at present, but if you leave your name, address, phone number and a short message, after you hear the tone, he will get back to you as soon as possible.'

'Goodbye.'

Help me.

Monday.

Non-day.

338

# 27

Bryan stood rooted in the middle of the crowded airport concourse, unable to move to right or left. Humans should have been created with more than just two hands, he thought, and preferably with wheels. *He* could do with a dozen hands, at least, so he could cope with all the luggage: the four huge bulging cases, the carrier bags of staple English groceries, which Lena feared they'd never get in Rome; the briefcase full of medicines (which covered every possible contingency from malaria to typhoid); the wellingtons, hot-water bottles, packs of cards and board games (in case of rain, or boredom), the tea-making equipment with special adaptor plug, so Lena could be sure of a decent (English) cup of tea, however far she strayed from Ivy Close.

Lena herself had vanished to the ladies' room – a dazed and dazzled Lena, still marvelling at the limousine which had whisked them from Upminster to Heathrow in greater ease and comfort than she'd ever known in her sixty years of life. They should have been going to Gatwick by common tube and train, not Heathrow by chauffeured Peugeot, but just last night everything had changed. The travel agent had phoned to say that unfortunately the airline they were booked on had suffered a grave crisis and been forced into liquidation a mere three days ago, so they'd be flying on another line from a different airport at a later time of day. He'd been totally distraught. He'd spent ninety-seven hours working out the journey plan to Gatwick, entering all the details in his new shiny scarlet notebook (which he'd dared at last, in Mary's honour – red for passion, danger, ardour, heat and lust), and then to have it overturned, with just one paltry night to change not just his schedule, but half the jammed compartments in his mind – a night he'd spent in anguish, pacing round and round his room, trying to cope with new arrangements, not daring to tell his Mother, finally calling up a car-hire firm as a bribe to stop her nagging.

It also seemed a most unlucky omen – chaos striking once again, proving the general Chaos of the Universe. If airlines could go bust, then why not Heathrow, also? He'd insisted on arriving with at least eight hours to spare, so if his hunch was right and he found the airport collapsed into a black hole, or just a pile of smouldering rubble, at least he'd have the time to make a third set of new plans.

They were not, in fact, required. The airport seemed all too vast and solid, almost overwhelming in its sheer size and scale and frenzy, jammed with traffic, tetchy jostling crowds. He was still wilting on the ground floor by the rows and rows of check-in desks, dwarfed by trendy jet-setters with their skis and winter tans; shamed by boyish yuppies still doing frantic business via cellular phones and dictating machines, as if their high-powered firms could hardly bear their absence for an hour. He doubted BRB would even notice he was gone.

Everybody else was checking in their luggage, striding off free-handed, or with just a stylish flight-bag looped across one shoulder, or a power-zoomed video camera slung around their necks. Only he was loaded down with castor oil and Heinz tomato ketchup, paralysed by the sheer weight of canned baked beans. The airline had refused to take his baggage yet, told him check-in time was two hours before the flight, so would he please return at half past three – *p.m.* He'd checked his watch – still only nine and morning.

'But . . . But I can't move,' he'd faltered. 'Not with all these cases.'

'We *do* have luggage trolleys, sir, and even a left-luggage office. Just grab yourself a trolley and wheel your cases over there.' The desk clerk gestured (vaguely) to the left, then turned briskly to the next man in the queue, a dark hirsute Adonis with one streamlined case so small and neatly compact it probably contained nothing but a few silk handkerchiefs.

Bryan peered up and down the seething hall. He couldn't see a luggage trolley – not one without an owner – and he dared not leave the cases to go and seek one out. Deadlock – as so often in his life.

'Bryan!'

He swung round, saw his Mother, exultant with a trolley, weaving through the jostling hordes towards him. He'd still not quite recovered from the shock of her appearance when she'd emerged at dawn, fully dressed, wearing a colour for the first time in his life, instead of the black or grey or beige of semi-mourning. He'd never seen the outfit, had no idea she owned it – an old-fashioned matching dress and coat in a vibrant cornflower blue, which seemed to transport him to another age. She looked like a character from some now dated film, in a dress too young (and short) for her, and in Mary's shade of blue. He had found it most unnerving, especially as she'd added a sparkling flower-spray brooch. He'd never seen his Mother wearing jewellery, nor any shoes but lace-ups. Yet there she was, lolloping towards him now in some low-slung laceless casuals, which only drew attention to her gammy foot, disfigured veiny leg.

He felt a wave of pity, curdled with embarrassment. Her leg was clearly hurting, yet she refused to sit and rest, seemed to have been galvanised this whole last week by the sheer peril and high drama of a trip to Foreign Parts; had even compared it to the war, which she'd also seen as a chance to live more dangerously, to espouse a Cause, pump excitement and adrenalin into her usual stagnant life.

'Watch out!' he called – too late. Lena was engulfed in a tide of foreigners – not just Europeans, but West Indians with dreadlocks, turbaned Pakistanis, pan-faced Japanese. Tarbooshes and yashmaks assailed her on all sides. What on earth were they all doing in this European terminal? They must have come specifically to goad her, brought their swarms of hypermanic children, to drive her back full-pelt to Ivy Close. His Mother hated children, felt they should be born with fully-trained bowels and bladders, good manners and good salaries, and preferably dumb. If children were bad news, then foreign children would be red rag to a bull. He could no longer see the bull, who was completely swamped in aliens; closed his eyes helplessly as he waited for her angry snort, her nostril-flaring charge. A sudden exhalation of Yardley's English Lavender and menthol liniment wafted in his face. His Mother was beside him, not bellowing or charging, but triumphant with her trolley.

'I stole it from a darky, dear. That deserves a kiss.'

He pecked her cheek, embarrassed. She was almost flirting with him, clinging to his arm like a loving bashful bride – not the faintest whimper about kids or crowds or foreigners, let alone the storm of protest he was ready braced to hear. He'd never seen her like this in his life before, almost longed for her to nag again, so at least things would be familiar. He couldn't cope with change.

'Careful, Bryan. You'll trip, dear.'

He *did* trip, cannoned off the escalator and landed on his bottom. He couldn't even remember going up an escalator. And where were all the cases? He leapt up in pain and panic.

'We've lost the luggage, Mother. Quick! Call a guard or something.'

'But we've just left it in that office.'

'What office?'

'The left-luggage place. They gave you seven tickets.'

He fumbled in his pocket, found the crumpled tickets, fought new and daunting worries. Would the suitcases be safe? Should he ever have abandoned them to careless cowardly staff, who might muddle up the tickets, or dash for safety if burglars smashed the doors down? He was still clutching the most vital things – his toy snake, Anne, which he'd hidden in a pillowcase, so that nobody would mock, and his large supply of notebooks labelled 'Rome', 'Mary', 'Check-list', 'Accounts', 'Expenses', 'Problems', 'General', 'Miscellaneous' and 'Emergency'. He should have brought a dozen for Emergency, the way that things were going, and a far bigger one for Expenses. That car had all but ruined him, and he'd taken out a dozen different insurances which had cost almost half as much again as the holiday itself.

'Oh, look, dear, all those shops!'

He looked. Not just shops, but banks and business centres, bars and restaurants, telephones and toilets, counters, kiosks, booths – endless signs shouting all around him. The signs were quite bewildering, required instant clear decisions, yet the very sight of all those choices reduced him to a vacillating shuttlecock. Wouldn't it be simpler just to bolt back home, unpack the brandy-butter and the Sennakot, fill the four hot-water bottles and put himself to bed?

'And what a huge great Christmas tree! Fancy Christmas decorations in an airport.'

His Mother seemed impressed, turning in amazement from shops to tree to baubles to flashing fairy lights. She was more used to Victoria Coach Station with its dreary concrete bays, its total lack of glamour, lack of all diversion save one shabby wilting café selling cardboard sausage rolls. Her eyes tracked from gift-wrapped chocolates adorned with flowers and bows, to a gigantic smiling Santa swinging from the ceiling on his sleigh. His own eyes followed hers, so he didn't see the real-life Father Christmas scurrying towards

343

him – or rather *Mother* Christmas. His body registered soft flesh as he collided with her ample jutting breasts.

'*Mary!*' he thought instantly, as he glimpsed fair curls, blue eyes, though the face itself was swallowed up in a froth of fake white whiskers.

'We've got a very special offer, sir, in duty-free today. Just buy two hundred Rothman's and . . .'

He crumpled up the leaflet she pressed into his hand. He'd been lusting for a billet-doux from Mary-in-disguise, and all he'd got instead was a page of panting prose about the smooth rich satisfaction not of his sweet mistress, but of filthy tar and nicotine. Yet at least his mood had changed. How dare he even contemplate bolting feebly home, when in just three days his Love would be arriving to share the Eternal City with him, reignite his faith and his devotion? It was Christmas Eve, a time for hope – and giving. He put down his bags (and snake), rifled through his pockets for his wallet, withdrew a wad of fivers, handed them theatrically to Lena.

'Buy yourself a present, Mother.' He could afford to be generous just once in his cramped life. If he was going to leave his Mother alone in Ivy Close, build a nest with Mary, then at least he should provide some compensation. 'Buy anything you like,' he urged. 'Don't fuss about the price.' He knew he was quite safe. Lena had never been extravagant in half a century's shopping; was so used to penny-pinching she would never dream of squandering his precious hard-earned cash, but would horde it in a biscuit tin, or save it for the groceries. He himself would do the squandering – buy a new silk tie to dazzle Mary. He stopped just inside the largest store, which appeared to offer everything from the *Daily Mail* and *Playboy* to huge slabs of chilled smoked salmon. 'You stay here, Mother, and pick out a scarf or something. I'll meet you by these teddy bears in exactly half an hour.'

★    ★    ★

Bryan mooched back from the tie shop, exhausted, empty-handed. Impossible to choose a tie in twenty-seven minutes. It had been known to take him months, as he'd keep returning and returning to the same shop or rack or counter, weighing up grey-blue against blue-grey, comparing stripes with squiggles, or dry-clean versus washable. He stood now amidst the teddy bears, searching for his Mother, couldn't see her anywhere, only sixty furry bodies, sixty pairs of brown glass eyes, most of which were mocking his alarm. He plunged the other way, darted up and down the aisles, fighting down the urge to cry 'Mummy, Mummy, Mummy!' like the lost and frightened child he felt inside.

'Mother!' He'd tracked her down, at last, at a counter labelled Travel Goods, which was loaded with appliances and gadgets – things he'd never dreamed existed: body-safes and siren-lights, combined mini-fans and mosquito-killers, a water-treatment system which claimed to kill every germ known to man and some still unclassified. Lena's hands were full, her trolley piled with packages – a trolley big enough to bankrupt him, if she continued in this fashion. He glanced around him fearfully. There were still racks and racks of other things she probably hadn't even noticed yet: jewels and scarves and dolls and scents, sunglasses and cameras, cassettes and Wedgwood china, tins of tea, jars of . . . No, he mustn't make his lists, not even in his head. John-Paul would disapprove.

Lena had moved on to the travel-irons, comparing prices, assessing weights and sizes.

'Stop!' he almost shouted. 'I've packed an iron already.'

'But *I* did all the packing, Bryan, and anyway . . .'

'I mean, they've got one in the seminary.'

'Seminary? What's that?'

'The . . . er . . . hotel. They're called seminaries in Rome.'

'Well, still best to have our own, dear. I expect Italian

345

irons are dangerous, like their government. And I'm sure we need one of these big . . .'

'No,' he hissed. 'We don't need anything. Except a cup of tea.' Tea would be much cheaper than a Ten-Way Torch or Tropical First-Aid Kit, or a foldaway umbrella which doubled as a walking stick and camping stool. He'd even offer her a bun, the nutty chewy kind which would take a while to masticate and so keep her from the shops. He helped her up the stairs to the Plaza on the floor above, where the restaurants were all clustered; stopped in shock as he heard his name booming over the Tannoy.

'Would Mr Bryan Payne, travelling to Rome, please report immediately to the Airport Information Desk. Mr Bryan Payne, please, to Airport Information.'

He gripped his Mother's arm, the blood draining from his face. John-Paul had summoned him back home, discovered some huge error in the last cheque he'd posted off. He could well have written seven pounds in place of seven hundred – even though he'd checked it twenty times. John-Paul would interpret that as an act of sheer contempt – his services, his expertise, worth peanuts. Or he'd start repeating all that stuff again about his fixation at the anal stage, which meant he wasn't just obsessional, but also parsimonious. An image of blocked faeces was poisoning his whole mind now. He tried to pull the plug on it, think less insalubriously. Of course John-Paul hadn't called him. The doctor was in Rome himself, had been there a full week. It was James who'd had him paged, a James crazed with murderous jealousy, now waiting at that desk with loaded pistols, or a Travel Muggers' Outfit disguised as a First-Aid Kit.

'Mother, you sit here. Promise not to move till I come back. This may well be urgent, a matter of life and death.'

'But what's happened? Why . . .?'

He couldn't stop to answer, hurtled down the stairs,

scanned the signs for Airport Information, found it almost opposite, joined the dawdling queue, every muscle tense as he jigged and fumed and cursed behind the loiterers.

'Payne,' he gasped at last, as he reached the counter, sweat pouring off his face.

'You're in pain, sir? Where's the pain? Look, you'd better take a seat here and I'll phone through to a doctor.'

'No, my *name*. Bryan Payne. Mr Payne. B.V. Payne. B. Vernon Payne . . .' He tried to stop the tide of names, heard his doctor's stern rebuke grating in his head. 'You wanted me. You called me – on the Tannoy.'

'No, I don't think that we did, sir, but let me check a moment.'

Bryan could feel his heart thump-thumping as the girl turned to scan her notepad. Perhaps it was Mary who had summoned him, disguised not as Mother Christmas, but as a pager or announcer. This could be the start of his new life. Any breathless minute her ardent message would be relayed to him by the freckled Miss in uniform still checking through her list. 'I love you, Bryan. I know it now. I'm leaving James – I have to. Meet me by the . . .'

'No, sir. We called a Mr Brian *Baines*, who's already reported here, in fact.'

'Are you absolutely sure? I mean there wasn't any message from a . . . lady?'

The young girl shook her head. 'No. Mr Baines had simply lost his spectacles, and we asked him to reclaim them from the desk.'

Bryan slunk away, suspicious. Baines could be a rival who had claimed not just his spectacles, but a crucial private message addressed to Mr Payne. The entire airport was swarming with his rivals, all bigger, broader, stiffer men, with larger bank accounts. And Rome would be far worse – hordes of Latin lovers with bold black

347

eyes and dark-furred chests ogling his own blonde and smooth-skinned Mary. And they wouldn't all be swathed in thermal underwear, which hardly helped his chances. His Mother had insisted he wear a long-sleeved vest and knee-length underpants in Thermolactyl Double Force, a thick and prickly fabric which fretted at his skin. The underwear was advertised for Arctic expeditions and assaults on Everest, not for modern airports heated to a sweltering over-eighty. He'd put it on quite eagerly that morning because he liked its virile promise, 'Double Force', especially when in contact with his groin, but it had let him down – of course. The only thing which had doubled (tripled, quadrupled) was his feverish sweaty heat.

He passed a vinyl-covered bench, miraculously empty as a whole family decamped from it: children, Grandma, Mum and Dad, trailing off together for their flight. He lurched into their place, now faint from hyperthermia; stretched out semi-supine, tried to turn the vinyl into John-Paul's stylish leather, begged his absent doctor to slip into his usual seat just behind his head. How could he have criticised John-Paul, panted for the blessed month when there would be no more appointments? It was already nine whole days since his last session on the couch, and he was missing them increasingly. Yet he'd wasted those last sessions, said hardly more than fifty words in each fifty-minute hour. John-Paul had interpreted the silence as being due to his mounting fears about the break. He'd never been away so long before, especially not at Christmas, and Bryan must clearly feel abandoned, and was perhaps even reliving the experience of his father's early death – an 'abandonment' so critical it had affected all his subsequent relationships, or lack of them.

'I *do* have a relationship,' he'd shouted *sotto voce*. 'I'm about to live with Mary, rescue her in Rome and secrete her back to England, buy a little cottage in Northumberland or Yorkshire or Hants or Wilts or . . .' John-Paul couldn't hear, nor his next remark that the sooner his psychiatrist pushed off to Rome himself, the happier he'd be. Since he could mention neither Mary nor his relief at John-Paul's imminent departure, he'd spent the remaining nineteen minutes imagining Mary's thighs. Were they white or tan, he'd wondered, voluptuous or slim, dusted with gold hairs or smooth as marble?

'What are you thinking, Bryan?' John-Paul had asked, at last, as perhaps his final offering before he said goodbye.

'Thighs,' he'd answered dreamily, as his hand crept higher, higher, inching slowly upwards towards Mary's moistening groin.

'Thighs?'

'Er, chicken thighs.' He'd bought some just last night – Sainsbury's frozen chicken thighs in egg and breadcrumb coating.

'You realise, Bryan, that "chicken" is the colloquial word for coward. It appears you're feeling cowardly today – weak, perhaps, and scared, worried by the fact I'm going away.'

'I can hardly wait!' he didn't say, just swung his legs rudely off the couch, even banged his shoes about as he tugged them on, decamped.

He groaned now, closed his eyes, did indeed feel orphaned and abandoned, in need of some support. He longed to hear his doctor's measured voice, investing things with causes, reasons, meaning. John-Paul had explained to him just a week or so ago how every time he gave himself some treat, he had to pay for it with still more guilt and worry; how he *needed* pain and problems to afford himself the punishment dictated by his stringent super-ego. John-Paul was right, as usual. He'd booked himself a holiday, and had never felt so vulnerable, so stricken.

He sat bolt upright on the bench. Was he in the right

349

terminal at all? Perhaps he'd come, mistakenly, to what they called 'long haul', which would explain the Japs and Indians. Any minute now he'd be jetting off to Tokyo, or Delhi, or Peking. How would he find Mary in an Indian bazaar or Chinese opium den? The agent had said Terminal Two, but supposing he'd misheard, as he'd mistaken Baines for Payne? Even his own language was full of traps and terrors: words not meaning what they said, people taking liberties with grammar, punctuation. A comma in the wrong place could initiate a tragedy. He was meant to be travelling with two hundred pious Catholics, yet he hadn't spied a rosary or missal; seen no one looking prayerful or accompanied by a priest. He checked his watch again. He'd been told to join his party half an hour before the flight, meet them by the departure gate at five. It was still only half past ten, but wouldn't *some* of them come early, be worriers like he was?

He zigzagged down the hall, searching for a dog collar, maddened now by the constant Tannoy messages which were telling other people where they were (and who); giving them instructions, clear direct instructions about flights and routes and schedules; finding things they'd lost; making them feel wanted, loved, secure. No one wanted *him*, or regarded him as important enough to call him to the desk, present him with a dossier confirming all his vital personal details: his name, his job, his blood-group, the colour of his eyes.

He trailed back to the Plaza, still nervous and confused, found his Mother studying a placard which offered a full English breakfast at a price so wildly high it must include diamond-studded eggs, and caviare to start with, instead of Sugar Puffs. He tried to steer her past the notice, ignore her anxious questions about why he'd been so long, why they'd summoned him at all.

'Oh, just a business matter. BRB find it hard to cope when I'm not there to man the office. Now, I think it's time we . . . we . . . changed some money, Mother.' He had changed it twenty times – sterling into lire, then back again, when his panic got so all-embracing he'd decide to cancel the whole holiday and claim on his insurance. Then hotfoot to the bank once more, praying for a different clerk who wouldn't recognise him when he passed the form across (*again*), requesting – yes, more lire.

'But we haven't had our breakfast, Bryan.'

That was his fault, too. He'd insisted they depart the minute they were dressed; had booked the car for dawn.

'And that restaurant looks quite pleasant, dear.'

It looked far more than pleasant – it looked completely ruinous. He could see it from the entrance, black with bowing waiters, jungled with exotic plants, which were bound to go straight on the bill, under 'cover charge' or 'extras'.

'It's never wise to eat before you fly, Mother – nothing heavy, anyway.'

'How d'you know? You've never flown.'

'I read it in a book.'

'You read too many books, Bryan. That's half your trouble really. Reading softens the brain. It isn't natural. Animals don't read. And it's ruining your sight. You'll be wearing glasses before you're thirty-five – and losing them continually, if I know anything about you. "I'm sure I put them here, Mother." Or there. Or . . .'

He felt a wave of sweet relief. His Mother was becoming her old self. He'd reward her with a cup of tea, a bun. He swept her past the blue-chip, five-star restaurant into the self-service one beside it, cringing as he saw its name: 'CHOICES'. The choices were impossible: a dozen different counters with a hundred different foods – even the drinks baffling and exotic. Every sort of tea from his Mother's standard brew to herb teas, fruit teas, and a range called 'Speciality', which included names like 'Sunrise', 'Country Way' and 'English Garden' – all fecund rural names reminding him of Mary. The sandwiches were hers, as well, crustless and refined; the fresh fruits plump and swollen like her breasts. He arrived at the cash-desk with Mary in his mind still, but nothing on his tray.

'Aren't you hungry, Bryan?'

'Er, no.'

'You've not been eating sweets again – in secret?'

'No, Mother.'

'Let me smell your breath.'

He exhaled into her face. She frowned and sniffed, then nodded grudgingly. 'All right. But don't start complaining you feel hungry in just an hour or so. You know the dangers of eating between meals.'

He glanced at her own tray in shock. She'd chosen foreign foods – cappuccino, when she never touched anything but Typhoo, and a Swiss-French croissant oozing melted Gruyère. He felt totally disorientated. This was not the Lena that he knew, the one who stuck to sliced white bread, Tesco's English Cheddar. His eye caught the Children's Menu tacked above the till – Hungry Bears' Bumper Burger and Snoopy's Dream Ice Cream. He longed to be a toddler strapped in his highchair, Mary bending over him, squirting in Dream Breast Milk.

No, he'd never keep it down; never eat or drink again, judging by the churning in his stomach. There simply wasn't room for food with all that terror clogging up his gut. They were sitting by the window which looked out on the runway and he could see the planes close-up now. Terrifying monsters which seemed far too big and lumbering ever to fly at all. He knew suddenly he'd die. By six o'clock this evening he'd be foundering at the bottom of the Channel, or impaled lifeless on a mountain peak. His Disaster Scrapbook was packed in the blue case. He should have kept it in his hand-luggage, so he could check up on the crashes – though half the gory details were already screaming in his head: Lockerbie, of course, and the British Midland horror just a shocking fortnight later, and the jumbo jet which crashed into a mountain range, killing all its passengers, and that other fated Boeing which mistook the M4 for the runway in conditions of dense fog. He peered outside again. It was already slightly misty. By five o'clock that touch of mist could have thickened into an out-and-out peasouper.

He fumbled for his pillowcase, removed his snake, clutched it in both hands. Okay – let people snigger – he no longer even cared, not with Death looming by their table, handing them his black-edged calling-card. Anne would die, as well – a case of callous murder. He should have left his snake at home, not dragged it into danger. He used its tail to wipe his clammy hands, felt wildly fiercely hot, as if he were escaping from the charred and burning wreckage, flames leaping at his hair, licking round his ankles. He mopped his streaming forehead on a paper serviette which wished him a good morning in bouncy yellow script. Good morning? Were they *mad*? This was his last morning with the living. He was about to plunge into the sky on a jet-powered death-machine; then hurtle down and down again until he hit the Void.

'Well, if *this* is what Italians eat, I'd rather have my usual toast, thank you very much.'

'What?'

'Don't say "what", say "pardon", Bryan. I've been telling you the same since you were six.'

He jerked up to his feet, Anne in one hand, steak-knife in the other, as if he were warding off some imaginary opponent, defying Death Himself. 'Mother! We're not going.'

'Not going where?'

'To Rome.'

'Don't be silly, dear. You've always been too highly strung. You get that from your father. Now put that knife down and drink this milky coffee. That'll calm you down. Cappuccino? They can keep their cappuccino. It's just a cup of froth, and at the price they charged, that's 15p a bubble.'

'Mother, we're about to *die*, and you're fussing about bubbles.'

'I don't intend dying, dear, except in my own bed and with a nice pot of tea beside me. You've gone too long without a meal, that's all that's wrong with *you*. I'll go and get your Coco Pops and you'll feel completely different with something in your stomach. Now, promise not to move, Bryan. I don't trust you on your own. While I'm gone, you can look out of the window and watch all those lovely planes.'

# 28

'Help, help! We're going down. We're crashing. Quick, jump out of the window, break the glass, get *out*! Oh God, the smoke! I can hardly breathe at all now, and the flames are . . . This is it – we're dying! Mother, Mother, hold me. I don't want to die alone. Not *you*, you fool! Let go of me, get back. Mother, please, where are you? I love you, Mother, honestly, don't want you to die. Get off, you brutes, I said. You're blocking all the exits and . . . Hurry, someone, hurry! The flames are getting closer. Let down the escape-hatch, ram open those two doors. Christ! Too late. We're dead.'

# 29

I killed myself last Friday. I had to. I couldn't stay alive with John-Paul dead himself. I lost a lot of bone and flesh, and parts of my insides just crumbled into dust. I never got them back. I'm much smaller now and lighter, take up far less room. I've also lost my voice, but that's just a cold, a bad one. I don't need a voice, in any case. There's nobody to talk to.

I mop my nose, blow on my numb fingers, walk slowly round the cemetery through spiteful sleety rain, stopping by my favourite of the gravestones. '*Quis separabit*,' it's asking me, as usual, though I never give an answer. There isn't any question-mark, and anyway I presume it's just an irony, like most of the inscriptions all around me – 'Resting', for example, or 'God Wanted One More Angel'. The only angel I can see has lost her nose and hands, and has obscene graffiti daubed across her wings. All the graves look old and tired, leaning on each other, or listing to the right or left; once-preening marble now choked with ivy, clawed by vicious brambles; everlasting granite chipped and stained.

I squat down on the ramparts of a showy mausoleum, stroke its fur of moss. I come here every day now, since it's obvious I belong. I should be underground with all the other inmates, where it's warmer and less lonely, but I somehow failed to make it as a corpse. I suppose if you fail in living, it's not all that surprising if you also cock up dying. I can't claim it as my resting-place, so I use it as a park instead, a sort of recreation ground, without the recreation. At least it's quiet and empty – empty save for bones.

I read the names of all the bones inside the mausoleum, which are inscribed in fancy Gothic script into stone plaques on the sides. They're mostly D'Acre Laceys, which sound far too grand for a cemetery in Bermondsey. 'Thomas D'Acre Lacey, called to rest 1852', 'Alice D'Acre Lacey, wife of the above.' Etcetera, etcetera. Until Simon D'Acre Lacey, who died last year, aged two. I had a brother once – or so they tell me. He died of meningitis the year I was conceived. I was intended as a substitute, but failed to measure up, even failed to be a male. I never told John-Paul. I knew he'd make too much of it, dig the poor kid up, do autopsies and inquests, disturb his peace, and mine. Some things are best left buried – maybe everything.

Yes, John-Paul is dead himself now, or dead for me, at least. I've traipsed back to his vacant tower fifty times, a hundred; gone at one-ten, two-ten, three-ten, even midnight; sworn at that dumb entry-phone, sobbed to it, implored it, but he's obviously decamped. I expect his other patients received notice of his new address, but he didn't want me back, just struck me from his diary, gave all my precious lunch-times to Beata. He's been telling lies for weeks, inventing trips abroad, so he could cancel all my sessions, threatening to increase his fees because he thought I couldn't pay them and would have to stay away.

I struggle to my feet again, blowing my sore nose, then trudge towards the gate; the rain following – and frantic – flailing at my shoulders, stinging in my face. It's a wrench to leave the cemetery, as always, as if I'm leaving home, or friends. I envy those snug dead. There was just one fleeting moment when I died – a quite astounding moment when I felt myself slipping from my body, letting go, letting go, deeper deeper deeper, like the most fantastic orgasm which I've only ever fantasised, imagined; never actually experienced with men. I was freed at last from body, or mind and thoughts, or gender, freed from

357

everything, just floating soaring nothing. Annihilation, like my name.

It was awful coming back. The vomit and the stench, the constant retching, retching; the slow dull creeping knowledge that I'd failed. No one found me, 'saved' me. I found myself – and hated it – but didn't have much choice. I'd no more pills, nor strength for knives, or drowning, or jumping twenty storeys. And you can't catch meningitis just to order.

I'm much better now, in fact – stronger altogether, can even walk and shop. I've been out since six this morning, window-shopping, wandering, seeing who's around on Christmas Day. No one much, apparently, but that's because it's wet again. (It was always raining, wasn't it, even when John-Paul was still alive – save for one strange burst of spring?) Scores of people have wished me Happy Christmas: radio announcers, television chat-show hosts, jokers in advertisements, Christmas cards in shops, the recorded Christmas carols in my local launderette. Well, not so much today, of course, with shops and laundries closed, but all last week continually. Christmas is a prison. The bars squeeze tighter, tighter, for several days before it, then snap completely shut on Christmas Day. Solitary confinement. Most other normal people are eating, drinking, jollying; part of some huge family – daughters, mothers, nieces, aunts – joined by genes and tinsel. I was once a daughter. I was even once a son, but things never last that long.

I turn right at the corner, trail down the grey deserted street until I reach the public library. That's locked and barred as well, though it's shouting 'Happy Christmas' still from all its lower windows, and has sagging drunken paper-chains looped across the ceiling. I dropped in there two weeks ago, not the lending section, but the solemn stifling reference room, asked a girl to point me out the medical register. I turned straight to the S's, to confirm what Zack had told me. John-Paul wasn't listed – nor any of his family, those brothers, cousins, nephews, whom Zack assured me were all doctors. The name just wasn't there, let alone the strings of letters after it. I asked the girl to double-check, in case I was mistaken. She was kind and took some trouble, but she finally agreed with me there was no one of that name.

'Are there any other books?' I asked, 'Where I'd find a doctor listed? Or any separate sort of directory for medically trained psychiatrists?'

'No point checking them,' she smiled. 'You see, this one is the Bible, so to speak. Every single doctor, psychiatrist or otherwise, has to be included in this register, which is updated every year and fully comprehensive. Are you sure you've got the name right?'

'Yes,' I said. 'Completely sure.' I know his name, for God's sake. It's tattooed across my body, engraved on all my organs.

I didn't leave immediately, just sat down where I was, among the damp old men and shuffling sad illiterates who use the library for its heating rather than its books, and wondered why Zack lied. Oh, I know everybody lies. I do myself, continually, so why should I complain? Yet somehow I keep longing for the truth, like I used to long for soul-mates, or God, or happiness – all things I've just let go now. Perhaps Truth is blurred and multiple, and we're wrong to give it one pompous abstract noun, but should think in terms of demi-truths (like demi-gods, who never promise much at all, and lose their capital). John-Paul was a demi-god and a con-man both at once, an artist and a doctor, married and a corpse. I'll never know him anyway – only just his name, and even that might be a fabrication. He could be in that register under Brown or Smith (or Freud), or churning out bad pictures as Jane Priscilla Steiner. Does it even matter now? I doubt it.

I drag on down the street, dodging all the puddles. It's

359

almost twelve o'clock, getting close to lunch-time. I'd better go back home and eat my Christmas dinner – a fag or two, an aspirin, half a bar of Twix. There's not much in my room these days. I've been trying to cut down – not just on food, on everything. I've thrown out every outfit I ever wore when I went to see John-Paul, which means almost all my clothes – burnt the ones I bought specially in his honour: the frilly 'female' dresses, or pretty pastel colours which wouldn't bite or scream at him. I've also stripped the shelves, trashed my books, which used to mean a lot to me, killed off all their characters. Most homes bulge for Christmas – presents, new possessions, fridge and larder crammed. I no longer see the point. It all rots and dies by January, joins the other corpses – dead Christmas trees, dead tinsel, dead happiness, dead truth.

I stroll across a huge main road, which is usually so clogged with cars you risk your life attempting it. Now it's silent, listless, just three bedraggled pigeons warring for a crust. The rain is easing off, at last. It's only semi-drizzling, though still leaden, very cold; the sky leaning on the buildings as if it's so weary and dispirited it needs a solid shoulder to support it. Everything is grey – clouds (and clouds in puddles), the wan faces of sick buildings which close me in, mock my dragging footsteps; the cracked uneven pavement which tries to trip me up. I toil back up the hill, stop from time to time to rest my feet (or breath), or decide what magic gift I'd choose from the windows of the toy-shops, if I were still a child, or still had parents who knew who or where I was. I select a large boy doll which says 'I love you' when you wind it up. Imagine getting love from just a few turns of a key.

I avoid a tide of litter, crumpled dirty placards from some march or demonstration, now flung into the gutter or left shouting at the pavement: 'SAY "NO" TO BOMBS AND DEATH!' How wrong they are, at least about the death.

I wish I hadn't walked so far. I'm feeling weak and faint,

my legs cold and stiff and aching as I turn into my own street, start hobbling down the steps.

I suddenly dodge back. There's someone at the bottom, an intruder and a male one, a tall but stooping figure, standing with his back to me, powerful shoulders hunched. Fear lasers down my spine. Christmas Day is the perfect time for break-ins, with so many folk away, the police careless or half-pissed. He could be armed and dangerous, so if I try to dart away, he'll hear me and swing round, maybe knock me flat. I stand transfixed with terror, just staring at his back, praying to the God I don't believe in.

'Help me, God,' I whisper, and He does so instantly. The man slowly straightens up, half-turns his head so I can see his striking profile – though he hasn't noticed *me* yet. I know that face, that profile, that dark hair black with rain; even recognise the duffel coat, its middle toggle missing, one pocket torn and stained.

'Seton?' I call desperately, but his name sticks in my throat, seems too large and rough for it. I'm glad he hasn't heard. I'm terrified he won't know who I am, simply look right through me, like that shaming time in hospital. That was several weeks ago, so he could be even worse now; forget we shared a boat – and life – one brief but vital fortnight. And I probably look much older, so he'll be still more confused. (I aged a lot while searching for John-Paul; lost whole decades scraping his dead cells off the streets around the tower, bottling his dead breath.)

I remain completely motionless, unsure what to do or say – even what to feel. Do I love the man, or hate him; invite him in, or kick him in the teeth? He's churned me up already. I'm no longer numb, but sweaty, and my blood and bones feel different, as if I've been given a transfusion, or changed to someone else. Yet I'm still half-paralysed. I keep staring at him, staring; scared that if I shift my eyes, he may change himself, or vanish. He certainly seems better than he did in hospital; no longer drugged or senile, but looking almost dapper, if you disregard the coat; wearing smart grey cords instead of shabby jeans, and decent shoes, not trainers. I long to touch those shoes, undo their laces, free their soft kid tongues, so they could speak to me and calm me, tell me what to feel. I always loved his feet – size eleven feet which made my own feet small – hairs on all the toes, the nails hacked cruelly short like the square ends of chisel blades. I suddenly know I've got to keep him here, claim him, as it were; not follow my first instinct and creep back up the steps, hide behind the railings, pretend I never saw him.

I force myself to move, edge down one step towards him, even clear my throat. He swings round at the noise, meets my eye, holds my gaze, unsmiling, for what seems like endless minutes, while I slowly die inside. So he doesn't know me, doesn't want to know me. Can I really blame him? I'm all bundled up in baggy shapeless sweaters, the last dregs of my wardrobe; still-ragged hair dripping down my neck. I look away, can't bear his vacant scrutiny, fix my eyes on a patch of grey stone step. More minutes creak and dawdle, then I hear his feet falter on the concrete, hear him spring towards me.

'Happy Christmas, Nial.'

I'm so touched I can't reply. Someone's actually wished me Happy Christmas, someone real and human, not an airwave or a poster or a sticker through the door. I try to say it back.

'Lost your voice?' he grins.

I nod, still overcome, not only that he knows me, but that he's made me real as well, used my name, remembers it, dragged all this way from hospital to find me, even dared a smile.

'Come in,' I mouth. 'Have lunch.' I try to keep things casual. Seton never liked emotion – not other people's anyway.

I open soup – my last small can – Campbell's Country

362

Vegetable, which seems a bit incongruous in the densest part of London. I even find a chunk of greying fruitcake, heat it in the oven so it's more like Christmas pudding and tastes less old and stale. Then we sit and smoke a while, and it's almost like old times, though neither of us says a lot. I can't; he doesn't want to; seems tense, preoccupied. I presume they turfed him out of hospital for Christmas. That's the policy these days. The birthday of the God of Love and you loose them on the streets without a sniff of turkey or a relation in the world. Where's Zack, I wonder? Cressida? His so-called friends and helpmates?

At least he's made my Christmas. I'm a couple now, a family, lolling at the table amidst the wreckage of the nuts and wine, the brandy, the liqueur chocolates. We're drinking coffee, actually, Tesco's cheapest instant. I haven't any booze at all, no chocolate but my Twix. But it's warm and quiet and peaceful, and I'm very nearly happy, soothed by soup and aspirin, contented Seton's there. We're both much older than when we met the first time; no longer need the charge of violent sex. He doesn't even touch me, but I'm flattered by the fact he actually sought me out, translated my address from two lines on a jotter to reality, desire. I think he sees me as a sister now, regards my pad as home. I've always wanted a brother, not a dead one or preferred one, or a substitute for me, but just a loving equal. I once felt jealous of his ten years with John-Paul, the fact that he seemed special, a favoured long-term patient, the beloved hoped-for boy. But now I realise we're both abandoned children, both rejected by John-Paul, which is another bond between us, and perhaps another reason why I shouldn't go to bed with him. It would be a kind of incest.

'Thanks for coming, Seton,' I whisper to him hoarsely. It's exhausting talking with no voice, but he seems to understand, says 'Ssh, don't strain your throat, Nial,' then reaches out his hand.

'You've got fantastic hair,' he murmurs, touching it a moment.

I nod. I haven't had it trimmed or tamed since I hacked it off myself, and it's grown very strange and shaggy, sticking up in places, uneven everywhere. I remember when he said those words the first time, how different we both were. Nothing lasts, not even hair, or pain.

I light another cigarette, stir sugar in my cup, try to concentrate on tiny things: the taste of sweetness in my mouth, the balm of nicotine, Seton's strong and sallow hand resting on the table by my own. I've learnt these last few days (or weeks) there are only little things – no fatted calves or silken robes, no wild rebirths, re-deaths. I edge my hand a little nearer Seton's, touch my thumb to his – a sister's touch, not sexual. He still seems a bit distracted, as if his body's here with me, but his mind is somewhere else, working on some problem. His feet are twisted round the chair-rung, fretting at it, nervous; a tiny muscle twitching in one cheek. I suppose he feels displaced, with no real home, no role. I never believed that story of him working as Zack's framer. He could hardly afford ten years of private therapy on a framer's meagre wage. Half of what Zack said was simply fiction, intended to impress me, or merely shut me up.

I squeeze his thumb, long to make him better, offer him some hope – though hope's like booze and turkey – in pretty short supply. I suppose I could invite him to live *here*. I've never lived with anyone for more than just a month or so, but things can always change. We could start some new small business, become partners, not just siblings. I reflect on that word 'partners', its overtones of mutual trust – closeness, continuity, sharing minds and plans. I've never had a partner, not in any sense. Though I'd have to introduce it really casually, so as not to scare him off or make him fear some trap or tie or cage.

'Seton,' I croak out. 'Don't laugh, but . . .'

He suddenly jumps up. 'It's time,' he says, pushing back his sweater sleeve so he can check his watch, compare it with my clock.

'What for?' I whisper, startled. 'It's time' is John-Paul's phrase, and always murmured softly; sounds wrong when Seton raps it out staccato.

'We've got to leave.'

'Leave for where?'

'You said you'd help me.'

'Help you?' I keep parroting his words in my eunuch of a voice. He's smashed the silence, and is pacing round the room now, disturbing sleeping dust. I pray he won't start ranting. I just haven't got the strength for those wild long-winded arguments we indulged in on the boat. I had less than two hours' sleep last night, and that was mostly nightmares.

'You promised, Nial. You said you would.'

'Would *what*?' I try to shout, but it only hurts my throat, comes out like a rasp.

'Help me kill the Pope.'

I stare. 'Seton, you're insane. I never said . . .'

'You did. You said it on the boat, the first time we made love. You said we'd kill John Paul together and . . .'

I'm suddenly back there on the bunk – naked, avid, furious; my nails scratching down John-Paul's small smug back, my whole body wild and fighting him. Yes, I said I'd kill him – Seton's right. The words exploded out of me, were part of my whole lust and rage and longing. I try to shrug them off now, embarrassed and ashamed. Could I have ever really meant them, or even cared that much? 'John-Paul, maybe,' I mutter, looking down to hide my guilty face. 'But not the Pope.'

'John Paul *is* the Pope.'

I sag back on my chair. How can I refute him with my cracked and crippled voice? Even simple chitchat proved too much of a strain, let alone a full-scale crazy argument.

Seton stops his pacing, pauses for a moment just below my window-bars, peers up into daylight. 'Though actually he's not. John Paul's a fucking actor – everyone knows that. He planned a career in theatre long before he ever joined the priesthood; got involved in student drama, played endless parts himself. Playing Pope is just another role for him. He's bogus, Nial, a joker. Those robes are just his costume which he strips off when the lights go down, strips off with his smile.'

I smile myself, to humour him. Here we go again. We'll probably have the wolfhounds next, or even the ex-wives.

Seton reaches up both hands towards the small barred square of sky, as if he's trying to pull it down, transform my gloomy room from dusk to day. 'He made my parents stay together. He *killed* them, do you realise, Nial, killed the marriage dead? They were enemies, sworn enemies, but he won't allow divorce, just wraps wives and husbands up in metal swaddling bands, then ties them tight together, till they choke each other, suffocate.'

I nod, a mite depressed now. I don't like this conversation. My own parents weren't exactly friends, died fighting to the last, tied not by any tyrant Pope, but by lethargy and habit. Seton strides back to my chair, leans down very close, till I see myself reflected (dwarfed) in his dark and angry eyes.

'He killed me, too, John Paul did. If you suffocate both parents, the child always dies as well. I'm *dead*, Nial.'

'So am I,' I whisper. The words shape themselves, unbidden. I never meant to say them, nor even thought them out, but I suddenly feel bitter, not just about my own parents, but Seton's too – *all* parents. No one should have children. It's too hazardous, too cruel. Yet Big Brother Pope insists, lays down the law for Catholics, even for the world. Not just no divorce – no contraception either. Unwanted children are the worst (and saddest); females forced on parents who wanted only males, huge great hulking daughters in place of dead and fragile sons.

'Well then, what are we waiting for? Everything's arranged.' Seton starts turning out his pockets, shows me airline tickets, passport, Italian currency. I'm astonished that he seems so . . . well, so *normal* – organised and practical like your average seasoned traveller who's thought of all the details. And without his grubby duffel coat, he looks very nearly smart, as if he's dressed up for the flight, wearing an expensive lambswool sweater and a rather dashing jacket the colour of wet slate. He must be better, surely, if he can plan like this, make bookings, buy himself new clothes, deal with banks and airlines. There's just one thing he's overlooked, one rather crucial matter.

'There won't be any flights, Seton, not on Christmas Day. Nobody would work today, not pilots or . . .'

'They do. I rang the airport earlier this morning. About ten per cent of flights still leave, including two to Italy.'

He's right. I scan the tickets, check the date and time: 25 December, 14.35. Alitalia to Rome. '*Rome*?' I gasp, as I re-read the tiny print; feel distraught and almost dizzy as I suddenly remember that Rome is where John-Paul is, my own John-Paul, my Pope. He wrote it down, didn't he, on the same white solemn paper he uses for his bills. I screwed that paper up, tossed it in the gutter, but not before I'd glanced at it; glimpsed 'ROME' in bold black capitals, and the dates he'd be away. I thought he meant next year, was totally bewildered, but now everything is slowly coming back – some Psychiatric Congress it was vital he attended, and how although he'd be away, I'd still be his patient and still in therapy – what he called therapy without the actual sessions. I was scornful at the time, saw it as a con, a way of getting rid of me, but now I'm so keyed up I can't sit still; keep jumping up, slumping back, trying to sort my thoughts out, stop them bursting through my brain or through the walls. If

I went to Rome I'd find him, raise him from the dead as he raised me. Double Lazarus. I'd be restored, his child again, his son. He might give me back my lunch hours – even give me lunch – let me share his table, feed me from his plate. And if I went with Seton and he accepted him as well, we'd be truly brothers, bonded. I'd have a proper family, a father and a sibling.

'Hurry!' Seton urges, collecting up his lire and heaving on his coat. 'There shouldn't be much traffic, but we're still pretty pushed for time.'

'Look, wait. I'm still not . . .' I curse my useless voice, feel paralysed, uncertain, full of doubt, suspicion. There's so much I need to ask first. Where will we be staying? How did he get that money, or afford two sets of tickets? Will I need to pay him back? Can I even find my passport and is it out of date? I start hunting through the drawers, still trying to voice objections, but it's impossible to argue. Seton's standing at the door, impatient fingers tapping on the handle, all objections swept into his pockets with the tickets and the currency, a last small knob of cake. 'Come *on*, Nial.'

'But I need to pack, and find things. I haven't got . . .'

'I've packed.'

'But not for me.'

'*Yes*, for you, as well. Just bring a coat, a warm one.'

I haven't got a coat. I used to wear my fur-trimmed gaberdine to go and see John-Paul, so it had to be thrown out. I grab my last old sweater, suddenly decisive. I can see this is a mission, something meant, and crucial, so I've no right to oppose it. Seton's scorching up the stairs, sprinting to his car, his whole body galvanised, his eyes burning and intent. It's not his car – it's Zack's – though no sign of Zack himself, thank God. The cases look like Zack's as well: cream leather with a lot of fancy straps, but labelled 'CUSACK, Seton'. I scramble after him, passport found, and ready in my hand, slam the door my side.

'Okay?' he shouts.

'Okay!'

The car revs from nought to seventy in seconds. My excitement does the same, as we hurtle through deserted streets, past a thousand Christmas dinners, surfeiting and sating all those protesting greasy stomachs. My own stomach's clear and clean – like the freshly vacuumed sky – no trace of rain at all now, no smuts of dirty cloud, just greedy sun sucking the stiff scum from the tops of sleety puddles, licking icing-frost from twigs. Everything is shining – gutters, roofs and raindrops; Christmas decorations hung in all the houses to greet us as we pass, flickering and dazzling, glowing gold and silver.

'*Faster!*' I rasp out.

Seton slams his foot down, rockets round a corner. I start to laugh, hoarsely but triumphantly. 'Wait, John-Paul!' I shout, with the last remnants of my voice. 'We're on our way. We're coming!'

# 30

Full in the panting heart of Rome,
Beneath the apostle's crowning dome,
From pilgrims' lips that kiss the ground
Breathes in all tongues one only sound:
God bless our Pope, God bless our . . .

Bryan forced his eyes to open. The lids felt nailed together, his whole body weighted down. What was that strange singing and where *was* he, for God's sake? Certainly not at home. He could see billowing blue curtains drawn around his bed.. He must have landed up in hospital, following the plane crash – or landed up in heaven – which would explain the triumphant hymn.

He tried to peer around him, could still see only blue. Could what he'd taken as curtains be sky, the firmament? No. There wasn't any heaven. Science had destroyed it, reduced it to a myth. Or maybe science was quite wrong, and all those books he'd tussled with were myths and lies themselves. He tried to struggle up, rouse his torpid brain. The hymn had died away now, but he could hear people banging about beyond the curtains, dropping things, conversing. The voices were all male.

'Mother?' he said softly, fighting sudden panic. He'd had the Parcel Dream again (mixed in with searing nightmares of falling, burning, crashing); wrapped Lena in stout cardboard and posted her to Bagabag (an island off New Guinea), but when she'd thudded back again, struggling from her wrappings, she'd seemed someone else entirely; a stranger and an interloper. She'd been dressed in shocking pink, with showy dangly earrings, and her face had changed as well as just her clothes; a face old and lined, but hideously painted, enticing him, and winking, like some raddled desperate whore.

'Mother!' he cried desperately, clutching at the bed-clothes, as if they were her skirts. 'Come back, come back! Come back the way you were.'

'Are you all right in there, Bryan?'

He froze. How did total strangers know his name – cheery voices hailing him as if they'd known him all his life.

'Happy Christmas, Bryan!'

'Wakey wakey, Bryan, old man.'

'Don't worry, Bryan. We're here.'

He pulled the thin grey blanket round his chin, was tempted to duck under it as someone popped a head between the curtains.

'Feeling better, mate?'

He was unsure what to answer. Had he broken bones, lost pints of blood – or limbs? He jiggled both his legs, panicked for a moment when he couldn't find his hands; eventually located them inside his green pyjama sleeves, which were far too big and belonged to someone else. He did a quick check on his fingers – all present and correct – groped between his legs in sudden fear. No, everything *in situ*.

The head between the curtains had now become a body, a stocky blue-jeaned body with a shock of ginger hair on top. It moved towards the bed. 'Hi, Bryan! I'm Colin Parfitt. We met last night, in fact, but I don't suppose you remember.'

Bryan muttered a vague syllable which could be 'yes' or 'no'. If he'd ever had a memory, he'd certainly mislaid it – along with his possessions. Where were all his clothes, his own blue-striped pyjamas, his precious snake, his notebooks?

Colin plumped down on the bed, let out a sudden

guffaw. 'Gosh! You really scared us witless, leaping up like that and yelling that the plane was going to crash. I've never said my prayers with such conviction.'

'But . . . But it did crash, didn't it?'

'You *are* a joker, aren't you, Bryan? How d'you think we got here, if the plane crashed?'

Bryan tried to peer through the gap between the curtains, glimpsed a row of narrow beds, all identical to his own, a stretch of plain white wall. 'Where's . . . er . . . "here"?' he asked.

'We're in Rome, mate.'

Bryan subsided on his pillow, smoothed his tousled hair. 'Ah, yes, I see. Of course we are.'

'And we're just going down to Mass, so if you'd like to sling some clothes on and join us in the chapel . . . Don't worry if you're late. This is just the first Mass – Father Campion's. There'll be two or three more later, then High Mass in St Peter's.'

Bryan nodded, closed his eyes, heard the scuff and tramp of feet beyond the curtains, a last carillon of voices, the sharp slam of a door, then sudden silence. Shreds and scraps of memory were stirring in his brain, images so shameful he wished he could disown them. Not much point in that, though, when Colin knew, the whole plane knew, the entire two hundred pilgrims knew – knew he was a coward – worse than just a coward: a madman and a laughing-stock. The whole appalling ignominious scene was now playing in his head: the aircraft taking off, at last; crowded, claustrophobic and clearly overloaded – bombs on board, and terrorists, not just priests and pilgrims – his panic taking off, as well, as he clawed his seat-belt open and plunged frantic down the aisle, shrieking out a warning.

He'd only meant to help, give the others time to snatch their snakes and notebooks, as the plane juddered, whined, vibrated, on its death-dive. Three stewards had grabbed hold of him, but he'd fought them fist and foot; punched

372

three solar plexuses, kicked three heaving groins. More braided arms assaulted him, till he was hopelessly out-numbered, and sobbing for his Mother. They'd held him down like a drunk, or common criminal, then strapped him in a harness thing and snapped on plastic handcuffs. He'd been so humiliated, horrified, he'd only howled the louder, until some bossy creepy cleric who seemed to think he was a doctor crossed with God and Billy Graham had started praying loudly over him, then tamed him with a handful of shiny purple pills. He sat up on one elbow, pressed his aching head. Those pills had furred his brain, turned his mouth into a cesspit.

The remainder of the journey was mercifully blank, though he did recall jolting through some nightmare of a city, which seemed far too bright and noisy considering it was night; lights flashing in his eyes, buildings looming up, then vanishing again; the constant noise of singing, very close and threatening. Fragments of the songs and hymns still echoed in his head – a curiously confusing mix of 'Ten Green Bottles', 'Tipperary', 'Faith of our Fathers', and 'Wake, O Wake with Tidings Thrilling'. He wished he *could* wake up – wake in some quite different room, without those galling memories; wake to sweet normality: a temperamental boiler; some strike or jam or go-slow on the news.

He eased slowly out of bed, explored the draughty room – though there was little to explore: no washbasins or wardrobes, no rugs or chairs or cupboards; nothing much at all save thirty beds (all with their blue curtains), and pathetic heaps of luggage – underpants and sweaters spewing from old duffel bags, dented cases leaking shoes and socks. He squinted through the one small deep-set window, glimpsed a blank brick wall, a row of battered dustbins. So this was Rome – and it was probably also Christmas, since he'd been wished a happy one. It didn't feel like either. Christmas meant his Mother rousing him

373

at five a.m. so she could complain about the dark, or the price of Tesco's turkeys, or the brown bits in the sprouts. And Rome meant warmth and fountains, exotic sun-kissed ruins, murals on the walls – naked-breasted goddesses, and nymphs without their fig leaves. He glanced around the drab walls of the dormitory – only cracks and stains and scribblings, and a patch of greenish mould. The cold was worse than London, not bracing sleety sharp, but a clinging clammy damp which reminded him of rubber gloves and mortuaries.

He picked up someone's shaving mirror abandoned on a bed, studied his own face. He didn't look the way he should, the way that he remembered; seemed to have become a stranger, foreign to himself. 'Happy Christmas,' he wished the face; watched the pale lips mouth it back. Then tense uneasy silence. He shouldn't be alone on Christmas Day. Yet worse to join that cheery singing crowd again, endure their false concern. He'd just have to find his Mother, brave her scorn, her fury. Anything was better than this chilly barren dormitory, this accusing solitude. He borrowed a fawn raincoat crumpled on a suitcase, limped out to the passage, bare feet flinching on the coldly naked stone. He could hear more eager singing from the far end of the corridor – women's voices, this time, which meant Lena might be near.

> Long live the Pope! His praises sound
> Again and yet again . . .

He shuddered for his Mother, who opposed the Pope on principle, as being doubly foreign (Roman and a Pole), stubborn, male, and Catholic, and dressing in a frock. He yanked up his pyjama bottoms, which were threatening to trip him up, crept towards the voices, tapped shyly on the door. No one seemed to hear him, so he pushed the door a crack, stuck a timid head round. The hymn broke off abruptly, embarrassed shrieks replacing it, gasps of wild alarm. He glimpsed a swarm of females in various stages of undress – droopy flesh bulging over corsets, or being hoisted into boned and bossy brassières; pink suspenders dangling over wobbly blue-veined thighs.

He slammed the door immediately, stood shaken just outside, dodged a bruised backside as it burst open once again and a terrifying female clapped him on the shoulder. He knew how he must look to her – a pervert and a flasher in the proverbial dirty mac, who invaded women's dormitories, stole their underwear.

'Look, honestly, I didn't mean . . . I'm not that sort of . . .'

'Hallo, dear. I'm Phyllis. It's Bryan, isn't it? Poor Bryan, you *do* look pale! Someone should be with you.'

'I'm . . . er . . . looking for my Mother.'

'Of course you are. That's natural. You've been very poorly, haven't you? Your Mother said you often get these turns.'

He couldn't speak for shame. Had Lena been maligning him, telling all those matrons his secret fears and failings – how he still slept with a nightlight, could only swim with water-wings?

'Look, I need to find my Mother. I'm feeling rather . . .'

'Don't panic, dear. She's quite all right – just sleeping in a single room, that's all. It's really Father Fox's room, but he moved out late last night, so she could have some peace and privacy. He felt it wasn't fair that she should have to share a dormitory when her leg was playing up so much, and she'd been through all that . . .' Phyllis broke off, tactfully, cleared her throat to fill the nervous silence. It was already filled for Bryan. Those mortifying memories had swarmed back into his head again as he completed her docked sentence: Lena coping heroically with her frenzied babbling son, being pitied for her

375

thankless role of being tied for ever to a retarded child of thirty-two.

'You come along with me, dear. Your Mother's fine – you'll see. I popped in to say hallo to her, earlier this morning. She's a brave soul, isn't she? That right leg's really swollen, yet . . .'

Guilt joined shame and fury, as Bryan shambled down the stairs, Phyllis clutching on to him as if fearful he might faint or fall, or simply run amok.

'That's it. Mind your head now. This place is very old. Sixteenth century, I think Father Campion said.' She paused to pull her socks up, knee-length woollen socks in thick green rib, worn beneath a tartan skirt and a knobbly home-knit cardigan. 'Right, we just continue down this corridor and your Mother's at the end here. It's a lovely little room, and sweet of Father Fox to give it up, but then he's charity itself. He's sleeping in the attic with Father Smithby-Horne.'

Bryan counted on his fingers. Three priests, at least, in just the last three minutes. His Mother would be virulent, surrounded by these Catholics, dragooned by Popish priests, still smarting at the 'scene' he'd made, humiliated, shamed. He hardly dared to face her, hung back behind the door, peered in through the crack as Phyllis knocked and entered.

Lena was sitting up in bed in a new pink (*pink*?) knitted bed-jacket, a young and handsome priest in a smart black suit and dog collar hovering at her side, pouring out what looked like proper English tea from a normal English teapot.

'Sugar, Lena dear?'

'Two, please, Father, thank you.'

Father! Lena *dear*? Bryan stared in disbelief. His Mother looked not furious, but smug – lolling on her pillows, handing back the sugar bowl to her attentive servant-priest, then greeting Phyllis effusively as if they'd been bosom friends since childhood. He remembered Phyllis now. She'd been talking to his Mother before the plane took off, drawn to Lena because of her role as VIP: the one and only pilgrim in a wheelchair. By five o'clock, when they'd met up with their party, his Mother's leg had swollen up so badly, the airline had offered her a wheelchair; laid on a smart young lackey in a braided uniform to push her to the plane. They'd even boarded first, been allowed to jump the queue; Lena scattering gracious smiles like the Queen Mother in her landau, as smarming stewardesses swathed rugs across her knees, offered embrocations.

'How's my son?' she was asking now, in an affected stagey whisper. 'Has the poor boy woken up yet?'

Bryan ground his teeth in fury, could hardly bear to listen to this parody of motherly concern, or watch Phyllis and that strutting priest contorting their smug faces into expressions of false pity.

'Yes, he's just outside, dear,' Phyllis whispered back. 'He looks a little peaky. I think he'd better rest today, take things really quietly.'

'He's very highly strung, you know, suffers with his nerves. He's actually seeing someone for it – been seeing him for years – one of those top brain-doctors they have on television. A brilliant man, as far as I can gather, though he keeps it very dark. In fact . . .' She lowered her voice still further, so he had to strain his ears to hear. 'He's no idea I know. He goes three times every week, first thing in the morning, before it's hardly light; claims he's doing overtime, or his firm is short of staff. He likes his little secrets, so I never say a word, just humour him, pretend I . . .'

'Ssh!' warned Phyllis, nervously, but Bryan had already turned and fled – back towards the dormitory, fighting total incredulity. Lena couldn't know, she *couldn't* – not when he'd all but killed himself with four years of lies, evasions; covered all his tracks, never left the bills around, or displayed the slightest shred of interest if the subject of psychiatry came up on TV. Yet she even knew what time he went, and how many times a week. Had she had him followed, gained access to his bank statements? He sank down on the narrow bed, all his pointless fabrications screaming in his head – the stolen wallets, plunging shares, the early starts or shiftwork demanded by his firm, the financial crises, pay-cuts. Disbelief and horror gave place to bitter rage. Even if she *had* found out, how dare she share his secret, broadcast it to Catholic priests, to mocking jeering strangers? She'd probably told them everything; his entire shaming childhood history confided to a party of two hundred – how he'd wet his bed till the age of five or six, had difficulty in swallowing solid foods, how he was scared of feathers, spiders, shadows, ghosts.

'Oh, God!' he groaned aloud, as the sheer unmitigated horror of his position as official party cretin burst into his already aching head.

'What *is* it, Bryan? What's wrong?'

He swung round, saw Colin's ginger head flashing like a beacon at the door.

'I feared something might be wrong, mate. I couldn't see you in the chapel, so I was scared you'd . . . No, don't get up. You're white as a sheet. Shall I call a priest?'

'No!' It came out like a yell. Didn't Catholics call their priests when they were dying? 'I'm always pale – it's nothing. Nothing wrong at all. I'm absolutely fine.'

'Well, you don't look fine to me. But maybe you're just weak from lack of nosh. I mean, you missed your dinner, didn't you, and the refreshments on the plane. And your mother said you've been off your oats for days – too keyed up to eat, she said, and with constant pains and wind. It's breakfast in ten minutes, so why not put your clothes on and I'll take you down to meet the crowd.'

'I . . . er . . . haven't got my clothes.' Bryan prayed he'd never find them, so he could stay in bed the whole two weeks, avoid all meals, avoid the 'crowd', that mob of giggling sniggerers who would enquire into his bowel habits, dissect his indigestion. His Mother had betrayed him, not only on the issue of John-Paul (did she even know his doctor's name, he wondered with a jolt?), but on still more intimate matters. His flatulence was painful – and strictly fiercely private – or had been till today. Now two hundred strangers knew the workings (or otherwise) of his alimentary canal.

'No problem, mate. We're roughly the same size.' Colin was rummaging in his suitcase, drew out a pair of denim jeans, an orange cotton sweatshirt with 'I'M BEST FRIENDS WITH JESUS' splashed across the front.

'No, really, I can't possibly . . .'

'Go on, take 'em, Bryan. I don't mind at all. It's only for an hour or so. Your mother's probably got your case, or Father Campion.' Colin tossed the garments over, drew the curtains round Bryan's bed, hovered just outside. 'Call me if you need some help, okay?'

Bryan had never dressed so quickly in his life. The thought of someone looking at his body, assessing his ·. . . his equipment.

'Ready, mate?'

'Er, no.' The jeans seemed worryingly tight, would reveal his lack of bulge and scrawny balls. He never wore jeans anyway, associated denim with hooligans and youth. The sweatshirt was still worse. He buttoned back the rain-coat across his Jesus-blazoned chest, slunk out through the curtains.

'Great! We're just in time for breakfast. It's the only meal we're served here. Apparently the kitchens flooded just this time last year, ruined all the ovens and what have you.'

'*Meal?*' thought Bryan bitterly, as he sat facing his dry crust of bread, his cup of watery coffee. His head was reeling from the noise – swarms of eager pilgrims jabbering and cackling, clattering cups on saucers – mostly dowdy

379

women, the males totally outnumbered and therefore more conspicuous. At least a hundred females had come up to his table, offered smiles or sympathy, whinnied little condolences as if he'd suffered a bereavement. Well, Lena *had* expired, for all the use she was to him, queening it in bed still, while someone took her breakfast on a tray – fresh fruit and coddled eggs, instead of prison fare. It *was* a prison, this gloomy basement refectory, with its cold stone floor and walls, its scrubbed wood tables, hard and backless benches – he its youngest inmate, bar the boyish priest he'd seen in Lena's room. The majority of pilgrims were his Mother's age or over, and though Colin looked much younger and a few other men were only in their forties, the women were all headed for their Maker.

He had hoped to lose his own Mother, and instead he was surrounded by a tide of mother-substitutes, all fussing fretting Mothers, telling him how pale he looked, or giving him advice about the dangers of the drinking water or the high risk of diarrhoea. The only mother he desired was young and very beautiful – and still in tranquil Walton, nine hundred miles away.

Would he ever meet with Mary in this maelstrom of a city? Rome was far too big. He'd pictured a small town the size of Bath or Oxford, packed with art and churches, and surrounded by soft olive groves – a laurelled Julius Caesar strolling through its Forum beneath a blazing sun, or a turps-tinged Michelangelo sipping rough Chianti in a pavement café open to the stars. And what he'd actually seen (from the bell-tower of the seminary, where Colin had escorted him before they descended to its bowels) was a sprawling grey megalopolis, half-lost in clammy mist, with constipated traffic clogging up the roads, and a few domes in compensation.

Another crowd of pilgrims was just breezing through the door; pals of Colin, obviously, since they were all heading for his table. Bryan drowned in introductions –

bad teeth, bad breath, bad accents assailing on three sides. All the names appeared to end in 'y' – Paddy, Polly, Johnny, Janey, Dotty – and all seemed overweight: bulky hips squeezing in beside him, jutting bosoms shadowing his plate.

'I can't wait to see St Peter's!' enthused a portly balding matron, sporting Christmas-bauble earrings in deference to the season, and displacing half her coffee with an overload of sugar.

'I can't wait to see the Pope.'

'You mean you've never seen him, Milly?'

'No. Last time we came to Rome, he was . . .'

'Have *you* ever seen the Holy Father, Bryan?'

He shook his head, his mind on Holy Mothers still, though his body was assaulted by Milly's thigh on one side and Dotty's on the other. If he didn't find his luggage, he couldn't even search for Mary; would hardly win her hand in Colin's cast-offs. Without a suit or neat grey slacks he felt totally disorientated. A smart suit gave him status, and pinstripes helped to tell him which way up he was. He was unravelling in jeans, becoming Someone Else – a layabout, a pop singer, a scruffy acned teenager. And the raincoat made him furtive, or maybe half-deranged. No one else was eating in their coats. A few kindly (bossy) ladies had tried – and failed – to coax it off his back, and now obviously regarded it as some sort of security blanket which he clung to night and day. But worse to be revealed in flimsy orange cotton with Jesus as his buddy. If he'd never had a mate in thirty-two long years, he wasn't keen to start today, with God.

'Hey, Bryan, are you going to have your rosary blessed?'

'Pardon?'

'The Holy Father blesses them when we meet him at the audience. I've brought thirty-seven with me – all my friends' and family's.'

He nodded vaguely to the beaming frizz-haired spinster

381

with three medals round her neck, one of which was dangling in her coffee cup. He was no longer in the refectory with Polly, Molly, Dolly, but had jetted back to England – Sylvan Gardens, actually – and was staring through the window of Mary's festive kitchen, streamers round the cooker, tinsel round the dog, the smell of roasting turkey mingling with her scent of milk and musk. He watched her three ungrateful brats tearing at their presents, scoffing eggs and bacon, blowing froth off mugs of steaming chocolate. Then James strode in – six foot six, at least, with new dazzling Christmas chest-hair sprouting from the gap in his pyjamas – claimed his master's chair, and Mary's kiss. The room was filling up now – cosy beaming aunties, snowy-pated grandpas, grandmothers with apple cheeks, home-made fudge concealed in apron pockets. He'd never had a family, never been coddled by a Nana, or cuddled on a favourite uncle's lap. Lena had one sister (the Anne who'd made his snake), and she had died of cancer when he was only eight. There were no other aunts or uncles, no grandparents at all – or none that he had seen. When he'd enquired about his relatives, his Mother changed the subject, or said 'Ask no questions and you'll be told no lies' – her standard answer to all his childhood queries, especially when he asked about his Father.

He suddenly added Skerwin to Mary's crowded kitchen, a Skerwin with a bandaged arm, who'd just spilled all his coffee. Mary didn't nag – just mopped his brown-stained Father up, consoled him with hot muffins. He stared down at his own cold crust – no butter, jam, or even plate. The bare wood was his plate, whereas Mary's kitchen table was swanking in a scarlet cloth, with pretty floral china. James banged his rose-sprigged cup down, strode towards his wife, dragged off her lacy negligée, and the wicked wisp of nightie underneath it. She was naked in his arms now, as he swept her off upstairs, ignoring the shrill protests of his three abandoned sons, the tut-tutting of the shocked and swooning aunts. He threw her on the bed, began planting violent kisses on her breasts, her thighs, her . . .

'*No!*' cried Bryan, leaping from the bench and spilling his own coffee, which scorched and stung his groin. 'She's mine, she's *mine*, you bastard!' He tried to hurl himself on James, who had changed quite unaccountably into a younger, stouter, shorter man in shabby jeans and a ruff of ginger hair.

'It's all right, Bryan, I've got you. Don't fight me, I'm your pal. Don't worry, Johnny, he's not that heavy, really. I can manage on my own. He needs his pills, that's all. Go and call his mother, could you, Peggy? I expect she's got his tranquillisers. That's better, Bryan. You just flop and take some nice deep breaths. That's it, that's really great. Now, if you lean on me and Johnny, we'll take you back to bed – okay – and Peggy here will go and get your mother.'

Mary opened her eyes. She could hear church bells pealing faintly from somewhere far away, James's snuffly breathing providing a soft descant. 'James?' she whispered, stretching out a naked arm towards the other (single) bed.

He murmured something in his sleep, something barely audible, though she caught the name Crawshaw, uttered as a groan. Poor James. She'd hoped he could leave Crawshaw back in London, along with Holdsworth, Pierce and Hampton; the mortgage, rates and overdraft; the debts, defaulting customers. Well, perhaps he would, given time and rest. It was only their first morning, after all. She threw back the lumpy duvet, crept softly to the window, lifted up the curtain, gazed in awe at the sparkling floodlit fountain – a tangled writhe of marble mouths and nipples, all spewing moon-kissed water, while gods and satyrs grabbed at thighs and breasts.

She looked beyond the square to the swollen dome which rose between an ornate and ancient building with a carved frieze of fruit and flowers, and what looked like a temple, with a row of fluted columns standing guard in front. The view from Sylvan Gardens was of sturdy double garages, burglar-proof front doors, a gnome or two, crazy-paving paths. Here, statues, churches, columns jostled in the distance – a stern-eyed saint gesturing to the moon, halo glinting in the street-lights as he stretched up from his plinth; a plunging horse in bronze seeming to leap towards the stars. Rome! The Eternal City, the centre of her Faith – of both her Faiths, now John-Paul was here.

She longed to be alone, so she could track him down,

call at his hotel, but she was tethered by six males – three sons, two fathers, and a spouse, all needing her, demanding. James's father and her own had both decided to accompany them, despite their myriad ailments and their years. James's father, Harry, had paid almost half of the entire cost of the holiday, offering it as his Christmas gift, and a contribution to what he called his grandsons' cultural education (which had swiftly overruled James's first objections to having a semi-invalid in tow). Her own workaholic father had decided to revise a book he had half-written in his fifties (abandoned due to lack of time) on the Food and Agriculture Organization, whose headquarters were in Rome, and which he'd need to visit to update his researches. He'd packed little else but reference books and file cards, bulky jotters, all his earlier notes.

Mary stifled a yawn as she watched a yellow taxi swivel round the near-deserted square. She'd had very little sleep last night, had been summoned in the early hours to each of the three other rooms in turn. The boys were sleeping together, in one three-bedded room, but the fathers had refused to share, despite the lower cost, since Lionel felt contempt for what he saw as Harry's hypochondria, while Harry objected to Lionel's midnight scribblings and the reek of his cigars. Harry already had diarrhoea and indigestion; Lionel had complained about 'disturbance' from the boys, while the boys themselves had giggled, quarrelled, blocked their basin, engaged in boisterous pillow-fights, and, in Simon's case, thrown up.

By the time she'd soothed and refereed, doled out medicines and warnings, and sponged two pairs of sheets, it had been after two a.m. The night before, she'd been up till nearly one, finishing off the ironing and the packing. It had been a strain to get away at all – to wash and pack for seven, coax Horatio to kennels and Aunt Alice to her niece's; transform the turkey relics into future freezer meals, and find willing 'flu-free volunteers for her various

385

good works. But she'd known that it was worth it as soon as they'd touched down, and she'd stepped out from the DC9 onto glittering Roman tarmac – a fat-cheeked moon competing with the floodlights, and one brilliant evening star seeming to promise help and guidance in her quest to find John-Paul.

The whole city was agog with the Blessed Edwin Mumford, but *she* was more concerned with her own private Blessed Doctor, who had surely as much right to be styled a saint himself, and certainly a martyr, since he martyred himself daily for the sake of all his patients. She'd been reflecting on the job of psychotherapist – its loneliness, its selflessness, the daily (hourly) listening to stories of distress, stoically enduring patients' anger, panics, violence; never fighting back or discussing one's own problems; unable to ask advice from family or friends, for fear of breaking confidences; unable to take a mid-week break or sudden unplanned holiday; always ruled and fettered by endless strict appointments, other people's needs. And 'fettered' was the word. John-Paul was tied to one small chair in one small smoky room; deprived of normal movement and activity, denied a change of scene or change of view. He could hardly yawn or slouch or sigh in the middle of a session, or get up to stretch his legs, and even shifting on his seat might lead to accusations that he was fidgety or bored. The sheer physical constriction must surely irk him sometimes, and it wasn't just his bodily health which was threatened by the job – psychiatrists also suffered mentally, or so she'd read just recently in James's *Sunday Telegraph* – often slid into depression, or became secretly addicted to amphetamines or alcohol, or even killed themselves with their own battery of drugs.

She was all the more impressed by her own serenely stoic doctor, who never showed a trace of even minor instability, and had never once cancelled an appointment because he was ill or 'indisposed'. And yet his life was one long battle against other people's suffering – always giving, giving, giving, with so little in return. He couldn't even accept a present from a patient (as she remembered to her chagrin from the débâcle of the mince pies). And his leisure-time seemed dismally restricted, as ascetic as a monk's. He'd told her once he hadn't time for reading, except professional books and journals, and he could hardly saunter off to clubs or pubs or theatres, with patients booked every night till ten. And if saints were proved by miracles, then John-Paul had worked his own – miracles as potent as the Blessed Edwin Mumford's: healing psyches, mending lives, resurrecting dead and cold libidos.

She ran one hand slowly down her body, stood stroking her mons veneris, praying to her saint. Was *he* awake, she wondered, maybe gazing from a window only streets away from hers, admiring the same vista, inhaling the same air; his pyjama jacket open in the warm breath of the night, the dark hair on his chest tangling past his navel to his . . .?

She drifted back to bed, touched her breasts, surprised to find them dry, and not spouting golden water like the fountain in the square. The nipples were erect, lacked only a god or satyr to fondle and admire them, excite them to a marble hardness. The satyr in the other bed was still breathing very hoarsely. (She would have almost called it snoring, except James forbade the word.) She longed to reach across and rouse him – rouse him in all senses – but John-Paul had suggested at their last December session that James was clearly threatened by her new eager sexuality; probably had a need to take the initiative in bed, to see himself as hunter and her as passive prey, and she had obviously undermined him by her reversal of their roles. He might also feel alarmed by her vibrators, he'd explained; their sheer size and power and stiffness arousing basic fears about his potency and manhood.

She'd been so upset, so worried, so galled by the fiasco

of their recent anniversary, which she had described with tears and shame, that she'd decided to disown her new miraculous libido (at least until the Doctor had worked a second miracle on James's own virility), and return to her old role – the bashful Mrs Frigidaire he'd once scorned and yet desired. But playing bashful wasn't quite so easy as simply being it spontaneously, and she'd become totally confused; a skirl of different voices discordant in the bedroom, some shouting 'Stop!', some begging 'More!', some urging both at once.

The last time they'd made love – a whole thirteen days ago now – she'd been so tense and edgy, she had infected James as well, and they'd both developed headaches, the thumping and disabling kind she'd once (wickedly) invented, to avoid sex altogether. But now they were away, she was sure things would improve. James had slept extremely well, had snored (no, breathed) through all the midnight crises; not even stirred when a drunken crowd of foreign guests paused outside their door to hoot and swill. With any luck, he'd wake refreshed – though if he slept much longer, the boys would wake as well, and instead of James lying groin to groin with her, it would be Jonathan jumping on her tummy. She checked her watch – ten to six already. The boys rarely slept past seven, and her ever-busy father would be pacing at first light, eager to have breakfast and start revising Chapter One.

She eased out of bed a second time, paused by James's pillows. She could always plead that she was cold, needed to slip in with him to warm her chilly feet. He jolted out of sleep as her shoulder brushed his own, tried to struggle up, both fists clenched aggressively, as if ready to do combat with the intruder in his bed. 'Larry?' he exclaimed.

'No, it's only me, dear. Larry Crawshaw's not in Rome. You've left all that behind.'

He fumbled for the light-switch, seemed bemused by the strange room, slowly got his bearings as he checked his watch and Filofax, blew his nose dramatically, then slumped back on the pillows. 'What a night! I hardly slept a wink.'

'Really, James? I'm sorry.'

'I've got too much on my mind. And this stuffy room is murder for my sinuses. I don't think I dropped off until two a.m., or later, and then I was woken by some hooligan.' He poked a finger in his ear, removed a scrap of debris. 'Well, at least the boys were quiet.'

Mary didn't answer. She was trying to play bashful while yanking up her nightie and arranging her bare thigh beside James's pyjamaed one. 'Never mind, darling. You'll have lots of chance to rest here. It's such fun to be abroad.'

James grabbed the slipping duvet, edged his leg away. 'I never like strange beds, though. They're always far too short. The Italians may be dwarfs, but they ought to realise Englishmen have longer legs and . . .' He broke off, head cocked sideways. 'What's that noise outside?'

'Just the fountain, darling.'

'No, that *other* noise. Good God! It's heavy traffic, at this hour of the morning.' James was already out of bed, frowning from the window as he surveyed the scene below. 'D'you realise, Mary, Rome has one of the most appalling traffic problems of any city in the world? Two million cars and damnfool motor scooters jammed into an area a quarter the size of London, and with no decent modern roads. The average speed of traffic has slowed to 3.7 miles an hour – I read it in that guide book on the plane – and the average noise during waking hours is well above the level which makes you permanently deaf. And they even said . . .'

'The fountain's rather pretty, though.'

'It's filthy dirty, Mary. That marble's almost black, and the nymphs have lost their noses. Most of Rome's monuments are literally crumbling away. They've got a

389

major problem with pollution, yet nothing's done about it. And d'you know why?'

She listened to the first half-dozen reasons, which ranged from graft and indolence to what he called Byzantine bureaucracy, then coaxed him back to bed, pretending to be concerned about his sinuses, which justified a close examination of his ears and throat and chest. Ears were erotogenic zones – or so the sex-books said – though James complained she tickled and jerked his head away. She could glimpse his little tassel through the gap in his pyjamas. Strange they'd never given it a name. According to those sex-books, penises had scores of names – Johnny, Willy, Percy, Peter, Rupert, Roger, Dick – and even her vibrators were personalized with nicknames, often rather brutish ones, which wouldn't quite suit James. His model looked a little limp and delicate, at least compared with 'Bully Boy' or 'Titan'.

She sometimes wished it was fashioned in gold latex instead of staid pink flesh, or came complete with thrill-frills or a probing light-up tip. Back in the old and frigid days it had always seemed too big. She was becoming far too critical, perhaps predatory, aggressive, as John–Paul himself had hinted; must really make an effort to appear passive and no threat. She lay back on the pillows, arms across her breasts, which she hoped would look virginal, whilst drawing his attention to them. He hadn't even said 'Nice tits', as he used to, pre-John-Paul. If only they were golf balls, or could be filled with best malt whisky which turned on like a tap, he'd probably show more interest. Ah! He was undoing his pyjamas now, slipping off the bottoms, and he'd swelled a little down below, reached the rough dimensions of her handbag-sized vibrator.

She still lay meek and modest, as if completely unaroused, ignoring the lewd urges pumping from her groin. James kissed her mouth perfunctorily, and she remembered not to open it, not to use her tongue; to reverse all the instructions in those emasculating sex-books. It seemed to be effective – James was now inside her – though he didn't feel as hard or stiff as her usual brute vibrators, left safe and sad at home. She didn't move beneath him, didn't make a sound, fixed all her concentration on acting the chaste virgin, so he could play the hunter, the rapist, the aggressor.

'Are you all right?' he panted, pausing for a moment to scratch between his shoulder blades, and sounding half-concerned and half-suspicious.

She nodded, face demure. 'Just be gentle, will you, darling? You feel so . . . so *big* today.' She watched him preen and brighten, relieved she'd got it right, at last. John-Paul had pointed out that many men needed to feel masterful, preferred their wives submissive, even cowering, in awe of their male powers. 'You're always big in the mornings, James, but today you're really wild!' She tried to shrink away, as if he were splitting her apart; bit her bottom lip in what she hoped would seem a gesture of fear and yet surrender, eyes fixed on his adoringly. She longed to make him truly wild, to mount her like a tiger, snarl his mating-cry. Tigers did it twenty times a day or more, when the females were on heat. She had read that in a book on mating animals; read about the wildebeest who could chase young hinds all day, mount one after the other, until they collapsed from sheer exhaustion.

'Don't move,' James breathed. 'I love you lying still. It makes it more exciting. Pretend you're a Roman slave-girl I've just bought in the market and you have to do exactly what I want.'

She made her voice as girlish as she could, added a faint tremor as she simpered through her hands. 'What *do* you want, Master?'

'Turn over and be quiet.'

She rolled over on her stomach, half-kneeling, half-crouching, like an animal herself; shut her mouth, shut

391

off her responses; lay, a sack, a duvet, while he mastered her, exulted. He seemed his normal self again; potent, energetic, relishing his power. So John-Paul had been right. James couldn't cope with any sexual rival, not even his own wife; needed an inferior, a position of command. She could feel him nearly coming, longed to shout 'Not yet!'; gnawed the pillow to occupy her mouth, so it wouldn't want to bite his lips, or fret and chafe his prick. He discharged with a tiny cry, withdrew immediately, patted her left flank as if she were Horatio; mumbled 'Lovely fuck, dear', then vanished to the bathroom.

She waited till she heard the roar of running water, then cried aloud 'John-Paul!', voice pleading, almost desperate; both hands between her legs. He was there in seconds, sitting just behind her as she writhed naked on the couch. 'Kiss me,' she insisted, now opening her mouth as wide as it would go, so he could thrust his avid tongue in, explore her teeth, her throat. He was still fully dressed in dark suit, white shirt, and highly polished shoes. She didn't want his clothes off, not even when he entered her. Clothes made it more exciting, kept him as a doctor, the smartly dressed professional who was examining her vagina while panting for her cunt.

'Cunt!' she whispered wantonly; knew he loved to hear her repeat those naughty words, as well as the exotic ones which he himself had taught her. He'd taught her everything, had made her Woman – Empress, not a slave-girl, with him as Emperor-Consort. 'Cock,' she gloated, reaching down to grasp it as he unzipped his bulging flies. 'Cupid's torch, connecting rod, fowling-piece, Aaron's rod, *arbor vitae*, holy iron, goose's neck, hanging Johnny, fiddlestick, tickle-tail, middle finger, womb-brush.' Her voice crescendoed through the list, yet lingered on each one, giving it its due, its appreciation, reverence. She had learnt those words just recently from a book of Sexual Folklore, and there were at least six hundred more – six hundred different names for one tiny towering organ. Some were very ancient, and 'cock' itself dated from the early seventeenth century. She was making up for her lack of education, learning new delicious facts each day from her vast library of sex-books (all hidden in the outhouse, where she'd once kept her home-made chutney).

Not that she could concentrate on history or statistics, not just at this moment, with John-Paul's *arbor vitae* swelling in her mouth, feeling almost as stupendous as in the dream she'd had last night, when she'd seen her ardent doctor as all prick – one engorged and thrusting organ from his ankles to his scalp. She smiled as she remembered, sucked him in still deeper, knew exactly what he liked now – her lips pursed tight and stiff, massaging the shaft, her swift tongue flicking back and forth across the swollen tip, then forcing down inside the tiny slit, exploring it and filling it until he overflowed.

Oh, she'd made such marvellous progress in just the last few weeks, had tossed away beginners' books, and moved on to advanced; changing John-Paul's coital outfits from dapper suit to morning dress, to tails and white bow tie; or sometimes having him examine her in a long white coat and stethoscope. The stethoscope was always stiff, always probing into apertures she didn't know she had, listening to her body, its private passion-noises. It was making noises now – wild uncensored noises, which she knew he'd hear amplified as he delved and groped and scrutinised, scribbling down his case notes about the swelling of her clitoris, the moistening of her vulva. She admired his sheer professionalism, his eager concentration – even now, with splashings from the bathroom, the traffic roar outside, the bray of a pneumatic drill throbbing through the square, a gang of raucous workmen yelling over it.

'Fuck me,' she said boldly. No need to pretend now, to play passive bashful maiden, so as to boost James's flagging fiddlestick. John-Paul *liked* her predatory, saw her passion

393

as a compliment, an enhancement of his manhood, not a threat or put-down. 'Harder,' she implored him, as he slammed between her legs. He was wildebeest and tiger, top buck of the herd. She loved his savage rutting-cry, loved the din outside: the discordant clash of church bells, hooting, drilling. No, the racket wasn't outside – the workmen had burst in and were drilling her own hole, their horny calloused labourers' hands chafing on her skin, their powerful tools ramming deeper, deeper. Their cries had changed, as well – no longer yelled instructions or cautions to the gang, but lewd and lustful Italian words bellowed in her honour as they stripped her down and filled her.

There was a second's startled silence as drill and church bells ceased, traffic thinned or jammed, and the men themselves switched off their brazen voices. She could hear the frantic fountain, overwhelmed before, now plashing in her room; gods and satyrs fighting into bed with her, water gushing everywhere from fecund mouths and nipples. She had never been so wet and hot, nor enjoyed such scores of ravishers; could feel herself exploding as tigers, satyrs, workmen, gods, all climaxed at the same astounding moment; John-Paul himself a fountain spewing out an arc of shimmering sperm. She came with him, with all of them, arching up her body, screwing up her face, gasping out that number she'd been so desperate to reach: 'Nine hundred and ninety-nine!'

'*Mary!*' hissed a frantic voice. She flinched, uncoiled her sticky fingers from her cunt. How did satyrs know her name, or a gang of Roman navvies? She was too flaked out to care, too sated-glutted-blissful even to find out what was wrong; just had to lie recovering, eyes shut, skin flushed and damp; replaying each sensation, exulting in John-Paul, hearing his wild compliments chiming through the church bells, his heavy gasping breathing a tribute to her skills.

'Mary!' slammed the voice again, sounding still more

394

agitated, and closer to her head. She squinted through her eyelids, glimpsed James's stripey dressing gown trying vainly to protect her from the prurient gaze of three young sons, two old and startled fathers, all gawping at the door.

'You told us not to yell last night,' primmed Simon. 'And you've been screaming out yourself, making so much din you've woken everybody up. And anyway,' he added, voice shrilling in reproach, 'it's extremely rude to sleep with nothing on.'

# 32

I walk slowly down the nave of St Paul's Outside the Walls, the fiery choke of sunset flaming through the alabaster windows, turning me to gold. Everything is gold – mosaics, frescoes, soaring granite columns – as if I've somehow got to heaven and left grey and gloom behind. It's been sunny every day since we first arrived in Rome; not a sickly schizoid sun like you get in grudging England, but a passionate and brazen one, wooing the brisk mornings, ripping off the frail blue mist which veils and blurs the city at first light. I've seen twenty churches, so far, but none to rival this. Its size is frankly dwarfing, the nave stretching to infinity, the gilded panelled ceiling as far above my head as the heavens from the earth. I know nothing of religion, yet as soon as I stepped in here, I felt I had to kneel. It was completely otherworldly, as if built by gods for God.

Many of the other churches left me somehow sated, as if I'd gorged myself on marzipan, washed down with double cream. All that elaborate decoration felt more like swank and swagger – man showing off his riches, or proving just how skilled he is, a rival to his deity. St Peter's, in particular, seemed to be screaming out its grandeur, insisting I admire it – admire its famous architects, its pride of peerless artists. Here, man is left behind. There's no glass to let the world in, just those alabaster slices which alchemise the light, and the golden blaze itself seems to make the columns tremble, the rich mosaics writhe. Everything is moving – apostles pointing heavenwards, angels' stone wings fluttering, the vast ceiling lifting off.

The church is called St Paul's because apparently he's

buried here, just beneath the altar, but it should be renamed Lazarus, since it rose again, from death. Almost the entire building was destroyed by fire in 1823. Thirty years later, it triumphed from the ashes, restored almost exactly as it was in AD 391, when it was the grandest church in Rome. You can feel the boast of resurrection shouting from the walls – which is perhaps why Seton likes it. He first brought me here yesterday, stopped outside the main façade, gazed up above the columns to the panel of mosaics throbbing in the sun. I could see a lot of stringy sheep grazing in the foreground, and then two shadowed cities, one on either side.

'Bethlehem and Jerusalem,' he muttered rather irritably, as if I'd asked him what they were and he didn't like my question, though actually I hadn't said a word. 'The beginning and the end.'

I shivered suddenly, despite the fact it was blazing noon, and warm. 'The beginning and the end' sounded somehow ominous, especially after Seton had been talking guns all night, with Giuseppe, Marco, Stefan, the three guys we're living with. They may be crooks or thugs (or Mafia) for all I know about them, and since none of them speaks English, I'm not likely to find out. Stefan's wild and angry-looking with a coarse black beard and black fingernails to match. Marco's very thin, as if whoever made him gave him bones but forgot about the flesh. Giuseppe is my favourite and the only one who smiles; a handsome, charming, jokey type, who's only in his twenties, but has one long strand of pure white hair startling from the black. At first, I thought he dyed it, but then I realised it was natural, as if just that lock had aged, or suffered some bad shock. It makes him slightly comic, like a two-tone tufted duck.

They were all a shade suspicious when Seton brought me in, Marco's frown a shutter closing off his eyes; Stefan chewing gum, only pausing for a moment to scrape it off his teeth, deign me a brief nod. But Seton introduced me as a member of the gang, someone useful and important who had to be respected, and would never blab, betray them. They took a while to thaw, but now they're pretty decent, share their food and wine with me, save me the best seat (a chair with broken springs), even lend me clothes. Seton claimed he'd packed for two, but the truth was rather different – all he had in duplicate was size eleven shoes. Giuseppe's the same build as me, so I'm dressed in his black cords (with balding zippered fly), a heavy short-cropped lumberjacket which smells of sweat and paint, and a pair of Stefan's Y-fronts, which only lack a prick. I rather like the outfit, which has somehow made me powerful, transformed my walk and bearing, given me new confidence, as if my dead father's looking down on me and finally approving.

I strut towards the heavy door which leads out to the cloister, a square of sun and shadow with barley-sugar columns and roses in the flowerbeds – yes, full-bloom scarlet roses in the tail end of December. The four men are still out there, huddled round the fountain, still jawing, jawing, jawing. They truly are a gang. Seton's bid to kill the Pope isn't just a personal vendetta, or proof that he's a nutter, as I assumed myself at first. The whole thing's far more complex, involves many other interests – political, financial, even moral. Seton seemed completely *compos mentis* when he started explaining it the evening we arrived. It was *me* who was confused as I tried to take on board the clash between the Communists and Catholics, the scandals in the Vatican, the involvement of the Masons and the Mafia, and why Stefan (who's Bulgarian) should be even more fanatical than Seton, want to bomb St Peter's, blow up every cardinal in Rome.

It didn't really help when the other three kept butting in, which made Seton switch immediately to very fluent swift Italian and left me still more flummoxed than before. But confused or no, I was still impressed with Seton, saw him in a completely different light. He's labelled 'mad' in England, whereas in Rome he's a skilled linguist and leader of the gang. The others all kowtow to him – I saw that from day one – and because he's my lover, I get to share his status.

The love is going well. We haven't got a proper bed, but that never hampered Seton, and it excites us both to know the guys are listening through the walls. They don't have any choice. The walls are just partitions, paper-thin and tactless, and if Giuseppe's sneeze or Marco's cough re-echoes like a bomb, then Seton's angry climaxes must all but knock them flat. He seems to need anger to get him roused at all, and I find it quite a turn-on – the violence and the ranting, the fact the Pope is there with us, on floor or rug or sofa, stripped naked, bound and beaten as Seton storms his name, mocks his flaunting titles; all his pomp and holiness reduced to sweat and sperm. I suppose sacrilege excites me, but it isn't only that. Even hate is proof of passion, and Seton's hate is consummate.

I drift towards the fountain, so I can see my lover's hands. They're gripping the stone basin, as they gripped my flanks last night. He's angry still – I can hear it in his voice, though I'm too far away to catch a word he's saying, and wouldn't grasp it anyway. All I've mastered in Italian is 'yes' and 'no', 'toilet', 'prick' and 'aubergine'; a few names of wines and pastas, which I picked up from a menu, and the brand name 'Crodino', which a girl crooned fifteen times or more on a television commercial (and which sounds obscene, but is actually a non-alcoholic drink). And 'Pope', of course – *Il Papa*. *Giovanni Paolo*, *Santo Padre*, *Sua Santità*. Seton mocks him in Italian, so I've come to know his titles, sometimes yell them out myself when we're heaving in our sleeping bag with *Il Papa* as a threesome.

In fact, I know all the statistics now – the nine hundred million Roman Catholic faithful, dictated to by a mere few thousand piddling Roman bureaucrats, all male, of course, and celibate; the seventeen thousand priests who've walked out on the job in America alone (while *Santo Padre* calls for even greater strictness, to chain them to their ministries); his forty-one international journeys, visiting seventy-seven countries, many several times (which Seton sees as a bid for power and showmanship, and a flagrant waste of money – though it pales beside the thousand million lire squandered by the Vatican Bank on the corrupt and murderous Mafia). I also know the adjectives – despotic and tyrannical, reactionary, oppressive. (Or fossilised and fraudulent, if he's bawling out the bureaucrats.)

Anger is infectious. I march back to the church, confront Giovanni Paolo, who's actually inside – gazing from a small gilt-framed medallion high above the columns. Every Pope who ever reigned, commencing with Saint Peter and ending with John Paul, is depicted in this church, each in a roundel of mosaic, with precious stones as eyes, and extending all along the aisles. I've counted them already, which took a bit of doing since the grand total was two hundred and sixty-three. I went prowling back through history as I paced up and down the nave, remembering not just tyrant Popes, but promiscuous ones as well – Popes with strings of mistresses, children by the score; Popes with violent bloody hands who poisoned, strangled, slaughtered, as they bumped off all their rivals, battled for new spoils.

'Your *Holiness,*' I say with heavy sarcasm, as I gesture down the aisle to Alexander VI, the most blatant of the Borgias, who spent half his papacy engaged in plots and scandals to enrich his bastard children (when he wasn't sleeping with them).

Silence. The church is empty save for Popes, and one devout (or drunken?) woman spilling like a sack on the patterned marble floor. I turn back to Pope John Paul, crick my neck to peer at him. 'So are you proud of all your predecessors?' I ask him, with a grimace. 'Do you all plot and fight and fornicate once the church is closed to tourists and the doors are locked and barred?'

He doesn't say a word, just gazes back with his supercilious face. I think of all the beggars I keep passing on the street, some kids of only six or so, some toothless crones, in rags. These Popes are robed in velvet edged with ermine; gold leaf on their mantles, gold ingots in their bank-vaults – wealthy wimps in fancy dress, laying down the law about women and the poor, when they're ignorant of both. John Paul looks smug and chubby, his jewel eyes hard, his narrow mouth set merciless.

I stand stock-still where I am, a rush of heat exploding through my body, as if I've received a revelation. I suddenly know I have to kill him, do the deed myself, save Seton and the others from jail or execution. If I die or get imprisoned, it makes hardly any difference. I was already dead a week ago, and my bedsit is a prison. *This* is liberation – to free nineteen million faithful from tyranny, corruption, and not just Roman Catholics, but idealists like Stefan, who are fighting scandals, burning for a cause. Okay, I don't quite grasp that cause, but if I espouse it as my own, then I'll become another Lazarus, kept alive in history like marble or mosaic, preserved in people's memory. I've always longed to achieve some perfect act, do just one thing successfully, to leave as a memorial, a present to my own John-Paul – not one he can return this time, or spurn as some base bribe. If I kill his namesake, then I prove my worth and selflessness, escape the mess and failure of my life (and death) to date, escape those endless sessions on the couch.

I grope towards a column, lean against it, dizzy; see John-Paul in my prison cell, an admiring awe-struck visitor, paying tribute to my courage; maybe even watching as I coolly pull the trigger at some solemn papal mass. I've been desperate to lay eyes on him since the moment I arrived, trudged to his hotel each day – one of the grandest in all Rome – braved the braided flunkeys who try to debar anyone who isn't dripping mink, or arrives on Shanks's pony instead of chauffeured Rolls. The conference hasn't started yet, but they still insist he's busy, won't divulge his room number, just shoo me out contemptuously, as if I'm a dangerous vagrant who's somehow fouled the air. The place is like a palace – chandeliers and marble, and a sumptuous curving staircase with cherubs on the balustrade entwined with languorous mermaids. (They ought to see Giuseppe's flat, where we all five camp and huddle. It's dark and mean and shabby-looking, with dust as decoration and half a rusting motorbike abandoned in the foyer.)

I struggle to the door again, so hot I need fresh air; relish the sharp slap of cold which reminds me it's still winter, despite the dazzling sun. The sun is dying, actually, dying in this cloister which was once an ancient cemetery and has fragments of old tombstones embedded in the walls. I can hear a siren shrilling from somewhere in the street. Even in Italy, I can't escape the sirens – in fact, they're louder here. I edge up to the group of men, who've forgotten I exist, touch Seton's arm a moment, keep my fingers on his sleeve while I tell him my decision.

Suddenly he's kissing me, and the kiss is part of sunset – blazing, bloody, dangerous, as we're merged with dome and palace in one furious scarlet pyre, which is kindling the whole sky from Ostia to Anzio. The other men are watching, encircled in that same fierce glow, which seems to gash their faces, frets their hands and hair. Seton frees my hurting mouth, turns back to his friends, who all nod and grin and gesture as he speaks swiftly in Italian, links his arm through mine. Giuseppe takes my other arm, Stefan on his left, Marco next to Seton, so we're all joined, arm through arm. Our shadows fuse as well, long dramatic shadows, which leapfrog walls and buildings, as we leave the cloister, surge on down the street, goose-stepping and laughing, blocking the whole pavement.

'*Vino!*' shouts Giuseppe, as we stop outside a noisy bar, claim a pavement table.

'No,' says Seton, tipping back my face again so he can run a finger down it, trace my open lips. 'Champagne!'

# 33

Bryan stood dithering at the traffic lights, which had changed to red three times, though still he hadn't dared to cross the road. Even when the lights said 'Stop', half the throbbing motorbikes appeared to totally ignore them, simply roared across his path, so he'd twice dodged back in terror, almost lost his legs. He was late for lunch already – if you could call it lunch, that sludge of boiled potatoes or tangled tepid pasta – no vegetables, no meat, no comforting hot puddings; just one tiny scoop of white ice cream in a guesthouse like a fridge itself, with draughts from all the windows, and a slimy cold stone floor. It was hardly worth the effort of getting there at all – the thirty-minute bus ride through hooting manic traffic, with all his fellow pilgrims jabbering like gibbons, or singing fervent hymns.

Fellow pilgrims phooey! He was no one's fellow. They mostly babied him or shunned him now, either regarded him as handicapped, a delinquent child and burden to his Mother, who must be humoured, chin-chucked, fed Valium and Smarties, or feared him as a psychopath, someone unpredictable, dangerously disturbed. A few women seemed quite terrified if he sat down at their table, edged away, or changed places with the men. He had always seen himself as a totally harmless person, gentle as a moth, yet he *had* been violent, hadn't he – attacked those stewards on the plane, even turned on Colin, punched him in the ribs, then had a go at Johnny, who was still walking doubled up. Bryan Payne a desperado, a Hun, a brute, a hoodlum.

Shuddering, he trailed away from the stream of panting traffic, mooched back the way he'd come. He couldn't face another meal with Colin cutting up his pasta for him, or

Mrs Carey-Cartwright whispering to her neighbour that it wasn't fair on normal people to allow 'cases' on the trip. He'd have to find a café, buy himself lunch out, except wasn't that as daunting, when he didn't speak the language, preferred Ribena to red wine? And Rome was clearly dangerous – his Mother was quite right. All five priests had warned them of pickpockets and muggers, wily gypsy children who pretended to be begging, but were trained professional thieves. And half the Roman drivers were murderers in disguise, only waiting for a chance to claim another corpse or three. But what was quite extraordinary was that his Mother was *enjoying* it – had warned him all his life of the perils of 'abroad', yet now seemed in her element; even loved the crowded streets, the shops which ripped you off, the brilliant bossy sunshine which felt just like a searchlight and made it impossible to hide. It was a sham, that sun, in any case – all glare without the warmth; had tempted him to venture out without his thermal underwear, so that now he was half-frozen.

He scrabbled in his pocket for his non-existent gloves, found a bag of birdseed which Phyllis had entrusted to him with excited eager cries about a black-necked grebe she'd spotted, feeding on the reed-beds of the Tiber. He could eat the seed himself. It would make a quick and easy lunch, without the need to risk diarrhoea trying out some Roman dish he could neither translate nor digest. And he could eat it by the Tiber, which Phyllis claimed was quiet and almost rural, if you walked down by its banks, followed it upstream.

He checked his map, found the Tiber coiling like a snake along the left-hand side. He missed his own snake desperately. A cad called Clive had nicked it, used it as a cricket bat, a doorstop and a muffler, put it on a dog-lead and hung it from the ceiling, doused it in the water-jug, and finally ran off with it and refused to give it back. He'd tried to ask his Mother to use her (growing) influence

405

to command or coax it back, but she'd been ensconced with Father Fox, whom she now called 'Alfred, dear'; and seemed always far too busy organising prayer-groups or helping 'darling Phyllis', to spare a word for *him*. She was on first-name terms with all the priests, who admired her selfless courage in devoting her whole life to a defective thankless son.

He increased his pace, braving narrow alleys or heart-stopping main roads; taking out his anger on the flocks of puffed-up pigeons who fled at his approach, or glowering at hirsute and handsome Latins who tried to edge him off the pavement, jeered at his new sunhat. He was tired of Rome already, had spent every free (or stolen) minute searching hopelessly for Mary. How could he find one person in a city of three million, with at least another million tourists – or so it seemed from the crushes in the cafés, the queues in the museums? And there were over a thousand hotels and *pensioni* in just central Rome alone. He'd checked only eighty-three so far (entering each in his red notebook with a dismal cross beside it when the receptionists shook their callous heads, or even failed to understand him); had found no Mrs (English) Hampton; was beginning to lose hope – as well as weight.

He plodded on morosely, his mind on Mary still. She'd probably never come to Rome at all, had changed her mind – or bookings – or been kept at home by a sick and feverish child. Which meant his own trip was a total waste of money; an ordeal and a torment with no prize at the end of it, no lovers' knot to make his pain worthwhile. He crossed another busy road, suddenly found himself gazing down at an expanse of jade-green water. The elusive River Tiber had unaccountably appeared, though he'd long since lost his bearings, concluded that the map had been drawn up by a Roman and was therefore clearly wrong. His spirits rose a fraction. The river looked deserted – no shipping like the bustling Thames, no busy built-up towpath; just that stretch of tranquil water reflecting plane trees on one side, bare and mottled branches rippling upside-down, sturdy trunks dissolving. He'd thought Phyllis was romanticising when she'd talked of rural peace – no chance of *that* in Rome – but as he tottered down the flight of steps to the bramble-tangled bank, the roar of cars and lorries faded to a murmur, and he found himself alone with weeds and water.

He trudged along the bank, crunching through the dead brown leaves, dodging burrs and nettles, half-hidden by the waist-high grasses which began to close him in. Swift white gulls skimmed across the water, perky sparrows quarrelled in the undergrowth, tussling over scraps. He was ravenous himself, had better eat his birdseed, not waste it on a grebe. He chose his picnic site with care, turned his back on the battered cans, twisted scraps of metal, piles of dirty newspapers, which had spoilt the view so far, and sat right down by the bank, spreading his grey raincoat underneath him, so he wouldn't develop haemorrhoids, or a chill in either kidney. He shook the seeds into his palm, chewed each twenty times; felt a sense of sweet relief as he imagined all the other pilgrims slurping down spaghetti with its dangerous lack of fibre, or fidgeting through grace (which often lasted longer than the perfunctory meal itself).

He lay back on the bank, lulled by sun and chewing, closed his eyes, tipped his sunhat over them, let his breathing deepen. He could hardly sleep a wink at night, what with the singsongs and the japes, the snorings and the sleep-talkings, and his own desperate wish for Mary – not to mention kidnapped Anne. He imagined his soft snake miraculously restored to him, coiled close against his chest, murmured to it fondly as he let himself drift off.

Twenty minutes later, he jackknifed to his feet, sweat beading on his forehead, despite the brisk December air. He'd actually been dreaming in that short sleep on the bank, despite his determination never to dream again. The last nightmare he'd endured involved a battle with the Vatican in which he'd queued for years and years to get official papal permission to go to bed with Mary, then spent so long filling in the forms (thirty sheets in triplicate) that his Love had shrivelled to a crone by the time he'd crossed the final 't' and signed his doddering name. Now he'd dreamed again – and things were even worse this time. He'd had the dreaded Parcel Dream, but with a completely different ending. He'd posted off his Mother to a new volcanic island, but instead of her returning thump-thump on the doormat, she had remained quietly on the lava in her corrugated wrappings; not even tried to force her string or struggle through her sealing wax.

He should feel thrilled, triumphant – to have reached that resolution, that denouement he'd been working for through four long years of therapy; to have achieved a major breakthrough and be freed, at last, from Mother. In fact, he felt quite terrified – alone and lost and vulnerable. Who would find his snake for him, or calm him on the plane, wash his thermal underpants, cut his horny toenails or the nails of his right hand? His Mother was neglecting him already, never seemed to speak to him, or even say goodnight; never joined him at the guesthouse or helped him through the meals. Her leg was very painful still, so she was spared the jolting bus-rides, ate at a taverna just three steps from the seminary with 'Alfred dear' and 'Snowy' (Father Smithby-Horne). According to the rumours, these meals were grand affairs – veal or sole or fillet steak, washed down with best Chianti. Breakfast she enjoyed in bed, waited on by the youngest of the curates, a tall and dashing fellow who looked as if he'd been rented from *The Thorn Birds*.

But what about this morning? Had she had her breakfast? Was she even *there*? Dreams could be prophetic – he knew that from John-Paul. His Mother might have vanished, and the dream be trying to warn him. He certainly hadn't seen her, not since late last night when she'd been sipping a liqueur with Father Fox. A liqueur! She never touched them, cautioned him repeatedly about the dangers of all alcohol – how wine upset your liver, spirits killed the brain-cells – yet here she was indulging with the clergy.

He tried to drag his mind back to this morning, remember some odd glimpse of her, maybe limping to the bookstall, or arm in arm with Phyllis, who had become her bosom friend. No. He hadn't seen a sign of her, and even Phyllis had asked him where she was. Fear choked his throat, hammered in his head. It was all his fault. He'd sent her in the dream to a terrifying island, a waste of bare black lava which had appeared several hundred miles from the barren coast of Iceland just a month or so ago, and been reported in the *Mail*: the most desolate island ever known (though not as bafflingly remote as Tristan da Cunha which was thirteen thousand miles from the nearest inhabited land, and where he'd already sent his Mother at least half a dozen times, though always had her back within the day). The new island was uninhabited and completely uninhabitable – no Post Office departments he could bribe or beg or bully, no bureaucrats to wheedle, no telephone to make an anguished call.

He paced up and down the bank, shivering in the snappy breeze which had sprung up from the east. The sun had disappeared; the water now looked black and almost curdled. Heavy clouds were snagging on the plane trees; the dead and bloated body of a water-rat floating slowly down the river. He shut his eyes, saw his Mother's corpse instead, battered by cruel northern seas as she was swept from her small lava-lump by a relentless tidal wave. He'd murdered her, destroyed her, and was now totally alone – no family, no hearth and home, no rules and meals and timetables to keep away the Terror, save him from the Void. It was only now he realised how desperately he needed her as Orderer and Bulwark, craved even her complaining, to prove she cared and noticed him, fill the endless silence. Four years with John-Paul and he was worse than when he'd started. All those shaming pricey struggles to wean him from his Mother, and he was still groping for her nipple, sobbing for the shelter of her strict and chilly womb.

Mary couldn't help him. There *was* no Mary, anyway. She was not in Rome, maybe not in Walton. All solid things were beginning to unravel, including his own brain. He suddenly longed to see the crowds again, even hear the traffic, speak to someone – anyone – prove he still existed. Fifty yards ahead of him was another flight of steep stone steps, leading up to street-level. He hurtled to the top, started sprinting down the pavement, headed for the seminary, praying he was wrong and he'd find his Mother digesting her *vitello*, or enjoying a Cinzano with Father Campion. A bus whimpered to a stop just a pace or two in front of him. He tried to jostle on, met curses and resistance, realised he was entering through the exit. He found the proper entrance, struggled with the bodies (which seemed all jabbing elbows), but was ousted once again, this time because he didn't have a ticket. In any normal country, you bought your ticket on the bus. But in Rome, you probably got it from the gypsies or the Vatican, filled in a form in triplicate.

He pounded on again, willing to risk a heart attack if it would bring his Mother back. He passed a Metro station, but dared not brave the tube. He'd tried it only yesterday, trembled down three escalators, found every filthy lurching train packed with mafiosi; panted vainly up again, back where he had started. If his Mother was still living, he'd insist that they went home, would lock the doors and stay there, never venture out again, not even to Kew Gardens, let alone to Rome.

'*Rivoluzione!*' screamed a graffito on the wall. He didn't

know Italian, but the word seemed oddly menacing, made his feet move faster, as he dodged past tourists, shoppers; dashed between fast cars.

At last, he reached the seminary, pelted through the gates. The pilgrims should be back from lunch and assembled in the hall for announcements and the rosary before their afternoon excursion to Ancient Ostia. He stopped dead in the courtyard, hair tousled, tie askew. At least a ·hundred of their party were seething round the fountain – pushing, shoving, jostling, most without their coats, some even in their dressing gowns or half-naked with bare feet, as if they'd rushed down from the washroom to witness some emergency. Dozens more were spewing from the building, trying to butt their way to the centre of the crowd, ramming with their heads, or heaving with their shoulders, more like hoodlum rugger players than pious prayerful pilgrims. Some were armed with cameras and were jumping up on ledges to get a better view, yelling 'Look this way!' or 'Smile, please!' to someone in the centre, someone totally obscured by the mass of serried bodies. Another group were on their knees, eyes closed in rapturous ecstasy as they recited a hushed prayer; a further large contingent pouring out a hymn of praise, arms outstretched to heaven. The noise was overwhelming – singing, shouting, cheering, clashing in a discord; a swell of mad excitement surging from the courtyard as two hundred eager voices expressed their joy and fervour.

A bow-legged blue-rinsed matron was hobbling swiftly past him, murmuring 'Praised be God Almighty!' He grabbed her dangling rosary, stopped her in her tracks. 'What's happened?' he cried hoarsely. 'What in God's name's going on?'

'A miracle! A miracle!' she shouted, almost breathless. 'Let that go immediately! I'm going to get it blessed.' She tugged her beads back rudely, started forcing through the crowd, swearing at two greyheads who tried to block her way. The mood was turning ugly, several women hitting out with handbags, fists or hymn books, as they wrestled with each other, tried to push in closer. Total gawping strangers had now appeared from nowhere and were swelling out the crowd, Italian peasants clamouring 'Miracolo! Miracolo!' as they fell onto their knees.

Bryan was still completely mystified, still lurking by the wall. He inched up very cautiously to the nearest group of women, hovered just behind them, shut out by their jostling backs, but listening to their babble.

'A shaft of light streaming from the altar . . .'

'Pierced right through her leg . . .'

'And she's not even one of us . . .'

'Hasn't been baptised . . .'

'Though she's marvellous with that son, of course . . .'

'And suffered all her life . . .'

'In pain since 1940 . . .'

'Always dragged her leg . . .'

'Could never dance or run, poor dear . . .'

'Even in a wheelchair on the plane . . .'

'Not fair on us good Catholics, though . . .'

'Don't gripe, Madge dear. God works in mysterious ways.'

Horrified, he backed away, tried to find a hiding place, make himself invisible. So his *Mother* was the centre of this crazy dangerous hubbub, cause of this hysteria; her private shaming history on every pilgrim's lips. He must leave himself immediately, hoof back to the Tiber, hide in those tall grasses, before he was pounced upon, derided. He started edging down the wall, skulking in its shadow, stopped in sudden terror as he saw three tall policemen swinging through the gate, armed with guns and truncheons. He wheeled the other way, almost collided with a woman who was trying to embrace him – Phyllis in a sweater and her flannel petticoat. He removed his face from her knobbly knitted bosom, tried to dodge her tickling hair which was tumbling from its bun.

'Bryan, my dear, you're here at last! I've been searching for you everywhere. A quite amazing thing has happened. Your mother has been healed.'

'Healed? She wasn't ill.'

'Not ill? Your mother's been in wicked pain since she hurt her leg in 1939. That pain's completely vanished. The leg is back to normal and she can gambol like a child. It's the Blessed Edwin Mumford's latest miracle.'

'But . . .' Bryan's voice died away. His Mother had no time for the Blessed Edwin Mumford, but how could he tell Phyllis so, explain that just a week ago she'd spoken quite contemptuously of 'unhealthy religious mania' and 'so-called jumped-up saints'? And miracles were moonshine, simply couldn't happen. There wasn't any kindly God to heal or intervene, only chaos and disorder, anarchy, blind chance.

'Now, I'm sorry, Bryan, I've got to dash. I'm on my way to the *Congregazione per le cause dei santi*.'

'*What?*'

'The Office for Canonisations. They've simply got to know about this latest splendid miracle. And I'll inform the press, of course. It's our duty, dear, isn't it, to spread news of God's goodness, when so many silly people blame Him for disasters?'

'Well, I . . .'

'You go and find your mother, dear. She'll want to share her joy with you, show you her healed leg. Now don't be frightened of the crowds. They'll let you through, you see. Just a second – I'd better brush your coat first. You've got burrs all down your back.'

She started pouncing on his coat, letting out a little yelp of triumph for every burr she loosened, then propelled him with a final lunge down towards the mob, whispering to a Franciscan friar (who looked a useful sixteen stone or

413

so, and was pushing in himself) to 'let the poor soul through'.

'No!' Bryan tried to shout. 'Don't want to . . . Don't believe in . . . It's all Chaos, all . . .' His voice was lost, his legs were lost, as he felt the Franciscan's rough brown bulk butting from behind, and he was bullied, bustled, bulldozed, through the first layers of the crowd. People tried to stop him, tugging at his coat, flailing with their elbows, yelling out abuse. No one seemed to recognise him, or allow him any rights as his Mother's only son. He was just a casual interloper, some rude and pushy upstart who must be kicked back where he'd come from. He was bruised and clawed both sides as the friar continued acting as a holy battering-ram, whilst the mob in front fought back with fist or boot. He closed his eyes in terror, bowed his bloody head, became a frisbee or a football, an object with no feelings and no bones.

Suddenly, miraculously, the frantic pushing ceased, and he saw light and air again; found himself cowering by the fountain, where he'd collapsed on to the cobblestones, the vast crowd now behind him. Slowly, he looked up to where all other eyes were gazing, saw his queenly Mother surrounded by an awe of priests, some he'd never seen before, all staring at her leg with expressions of bewilderment or triumph. He clutched the fountain basin, dragged up to his feet. Never mind her leg – her whole being was transformed: her face no longer putty-pale, but flushed and even youthful, her eyes lifted up to heaven, both arms outstretched in prayer; a new radiance about her, as if she'd changed from flesh to flame.

'Mother . . .' he said weakly, though he hardly dared to speak to her she looked so otherworldly. She didn't hear him, didn't turn her head. 'It's Bryan,' he said. 'Your son.'

Had she ever had a son? He doubted it, the way that she ignored him; seemed aware only of the clergy and their powerful God above, who appeared to be conversing with her; he a mere intruder, or perhaps not there at all. He felt himself dwindling into nothingness, extinction. Could *no one* hear him, see him, plead his cause with Lena, inform her of his presence, his existence? He glanced back at the crowd. Faces, faces, faces, as far as he could see, but not one who seemed to recognise him, or care about his plight. Every single one of them was goggling at his Mother, rapt and near-ecstatic, as she began to walk a circle, to demonstrate her healing, intoxicate the mob. He stared in disbelief. As long as he remembered she had always dragged her leg, always complained of pain and inflammation, but now the leg looked normal, the recent angry swelling completely disappeared, and she was moving with an ease and grace unthinkable before – as Phyllis said, frisking like a ten-year-old.

The crowd was pressing closer; cameras clicking, frenzied flashbulbs snapping, rosaries and prayer books waved beside her nose, or rammed into her back, as if she could bless them by her touch or just her aura. Someone seized her handkerchief, ripped it into shreds, two dozen frantic jealous hands fighting for a relic. A prostrate sobbing woman was kissing both her shoes, a younger girl trying to snatch her coat belt.

'Get back!' the priests were shouting, as they tried vainly to control the mass of heaving bodies, reassert their power. 'Clear the square immediately and assemble in your dormitories. We can't call this a miracle. It's far too soon. We'll need to . . .'

'A miracle, a miracle!' defiant voices roared, as they kept mobbing, jostling Lena; one man trying to prise the cobbles loose where her sacred feet had trodden. 'God has shown His favour. God is here amongst us!'

Bryan was blinded by a flash of light, saw not God, but two professional photographers who had somehow sweated to the front and were filming the whole uproar, one on video. He used his scarf to mask his face as he dived into the crowd, battled back the way he'd come, hitting out himself now as he stampeded through the tide of mad humanity. Supposing someone saw him in the film – his boss at BRB, or Fletcher in Accounts? He'd never live it down. He'd told his firm he was going on a cultural trip to study ancient art, not cavorting with a horde of religious maniacs.

At last, he struggled free, severely bruised and battered (and having lost one shoe and half his coat to the more ferocious of the pilgrims). He heaved the other shoe off, hurtled towards the gate – feet screaming out their pain – almost hit the bonnet of a huge black shiny limousine gliding slowly through it. The car swerved to avoid him, then skidded to a stop. All four doors sprang open and a bishop in full purple strode majestically towards him, flanked by four more dignitaries, all dressed in formal robes; a posse of armed policemen bringing up the rear.

'No!' he yelled. 'It's all a big mistake. It's a fluke, that's all, a freak. She's not even my Mother. She . . .'

He tripped and fell, landed on his face, lay bleeding on the cobblestones as the bishop's lowering shadow marched across his feet. He glimpsed truncheons, holsters, brute black boots, closed his eyes in terror.

'John-Paul!' he cried. 'Come *back*!'

# 34

Mary skittered down the Via della Scrofa, free at last, alone at last, exulting in the brisk and brilliant morning, the freshly laundered sky – best of all, in the lack of any ties. No small and sticky hand in hers, no heavy husband tethering her arm, no two testy fathers demanding sweets or smokes or toilets. James had hunted down a golf club, disappeared all day, complaining almost happily about the long drive out of Rome and the fact he'd have to hire his clubs, which were bound to be inferior. All three boys had gone with Grandpa Lionel to the zoo in the Borghese Park. She was surprised he'd spared the time for them, but he seemed obsessed by lions, had found his noble namesake everywhere in Rome – marble lions and stone lions, lions rampant in museums, or reverent in churches – and now wished to see the living kind, admire the king of beasts. (She suspected that he saw himself as a rampant king of men – yes, even in his eighties.) Poor Harry was laid low in bed, afflicted at both ends, blamed his sickness on the Roman food; his diarrhoea on the water. She couldn't leave him long, but she'd dosed him with a mixture which contained a dash of morphine, so with any luck, he'd sleep – at least until she'd carried out her all-important mission.

She dithered at the crossroads, unsure which way to go, though Lionel had drawn her what he called a simple sketch map, with Sant'Agostino's clearly marked – well, clear to *him*, perhaps. She found Rome rather baffling, not just the roads, the money. She still hadn't quite worked out how many lire to the pound, except it seemed an awful lot, and the prices in the fashion shops looked really rather frightening with those daunting rows of noughts. And the dates were tricky, too. Back in simple England you could stick mainly to AD, but BC was just as vital here, at least in Oliver's classics course. She was really proud of Oliver, who knew all the different emperors without muddling them, as she did (even though she'd watched all twelve parts of *I, Claudius* and a series called *Decline and Fall*, which had starred Jeremy Irons in a laurel wreath and toga). He could even tell one ruin from another, and had spent ages in the Forum, not just rounding up wild cats as Jonathan had done (or getting bored like Simon), but studying his guidebook and making sudden brilliant comments, which even James admired.

She hadn't said a word, of course, but she'd found the Forum really quite a mess – all those crumbling piles of stones and depressing heaps of rubble, and all in such a shambles – expensive broken columns lying where they'd fallen and nettles choking everything. She'd have liked to sort it out, tidy things away, dump the debris in black dustbin-bags, do a bit of weeding. No point labelling something the Temple of Vespasian or Julia's Basilica, when it was just a few old dusty bricks or half a dirty column. And even Trajan's Market, which was very nearly whole, was really only a BC variation on the huge Tesco's in New Malden. It was a treat today, to tell the truth, not to have to view another decomposing temple, or admire another ruin, or trek through a museum with her neck cricked at an angle. She had something far more crucial to carry out – alone.

She turned right, then left, still studying the sketch map, which was crumpled now and more or less illegible. Her sweaty hands had made it damp and smudged. The December air was still shock-cold, despite the glittering sun, but she was perspiring from sheer nerves. She could hear the fevered murmur of a fountain, plashing some-where close, doubled back to find it, so she could cool her wrists, rinse her clammy fingers. The water in the basin was steaming like a bath, obviously warmer than the chilly air around it. How passionate it looked, that excited breath of steam panting from the seething fretted water. All the fountains which she'd seen so far appeared to be in a perpetual state of orgasm – gushing forth, spewing out, never still or sated. And there were at least three hundred of them, or so the guidebook said – three hundred endless climaxes, spurting day and night.

This fountain was exotic, and clearly overcrowded – not just nymphs and satyrs, but dolphins, eagles, porpoises, and some rather rude young men who were doing nothing to conceal their all-too-public parts, but sprawling with their thighs apart, as if to show them off instead. She compared each, size for size, wished they could be sculpted erect and really stiff, like an Etruscan god she had spotted in one of the museums. Since she'd arrived in Rome, she'd seen more sets of genitals than ever in her life before, so that all those recent words she'd learnt were coming in quite handy. She'd gawped at sculpted satyrs' tickle-tails, painted gods' flap-doodles, stallions' huge bronze master-tools, cherubs' marble joysticks. Some were chipped or broken off, some fig-leafed, draped or veiled, but they couldn't veil the passion – naked passion everywhere, on walls and plinths and ceilings: swoonings, orgies, blatant rapes – and her own sex just as shameless: flagrant females twined with swans, or fondling stiff-horned unicorns, or stroking their own nipples.

She had seen the brazen hussies even carrying on in churches: marble saints and angels who were clearly counting orgasms and had long since reached the million mark; nude men flaunting muscly thighs on the Sistine Chapel ceiling; Adam with a coupling-pin she'd examined through binoculars (which Lionel had kindly bought to assess the brighter colours in the recent restoration, compare them with the dingy ones he'd deplored in 1950). And even the Vatican Museum writhed with near-pornography: sixteenth-century swingers doing outrageous things on ceilings, voluptuous blushing murals more suited to a brothel, and so many different sizes of scrotums, pricks and testicles, she had begun to wonder if six hundred words were really quite sufficient.

John-Paul was right – as always. He'd explained several times already that sex and religion were not necessarily incompatible and she had no need to feel guilty because she'd helped herself to pleasure and release. Here in Rome, the centre of her faith, unbridled lust was commonplace, merely labelled 'Art' and allowed to grace the churches, even the Vatican itself. She'd said 'cunt' and 'prick' out loud in St Peter's great basilica, felt no trace of guilt, only wild elation. Her own passion and excitement were now part of something higher, had been sanctified and vindicated, allowed the imprimatur. John-Paul had transformed her from a confined and lowbrow housewife to an artist and an intellect – even something of a linguist. She'd learnt several colloquial French words for the penis (*la queue*, *la verge*, *la bitte*) and also Anglo-Saxon ones, such as *gesceapu* and *teors*. She felt different altogether – uplifted and creative, leavened like her home-made bread (which she no longer had the time for). And in Rome she was a star, her blue eyes and blonde hair attracting constant glances, even blatant whistlings, whispered assignations. Even now, a youth was strolling up to her, not more than half her age, yet leering at her breasts, trying out his bad but bawdy English.

She shook him off, continued on her way, found herself at last in the Piazza Sant'Agostino, staring up at its tall and stately church. According to the guidebook, famous sixteenth-century courtesans had come tripping to this church, artists' models, mistresses of Popes, even common prostitutes. She shivered with excitement. It all seemed fitting, somehow, consistent with her mission. She was here to beg the special help of the Madonna del Parto, a statue of the Blessed Virgin famed throughout all Italy, visited by women from Palermo to Milan. She might not know Italian, but *parto* she had learned – five letters which were swelling to nine months.

She entered the dim church, admiring its rich splendour, the gold and marble majesty which seemed commonplace in Rome. She found the statue just inside the door, gleaming and dramatic amidst its blaze of dazzling lamps. The shrine was overflowing with offerings from the satisfied: jewelled medallions, solid silver hearts, priceless gems and treasures. If her own request were granted, she'd donate her sapphire ring, a piece of antique jewellery which had been left her by her mother (and which James had often tried persuading her to sell). She did her best to lose her debt-plagued husband on the golf course as she showered all her heavy change into the boxes by the candle-stands, watched every dead electric bulb spring to instant life. Each candle was a wish, a prayer, a strengthening of her hope. She knelt before the statue, kissed its marble foot, worn smooth by countless women who had come for the same reason, come secretly and desperately, as taut with nerves as she was.

The Virgin seemed impassive, her eyes cast down, ignoring all her trophies. Supposing she were deaf, or chose simply not to hear? Yet she was lauded as all-merciful, renowned for her compassion. Mary gazed up at the marble breasts, which looked engorged with milk, then down at the wide hips – perfect hips for child-bearing, the strong and powerful Mother. She could hear the prayers of would-be mothers vibrating through the church – twentieth-century typists, sixteenth-century peasants, women rich or ragged, young or middle-aged. She joined her prayers to theirs, then tiptoed to the door again, closed it very gently, reluctant to disturb the hushed fervour of the church.

She stepped out into sunlight, blinking in the glare, wincing at the traffic noise as she jumped five centuries. She dodged between two taxis, turned into a side street, searching for a bar. Step One was completed; Step Two far more daunting. Would she ever have the courage, ever dare that tiny test – tiny yet momentous; three brief and trifling minutes which could change the whole remainder of her life? She'd been dreading it all night, a dread confused with longing, as her fear was mixed with hope.

She found a small and sleazy bar, propped up either side with scaffolding, as if it needed crutches. Never mind how rough it was, so long as it had a lavatory. She had learnt the word for toilet, now blushing as she stammered it, and ordering a coffee first, to justify her asking. (Public loos were rare in Rome, as poor Harry had discovered.) She left her coffee steaming, slunk out to the back, found a cramped and smelly cubicle with sawdust on the floor. She pulled her knickers down, crouched above the toilet, mouthing one last desperate prayer as she watched the stream of urine falling in the bowl, and catching a few vital drops in the little pot she'd brought.

She scrabbled for the dipstick with its two embedded circles. No need to read the instructions – she'd done that twenty times or more, knew them off by heart, knew the crucial colour-code. One circle would turn purple if she were genuinely pregnant, but remain completely colourless if she were mistaken or imagining things. The test took just three minutes, which was really quite miraculous, and you could do it at an extremely early stage – as early as the very day your next period was due. When she'd been pregnant with her first child, she'd had to wait six weeks, and her doctor sent the specimen to a hospital laboratory, which meant hanging around another week before her condition was confirmed. You couldn't buy these quick home-kits from any local chemist, expect almost total accuracy, yet bypass all the doctors and laboratories.

The only thing you needed was a fairly steady hand, and hers was really trembling as she used the tiny dropper to transfer the precious urine to the tube of purple powder, then plunged the dipstick in. She shut her eyes immediately, not daring to watch the circles in case they stayed unchanged. She counted to a thousand, then began at one again, eyes still tightly closed; only jerking to her feet as someone battered on the door, a drunkard by the sound of it, hollering in Italian.

'Yes, I'm sorry. Yes, I'm coming. Just wait a moment, would you? This is absolutely crucial . . .' He didn't understand, couldn't even hear her, was swamping her tense whisper with new and louder curses. She crumpled up the instruction sheet, smoothed her skirt and coat, glancing at the circles with a hopeless desperation. Of course they would stay colourless, of course she wasn't pregnant. It was simply wishful thinking, fantasy, delusion. No, wait – that vital right-hand circle was beginning to change and deepen from a listless chalky nothing to a weak and wavering lilac. She blinked and looked again. No mistake. The colour was now deepening to the triumphant vivid purple of a bishop's flaunting robes. She clung on to the cistern as she tried to take the truth in, relish its full meaning. She was pregnant by John-Paul, carrying his child, had his genes inside her, fusing with her own. The child would be a prodigy, combining all his skills; his intellect, his brilliance, his insight, his . . .

'*Chè cazzo c'è là dentro? Vuoi uscire brutto stronzo?*'

She almost dropped her dipstick as she struggled with the bolt; could hear the rudeness in the words without grasping what they meant; feel the man's impatience shudder through the door as he hammered it and kicked it. She flurried from the cubicle, stammering her apologies as a ruffian in ragged jeans cannoned roughly past her, clutching at his flies.

'I'm going to have a *baby*,' she mouthed in explanation

423

as the door slammed shut behind him; repeated the same awesome words as she walked along the passage, almost in a daze. She longed to tell the world; flung a marvelling smile at two dozen surly customers as she re-entered the drab bar, gulped her scummy coffee standing up. She still couldn't quite believe it, kept peeping at the dipstick which she would never throw away, keep as a memorial, a glorious purple trophy. Two young men were ogling her from further down the counter. She nodded to them graciously, received their adulation as her natural right and privilege, now John-Paul had made her Mother, changed her from mere patient to sacred vehicle.

She left a generous tip, swept out to the street again, passing festive Christmas streamers which seemed strung up in her honour. The air was now much warmer, old stone glowing golden, glints of dazzling sunlight flickering on the cobblestones. A withered cringing gypsy came hobbling up beside her, holding out her hand. She'd used all her change on candles, so she filled the dirty paw with crisp new banknotes. She could afford to be magnanimous now she'd be saving James a fortune every month. No need to continue her sessions with John-Paul, when she had him deep inside her and was cured in any case. She'd first sought his help for coldness, sexual prudery, then become his torrid mistress, avid and awakened. She would replace his shrine in the spare room with an exquisite wooden cradle, hand-carved from precious wood, lined and ruched with silk. It would no longer be a 'spare' room, and she no longer spare – her life's work now to nurture John-Paul's child.

She could see babies everywhere, in prams and push-chairs on the streets, in posters and advertisements, in the straw-and-plaster mangers set up in the windows of several shops and cafés. She stopped at one such crib, glanced at the Madonna kneeling by the Christchild – a princess, not a peasant, robed in real blue velvet. She touched her sapphire ring, the same vibrant shade of blue, slipped it off her finger. It was no longer hers to wear, belonged to the Madonna in the church of Sant'Agostino, the all-merciful Madonna of Childbirth. She must return there right away, beg the powerful Virgin for one last grace and favour as she offered her the ring: John-Paul's child – and hers – must be a girl.

# SHOPPING LIST

wicker cradle
nappies
vitamins and iron pills
babygros (all pink)
check bottles, bath and pram
*Rome in Pictures, Pop-Up Rome, A Children's Guide*
   *to Ancient Rome*
currency converter
Italian dictionary
Diocalm (for Harry)
binoculars
pink lion

# 35

I'm bored, completely bored. Yes, I know this is meant to be a fucking papal audience, my first glimpse of *Sua Santità* in the living breathing flesh. The trouble is I've been sitting in this huge oppressive hall for an hour and twenty minutes (having queued outside another hour with the rudest so-called Christians I've ever had the misfortune to meet, who'd kick you on the shins or tug your hair out by its roots, if it would help them push in faster) and not a sign of the Great Man yet. We've had hymns from Negro choirs, carols from a shrill of nuns, and some rather schmaltzy warbling from a troupe of hateful children, all kitted out in frilly shirts and braided scarlet waistcoats. They sang in every tongue but English, and the babel all around me is equally confusing. I'm surrounded by foreigners, a good six or seven thousand of them, gabbling on all sides, with not one mate to talk to in a lingo I can grasp.

I saw a picture of the Tower of Babel in a gallery in Greenwich once – a gloomy pile lost in cloud, while further down the canvas the gang of navvies building it had dropped their tools, confounded, or were shown writhing on the ground in what looked like frothing fits. The tale is most depressing, as I remember from my Bible, and means the peoples of this wretched earth can't understand each other, are divided by their different tongues, which prevent any basic harmony, any sense of unity, make them mutual aliens. I feel that way right now. There's a couple on one side of me who keep flirting in Italian, little whispered intimacies which shut me out twice over, and on the other side is an obese and raucous woman who's yakking to her neighbour in a language so obscure it could be Serbo-Croat or Tibetan. Even with our so-called gang I'm the odd man out, since they can all communicate, while I'm restricted to my dozen words of primary-school Italian, which hardly cover all the vagaries of human feeling and experience.

I crane my neck, to see if I can spot them amongst the rows and rows of heads – dark heads, greyheads, baldies, berets, school-hats, veils and wimples. It's totally impossible. They're right down near the front, while I'm stuck here at the back; so far away, in fact, the proceedings on the stage look as if I'm viewing them from the wrong end of a telescope. I'm not sure why we're parted, except Seton insisted that we enter through different doors and be searched by different security men, as part of what he calls his recce. I wasn't turned away myself, though I'm lumbered with a large umbrella which doubles as a shooting stick (and which Seton plans on using later, to secrete a sawn-off shotgun). The police didn't even check it, just rummaged through my handbag and ran their metal-detector up and down my body. This is all just a rehearsal, a testing out the ground, an improvement and refinement of techniques.

Seton tried a second ruse. He's carrying a camera-case with a concealed compartment at the bottom, which he'll use to hold a smaller gun. Today he put a small bronze statuette inside, merely to see if it was spotted, picked up by the metal-detectors. I presume it wasn't, since he's still carrying the case, and gave me the thumbs-up sign when he first came in, climbing on a chair-seat to locate me at the back – which wasn't quite so difficult, since the crowds were far less dense then; have been building up each minute ever since. I was scared to death they'd stop him, confiscate that camera-case, but he's told me twice already that though the searches appear thorough, the officers are often lax, in fact; worn down by the sheer mass and press of numbers, the rude bad-tempered crowds. Apparently, the police force here is not exactly renowned for its efficiency, but is pretty damn disorganised, like so much else in Rome. There've been some recent scandals about lapses in security at both the airport and the Senate (which Seton read with pleasure), and I've seen several *carabinieri* smoking quite openly on duty. Mind you, I'd probably smoke myself if I had to cope with hordes like this each week – seven thousand ruffians, disguised as papal groupies, threatening law and order. They hold these general audiences almost every Wednesday of the year – servile Catholics swarming from all corners of the globe, to toady to their Tyrant, grovel at his feet. When we first joined the jostling queue, it was more like Wembley Stadium than St Peter's solemn Square – tourist coaches parked in droves, disgorging eager fans; swarthy souvenir-sellers closing in with their hideous papal knick-knacks, their tea towels of the Vatican and John Paul coffee mugs.

A pity they weren't selling John Paul guns, or I'd have bought one with his name on, shot those six smug bigwigs strutting up and down the stage in their preening prelates' purple. All that male pomp riles me – all that wasted cock. Celibates should be officially castrated, their flaccid pricks donated to normal but unfortunate men, who have suffered in bad accidents or got entangled in machinery and would love a working penis. I look round in surprise, jolted by a sudden storm of riotous applause. At first, I think my thoughts have been picked up by some Orwellian mind-machine, and they've awarded me a medal for the best idea since heart transplants, then I realise the acclaim is for the Pope. Yes, *Il Tiranno* is here.

All the lights snap on as a tiny white-robed figure enters from a side door on the stage, glides slowly to his ritzy golden throne. The hordes are going wild – clapping, shouting, stamping, unfurling flags and banners – but as far as I'm concerned, the moment is a definite anticlimax. So this is *Sua Santità* – the Prince of the Apostles, the Successor to Saint Peter, the Primate of all Italy, the Patriarch of the West, the so-called Vicar of Jesus Christ Himself, who's been seen in person by more gawping cheering millions than any other single individual in the whole course of human history; the High and Holy Autocrat who rules nine hundred million. Admittedly, I can't see very clearly from this fag end of the hall, but the guy looks old and past it, a peasant with a weight problem, and not much left of his hair. He doesn't even greet us – well, not with any passion or panache, just a few brief nods, a wave or two, before he plumps down in his chair and starts maundering in Italian, droning on and on, reading from a sheaf of notes in a soporific monotone.

I fidget in my seat (which is naked wood with no arms or kindly padding, and probably meant as penance); glance around the hall. It seems slightly less oppressive with the lights on, the two hideous stained-glass windows glowing neon-bright, but it's still quite the ugliest place I've ever seen (and that includes the Millbank Tower and Brent Cross shopping centre). The ceiling looks like polystyrene concrete, with the worst features of both, and is dimpled with small padded indentations in a dreary (dirty?) white, like the inside of an egg-box – the cheapo cardboard sort. Yet they boast it cost a bomb – money probably all extorted from the poor and shabby faithful, including those starving in squalid Third World slums.

They're still extremely faithful, though, judging by the reverent hush which greets the pontiff's words; then more rapturous applause when he finally lets up, and another portly celibate in a long black buttoned frock starts spouting in a different language, which I recognise as German – thanks to Wilhelm – though it's prayer and priests and pilgrims, rather than fellatio or death-camps. The Germans in the hall go more or less hysterical and start leaping to their feet, or breaking into neo-Nazi hymns, as their various different groups are introduced – high-school kids from Munich, seminarians from Hamburg, a youth brigade from Ludenscheid, and several (boring) others I can't quite understand. Then it's *Il Papa*'s turn again, this time speaking German, though I hardly grasp a word of it since he enunciates less clearly than the priest, and sounds distinctly weary. Join the club, John Paul. I had two hours' sleep last night and would gladly doze off here and now, if these penitential seats allowed.

Another aching hour drags by, as we move from German into Spanish, from Spanish into French (both Frogs and Spaniards cheering as they're introduced by group), and then a couple more weird languages which prove the curse of Babel and could be gibberish. I feel shut out and excluded, and also pretty dense – the alien, the moron, who hasn't bothered with her Linguaphone. There's just one welcome respite when a priest from Dallas, Texas, in a stylish purple dressing gown introduces the English-speaking pilgrims, who include Japanese, Australians, swarms of charismatic Yanks (with a squad of female choristers whose dress outswanks the bishops'), and an embarrassingly jolly contingent from Old England, whom I haven't even noticed since they're mostly at the front. There's a lot of talk about the Blessed Edwin Somebody, and then an old bag in a kilt whom the Texan priest calls 'Phyllis' stands up and sings a solo in an ardent baritone. And once everybody's recovered from the shock of her low G, the Pope tries out his English, which is halting, slow and guttural, and centres mainly on the Blessed E., who sounds a cross between a sadist and a screwball.

I still don't understand. Oh, I grasp the actual words this time, but I can't fathom for the life of me why a sixteenth-century schizophrenic who sounds in need of daily sessions with John-Paul, and used to share his bed and broth with seven devils (whom he cast out of a bishop, but who stayed to take revenge) should be the toast of all those pious worthy matrons. If they met him in the flesh, they'd probably run a mile, or start drawing up petitions to have him put away, as a danger to their daughters or the peace.

I'm really quite relieved when he's consigned to his coffin in 1588, though according to the Pope, he refused to rot or decompose like any normal corpse, and is apparently still pink and plump, despite his grisly martyrdom. It all sounds most grotesque – and an obvious downright lie – so I'm glad when the Pope decides to leave him underground. (He's been exhumed three times, in fact, which must be quite disorientating for a man of unsound mind who assumed he was terminally dead), and move on to something else. His Holiness starts talking about suffering, and time: how the old year's creaking to its close with its sadnesses, its losses, its sense of disappointment, and how even a New Year may not bring us what we crave. I sit up and take notice, not just of what he's saying, but the tone in which he's saying it. I can actually hear the suffering in his voice, which has suddenly clouded over, seems to darken, falter, as if he's remembering some personal loss which he's experienced first-hand.

My thoughts shift to John-Paul – my *own* John-Paul, the elusive one, whom I've still not glimpsed at all. I flogged back to his hotel again, was told that he was out; not expected back till midnight, and would I kindly leave myself. Yes, the receptionist spoke English, but still we couldn't communicate. There was no sense of fellow feeling, no basic human sympathy. Even John-Paul's name divided us. Her accent made it comic, as her manner made it casual – just a scrawled line in the register, another routine visitor; whereas it's branded through my flesh with molten iron.

I dragged Seton with me next day, lured him there on some deceitful pretext, hoping his snazzy clothes and silver-tongued Italian might impress the girl and conjure up John-Paul. Perhaps it was just as well they didn't, since Seton might have bashed him, or started paying off old scores, but he did succeed in wangling a copy of the conference programme. God! It made me sick – John-Paul's name still swanking with those deceitful strings of letters, and all that pompous empty jargon inflating him to king-size – lectures on Narcissistic Introjective Denial, or the Role of Illusion in Symbol Formation, and other equally riveting subjects; while his patients die, despair. It's like the Vatican again – power through pomp and posturing, keeping normal people out because they don't understand the concepts or speak that arcane language; haven't wrapped the world up in one closed and biased system which brooks no opposition. *Both* John-Pauls lay down the law, follow rigid rules, insist on fixed procedures, live life by their bibles. They're also both Big Shams, offering hope and comfort, which never actually materialises; proclaiming cure, salvation, when there's neither health nor God. We're all panting for a saviour, but that doesn't mean there *is* one.

My shrink's a double sham – if Zack was lying and Seton speaking truthfully, which I suspect now was the case – a bad artist and a plumber's son, gatecrashing a congress where he's no real right at all; deceiving not just patients, but all those bona fide doctors and genuine conference members. He breaks all the rules himself, yet insists on patients keeping them – more rules than back at school: arrive on time, depart on time, and not a second later; don't dare be ill or cancel any sessions; don't make demands, don't phone, accept his interpretations as God's Holy Law which cannot be denied; no silly chat, no shirking, no invasive personal questions, and most important, pay all bills by return. Yet some people say it's rules like that which can actually make you a patient in the first place – domineering parent-figures insisting on a compliant child who's allowed no space nor freedom, but dragooned into obedience and neurosis.

I'm beginning to feel quite wretched, as if the sudden

433

change of weather which taunted us with clouds this morning, instead of jaunty sun, has affected my own mood. It's a heavy day outside, the Tiber rippling sluggishly, St Peter's usual blazing dome lost in sullen mist. Mind you, I wouldn't mind a glimpse of cloud or water, however dull or grey. It's so claustrophobic in this hall it's like being underground; the outside world completely barred, no view at all, no air. I keep groping for my cigarettes, then remembering I can't smoke here. The Pope has probably banned it not only in this audience-hall, but totally, infallibly, for all Roman Catholics everywhere, as he's banned divorce and contraception, even masturbation.

He's prosing on and on still. I'm trapped in words, foreign words, which make me feel totally alone – alone among six or seven thousand – as if I've landed on a planet where I don't belong at all, and where people's mouths and larynxes are shaped differently from mine. He's switched from halting English to what I guess is Polish, judging by the speed with which he rattles through his notes. I hate those notes – they're so unspontaneous. (I wonder if John-Paul makes notes – notes on all his patients, and whether he's chucked all mine away, or marked them 'Case Concluded'?)

I peer along the row to check if anyone is smoking, and whether you're skewered on those Swiss Guards' lethal halberds if you dare to disobey. No one's even chewing gum or fingers. The lovey couple next to me are joined at hand and knee; the stout woman on the other side has linked arms with her crony. My own arm fidgets to my bag, hand closing round my pack of boring Rothmans (I couldn't find Capstans – or Chesterfields – in Rome), turns it into a gun, a small but lethal Mauser, fumbles for the trigger. Bang-bang, John Paul, you're dead. It would be a relief to shoot him, actually. I've been sitting here so long I'm dying for some action, need to use my restless hands, which are cold and all but trembling without their fix of nicotine. And it would force my own John-Paul to turn his mind to Nial, remember who she is, even if he only saw her picture in the paper – a picture of a heroine-assassin. It would also shut His Endless up, and I doubt if anything else will. I suppose that's part of being an autocrat – he pontificates, we listen.

I'm wrong – he's stopped – spontaneously, without a bomb or bullet. At least he's praying now, not preaching, and everyone is standing up, so I presume we're near the end. Yes – he gives his final blessing and all the pilgrims thresh and writhe and wave their flags or banners, then half the hall starts swarming out, stampeding for the exits. I'm about to join the scrimmage when I see the other eager half surging towards the centre of the hall; packing close against the barriers which line the middle aisle, leaping up on chairs with cameras poised. Although I'm stuck right at the back, I actually chose a seat smack-bang in the centre, adjoining that wide aisle – simply because it seemed less claustrophobic. Now I realise that position is like gold dust, and several hundred pilgrims are intent on ousting me and stealing it, even at the cost of a dislocated shoulder or painful trampled foot. I've no idea what's going on, but I stick fast in my seat, refuse to give it up, and it's only when I eventually jump up on it (copying my neighbours), that I realise what I've battled for – access to the Pope.

I assumed he'd disappeared, left with all his entourage by the small door on the stage, but he's actually ploughing down that centre aisle, flanked by just one purple-robed disciple, two Swiss Guards and a few assorted lackeys and photographers. I peer at him, amazed. He's stopping every second to squeeze hands, or bless the sick, talk to dribbling morons, cuddle little children. I've watched politicians do the same when they're trying to mop up votes by wooing hideous females or kissing bawling brats, but it's always a performance. However hard they kiss and coo, you can tell they're insincere; can't wait to hand the babies back,

435

shake off the smirch of common hands and escape into their elitist clubs for pheasant and champagne. This is absolutely different. I can't explain it really, except Giovanni Paolo seems to love his flock – yes, even its most poor and abject specimens.

I watch as he embraces a stooping shrivelled man whose gaunt and haggard face seems marked by death. He takes both his hands in his, speaks to him intently, his own face creased with genuine concern. Then he reaches out to hold a baby, an ugly lumpy creature which would tempt most normal people to infanticide. Not *Il Santo Padre*. He loves that kid – you can see it on his face. I register a jolt of griping green-fanged jealousy. That's how *every* father should hold and love his child, with that total deep commitment, that expression in his eyes. This man loves the world, and not the world in abstract, or sterilised or sanitised behind a cold glass wall. He's face to face with a really grubby woman now, a gypsy by the looks of it, her vulgar beads tangling in his buttons, her hair greasy on his neck. He doesn't shrink away from her. She could be his own mother, the affectionate almost reverent way he treats her.

John-Paul would rather die than touch a patient – except to fling her in an ambulance, or hold her down by force. He might 'verbalise' about it: what does touching signify; what pictures does the word bring up? – but actual contact, never. Even if I had a stroke, or fainted, he'd leave me where I'd fallen, gasping on the floor, rather than risk an arm around my neck. Both Giovanni Paolo's arms are wrapped around a young girl in her twenties. It's not sexual – she's a spastic – he just understands that all of us crave comfort, the physical maternal sort which is so rationed in this lousy world, especially if you're old or sick or hideous.

Almost every single person is stretching out their hands to him, as if his touch can heal, like the Royal Touch in

Stuart England, when God's Appointed Monarch could cure anything from syphilis to scrofula. I leave my own arms strictly by my sides. This may be mass hysteria and I shan't let myself succumb. Anyway, he's still a few yards distant, and my wretched arms would be dropping off their hinges if I kept them horizontal until he finally inched up to us. He certainly takes his time, refuses to stint anyone of their individual chat – and that includes the small fry. He's heavily involved now with a skinny little five-year-old who presents him with a painting of a matchstick Pope with spots – a smudged and messy botch-up without a shred of talent, but accepted with such reverence it could be a Velasquez. He's being showered with offerings from all sides – baskets of exotic fruit, swanky hothouse flowers, but he's equally delighted by a few mangy stems of rag-wort proffered by some nutcase who keeps clutching at his sleeve. He doesn't brush her off; listens to her, bothers, despite the impatient bodyguard who tries to hustle her away. He must be tired and hungry, gasping for a drink. He's been speaking for two hours in at least eight different languages, and it's already well past lunch-time.

I must say I'm impressed. I've always been suspicious of words like humanity or piety. You say a man is holy and most people cringe or shrug. Holy can mean priggish, sanctimonious. Not with *Sua Santità*. The title's apt, I see now. He spreads holiness like ointment, rubs it in himself. And it isn't just a duty, an empty show to impress us gawping pilgrims. I keep a sort of lie-detector somewhere in my head, and it's not registering at all. This guy is bona fide.

He's much nearer now, and I can see his face close up. Okay, he's old and plain – that I don't retract – his receding forehead lined, his face sunken around the eyes, but it's the face of a good man. There's a minor sort of hurricane swirling all around me – hands reaching, waving, clutching; bodies lurching perilously on seats. Everybody's

437

trying to kiss his chunky ring: lips smacking, missing, moueing in midair. Others offer gifts instead of kisses. A huge bouquet of roses grazes my left cheek as it's passed across in front of me; someone else is shelling out what look like gold doubloons. I've nothing to present, just a crappy hand which probably smells of nicotine, and that deceitful cruel umbrella.

I let the brolly fall, climb down from my chair, stand absolutely silent while a hundred-hundred imploring mouths yammer on all sides, begging for a hand-clasp, a private word, a hug. John Paul stops a second, looks at me directly, as if he's picked me out from all those other faces, prefers my wary silence to their din. He takes a step towards me, servile lackeys following, tall guards Argus-eyed. Suddenly, he's there, standing right in front of me, so that I can smell his stalish breath, see the tiny craters in his skin. His hands close over mine – hot and rather clammy hands; solid, stumpy-fingered, the skin roughened round the thumbs. I'm not idealising the man. His piggy eyes are all but lost beneath the frowning brow. His neck is slack and fleshy, and I'm taller by an inch. It's his touch which counts, that rare and dazzling sense of being cherished and enfolded, as he lets my hands go, dares to hold me right against his chest, pressed close into his body, to his heart, his warmth, his sex. I've been held like that in dreams, in endless lying fantasies; held by my cold father who wouldn't hold a dog; held by cruel John-Paul who'd let me weep my eyes out rather than reach across and dry them.

The whole vast crowd has vanished. There's only him and me now, from some era long ago. He's chatting to me, questioning me, but I've become an infant and can't speak any language, including my own tongue. Is he talking English or Italian? I've no idea at all, though I suspect he's granting me forgiveness for what I haven't done, the years I haven't lived yet, the shot I haven't fired. Whole centuries seem to lumber by, yet still he makes no move to cast me off. The Prodigal Son was never held so long. I'm fatted calf and silken robe; I'm rings on every finger; I'm wine and oil and sweetmeats at the feast. Then, at last, he pulls away, but holds me with his eyes still, my own eyes faltering from his gaze as I recall that sawn-off shotgun concealed in Giuseppe's flat.

I jerk back in surprise as I feel his hot and sweaty thumb trace a cross on my cold forehead. *Il Santo Padre*'s blessing me – which no one's ever done before, not even in a fantasy. You can only bless something which is good. I'm good – despite the guns – become so instantly, as he keeps his thumb pressed against my head. Everybody's staring, cameras flashing, jealous women shoving, impatient children tugging at his arm. He's been longer with me than anyone, as if he knows how much I need him, knows exactly who I am.

I'm suddenly aware of all the noise again: pilgrims gabbling, clamouring, shouting out what sounds like '*Papa, Papa!*' as he slowly turns away from me, moves on down the aisle. I touch my blazing forehead, can feel that cross transfiguring my brow. They're right – he is a father – *mio santo padre.*

# 36

Mary gazed around her, eyes tracking from the lustrous sky with its swathe of silver moonlight, to the tiny stars and coloured lights looped across the streets for tonight's big celebration. A full moon and New Year's Eve! The two seemed to contradict each other – the year only just conceived and not yet formed; the moon already at full term. Yet both were so exhilarating; the flurry of New Year throbbing in the shops and squares, as the whole of Rome prepared for fevered midnight; the moon elusive, teasing, as it dodged behind the Pantheon, then courted her again, springing out between two towers, flirting with the clouds. It was a treat to be alone, if only for an hour or less, a snatched but vital hour in which she would know her fate once more.

She'd left the three men and three children deep in teddy-bears and tinsel in the Piazza Navona, where they were enjoying the huge toy-fair – brightly coloured market stalls selling sweets and games; Father Christmas quaffing rough Chianti among a group of sozzled gnomes; streamers and balloons strung along the pulsing pavement cafés. Lionel had been buying lions – sugar lions and chocolate lions, lions with manes of marzipan or sleek black liquorice noses, as his own small contribution to their celebration supper, which they'd planned to eat picnic-style in the safety of their room. Their courier had warned them of the dangers of the streets tonight – how the native Romans followed the old custom of flinging out the old, to symbolise the ending of the year. And 'old' might mean old beds, old junk, old pots and pans, even huge old wardrobes, which could kill a person strolling underneath. It was also Fireworks Night in Rome, like Guy Fawkes back in England, and the fireworks were reputed to be perilous as well – two fatalities last year, and over ninety injuries, despite the constant warnings to stay inside, avoid all public places.

Mary turned into the Via del Pastini, looking back anxiously to make sure James wasn't following, or Simon pounding after her, demanding to 'come, too'. She had told them all – quite truthfully – that she had to do some shopping, buy a few last items for the supper, including a celebration cake. She'd seen some quite amazing cakes in a shop just round the corner – airy cream-filled sponges in the shape of the Colosseum, or special New Year cakes with '*Buon' Anno*' piped across them, or beribboned figure ones, to depict January the first. She stopped outside the window, admired the range again, decided on a clock-cake with a stark white-icing face and two black hands pointing dramatically to midnight. She was obsessed with time at present, trying to work out when she had actually conceived. Her last (apparent) period could have been a fluke. It had certainly been light, perhaps not a period at all, just a fleeting show of blood, which she'd read did sometimes happen in early pregnancy. Could she have conceived a whole two months ago – or maybe even longer? Certainly her breasts felt full and tender, and, looking at these creamy cakes, she felt a wave of nausea very similar to the sickness of her previous pregnancies. As soon as she got home, she must make an appointment at the surgery, be properly examined, replace her Orgasm Chart with a Calendar of Pregnancy, start ticking off the days until the birth.

She tripped inside the *pasticceria*, still marvelling at their opening-hours – a full spread of cakes and pastries at seven in the evening – examined all the other gâteaux while the girl was wrapping hers, so she could pick up some ideas. It was time she made some fancy cakes herself, gave up

441

'Science and Society' for family and home, returned to her old skills. With her own deep needs fulfilled, she could concentrate on James, try to resurrect the softer, more romantic man she'd married. He was probably jealous of John-Paul, maybe felt excluded, but that jealousy could cease now – along with the steep bills. She was married to John-Paul in the most sacred, fundamental sense, bonded to him, one with him, carrying his child, but that would stay their secret, and outwardly and publicly she'd devote herself to James – yes, even on this holiday. No need to try to find the Doctor, search out his hotel, when his genes, his vital essence, were encompassed in her womb.

She stepped into the street again, treading the red carpet which many of the smarter shops laid outside their stretch of pavement for Christmas and New Year – or had it been laid down in her honour? The whole city seemed to know about her pregnancy, and be celebrating, revelling – fairy lights in all the shops, wreaths of fertile evergreens hung on doors and windows; the moon itself so brilliant it seemed to have been lacquered just to please her, reflect her buoyant mood.

She stopped to buy oranges from a stall heaped high with gold – tangerines and clementines, fat and fragrant melons – golden flowers to match: huge shaggy bronze chrysanthemums, the first frail daffodils. A beggarwoman clutched at her, dragging one thin leg. James complained Rome's beggars all dissembled, inventing gammy limbs or hacking coughs, wrapping blooming babies in pathetic dirty rags. No matter. She was still more fortunate than they were; the most blessed happy woman in all the world today. She gave the crone her oranges, then crossed the road to dodge her. She needed all her cash today, must keep it for the *maghi*.

She rolled the word around her tongue, shivering with excitement. Magi back in England meant three kings. Here it meant magicians. She'd first spotted them herself in the

442

Piazza Colonna, setting up their little makeshift tables just behind the colonnade; had learnt their name from the man at the hotel, whose English was impressive and who always smiled and flirted with her each time she left the room-keys. He had told her the magicians were really basic fortune-tellers, but not just meddling amateurs; some of them true psychics who could see into the future, had access to a depth of knowledge unplumbed by normal reason. She was already quite aware, from the Church, and from John-Paul, how reason never took you very far; how you had to leap beyond it to faith or intuition, had to trust to instinct, or explore the seething id, plunge deep into the coils of the unconsciousness; could learn things on a level quite apart from proof or logic, learn through dreams, through prayer. John-Paul had made her clever, expanded her whole outlook, taught her there were other things besides GCEs, diplomas.

She checked her watch anxiously as she dithered at the crossroads, unsure which way to go. It was difficult to walk now through the dawdling jostling crowds, especially with her cake-box, her bulky sheaf of flowers. 'Sorry,' she kept saying to the people who bumped into her, reflecting on a word they probably didn't understand. Of course she wasn't sorry – not about the baby, felt no shred of guilt, not even towards James. He would accept it as his own, and it might even come to bond them, become the focus of a new stage in their marriage, a more tranquil fruitful stage.

She stopped in shock as she turned into a square, recognised the column in its centre. The little street she'd taken more by chance than by geography had led her straight into the Piazza Colonna. She had found it with no mishap, without once getting lost. That itself was magic, could mean she was being guided to her fate. She crossed the square, slipped between the solid grey-stone pillars of the colonnade, found the three magicians sitting in their

443

shadow, each at a small table with a lighted candle on it. She glanced from the three tiny flames to the radiant moon above. It seemed larger and much closer, as if it had moved down the sky to eavesdrop. She hovered by a column, trying to choose between the *maghi*. The tallest, most exotic one wore a full-length coat with a dramatic fox-fur collar and a black topper on his head. The youngest looked a gypsy, with his swarthy skin, his one gold dangly earring, and his casual grubby clothes. She was attracted by the third – a dark and wiry man with long artistic fingers, intensely serious eyes, a silver salamander pinned to his lapel. All three were occupied, clients tête-à-tête with them – people like herself who had come to learn their fates, had placed their happiness, their future, in these fortune-tellers' hands.

The third man was just finishing, accepting two crisp banknotes from an ecstatic-looking girl, thanking her and smiling, his silver brooch glinting in the candlelight. 'ENGLISH SPOKE,' read a roughly crayoned notice propped up on his table. Wasn't that an omen – the fact they could communicate, the fact his chair was empty now, as if it were urging her, inviting her, to sit in it herself? She was sure this man was right for her, trusted him instinctively, was drawn by his resemblance to John-Paul – not so much his looks, though both were dark and slender – but his air of passionate solemnity, his sharp-boned sensitive face. She edged towards him shyly, sat down at his table, still clutching all her packages.

'You Engleesh?' he asked softly.

She nodded, shrinking at his scrutiny, the way he was gazing right into her face as if to drag her soul out; his black eyes so expressive she felt he was speaking with them, through them; pouring out predictions, revelations, though as yet he'd said only two brief words. He gestured to her to put her shopping down, then placed both her hands palms-up on the table, started examining the left

444

one, brow creased in concentration as he traced its curving lines, his own hands bony-cold. Still he said no word, appeared to be picking up her character, her basic fears and feelings, not through any confab, but as if he had antennae. That, too, was like John-Paul.

At last, he spoke, his eyes returning to her face again, and seeming to pierce through flesh and bone. 'You good lady – very good.'

'Oh, no,' she said, embarrassed. 'I'm not good at all, honestly I'm not. In fact, I've been neglecting things just recently – back at home, I mean – haven't really bothered with the cooking or the . . .'

'You good, I say. You strong. But many other person drag your strength.'

'Drag it? What d'you mean?'

'Peoples take your time, always – how you say? – pulling you and fretting you, so you gives your strength away.'

Mary's mind tracked back to last night. She had been up with Harry once again, from one a.m. till three. He'd been complaining of a buzzing in his ears, which he feared might be tinnitus, or even an early warning-sign of Alzheimer's disease – until she realised she could hear it, too, and it was actually an extractor-fan, set high up on the roof above his window. 'Well, I suppose Harry *is* a trial just at the moment, but then he's always had trouble with his digestion, and it wasn't fair to bring him, I suppose. But we couldn't really . . .'

'Harry is your lover?'

'Oh, no! He's almost eighty.'

'You have other lover – yes?'

'Er, yes.' Her cheeks were flaming, as scarlet as the woollen scarf flung casually round his neck above the thin black jacket, the grubby once-white shirt, open to the chest, and revealing coarse black hair.

He nodded, seemed to know about John-Paul, started laying out a deck of cards on the dirty gingham tablecloth,

445

arranging them in two long rows, face-down. 'Take card,' he said, pointing to the bottom row. She picked one, turned it up, flinching at its symbols: a jewel-eyed serpent wreathed around a pillar, a strange broken wheel above. She had no idea what cards these were. They seemed nothing like the ordinary pack Harry used for rummy, nor even like the tarot cards Oliver had borrowed once from an eccentric chum at school (and which James had later confiscated as being what he called both bogus and bad taste).

The fortune-teller was staring at her card, one hand half-concealing it, the other twitching restless on the table. 'He great man,' he murmured.

'Er . . . who?'

'The man you love. He powerful man. He big.'

Yes, big, she thought – he's right – big in all the vital ways, colossal in his influence. Even here in Rome, John-Paul seemed to loom in every street; tower on every column in place of emperors and saints, controlling rampant stallions or brandishing a sword.

'You waiting something, you and lover, yes?'

'Yes,' she breathed. 'We are.' How amazing that he knew; had stumbled on her secret so precipitously, discerned the very reason she was there. No point sitting silent any longer. She must ask him that one question which obsessed her. Never mind the rest. She had no interest in the future beyond that huge concern – no wish to hear about legacies or journeys, chance encounters, strokes of fate. She shifted in her seat, aware of idle tourists strolling by, whispering to each other, or pointing at the cards. The candle had burned low and was guttering in its glass, making sudden frantic flurries, then wavering, half-dying, as if its time was nearly up. Her time was rationed, too. James would be annoyed by now, Lionel bullying Harry, the boys ruining their teeth with sugary snacks. 'Look,' she said, lowering her voice, and glancing down to avoid the vulgar stares. 'I . . . I'm going to have a baby. *His* baby. You understand?'

The man looked pained. 'My Engleesh very good. This baby good as well. This baby very good.'

Mary gripped her chair, astonished. 'You *know* about the baby?'

The man nodded, stroked his chin, where he was growing the first stubblings of a beard. 'I see it in the cards. This baby very special. It grow up to be saviour.'

'*Saviour?*'

'Yes.'

She stared at him, enchanted. He was confirming what she knew – knew from instinct, intuition, in the depths of her own heart. She leaned forward in her seat, hardly caring now whether anyone was watching, her voice hoarse from hope, from nerves. 'There's something I've just got to know – will it be a boy or girl?'

There was a sudden nervous pause. She could hear the drone of traffic, the drag of passing feet, filling in the silence. Restless leaping shadows flickered up and down the columns from the last throes of the candle-flame. The man held her with his eyes again, one tiny muscle twitching in his cheek.

'You want boy, or you want girl?'

'I want girl.' She was picking up his accent, transfixed by him, his presence, that strange light in his eyes, the silver salamander which seemed to wink and writhe, his dark and mobile face which registered each fleeting change of mood.

'I've got three sons already,' she confided in a whisper. 'They're marvellous boys, so clever and . . . But I always wanted a girl – yes, right from the beginning. I've never told my husband. It seemed disloyal, ungrateful. But this time . . .' Her voice faltered to a halt. 'I can't explain it really. It's just – you know – important.'

The man said nothing, simply swept the first cards

447

fiercely off the table and started flicking through a second pack, picking out a couple – one with one dot, one with two – and holding them both up to her. 'This positive card,' he explained, pointing to the single dot. 'This negative – with two dots.' He reshuffled the whole pack, then laid them out in two long rows again.

'We ask question of the cards,' he said. '"Will child be girl?" Okay? And then you start pick card – one card, two card, many card – till you holding card with dots on. If one dot, *yes* – so girl. If two dots – *no*, so boy.'

Mary sat half-paralysed, agog to know, yet dreading those two dots. She glanced up at the fortune-teller, who was still watching her intently, her tiny form reflected in the dark pupils of his eyes, as if he knew her now so well, he carried her inside him. She shivered suddenly. The night seemed colder, darker; the candle-flame burnt out, the moon behind a cloud, as if it, too, feared the answer. The fortune-teller prompted her, touched her cheek a moment, the gesture strangely intimate. 'You ask question now, please.'

'You mean ask it out aloud?'

He nodded. 'Yes. Important. Words important. Words have power.'

She swallowed, cleared her throat, spoke as distinctly as she could. 'Will my baby be a girl?' she asked the cards. '*Our* baby. John-Paul's child.' There was a moment's total silence, as if by speaking John-Paul's name she had brought all Rome to a halt, somehow stopped the traffic, stilled the universe.

'Take card,' the *mago* whispered, seeming to catch her mood of breathless expectation. Mary's hand moved confidently to the far end of the table, as if somebody were telling her which card she had to pick; some power beyond her own directing her tense fingers to that last one on the row. She paused a moment before turning it face-up. Could she be mistaken? Perhaps it was a picture-card with

448

no dots on it at all. As the man had just explained, she might need to pick up several cards before she got her answer. She turned it over: one dot.

'*Positivo!*' cried the man, switching to Italian in excitement. '*Ragazza!* You have girl-child.'

'Girl-child,' she repeated, both hands round the card now, as if cradling it, embracing it. She kept staring at the tiny dot, watching it burgeon from an egg-cell to a perfect eight-pound baby. The man was half out of his seat, jabbing at the card with one thin excited finger, his whole face alive, elated.

'Very special girl-child! She make happy everyone. She have *gioia*, *providenza*. She do big things, like father. Very special father. You leave him soon, but . . .'

'Leave him?'

'Yes.'

She knew it, had prepared for it, realised that once she stopped her sessions with John-Paul, she would not be simply leaving him, but would probably never see him in her life again. Yet it still hurt to hear the *mago* spell it out; hurt as fiercely, cruelly, as if she'd held her hand in the new and ardent candle-flame he'd just lit in its glass holder. She kept her eyes fixed on the flame, felt them prick with tears.

'You not cry, dear lady. You strong, you very strong. You leave your lover, but him not leave you ever. He always there. He with you. He inside you.'

She suddenly scrabbled for her purse, started pouring all her banknotes on the table, almost covering the two long rows of cards. 'Thank you,' she said wildly, kicking back her chair and reaching for her flowers. She deposited the huge bouquet in the fortune-teller's arms. She had meant it for the children, to decorate their room, add a splash of scent and colour to the celebration meal. But she had to give this man some token, not mere humdrum money, some more personal offering to repay him for his words.

449

She could hear him calling after her in English and Italian, the two tongues oddly mixed, but she had no more time to spare, was already darting back the way she'd come, crossing the piazza, squeezing through the crowds.

She turned left, then right, then left again, miraculously remembering the streets she'd taken, the shops and bars she'd passed; found herself back beside the Pantheon. She stared up at its massy bulk, chequered in the moonlight. What had Oliver told her – that it had been built two thousand years ago as the temple of all pagan gods, then became a Christian church, re-dedicated to her namesake, Mary, and all the saints and martyrs? Her eldest son was intrigued by pagan deities, kept questioning the Christian one with arguments which flummoxed her; insisting he preferred the idea of nature-gods and emperor-gods to a one-and-only abstract God which nobody could prove. The whole subject quite confused her, especially since she'd heard last month on *Woman's Hour* that at least a thousand people in Britain today claimed to be gods themselves, and that this was still more common in the East, where gods could (and did) manifest themselves in the guise of ordinary men.

She paused a moment by the stained but robust portico, touched the dank stone columns. Could John-Paul be a deity himself – not just a saint, a god? If there were so many different gods around – Egyptian ones and Roman ones, emperors, gurus, yogis, even common English bank-clerk gods, then why not John-Paul, too? It was no more inconceivable than Jesus being God – in fact, less surprising, really, since Jesus was a hippie-type who dressed in beard and sandals, and had sometimes sounded rude and quite unmannerly, whereas John-Paul was never anything but courteous, considerate, and impeccably turned out. And it would certainly explain the *mago*'s strange word 'saviour'. After all, a god's child would be special, destined for future greatness. She had seen statues of ten dozen gods in the museums they'd been visiting – river gods and sky gods, gods of wine or war. John-Paul should have his plinth as well, as he already had his cult, his obedient marvelling votaries – as God of Love, Libido.

She heard a clock strike eight, jogged the last three hundred yards, panted to the Bar Navona where she had arranged to meet the menfolk at seven forty-five. She was twenty minutes late, yet she couldn't see a sign of them; scanned the pavement tables, even checked inside, though the boys had all insisted on a table in the open, so they could see the fountains and the buskers, watch any early fireworks which might be let off in the square. They'd probably got distracted by the stalls, or Father Christmas, and if she tried to track them down they were bound to miss each other. Best for her to wait, sit tight, bag that last free table.

She ordered herself a glass of sparkling wine, watched the press of people drinking, laughing, guzzling – well, all except the sullen group at the table right beside her, where a girl was actually in tears; their mood obviously quite different from the general festive merriment. The girl was tall and handsome, despite her tear-stained face, with fine bones, striking features – though with a strangely ragged haircut, as if she'd hacked it off herself. She was also dressed in man's clothes, though the garb looked almost stylish, accentuated her slim but shapely figure. She was sitting with four men, who all seemed rough and brutish; none bothering to comfort her, but ignoring her completely as they smoked and downed their beer. She longed to lean across and say a word of sympathy, though the girl wouldn't understand it – looked foreign, as the men did, dark and slightly exotic, as if several different countries had left their mark on her.

She sipped her wine uneasily as she listened to the sobbing; hated anyone to cry, least of all today, when she herself had so much joy to share. Could the girl

451

be pregnant, too, but perhaps not want her baby, and that surly man beside her be the unwilling angry father? She suddenly rummaged in her handbag, drew out her handkerchief. This girl was in distress, nose running into her mouth, tears soaking into her shirt, and with nothing but her sleeve to mop them up. She might not know the Italian word for hankie, but that needn't stop her offering it.

'Th . . . Thanks,' the girl said, startled, as she scoured her nose and eyes, edged her chair round sideways, so it was almost touching Mary's.

'You're English!'

'Yes. And I never cry on principle, least of all in public.' She was laughing now, as well as still half-crying; seemed extremely overwrought, her legs twisted round the chair-rungs, an ashtray full of mangled cigarette-ends beside her empty glass.

'Well, it's very nice to meet you. My name's Mary Hampton.'

'Nial.'

'I beg your pardon?'

'*My* name. Blame it on my father. In fact, you won't go too far wrong if you blame everything on him.'

'Cut it out, Nial, can't you? The whole of Rome doesn't want to hear your hang-ups.'

The bad-tempered man beside her had risen to his feet, tossed Mary's hankie back to her, yanked Nial up by the wrist. 'It's time to go, anyway. You ready?'

'Yeah.' The girl seemed subject to him, didn't spare a look behind her, or even the briefest of goodbyes, as she shuffled out morosely, the three other men getting up as well.

Mary watched them go, smoothing out the saturated hankie. That girl should see John-Paul, learn what she was doing to herself – how she'd probably chosen that uncouth and fractious boyfriend because she was trying to reproduce the situation with her father, force an unloving man to love her. She sighed and checked her watch, trying not to fret about the boys. At least the piazza offered great diversion, all her senses titillated by the sound of plashing water, the pulse of a rock band, the smells of roasting chestnuts, cloying candyfloss, the gaudy tinsel colours of the sweet-stalls. She kept her eyes scanned for her menfolk, though it was hard to distinguish anyone in the tangled crowds, the pools of murky shadow which alternated with swathes of light from the dramatic floodlit fountains. And she was continually distracted – by a poodle in a real fur coat, a lad in scarlet pantaloons juggling with six balls, a furtive man in a raincoat and a sunhat just skulking past her table, eyes fixed on the ground.

'*Bryan*!' she called, astonished. 'What *are* you doing here? I thought you said you had to fly to Tokyo on business?'

Bryan lurched towards her table, his face draining of all colour, seemed to stagger, reel. Mary caught his arm. 'Are you all right? You've gone quite pale. Sit down a moment, and I'll order you a brandy.'

He stared at her, unspeaking; looked haggard and unkempt, dark rings beneath his eyes, his raincoat buttoned wrongly, so that it hung lower on one side. He stroked his crumpled sleeve where her arm had touched his own, kept gazing at it wonderingly. 'I'm dreaming,' he said slowly. 'This is just one last cruel deception. You're not Mary Hampton, are you – the Mary of the class?'

She laughed. 'Of course I am. Look, do sit down and join me. I'm just waiting for my family. It would be nice for you to meet them.'

He backed away immediately. 'Oh, no. I'm . . . er . . . busy, very busy – preparing for a seminar.'

'A seminar on New Year's Eve? They must be awful slave-drivers. You can spare five minutes, surely?'

He peered a moment at his watch, then glanced

nervously around him. 'It's dangerous to be out at all, especially on your own. Father Campion warned us. It's the most dangerous night of all the year in Rome. He said we might get killed or . . .'

Mary pulled a chair out, patted it encouragingly. She could think of more exciting companions than poor perverted Bryan, but until James and co turned up themselves, she'd rather have a chaperone than sit here on her own and be subjected to rude leers. Anyway, tonight she craved for company, almost any company, longed to pour her news out, share it with the world. 'We're safe till ten, at least, Bryan. It's only nearer midnight that things get really violent – or so our courier said.'

He sagged down in the chair, as she ordered him a brandy, herself another wine. She already felt just slightly faint and fuzzy, but it surely wouldn't hurt to get a trifle tipsy on this one night of the year, and when she'd received such marvellous news.

'Isn't Rome *fantastic*,' she said, leaning forward to clink her glass to Bryan's.

'Yes,' he mumbled tonelessly.

'How long have you been here? And is it strictly business, or a holiday as well? And why Rome and not Japan?'

He shook his head, as if he'd hardly grasped her questions; really did look ill. Perhaps he'd caught that 'flu bug which had been going round at Christmas time, and was still feeling weak and low. She must try to cheer him up, rummaged through her mind to dredge up Simon's little jokes, or the priceless things that Jon had said about what he called the cattycombs. His face remained quite tragic, his posture slumped and stooping. Recklessly, she ordered still more drinks, as much to lift his gloom as to calm her own anxiety about her husband and the boys. It was almost half past eight now and no sign of them at all. Had her precious Jon been injured

454

by a firework, her precocious brilliant Oliver had a bed thrown at his brain?

She drained her third Spumante, felt better instantly. Of course the boys were fine; everything was fine; and she was pregnant with a daughter, a rare and splendid girl-child who would lighten the dark world. 'Bryan,' she said, giggling rather nervously as she flirted with her beer-mat. 'Can I trust you with a secret?'

He suddenly leaned forward, as if at last she'd caught his interest, roused him from his torpor. She looked away, still nervous. 'I shouldn't tell you really. It's something very private, and you might not understand, might think I'm – you know – loose.'

'Mary, what are you trying to tell me?' His hand was groping after hers, his face no longer pale, but flushed and almost galvanised.

'Er, nothing. Look, forget it. It was just a . . . silly joke.'

'No, Mary, not a joke. I know you're serious.'

'Well, yes, I am, but . . .'

'You *are*? Oh, Mary! I never thought you'd say it, never thought you'd actually dare to . . .'

'Well, I suppose I shouldn't really. I mean, I haven't even mentioned it to James yet.'

'You're going to *tell* him?' Bryan's eyes were wild – fearful yet triumphant, the flush deepening on his cheeks, exulting down his neck.

'Well, of course I am. I can't keep it a secret any longer.'

'Oh, Mary, I'm so happy!'

'But I haven't told you yet.'

He shook his head, both hands seeking hers now. 'You don't need to spell it out. We don't need boring words.'

'You mean it *shows*, already?' Mary moved her hands to the safety of her glass, glanced down at her stomach. She had known John-Paul for only fifteen weeks, but then fifteen weeks was just exactly long enough for a pregnancy to show: the first swelling of her belly, rounding of her breasts.

Bryan sprang up from his chair, started waving to a waiter. 'Let's celebrate! I'll order some champagne.'

'No, really, Bryan. It's sweet of you, but I've had three drinks already and I shouldn't really touch the stuff, not in my condition.'

'What condition? Mary! You're not ill again, for God's sake? Oh, no, please no, not that!' He sank back in his chair, hid his face a moment, groaning through his fingers. 'Just when everything's come right, to have you dragging back to that dreadful hospital.'

'What hospital? I don't know what you're talking about. I've never been ill in my life. I was just referring to the baby.'

'Baby?'

'Yes. The one I'm going to have.'

'You're . . . You're going to have a . . . a baby?'

Mary stared at him, concerned. This wasn't just the aftermath of 'flu – he really was far gone. His AIDS must be much worse, striking at his mind now, as well as his poor body, attacking memory and brain-cells, not just the immune system. He had no recall at all of what they'd just been talking about, appeared to have blanked it out entirely. And he even seemed uncertain who she was; had questioned her identity when she'd first called out to greet him, and was now confusing her with some invalid in hospital. She must treat him very gently; made her voice as kindly as she could as she explained to him again in simple words. 'Yes, I'm pregnant, Bryan.'

'Pr . . . Pregnant?'

'Yes.'

'It's a lie, a lie! You *can't* be.'

She laughed, despite herself; was feeling really strange now, giggly and yet anxious, distressed for Bryan, yet

456

reckless. 'That's what *I* thought, first of all. But I've done a test – well, two, in fact. I wanted to be absolutely certain, so I repeated it a second time and there's not a shred of doubt. And it's going to be a girl, a very special girl. Oh, I know I shouldn't tell you this, but I'm just bursting to tell someone.' She leaned across, gulped Bryan's untouched brandy, wrestling with herself about the advantage of discretion against the release of speaking out. She longed to shout her news from the highest point in Rome, boom it through a megaphone, but if that were neither wise nor even feasible, then why not whisper it to Bryan across the table? Her secret would be safe with him, and it would be a mark of trust to take him into her confidence, let him share her happiness. The poor wretch seemed so friendless, so utterly alone; might appreciate a private bond between them. She edged her chair up closer, voice lowered, yet intense. 'Bryan, I think the baby's father's may be what they call an avatar.'

'A *what*?'

'It's a Hindu word – means he's actually a god, but he's come down to earth in human form. They explained it all on *Woman's Hour*.'

'Your husband is a . . .?'

'Oh, no, not James. It's not my husband's baby.'

Bryan rammed his chair back violently, hurled both their glasses to the ground, and began pelting across the square, scattering chestnut-sellers, jugglers, and alerting an alsatian which bounded in pursuit of him, barking near-hysterically. Mary tried to follow, felt a dragging weight behind her; found she was tethered to her seat by one end of her coat-belt, which had tangled in its plastic slatted back. She tugged it free, at last, shouting at his disappearing form. 'Bryan! Come back. Please wait. You don't understand at all. Let me just . . .' She lurched two steps from her table, bumped – smack! – into a group of men and children, was caught in two steel arms and a whiff of strong Havana; heard her name spat out with clear distaste.

'Mary! Whatever are you doing? We've been waiting a whole hour for you – *and* worrying our guts out. We said seven forty-five at the Café di Nerone, and we finally catch up with you at nearly ten to nine, at a different bar entirely.'

# 37

'*Buon' Anno*, Nial,' I mutter to myself, as I sip my tepid lager, check my watch again. It's already ten to midnight, yet no sign of them back. I'm sitting on my own in Giuseppe's shoddy flat, listening to the hullabaloo outside. The entire street is warming up for that final stroke of twelve – drinking, hurling streamers, setting off fire-crackers under cars (or women's skirts), shrieking with mixed terror and elation. Seton said they were going to buy champagne, though I doubt that story actually. You don't need four strong men to carry back one bottle and a few bags of crisps and nuts, and anyway it wouldn't take two hours. God knows what they're up to – they didn't deign to tell me. They're much less trusting of me now, since I refused to kill the Pope; see me as a turncoat, treat me like a Judas. And my stupid tears this evening didn't help. They loathe tears – all of them – especially in a public place, and I tend to see their point, hate myself for cracking up, behaving like a fool. I don't know why I did it, though I suspect the Pope changed something in my gender by holding me like that, made me more a woman, or a daughter, the kind who weeps and clings.

I was also very angry that Seton had deceived me, fed me propaganda about a rigid tyrant Pope, censored his whole human side – the concern he feels about poverty and violence, the way he makes a point of visiting the slums and shacks of Rome, so he can see the filth and vermin for himself, then nags his parish priests to put things right. All the cuttings Seton showed me centred on his bigotry, never on his decency, yet he's made some pretty stirring speeches which I've managed to get hold of

– about sharing one's last cent (or crumb), breaking the chains of selfishness and sin. I could almost hear them snap, see the whole mean sated Western world reaching out to feed its startled neighbour.

Seton says it's cant, the oppressor shamming concern about oppression, but would *he* be able to forgive his own assassin, as Giovanni Paolo did in 1981? He broadcast that forgiveness while still racked with pain in hospital; later visited the prison cell and embraced the desperado who'd tried to bump him off. He's still disabled from that shot, yet he continues with the audiences, despite the obvious risks; still mingles with assassins, because he feels his people need him – even murderers like Seton and myself. And he's suffered not just physically, but mentally – lost his mother as a kid of eight or nine; was brought up by his brother who died himself at the raw age of fifteen; saw his only sister snuff it when she was just a babe in arms, like my own dust-and-ashes brother.

I've been reading all about him, feeling some strange bond with him, which I can't explain to anyone, since we couldn't be more different in most outward obvious ways. I keep thinking of him praying – praying for prodigals and prostitutes, praying for the world, and therefore me. I've always rather scoffed at prayer, but now I realise it's caring and attention, so I'm in his thoughts, on his mind, one of his concerns.

'Pray *harder*,' I implore him. It's exactly five to twelve and I'm still horribly alone.

I dawdle to the window, use it as a mirror. I don't look bad tonight, tarted up in Giuseppe's best black cords and a rather stunning scarlet shirt which I coaxed from surly Stefan. You're meant to dress in red on New Year's Eve – it's an ancient Roman custom – especially for the women, and especially underneath. All the shops are full of scarlet underwear, and Seton actually bought me a pair of red lace panties, so skimpy-brief my pubic hair froths over them.

460

It seems odd to have them on beneath men's trousers, as if I'm a girl and man at once. I suppose that's what I feel – a man who's been castrated and now cries too easily; a hulking macho woman who's learnt to fire a gun.

I wince at the shrill wailing of a siren. Tonight should be in the *Guinness Book of Records* as far as siren-power's concerned. The ambulances sound frenzied, the fire engines berserk, and every policeman in Rome seems to be hurtling through this neighbourhood with horns and screechers blaring. John-Paul's piddling sirens which whisper round his tower would be completely overshadowed here, hardly register at all. But then he doesn't register himself now, not as fiercely as he did. How could he, when he doesn't touch, or pray?

I did find out his room number, plucked up all my courage and rang through to his hotel; simply asked to speak to him, as casually, as nonchalantly, as if we were bosom pals who indulged in daily chats. 'He's in room 142,' I lied, picking the first number which came into my head. There was some delay, cross-checking, mumbling in Italian, then the woman on the switchboard came back to me, at last. 'It's not 142, it's 313, and I'm afraid he's out, signora.'

313 alarmed me. Thirteen is unlucky – though three itself is lucky, so I suppose I could regard it as two threes with just a one or 'I' between. Threes are everywhere: in religion, folklore, fairy tales – three witches, fairies, wishes; three persons in one God. In the end, I shrugged it off. I'd lost interest, actually; was more concerned with Giovanni Paolo, his own three roles as orphan, victim, Father.

I grab a shrivelled olive, abandoned in an ashtray, crunch it, stone and all. I'm absolutely starving – nothing much for breakfast, two dry rolls for lunch, and a pint of beer for supper. Most other lucky people – tourists, natives, families – will be more or less blown out by now, having just devoured their special New Year's dinner: at least half a dozen courses (and sometimes double that), with fantastic wines and party hats, nuts and fruit and sweets. It's called a *veglione* – my Italian's getting better – then at midnight they start stuffing once again: lentils and a pig's foot, which sounds pretty damn disgusting, except it's another ancient custom, and meant to bring you luck – no more cruel thirteens.

I need some luck myself. Still no sign of Seton, no welcome thud or shout. I start pacing round the room, trying not to watch the clock-hands which have all but come together. If I'm on my own at the vital stroke of midnight, I'll take it as an omen, conclude I'll be alone all year. I hear the clock begin to strike – slowly, almost tauntingly, as if it's gloating at my pain. I block my ears, still hear its heartless chiming through my hands. 'Two,' it says. 'Alone.' 'Three', it jeers. 'Alone still. They've totally forgotten you. So what did you expect?' It spins out four and five, chortles over six. I burst into the smaller room, the one I share with Seton, fall onto the pile of rugs we've been using as a bed, howl louder than its seven, eight and nine.

I don't even hear the door open, until Seton's actually shaking me, pulling at my arm. 'Come on! Get up! We're celebrating.' There's a rush of freezing air and we're suddenly outside, part of some huge crowd who are all dancing in the street, whooping, cheering, singing; not foreigners or strangers, but all one excited family. Champagne corks are popping, arcs of foam ejaculating, and a storm of brilliant fireworks seems to explode away the sky. I've never heard such uproar. Those rockets must be bombs, the Roman candles sticks of naked dynamite. The noise re-echoes from the buildings, which add their own applause; heads at all the windows, hands flinging squibs and streamers. Sirens yelp and caterwaul, blue flashing lights from police cars compete with showers of sparks – so many rockets shooting up, the sky turns blue and gold. Someone hurls a chest of drawers from an upper-storey flat. It crashes to the street, people fleeing terrified, then doubling back to loot its shattered drawers.

Empty bottles are smashing on the pavement, a huge bouquet of bright balloons bursting in midair. And, suddenly, another clock is thundering – a hoarse clock on a church-tower, striking mercifully late. I'll date *my* New Year from that one, ignore the mocking bully on Giuseppe's mantelpiece. I drain my pink champagne, hold the last gulp in my mouth, then press myself to Seton as I tongue it into *his* mouth. The final stroke of midnight seems to chime right through our bodies, vibrating in our bellies, shuddering down our spines. We're joined and sealed by midnight, by the sudden squall of firecrackers which seem to celebrate our kiss. I open my eyes a second, see the bloated moon watching like a voyeur as Seton slips his hand between the buttons of my shirt, finds my naked breasts. Giuseppe's watching too – excited, maybe jealous – suddenly scorches over and breaks me and Seton up; kisses me himself, hanging round my neck like a crazy younger brother. Then it's Stefan's turn, suspicious surly Stefan, except he's laughing now and teasing, as if I'm not a whingeing traitor and there's been nothing wrong between us. Marco's pumping both my hands, filling up my glass, skittish bubbles exploding in my face. We all toast each other, hug each other, try to chain ourselves with streamers, so we're all five looped together; five brothers, five best friends.

Eager church bells start to peal from somewhere just behind us, cracked and rather drunken bells ringing in New Year. 'Wait!' I shout. 'Not yet.' I can't celebrate the new until I've chucked away the old, added my own rubbish to the debris in the gutter – broken glass, dead fireworks, trampled dirty tinsel, empty cans and bottles, even a dead pigeon. I stand absolutely still a moment, amidst the tangled revellers. This is serious and difficult. I must throw away my hate, my bitterness and anger – anger with my father, fury with the world because it's not the shape or flavour that I ordered in the womb. I snap the streamers round my neck, take a step away, remove myself a yard or two from Seton and the gang, then hurl my full glass of champagne into the street. I watch it foam around the corpse of a spent rocket, dribble down a drain; shards of glass ricocheting high into the air. Seton lunges after me, grabs me by the arm. 'Are you crazy, Nial? That's best champagne. It cost us.'

'It cost me too,' I yell above the din. He doesn't understand, can't hear me anyway. Those raucous throaty church bells have started up again and are pealing so exuberantly they're almost drowning out the sirens. 'New Year!' they bray and jangle. 'New leaf, new life, new deal.'

'New *hope*,' I whisper soundlessly. 'New start.'

# 38

Bryan eased up from the toilet seat, stared into the bowl. Absolutely nothing. No result at all from the castor oil and senna-pods. His bowel had all but atrophied these last few days in Rome. He'd always blamed his constipation on his Mother; the way she stood outside the bathroom door, rapping out warnings and commands. Now he actually missed her there, longed to hear her telling him not to waste the toilet-paper, or reminding him how many germs could live on just one finger. She had more important things to do – consult with priests and bishops, grant interviews to media men or hordes of goggling locals, pose for preening photographs. She had already become so famous that virtual strangers were fighting for her autograph; reverent pilgrims collecting up her toast crusts or the leavings on her plate, to take home as precious relics. Even at this moment, she was the centre of attention. Their party had arranged a special New Year's vigil, from ten o'clock till midnight, in which prayers were being offered in thanksgiving for her miracle, hymns of joy and triumph sung; candle lit from candle until the whole chapel blazed with light.

He himself was sitting in the gloom, the toilet light switched off and only a beam of moonlight patterning his pale and ghostly thighs. The room was chilly-dank, drops of condensation oozing down the shiny sallow walls. The pipes were old and rusting, with strange bulges in their length, as if they too were blocked with faeces, poisoning themselves. Yet where else could he hide? Every other room was communal, even the dark washroom, with its row of matey basins, its asthmatic wheezing shower, which took almost thirty minutes to change from melted ice to grudging tepid. He himself was cold, and very cramped. He'd been squatting there for nearly two whole hours, had bolted in at ten to ten to avoid the tide of pilgrims surging to the chapel. He couldn't let them know that he'd been crying, endure their pity or contempt, be unable to explain the sheer horror of that moment in the café when his pure and perfect Mary revealed she was a whore.

He closed his eyes, heard her nervous voice again about to tell him that she loved him; the first woman in his life who had ever needed and desired him. He knew at that wild moment he was saved; saved from misery, extinction, saved even from John-Paul. It had been so wonderful to find her, track her down, at last, when he'd given up all hope, even started to believe she was just a mirage, a vain dream. He'd checked eighty-seven more hotels, and at least two hundred cafés, but failed to catch a glimpse of her until that startling stroke of fortune when she'd actually called his name, begged him to sit down with her; seemed as eager, as solicitous, as in his wildest fantasies. He had even touched her hand across the table, felt its warmth, its pulsing life; imagined it stroking down his body, kindling him, reviving.

And all that had been kindled was a bastard – a child conceived by some promiscuous pervert who attracted her so madly she actually saw him as a god. A god! Some lewd bed-hopping womaniser she'd probably picked up in a bar, who was unworthy even to look at her, let alone seduce her. It had been bad enough imagining she still had sex with James, but to think she might be sleeping with maybe *swarms* of men – waiters, wastrels, window cleaners – conceiving babies indiscriminately, even boasting of the fact. He had never seen her look so smug and satisfied, and on top of all that lechery she'd been knocking back the booze, even snatching *his* glass, once her own was empty. He should have realised her true nature when he'd discovered those vibrators, but he had tried to blame her husband, kid himself she was still the pure unspotted woman he'd idealised.

A sudden loud explosion re-echoed from outside. He crouched lower on the toilet seat, head huddled to his knees. They'd been setting off bombs since early evening. Thank God the seminary was solid as a fortress, protected by stout walls, well-defended by outer gates and barricades. And with all his party safely in the chapel, none would risk their life or limbs in the mayhem of the streets tonight. But perhaps he should be down with them. Wouldn't it be safer than cowering all alone here, with no one to instruct him if there were an emergency, a crisis? He shuffled to the door, trousers round his ankles still, opened it a crack, heard a hymn surging from below.

> Songs of thankfulness and praise
> Jesus, Lord, to thee we raise . . .

No, he couldn't face it. Their Lord wasn't *his* God. He didn't have a God, didn't have a Mother. Lena had become no longer simple Mrs Payne, but what Father Smithby-Horne called a 'vehicle' to display God's might and mercy to the faithful. And the 'vehicle' was revelling in her power. Everyone was pandering to her; ardent Phyllis acting as her handmaid, priests rushing to escort her if she so much as moved a step, special meals and privileges laid on throughout the day. They were even setting up a bronze and marble plaque, to record the details of her miracle, and once engraved, it would become a solid fact – at least to half of Rome.

The whole business quite disturbed him. How could he square miracles with anarchy and chaos, except miracles were chaotic in themselves, broke natural laws, upset normal reason? He'd tried to stick to reason, to explain the cure away as what doctors called a natural remission, or argue, John-Paul-style, that Lena had been healed because she no longer had a need for her affliction; had been enjoying herself for the first time in her life; been cosseted, respected, since she was first wheeled onto the plane. John-Paul had once explained that certain people could aggravate their pain, or even induce it in the first place, to win sympathy, attention, but if they could get this in another way, through esteem or some achievement, their injury or illness might diminish quite dramatically. Now he was less sure. You could no more prove John-Paul's ideas than a miracle itself. And when he thought back to his Mother's life, there were indeed things which truly baffled him. The whole business of John-Paul himself, for instance. How had she discovered that, save through supernatural powers, when he'd done every last thing possible to keep it secret from her? And even minor matters, like the way she always knew when he'd been eating between meals – and not just when, but what. Once, he'd chewed up the whole chocolate wrapper, as well as just the Fruit and Nut, so she'd never find it in his waste-bin; washed out his mouth with Listerine, in case she smelt his breath, yet she'd still remarked acidly at dinner time: 'Bryan, I don't know why I even bother cooking, when you prefer Cadbury's Fruit and Nut bars to my macaroni cheese.'

Now, she wouldn't notice if he devoured a whole sweet-shop full of chocolate; would probably never cook for him again; maybe never return to Ivy Close at all, but stay in Rome where she'd be famed as a celebrity, surrounded by an entourage of local Catholic fans. He'd lost his home, lost her as his Mother – and it was partly his own fault. He'd *tried* to lose her, hadn't he, almost all his adult life; packed her off to islands or hostile barren wastelands, using double string and cardboard, so he wouldn't hear her screams? Well, this time he'd succeeded. She was indeed as far from him as if she'd been delivered by a postman three hundred thousand miles away.

He pulled his trousers up again, struggled with his belt, stood slumped against the wall, staring dully out through the tiny smeary window. A full moon was very dangerous on a night like New Year's Eve, when passions were already high, and fuelled by alcohol. Even on a normal night, a full moon could drive you mad. He'd read it in the *Mail* – how staff in mental hospitals had twice as many crises on the days around full moon – patients cracking up or running wild. He drew the dirty curtain to try to shut it out, sank back on the seat once more, head drooping, eyes half-closed. 'God of might and mercy' they were trilling from downstairs. There wasn't any mercy – that at least was clear. His stomach griped, his tongue was furred, his body had stopped working. Impotence. His pale lips mouthed the word. Constipation was just another term for it, another symptom of paralysis, stagnation. Even if he outflanked all his rivals, won Mary for himself, he'd probably prove a laughing-stock, unable to perform. He could see the shameless father of her baby thrusting wildly into her, pistoning and pumping her in every bar in Walton, every bed in Rome. If he ever met that maniac, ever had an inkling who he was, he'd . . . he'd . . .

He unclenched his fists, wiped his clammy palms. His own fury terrified him – those jumbled lethal images of cudgels, choppers, hatchets, daggers, guns. They locked up violent psychopaths, strapped them into straitjackets. 'Go away!' he shouted to the flint-faced psychiatric nurse who had reared up in his head. He must calm down, wash his hands and face, scour his *mind*, for God's sake. Impossible to wash, though. There wasn't any water. And yet he could feel germs crawling over him: germs of jealousy, revenge, germs of fury and confusion. He reached behind the cistern for the bottle of disinfectant

– Sainsbury's disinfectant which must have been brought by one of the English to counter Roman squalor. He could sluice his hands with that, perhaps even swab his body, pour some on the cleaning-rag and have an instant sponge-down, sterilise his brain with it, remove those deadly weapons.

Except it was *Mary* who needed sterilising – and in both senses of the word. It was she who'd made him violent, she who'd tainted, taunted him. He closed his eyes a moment, saw her lying naked while he swilled the disinfectant between her open thighs, scouring all the men off her, their fingerprints, their sperm; trying to reach inside her body, so he could fumigate her womb, flush that hated foetus out. He could see her flesh glistening-wet and quivering, as it shrunk from his cruel hands; watched her flinch and tremble as the undiluted fluid smarted on her nipples, stung inside her groin. No – he flung the rag away, couldn't bear to hurt her, even with such flagrant provocation. Inflicting pain on Mary didn't heal his own.

He turned back to the window, bottle in his hands still. It had become a baby's bottle now; Mary's baby swelling from a speck to a Goliath, gobbling down her milk, her breasts, her life. Of course he hadn't managed to abort it – it was growing every moment, expanding as he dwindled. How would he endure the next nine mocking months; how even find the courage to bear the next two hours – that loathsome pilgrims' party planned to start at midnight: the jollity, the singsongs, the charades and childish games. He checked his watch – exactly ten to twelve. Just ten brief minutes left until New Year. Could he face another year, its loneliness, its pain; face another two hundred sessions on John-Paul's fruitless couch; maybe twenty times two hundred if his analyst was right and he was resisting his own treatment, one of those psychotics who needed half a lifetime before they could be cured, or even move from

470

desperate to plain miserable? He could hear John-Paul's impassive voice repeating those grim phrases he'd heard so many times – resistance, negative transference, persecutory anxiety, repetition-compulsion. How could he ever win against such odds?

He tugged back the tattered curtain, gazed out at the night, the callous moon pretending there was some event to celebrate as it poured its tinsel beams on roofs and walls. Even the disinfectant bottle shimmered in its light, like some festive gold liqueur. 'POISON', read the label. 'Not to be taken.' He fought a wave of dizziness as the letters blurred and rippled in his head. If he disobeyed the label and drank that potent poison, he could miss the party, miss New Year, miss the birth of Mary's baby, the transfer of his Mother's goods and furniture from Ivy Close to Rome. His body seemed to spring to life as the idea took hold and rooted. He could feel the blood drumming through his arteries, pounding in his head. He was no longer blocked or paralysed, but untrammelled, freed, released. He had actually made a decision for the first time in his life, without agonising, dithering, setting out long lists of pros and cons.

There *were* no cons as far as dying was concerned. Even John-Paul had written a book on *Thanatos* (which at first he'd feared was a new and dire disease, until he discovered from the dust-jacket it was simply the Greek word for death, used by Freud to personify the death-instinct). He'd borrowed the tome from his local public library, struggled through the close-packed text, given up halfway; but still been struck by his doctor's obvious interest in the pull and lure of death – man's longing for oblivion, negation. Oblivion was his now, and oblivion came free – no monthly bills charging him for pain. All he had to do was make sure his death was orderly, time it with precision, not shamble out casually with no strict and tidy plan. He had his plan already.

As the first loud stroke of midnight resounded from the courtyard clock, he would tip the bottle up, gulp the first long draught, and as its last chime died away, he would drain the final drop.

He put the bottle down a moment, so he could comb his hair, straighten up his tie, brush any speck or loose thread from his clothes. Thank goodness he was wearing a clean white shirt, a decent formal jacket. It seemed important to be neat, to have his shoes and nails clean. He positioned himself ·squarely on the seat, feet together, back and shoulders straight, then held the bottle ready, unscrewed its rusted cap. He wasn't even frightened; more elated and amazed that he had cut through all the torment of a lifetime; the vacillation, seesawing, the endless indecision. Just four minutes to go now. He started counting seconds to calm himself, still the frantic judder of his heart.

At last, he heard that sudden throaty in-breath from the courtyard, which always meant the clock was about to strike. He panicked for a second as he confused it with the clock outside John-Paul's Gothic tower – that cracked and strident voice cawing eight o'clock each Monday, Wednesday, Friday of his life; inducing sweet relief as it released him from the couch, yet also deep frustration, since he knew he would be back there morning after morning, as year succeeded year. '*No*,' he whispered to himself. 'I shall stop my clock, run down. Just twelve more chimes, then silence.'

The first chime seemed to vibrate through his body, thunder through his brain. His hands were clenched and sweaty on the bottle, his whole body tensed, prepared. He tipped his head back, raised the heavy bottle to his mouth; his last thoughts not on Mary, but on the triumphant fact he'd escaped John-Paul for ever, outwitted him in death. The bottle grazed his trembling lips, as he closed them round its nipple, closed his eyes as well, let the bitter golden liquor lacerate his tongue.

# 39

'Mary, this noise is quite ridiculous! I was prepared to put up with it at midnight, but it's nearly three a.m. now.'

'I know, dear. Try and read. It's the only thing to do. The man downstairs told me a lot of youngsters celebrate till dawn.'

'Celebrate? It sounds more like a war. I'm going to complain.'

'Oh, don't, James! No one can do anything. And if you go outside yourself, you may get hurt.'

'I wouldn't dream of going out. I just want a word with that moron of a desk clerk. Maybe he can't control the fireworks and the yobbos, but at least he could restrain the hotel staff. There've been half a dozen porters banging around with luggage for almost a full hour now. I mean, what in God's name's going on? People arriving in the middle of the night, or changing rooms or something? And can't he have a word with that ass in 207? Okay, if he wants a knees-up in his room, that's quite all right with me, but does he have to leave his door open and have half his guests lurching down the corridor and battering on *our* door?'

'Only one did, darling.'

'There'll be more – you see. Just as we've nodded off at four or five o'clock, he'll send out for indoor fireworks or start playing the accordion . . .' James erupted from the room, coat atop his dressing gown, bare feet in bluff black shoes. Mary put her book away, switched on the main light. New Year's Eve hadn't gone too well, starting with the picnic meal which had been mainly cream and sugar – chocolate lions, sickly cake, followed by more lions –

473

which, as James had pointed out, was hardly very healthy for his cholesterol levels. She'd been so elated by the *mago*, so excited by her future, her mind had been on higher things than coleslaw and salami. She had totally forgotten to buy salads and cold meats (or even bread and cheese); had left her bag of apples by the fortune- teller's chair. The boys had been delighted by a meal of mainly sweets, but James kept asking anyone who'd listen how a normal rational female who'd kept house for thirteen years could spend five thousand lire and two hours in a food shop and return with just one gâteau and no change?

Even the fireworks had been something of a let-down – all bang and not much spectacle – and with none of those set-pieces of flowers or shapes or buildings which you got back home in England, and no real show of colour. Just what James described as a 'God Almighty racket', which had terrified poor Jonathan, and put Lionel in a paddy since it continued well past midnight when he'd been trying to sort out his research notes on Third World artesian wells. And it wasn't just the rockets or raucous fellow guests. James had been complaining about the din from 207, but there had been even more disturbance from her own immediate family. First Simon had come bursting in with stomach-ache, then Oliver with nightmares and Harry with a heart attack (which she re-diagnosed as flatulence and dosed with Pepsidol). And, lastly, Lionel himself, just half an hour or less ago, summoning their help to remove a drunken Lithuanian who had collapsed outside his door.

Mary sighed, trailed into the bathroom. Even her bladder seemed irritable tonight. She'd blamed it on the wine at first – three glasses in the café, and then champagne on top. But it could be just another symptom of her pregnancy. She had planned on telling James about the baby in the first hour of the new year, which would surely be symbolic; mark the new start in their marriage and their hopes. She had imagined a romantic lull with all the fireworks spent, the children sleeping peacefully, and even Harry anaesthetized by his tumbler of champagne. She could hear him through the bathroom wall, splashing water, coughing; guessed he might lurch in again with some new and fatal symptom. She didn't want her baby's birth mixed up with Harry's death. Maybe safer not to tell James until they were actually back home, had off-loaded both the fathers, waved the three boys off to school. She could choose a Sunday afternoon when he was relaxed from golf, replete with beef and trifle; take his hand in hers as they sipped coffee by the fire, draw it gently to her tummy and . . .

She jerked back from the basin as a shattering crash outside aborted her soft thoughts – the noise of broken glass, maybe broken bodies. She fretted to the door, opened it an inch, glimpsed the man from 207 dancing with the pie-eyed Lithuanian; his party guests storming down the corridor, hurling glasses at the picture-frames. Then, suddenly, another figure came limping into view, one whose legs and hips she recognised, though his head and neck and torso were more or less obliterated by what looked like yellow porridge.

'James!' she cried, darting out to grab him, steer him safely to the room, since his eyes were yellow-poulticed and he was carrying his shoes; in danger from the broken glass, the pools of spilt champagne. 'How . . .? Who . . .? Why . . .? What . . .? What *is* it?'

'Lentils,' James groaned softly, as he scooped them from his mouth, shook a glutinous coating from his shoulders. 'Six pints of lentil stew. It's some special dish they make for New Year's Eve.'

She slammed the door and locked it, snapped the safety-chain in place, led him to the bathroom, found flannels, soap and towels. He no longer smelt of aftershave – the Brut he'd splashed on earlier to celebrate New Year –

but overwhelmingly of garlic. 'I'm sorry, James, but I just don't understand. Why lentils on your *head*?'

He sank down on the bathroom stool, let her sponge and scrape him, unplug his ears and nose. 'Well, I was just talking to that desk clerk, telling him it was high time we got a bit of shuteye, or was that infernal bloody bunfight continuing till dawn? I suppose he imagined I was threatening him, because he summoned three more staff, and this damn great slanging match breaks out, with total strangers joining in – other guests and waiters and some riffraff from the bar – and soon everybody's shouting and even using fists. I didn't stand a chance, Mary. I lost my coat and dressing gown – could have lost an eye, as well, the way those nerds were carrying on. Then this jackass of a chef in a tall white hat and apron and pissed out of his mind, comes prancing from the kitchen with a bloody great cauldronful of what he calls *lenticchia alla toscana* and dumps the whole lot on my head.'

'He could have *killed* you, darling, or blinded you, at least. Were the lentils hot or cold?'

'Tepid and congealing – and with enough garlic in the mixture to halt a Roman legion. Yet he even had the cheek to say they'd bring me luck. Apparently it's some old Roman custom. You eat lentils at New Year and they're meant to make your fortune – "many many monies", as he put it.'

'Well, that would be a change, dear. Now you'd better have a bath. I've scraped off what I can, but your hair's still plastered with the stuff and it's sort of hardened round your chest-hair. While you're soaking, I'll wash out your pyjamas and try to clean your shoes.' She ran his bath, found shampoo and bath-foam, cleaned the stool and floor where he'd been sitting, then dragged back to the basin with his lentil-soggy shoes. The left one felt much heavier than the right; seemed blocked not just with garlic-pungent sludge, but with something hard and knobbly, which had been rammed inside like a gross dismembered limb.

'James! Whatever's this?'

James had discarded his pyjamas in a damp heap on the floor, was just stepping into the bath. 'What?' he said. 'Oh, that. A present from the chef. It's a pig's foot – a *zampone* – meant to bring you luck again; in fact, not just luck, but health, wealth, happiness, the rainbow's end, delirium – you name it. Another of their damnfool New Year customs. It's served up with the lentils. You get a wish or something with the first slice that you cut. The chef's English was atrocious, so I couldn't really follow it. And frankly, I wasn't all that riveted, not with half a hundredweight of lentils dripping down my neck.' He plumped into the bath, still railing and complaining; tipped right back, so his head was half-submerged.

Mary ran more water, sponged the pig's foot clean. Perhaps it was an omen and James's constant worries about debts and bills and creditors would be miraculously relieved; the brave New Year be filled to overflowing with 'many many monies'. She'd be contributing herself by giving up her therapy, axing those substantial monthly bills. And if lentils brought you luck, then their luck was running over – oodles of thick golden luck still smeared across the floor, floating in the bath-water, blocking up the basin, clinging to her nightie. She heard the clock outside strike three, savoured each long chime, touched her swollen breasts a moment as she paused in swabbing shoes. Never mind the problems. If Simon sicked his cake up, or Lionel decided he was flying home that night (as he'd already threatened twice), or Harry staggered in again with rabies or Bell's palsy, or that jackass of a chef appeared with a saucepanful of boiling ravioli, did it really matter? Those were simply trivia, life's minor snags and hitches. She let her hands slide lower, pressed them to her belly, could almost feel the foetus quickening in her womb. She had her luck already. The New Year was growing, swelling, already three hours old – the most blessed year she'd ever know, in which she'd give birth to a daughter who would explode like a bright rocket on the dark face of the world – Joanna-Pauline, her dazzling saviour girl-child.

# 40

Bryan lay back in his tomb, wincing at the dank chill of the stone, drawing in his legs and arms to fit the cramped and narrow grave. Hundreds of thousands of bodies had been buried in this place, wrapped in lime-encrusted shrouds and racked in simple niches sculpted from the rock. The air smelt musty, fetid, as if the corpses were dissolved in it, or some left simply rotting. There was no chink or glint of daylight, just an unhealthy sallow glimmer from the crudely-wired lighting-system filtering down the black and bleary walls. He could just make out the carving of Jonah and the Whale, depicted on a sarcophagus above him. The guide had told them it symbolised redemption, deliverance from death. He shut his eyes to block it out, had no wish to be reminded of his own release from death, his own bungled suicide.

This attempt would be surely more successful. Nobody could live long in the catacombs, survive a night unscathed. He'd deliberately lost his party, darted left while they were turning right, got entangled with another group of tourists – Japanese with cameras and interpreters – but had thrown them off as well; hurtled down a flight of steps marked 'VIETATO ENTRARE!', with a scarlet-painted hand held up in warning. No one had come after him, no one called his name – no Colin yelling 'Bryan, mate!', no frantic Lena searching for her son. This particular catacomb closed at five o'clock, and it was already twenty past. They'd never find him now. There were seven miles of subterranean passages, on at least five different levels. Even if they dragged through every passage, climbed every stair and storey, they'd hardly spot him hidden in his niche.

He rubbed his arm, which had developed pins and needles, wished he had his snake. He had always hoped to be buried with poor Anne, had even left instructions in his will. But the snake was dead already, its grave some dirty gutter or unknown rubbish-tip. Clive had tied it to a rocket, exploded it away on New Year's Eve. He should never have brought it with him in the first place. Even at the airport it had proved a real embarrassment; dragged out of his suitcase as a possible security risk, held up by its tail for all the giggling pilgrims to deride. The only child he'd ever have, and he'd still failed to protect it. He was a useless mother, useless son as well. He hadn't even said goodbye to Lena. He'd tried, in fact, but she'd been closeted with Father Smithby-Horne, receiving her first lesson on transubstantiation. Yes, his Mother was taking instruction in the Roman Catholic faith – a faith she'd disparaged and decried for over thirty years. It had genuinely shocked him, redoubled his resolve to seek extinction for himself. Once she was a Catholic, she would be even more cut off from him, shun him as an unbeliever, a danger to her new beliefs. He might join the Church himself, of course, as a last desperate bid to regain her attention and approval, but the prospect horrified him – not just the shabby compromise of all that he believed, but the thought of Lena hovering by the confessional box while he stuttered out his sins, reminding him of heinous ones he was too ashamed to tell.

Was it a sin to worship Mary, still hope to . . .? No, he mustn't dwell on Mary, had vowed to die without sparing her a thought. He had neither a mistress nor a Mother now, was orphaned and abandoned, a near-corpse in a lime-encrusted shroud. His clothes felt stiff already, stiff from cold, stiff from grime and rock-dust. This form of death took courage – no instant poison, merciful sharp knives. He might linger on all night before the airlessness and fetor, the total lack of drinking water, finally snuffed him out – maybe even two nights. The catacomb was shut all day on Thursdays, so no one would disturb him, no one interrupt his slow demise; no tramping bands of sightseers, no multi-lingual guides.

He'd been impressed, despite himself, by their own old but ardent guide – the way he'd made those early Christians spring to instant life. Eighteen centuries had rumbled back and he'd seen them milling in these warrens, weeping for the death of some trusted friend, or child, yet rejoicing in the afterlife, the promise of reunion; living in a spirit of serenity and hope. Saints and Popes had been buried here, as well as ordinary men – even famous martyrs. He'd heard about the martyrs from yet another guide on their party's recent expedition to the grisly Colosseum, where swarms of naked Christians had been thrown to ravening lions.

He shivered, would have welcomed a fierce lion, to dispatch him sooner, remove the clammy aching chill spreading down his slowly numbing limbs. He really ought to move, even jog a pace or two to restore his circulation, and anyway, he was bursting to relieve himself. How undignified it seemed that even a man's final hours could be so crudely interrupted by the need to obey basic calls of nature. He struggled from his niche, stood embarrassed, clutching at his flies. It seemed a desecration to pee in front of Jonah, and with so many graves surrounding him. A skull in the top niche seemed already to be staring, empty sockets wide with disapproval. He skulked along the passage, lowering walls threatening to engulf him, blackened roof pressing grimly down. He waited till he found a shadowy corner, then unzipped his trousers furtively, let his urine flow. Every time he peed now, he had to shut his eyes, couldn't bear the sight of it, the humiliating memories. He tried – and failed – to quash them, blushed with shame and horror as he saw himself sitting on that toilet seat, just two days ago, gulping disinfectant. Except it wasn't disinfectant – it was pee.

Some cruel or cranky pilgrim had left a disinfectant bottle full of fresh-passed urine concealed behind the cistern – God alone knew why – a joke, maybe, or perhaps some test or sample needed for a doctor, or . . .? Never mind the reason. He'd retched in sheer disgust as the first drops hit his tongue, bolted from the lavatory, bumped smack into the swarm of eager pilgrims surging up the stairs from chapel. They'd no idea how desperate he was, how close to death, extinction; had merely clucked with disapproval at 'Payne in the Arse' (as Clive had christened him) up to one of his silly little tricks again, the despair of his poor mother. He'd just started to explain, when suddenly, dramatically, the senna pods decided to take action and he'd dashed back to the toilet, remained there a good hour, as wave after wave of griping churning spasms reduced the entire contents of his body to an awesome liquid deluge.

He shuddered at the memory as he shook off the last drops of shaming urine, rezipped his flies, wandered on forlornly down the passage. He had no more heart for reclining in his coffin, could surely die as well in a common stretch of corridor, lying where he fell. There were at least fifty separate catacombs encircling Rome – or so the guide had told them – six hundred miles in all, if you placed their cavernous tunnels end to end; six million bodies buried there *in toto*. If the passages were linked, those tunnels all connected, he might stumble on for endless miles, haunted by six million ghosts, until he finally expired from sheer horror and exhaustion. Would his Mother miss him, even notice that he'd gone, or would she be too busy mugging up the Seven Works of Mercy or the Eight Beatitudes? He had tried composing letters in his head to the Government of Iceland, regarding the new volcanic island off its shores. Could a parcel (Mother) delivered there mistakenly be in any way retrieved? Could he call on their emergency services, helicopters, lifeboats? Never mind the cost – he'd find the money somehow. He'd also written to the Foreign Office, the Chairman of the Post Office, the Ministry of . . .

His thoughts and feet faltered to a stop. The dark confining passage had opened out to form a murky chamber on his left, with an altar at one end of it, surmounted by a rough stone arch hacked crudely from the rock. The guide had told them that Roman Catholic Masses were still said in these small rooms; twentieth-century pilgrims recalling those of seventeen hundred years ago as they offered bread and wine. A large but artless loaf of bread was actually carved into the stone – the bread of life, the guide had said, the bread of our redemption – along with other Early Christian symbols of hope and resurrection, depicted by those second-century faithful. He was tired of resurrection, longed to see some symbol of certain fool-proof death, unalterable, irreversible, mined with worms, crumbling into dust.

He heaved himself up towards the altar, lay stretched out flat on top of it. At least he had the space now to spread his legs and arms, felt less claustrophobic beneath the curving roof. No point cowering any longer in some cramped and choking niche when there was nobody to find him, not one single member of a party of two hundred even to realise he was missing, let alone to care. The stone felt hard and clammy underneath him. He longed for a soft pillow to relieve his aching spine; seemed to have no flesh nor clothing between the altar and his vertebrae, only rock embracing bone. He kept thinking of the Christians, not the fatuous pilgrims in his party, but that intrepid band of rebels in the first and second centuries, who had never been alone in life or death. The guide had pointed out their epitaphs, all so confident, assured – not the hopeless pagan '*Vale*', which bade farewell to life, but '*Vivas in Deo*', which welcomed Life Eternal. He envied them their faith, their sense of camaraderie, their dangerous secret meetings which must have bound them even closer, their shared beliefs and hopes. How different was his own case. He was dying as he'd lived – solitary and friendless; believing, hoping nothing.

Suddenly, he started, groped out both his hands. The chamber he'd called 'murky' was now a terrifying black, as if he'd been swaddled in a winding-sheet made of dark and stifling serge, which was drawn so tight around him he could neither see nor breathe. They must have switched the lights off, those dim but vital lights which had kept alive the boundaries, given him his bearings, showed up the distinction between wall and ceiling, sarcophagus and niche. He was plunged now in a darkness so relentless and disorientating, he could only lie in horror, trying to tear away the blackness with his hands. 'Help me!' he kept crying. 'Mother! Mary! Anyone! Please come back. Please help.'

Nobody could help him, nobody could hear. He had courted death, and not been spurned, refused; except he was *alive* in death, still flinchingly alive, as every nerve and brain-cell in his body registered its panic and alarm. Surely fear would kill him. No one could experience such naked jolting terror and still survive. Yet he *had* survived, was still lying fully conscious, desperate, despairing; fearing fear itself as much as death. Perhaps he'd never die, just lie here for eternity as time and terror both dragged on, dragged on; mocking him, enfeebling him, yet never actually granting him extinction.

The idea so appalled him he jerked up from the slab; felt he had to move, just to prove he still had power to do so; had to take some action, distract himself, exert himself, try to outwit fear. He inched down from the altar, feeling with his hands, a blind man without stick or dog, lost in a blind alley. Should he stay put in the chamber, where at least he had more space, or try to struggle down the corridor, in search of light, escape? Both courses seemed impossible. The dark itself had paralysed his brain, prevented any choices. He took a faltering step towards the passage, groping for its walls, shambled back immediately in panic, clutching at the altar as his only certain landmark. The silence was as total as the darkness. Yet would noise be any better – rustlings, shufflings, the stealthy tread of ghosts and wraiths, which must haunt this place, pace its endless galleries?

He could feel his legs trembling underneath him, sank down on the rough stone floor, crawling into a gap between the altar and the wall, which seemed to form another tomb. He closed his eyes, which made the darkness darker; a darkness made of centuries and of rock, both solid and unending, like his fear.

'Bryan!' a voice called softly. He took no notice, must obviously be shifting from terror to derangement; imagining voices which weren't there. No one could have spoken when he'd heard no breath or footstep, felt no human presence. '*Bryan*,' the voice insisted – an English voice, a kindly voice, gentle, almost shy; the sort of soothing Mother's voice he'd imagined in his dreams, except it was softly male, not female. 'Go away,' he muttered to its echo in his head, that tantalising whisper now threatening him with madness. 'There's no one there. Nobody. You're just . . .'

His sentence petered out. A sudden fierce and dazzling light was shining in his eyes, half-blinding him, so he had to turn away. So someone must have found him after all, some pilgrim with a flashlight, or soft-footed furtive guide. He remained huddled where he was, still not quite believing it; sweet relief struggling with astonishment. How could they have reached him without the slightest noise or warning? Surely he'd have heard their steps, however quiet and muffled. The silence was so absolute he'd have almost heard an insect crawling up the rock-face. The soft voice spoke again, lingering on his name with affection,

485

familiarity, as if he'd known him years. Bryan braved the dazzling glare, turned towards the speaker, who seemed to be hovering in midair, made not of flesh but light. A shortish, fairish, slimmish man with greyish hair and light-ish hazel eyes was smiling down on him, the neatish nose and smallish squarish face-shape reminding him instantly of . . .

'Skerwin!' he exclaimed. How in God's name had his Father ever got here, or even known he was in Rome? Shouldn't Skerwin be at the Winston Churchill Centre, starting a new term, or at least polishing up his lecture-notes?

'Skerwin *Senior*,' the man corrected gently. 'Your Heavenly Father, Bryan.'

'My . . . My *what*?'

'Your Heavenly Father.'

'You mean . . . God?'

The man nodded, smiled his 'yes', seemed to shimmer in the light, a vibrant otherworldly light which had no source except itself.

'But there isn't any God.' Bryan's voice was just a mumble, but he had to make his point. Science had destroyed God, chaos overthrown Him, every book he'd read denied Him, every new disaster mocked and undermined Him. He kept looking down, then glancing back, trying to clear his vision, pummelling his eyes, blinking them and rubbing them, shaking his whole head. Could he be hallucinating, suffering from some brainstorm? No. The man was truly there. He could see every smallest detail now – the knobbly wrists and broad blunt-fingered hands, the faint and palish eyebrows, uncertain weakish chin. Would God have a weak chin, though, or be wearing an old mac?

'I'm afraid I'm extremely busy, Bryan, keeping things in order, but I just wanted to assure you that Order's the key word – everything's under control and working very smoothly.' He rummaged in his briefcase, brought out a cache of notebooks very like Bryan's own – feint-ruled with narrow margins, A5 and spiral-bound. He began leafing swiftly through them, displaying them to Bryan. Each page was neatly written, headings underlined, sub-headings in capitals, some pages ruled exactly down the centre, with lists each side of what looked like pros and cons.

'Natural Laws,' he murmured, pointing to the largest book. 'Universal Principles. First Causes. Basic Rules. Proofs of My Existence.'

'Proofs of your . . .?'

'Oh, yes. Some have tried to deny me, as of course you're well aware, Bryan, but logic and mathematics both come down on my side.'

Bryan struggled to his feet, agitated, mystified; objections tumbling out of him. 'But I thought logic was discounted now and maths just empty figures, since the quantum revolution and chaology and . . . I mean, I understood you couldn't prove a thing – that we'd lost all sense of absolutes, and "proof" was just a play on words and . . .'

The man shook his head, reached out a soothing hand. 'Ripples, Bryan, just ripples on the deep white pool of truth. Give them time to settle, and you'll see the surface steady and serene again, and know I am your God.' He started replacing all his notebooks, opening up his briefcase which looked not a little battered, a piece of hairy string wound round one broken handle. Bryan peered inside, glimpsed rulers and dividers, a time-switch and a tide-chart, compasses, a T-square, a chronometer, a calculator, three separate stiff-bound books labelled 'Past', 'Present', 'Future', with attractive matching covers. And stuffed right at the bottom was a crumpled scholar's gown, black, with scarlet lining and an impressive ermine trim, the sort he'd imagined for his

Father, B.K. Skerwin, and which he'd seen on *Dreaming Spires*. So this God was a scholar, an intellect, a brain; an Oxbridge man, who might be slightly shabby with his torn and bulging pockets and at least two buttons missing on his grubby chain-store mac, but a shrewd efficient Mastermind who had his adroit finger on the pulse of every system in the universe; had it measured and gradated, calculated, quantified, could plumb and probe its depths; outwit chaos, anarchy; probably even deal with miracles, make sense of them, account for them, fit them in his Scheme.

Bryan sank back on the floor, peace and sheer elation bubbling through his veins, as if he had just received a transfusion of champagne. The old universe he'd mourned with its certainties, its laws, its coherent truth and logic, was miraculously restored. Things had Causes once again, and two and two made four, not five – or zero. Past and Future had been rigidly nailed down, sequestered from each other, forbidden to encroach or even fraternise; held in check by sandbanks and ruled lines. And space and time were no longer spliced together, but each put strictly in its place in a separate (tidy) notebook. Time ran only forwards now, not backwards or in circles – did what it was told. Everything was labelled, everything in pigeonholes; anti-matter banished, black holes filled and levelled, light-years trimmed to size.

He touched his face and body, felt them solid, real, defined. He could live again, hope again, believe in Sense and Shape again, take bold steps in a universe which would no longer flake and crumble, or threaten to extinguish him along with his surroundings. He clasped the man's firm hand, a hand so like his own in its shape, its bony detail, he realised he was part of God, truly this man's son.

'We may not meet again, Bryan, but there's no more need for fear. I see every sparrow fall, you know, and any son or child of mine is worth more than many sparrows.

My eye is on you always, and my right hand will be guiding you, as it guides the universe.'

Bryan stuttered out his thanks, so deeply moved his words were incoherent; then realised that the man had disappeared, left just his light behind. Yes, the crippling blinding darkness was no more. He could make out walls and carvings once again, as if some magic hand had switched back all the lights – still low anaemic lights maybe, but no longer choking blackness. He moved towards the rough-carved loaf gleaming on the wall, touched its crusty surface, as if it had the power to feed him and sustain him. The bread of life, the bread of his redemption. Where were all those other symbols the guide had pointed out – the flowering tree which stood for Hope, Noah saved from death and flood, Isaac spared from sacrifice? He had no more need to sacrifice himself, seek death, annihilation. He didn't even need his Mother, now he had a Heavenly Father; one who would watch over him for ever, maybe had a notebook devoted exclusively to him – the neatest book of all, with equal margins on each side, not one smudge or error in one single line of writing; beginnings, middles, ends, on every ordered page.

He was frisking, almost dancing down the corridors, hardly even caring that he was trapped there for two days. He had light now, and new hope, and water was no problem. He would strike it from the rock, as the great Moses had himself – or so the guide had told them; brought refreshment out of aridity and drought. He stopped a moment, frowning, suddenly remembering a session with John-Paul, at least three years ago now, when he'd asked his doctor if he could have a glass of water. He'd been feeling rather faint, after a disturbed and restless night, a panic on the tube. He'd never got the water. John-Paul had spent a good half-hour examining his reasons for requesting it. Perhaps he was dissatisfied with the progress of his therapy, and thus demanding more than merely words; craving mother's milk, maybe, regressing to the infant state and begging to be fed. Or experiencing some inner sense of poison or pollution, which might make him ask for water as a symbol of purification.

He had sat in (thirsty) silence, quite unable to respond, until John-Paul tried another tack, exploring that word symbol. Water was a symbol of fertility, rebirth, so they'd sidetracked on to Lena's womb (he still dry and gasping); then plumbed the Seas of Chaos, and finally examined 'healing waters', 'troubled waters', 'still waters running deep', the metaphor of 'being in deep water', and the waters of the Spring (or Tree) of Life. In the end, he'd settled for a cup of tea in BRB's canteen, feeling baffled and defeated and still more faint and parched. He had forgotten the whole incident, merely shrugged it off, but now it had come surging back and seemed symbolical itself. John-Paul had never granted him a drop of healing water, not in all that time; not one draught of hope or life, nor one beaker, even trickle of refreshment; had merely threatened years and years more painful arid therapy.

He was standing in a corner, an ancient stone sarcophagus bulging to his right, its carving worn and crumbling, so that the figure in the centre had neither face nor eyes. John-Paul! The likeness was astonishing – both lean and foreign-looking men with elaborate snaky hair, and both obviously tyrannical, with vassals, servants, patients, cowering at their feet. He'd always seen John-Paul as faceless; his features just a bland impassive mask, his eyes black holes gazing into nothingness, his heart as cold as stone. Stuff his years and years! He would never see the man again, never stretch out on the couch for even half a minute, let alone an hour. A fifty-minute hour! That alone proved his shrink was bogus. In his Heavenly Father's Universe, every hour was exactly sixty minutes, give or take no fraction of a second. Once you started docking time, contracting it, insulting it, then you'd moved away from exactitude and truth; were misleading people, conning them, tampering with the basic rules and structure of the cosmos. No point seeking healing from a con-man, wasting money on a charlatan. 'Shrink' was all too apt. John-Paul had shrunk too many things – his mornings, wallet, self-esteem; his bank account, his genitals – and even time itself.

He turned to face the sarcophagus square-on, punched his fist into the flattened flaking features. 'Take *that*!' he said. 'It's over. I'm free at last – free from bills and lies, free from dawn ablutions, stumbling in the dark from bed to tower, from nightmare to bad dream.' Okay, so he hadn't yet resolved his negative transference, or come to terms with his anal-sadistic regression and ambivalence, but half his so-called problems had been invented by John-Paul, endowed with fancy names so that they'd take longer to eradicate, keep his natty doctor in silk shirts and calfskin shoes.

Anyway, he wouldn't have the time now for long-winded psychotherapy. He had decided to enrol in the Open University or start a course at night school – not 'Science and Society' one footling night a week, but a proper university course, worthy of the son of Skerwin Senior – and in theology, not science, so he could get to know much more about the real and ordered universe, the Great Father who controlled it. He must send up for prospectuses, buy new pens and notebooks, list all the things he'd need. He would actually have money for the first time in four years, could stop his endless scrimping and economising; splash out on a car, invest in some new clothes, even book a proper holiday; not a vulgar pilgrimage, but some highbrow course or cruise, with cultured intellectuals as his friendly fellow voyagers. He might even meet a girl, a woman all his own, not pregnant and promiscuous and tied to seven males, but a fair and lovely innocent who'd . . .

491

He grabbed the rough stone tomb. Frantic thudding footsteps were careering down the passage just above his head. 'Barbarians!' he gasped, recalling the guide's tirade on the waves of ruthless tomb-robbers who had looted Christian corpses for their jewels, their precious relics; Lombards, Goths and Saracens pounding through the centuries, plundering these catacombs. And here they were again – no respect for death – just breaking in and battering down, snaffling what they could. He dodged right, then left, then right again, panicked by the sound of feet on steps. They were crashing down a staircase; must be on his level now, only dangerous yards away. If there were no dead to rob or ransack, then they'd rape and mug the living. The guide had stressed how cruel they were, how savage and rapacious. He didn't want to die – not now – not with an ordered universe, a loving caring Father, the prospect of some money in the bank. Desperately, he tried to run, despite the gloom and shadows, the rough uneven floor; hurtled round a corner, cannoned smack into the rear wall of a cul-de-sac, dashed the other way, straight into the outstretched arms of a tearful flurried Phyllis, with Colin, Father Campion and two distraught Italian guides cantering out-of-breath behind her.

'Oh dear,' he said, embarrassed. 'I thought you were the Goths.'

He hardly heard their reprimands, their naggings, trouncings, censure – how irresponsible he was, how selfish, stupid, careless; to lose his party, drag behind, frighten them to death; even risk his own death, or at least a nasty chill. He had eyes only for Colin, the object in his hand – something long, bedraggled, limp and very precious.

'*Anne!*' he breathed in wonder, as the wet and wounded body was shoved into his arms, its tail half-burned away and dripping dirty water, its felt tongue hanging loose, its colour strangely faded, and an unpleasant pungent odour clinging to its skin. Never mind the smell. His Heavenly Father had sent his absent child back, made his joy complete.

'Yeah,. I reckoned you'd be chuffed, mate.' Colin grinned and shrugged. 'Though I had to fight Clive to the death for him, you realise. In fact, I jolly nearly . . .'

'Now, come along, Colin.' Phyllis jabbed him with her torch. 'We haven't time for chitchat. You're in charge of Bryan. Hold on to him tightly and make sure he doesn't slip away again. I'll lead the way with Father.'

Colin marched behind obediently, but slowed his pace a little until Phyllis and her entourage were safely out of earshot, then continued with his saga. 'I reckon this whole thing was *meant*, Bryan – I mean, your getting lost like that. Not one single pilgrim remembered seeing you down here, or even on the coach, so we all assumed you'd decided not to come and were skulking in the seminary. They sent me off to find you in the pigsties, and instead I found your snake friend, lying in a pool of liquid pig-shit. Well, I took him to the washroom and was trying to sponge him clean, when Clive comes in and sees me, and we start this tug of war. Clive wins, of course – he's brawnier – and says "Listen, lad, if you want to get the bugger clean, let's do the job properly, okay?" And he turns the shower full on and dunks Snakey underneath, holds him there forever, till the dye's all streaming out of him. But that's not enough for Clive-mate. He starts stuffing your poor pal right down the plughole, with the water still cascading down on both of them. Well, at that point I saw red. I really beat him up, Bryan – I had to, didn't I? – to save poor precious Snakey, though it cost me a few bruises and a sodden pair of jeans. In fact, I was just dashing off to change my clothes when Father Campion nabbed me, said he was driving back to the catacombs to find you, and would I come as well, and make it sharp. He didn't even give me time to grab a towel . . .' Colin's words ran out, at last, as he gestured to his streaming clothes, tweaked the snake's wet tail.

Bryan himself said nothing, just shuffled, stumbled on; victorious Anne clutched close against his chest. The guides, the priest and Phyllis were already far in front, though he could hear their steady drone. They were probably still complaining about careless thoughtless pilgrims who were a constant bane and worry and would be better off at home. He must say his sorrys later, thank brave Colin later, buy him several pints, but at present he was too overcome to speak. His mind was on his snake, his Noah-snake, saved from flood and drowning, his Jonah-snake, his dear beloved Isaac, who, like himself, had been snatched from vengeful death, to live again, enjoy again – a life not shrunk and jargonised, but transfigured and expanded.

'Thank you, God,' he murmured, saw a smuggish Skerwin Senior part the clouds a moment and flash him a shy smile.

# 41

I pour glistening virgin oil into the salad-bowl, watch it gleam and tremble in the light. I'm an untried virgin myself when it comes to preparing food. I never cook for anyone, and my own meals are mainly snacks or just apologies. I'm not cooking now, in fact, just using every skill I have to make this supper special – a last supper, you might call it. I could be dead tomorrow, mobbed by furious crowds, and if not killed – in prison. I toss a few crushed walnuts in the bowl, add a grind or two of peppercorns, a trail of honey, splash of wine, a final kick of mustard, fierce and hot. The dressing's ready. Now I make the salad, shredding curly crinkled lettuce the colour of dark blood; quartering tomatoes – large misshapen lumpy ones with yellow wounds blistering their skins. I slice beetroot into gory discs, cut carrot sticks so sharp and thin they could be tiny scalpels. It all looks very pretty, dangerously pretty.

Seton isn't back yet. I'm Woman in the kitchen, waiting for him, waiting on him, setting out his meal. The flat is clean and tidy – I scoured every room myself, bought tulips for the table, arranged them in the coffee-jug because I couldn't find a vase. I didn't buy a lot of food – there didn't seem much point when Giuseppe, Marco, Stefan have already gone to ground (disappeared last night, mysteriously and late), and Seton and myself won't be eating here again. But everything I did buy I made certain was the best – the freshest bread, the moistest cheese, the most expensive olives. I kept it very simple. I feel this need to strip things down, slough off fuss and frills, focus on the basics – life and love and death. I've even stripped myself off. I'm working absolutely naked in nothing but

495

my skin. The flat is stifling hot tonight, but it isn't simply that. Clothes make you Man or Woman, and I've no wish to choose between them, know I must be both – Woman in the kitchen and in Seton's bed tonight; Man with my Beretta.

I leave my carrot-shrapnel, go to check the gun. It's still hidden where I left it; looks bigger somehow, treacherous, as if it's decided to betray me, rat on me itself. I keep trying not to think about the morning – the canonisation Mass with ten thousand pilgrims packed into St Peter's, two of them with plans to kill the Pope. Yes, I've changed my mind again, agreed to fire the shot. I sag against the wall, feeling sick and really faint, which happens every time I allow that thought to surface, remove it from its lock-up in my head. It was not my own decision, but a message sent from some power outside myself and relayed through a fortune-teller. 'You must kill the thing you love,' he said. How weird he understood. I mean, I'd hardly told him anything, yet he knew about my mission, used that very word. I thought I'd found him just by chance, but I see now it was meant. I was idling down the Via del Tritone and turned into a square I'd never seen before, and there he was, sitting by the colonnade. I only stopped to talk to him because he looked so like John-Paul – the same short stature, foreign looks, and religious-like intensity – even eating like John-Paul; chewing on a stump of hard salami with such passion and solemnity it seemed more than merely food. I was attracted by his eyes, fervent burning black-bruise eyes which never left my own as I sank down at his table, let him take my hand. 'You are being *used*,' he whispered, once he'd studied both my palms and then the exotic-looking picture-cards I'd picked out from his deck. 'But that is good thing – very good. You not fight it. You say "yes". You kill the thing you love.'

Kill the thing I love. It sounded like a poem and I knew instinctively he was right. It's because I love the Pope I have to kill him – save him, if you like; save him from senility, despair and disillusion. Last night, I read a speech he'd made a year or two ago, about our twentieth century being not the height of human progress (as so many cretins think), but a new Dark Age of poverty and violence. Giovanni Paolo has had seventy years of violence; needs releasing into unconsciousness, allowed peace and sleep, long sleep.

The fortune-teller didn't say a lot. He seemed restless, almost edgy, somehow bothered by my presence, but just as I was going he unpinned the silver brooch he was wearing on his lapel and pushed it into my hand, so hard its sharp pin jabbed my palm, actually drew blood. I thought it was a newt at first, or some weird sort of snake thing, but he called it *salamandra*. Salamanders leap from flames, escape from fire and danger, so I presume he must have meant it as a sort of badge of courage. I've wrapped it in a handkerchief and left it with the gun. I'll need them both tomorrow – courage and eight bullets.

I've learnt to load that clip of bullets, arm and fire the gun. We drove out to the country on a borrowed motorbike, found a dark secluded wood where some other guys were already shooting birds, gunning down anything that flew. I felt sick from bloody feathers, the thud of falling bodies; remembered my own martyred bird – the one my father burnt alive when I was only five or so, and still in love with him. Seton loathes weak women, so I pulled myself together and tried aiming at the oil-can he'd strung up from a tree. I only had eight bullets, and the first two missed completely. He let me move from twelve feet in to nine, and then I hit each time; hardly even shuddered at the kickback of the gun. It's the smallest lightest handgun Seton and his cronies could hunt down here in Rome – a nine-millimetre Beretta semi-automatic (which are issued to the Spanish secret service and the police in Buenos Aires). I'm relieved I won't be using that brutish sawn-off shotgun, which is heavier and larger and more difficult to hide. Seton planned to pare it down, then tape it to the stem of his bulky golf umbrella – remove a few spokes first and bag the folds around it, so it would look badly furled, but otherwise quite innocent. But once it was decided that it was me – not him – who'd fire the shot, and at a solemn papal ceremony, he realised the umbrella would seem suspicious, out of place. He wants me to be tarted up in a snazzy dress and coat, to match the snazzy ticket which will admit me to a seat right up the front, and a hulking great umbrella would hardly match my gear. Also, I somehow like the feeling of having those eight bullets – eight chances, if you like, instead of only one or two.

'You'll need to fire as many times as possible,' he told me in the wood, as he snapped open the Beretta, removed the empty bullet-cases. 'Before you're overwhelmed.' Overwhelmed. I left the word behind, lying in the undergrowth like another stunned and bloodied corpse, drove back to beer and skittles – or at least beer and backgammon.

We practised all the other stuff indoors: how to make my movements quicker, but to slow and calm my breathing; appear casual and relaxed when just about to kill – how I'll ease the gun from the false bottom of the camera-case, slip it up my coat-sleeve (the left sleeve with the steadier right hand); conceal it there until I've edged up closer, closer, then whip it out – and fire.

Just thinking of that lethal drill makes me almost faint again. I need a cigarette, a breath of air. I fret back to the kitchen, place the salad on the table with the bread, the wine, the cheeses, then grab my Rothmans, drift to the back door. Giuseppe's square of brute back yard is dark and very private, so nobody will see me save the stars. They're very bright tonight and very high, as if someone's stretched the sky out, like pastry or elastic, put more space and void and darkness between earth and highest heaven. (I doubt that there's a heaven, but the concept's quite appealing and I'm glad somebody believed in it enough to coin the word. Weird if we both got there after all – myself and *Sua Santità*, found ourselves together after death.)

The streets are strangely quiet. With the canonisation only hours away now, the Blessed Edwin Mumford almost a full saint, I'd have imagined there'd be wide-scale celebrations – fervent pilgrims processing through the city with banners or brass bands; maybe more wild fireworks, or noisy public parties. But I can only hear one whispered pulse of music, very faint and blurred like smoke, curling from a basement room below me. Perhaps the pilgrims are all safe inside – in church or chapel, praying – preparing for tomorrow. An event like that must take such mammoth planning: St Peter's vast basilica to be primped from floor to roof; all the vestments to prepare, the mitres, Mass-books, music, candles, flowers; all the speeches to rehearse; the security, the crowd-control, the coaches, the Red Cross. I shiver as the sharp night air cuts my naked skin, dodge indoors again. We're prepared, as well – our last decisions made: when I'll enter, where I'll sit, how I'll pass security (or hope to); exactly at what point I'll fire the shot.

Seton's still not back. He warned me he'd be late and I'm not even apprehensive, let alone plain panicky as I was on New Year's Eve. We're much closer now, more trusting of each other, bonded by our mission and our plan. He told me to start supper if he wasn't in by ten. It's already quarter past, so I sit down at the table, pour myself a glass of wine, sip it very slowly. It's a brusque and rugged red wine which tastes of basic powerful things like iron and dark wet earth. I try to wrench that taste out, hold it in my hands. I want to relish everything tonight, make it an experience, a ritual. I cut myself a slice of bread –

best white bread with a crisp and powdery crust which snows my hands with flour, a springy crumb so soft you could lie down on it and sleep. I break a small piece off, sniff its yeasty fragrance; crunch a radish first, so the two conflicting tastes and textures startle in my mouth – the radish hard and harsh, the bread doughy-bland and sweetish. Everything seems perfect, as if it's reached its full fruition and been held there for this evening: cheese ripe but not yet oozing; salads sheeny but not limp; scarlet tulips opened out, yet not one petal fallen or stalk sagged.

I'm so alert, my taste-buds jolt and tingle with every smallest mouthful, as I register its savour and its smell: blue Brie slightly gamey; Dolcelatte velvety; olives brackish, dour. It's months since I've had adult food – grown-up cheese with stink and rind (instead of those Kraft triangles which are mainly milk and soothe); dark and bitter lettuce. Even here in Rome, I've been eating children's pap: strawberry yogurts, pink ice-cream, plain pasta with no sauce. But childhood seems a mirage when I think about tomorrow. I've aged in just a day; grown from stripling to assassin; have to eat to keep my strength up now; fuel my murderer's courage.

I pluck a frond of lettuce with my fingers, let its rough and ragged texture graze against my lips; the confused taste of the dressing imprint my tongue with its contradictory messages – now sweet, now bland, now sharp. I watch a trail of salad-oil dribble from my fingers and ooze slowly, slowly down between my breasts; will it not to fall or disappear. I want to preserve this moment, keep it as a memory, wrap it like a precious gift, embalm it under glass. I blot my chest with bread, leave a floury smear, kick my chair back suddenly as I hear Seton at the door. I've still got lettuce in my mouth, but he doesn't wait for me to swallow it. It's his tongue I'm almost swallowing, the urgent tastes of nicotine and aquavit ousting cowardly salad. 'It's supper time,' I tell him, when at last he's freed my mouth. He grabs three olives and a piece of cheese, eats them standing up, still touching me and nuzzling me, his outdoor clothes cold against my flesh. I suppose he's turned on by my nakedness, the fact I'm sitting at the table in the buff, when I'm usually in sweaters, muffled to the neck.

I butter him a piece of bread, feed him like a child, excited by the teeth-marks imprinted on the buttered stub I'm still holding in my hand. I cram it in my own mouth, offer him some wine. 'No.' He shakes his head, takes a gulp from *my* glass, then steers me to the bedroom, to the pile of rugs and pillows we call our double bed. He dumps his coat, starts peeling off his clothes – all of them, and straight away, which he's never done before. Often, he seems scared of his own nakedness, as if clothes were power or armour and he's reluctant I should see him stripped and vulnerable. Many times he's made love fully dressed, with just his zip undone; his dirty jeans or nubbly cords chafing my bare thighs. Tonight is very special. He's as naked as an olive, his skin as smooth and dark, as I run my hands along his bony back, across his curving buttocks, down between the crease. We rarely lie and just embrace – there's never time or tenderness enough, but time has stopped this evening, literally. Giuseppe's bossy clock says five to three. It ran down this afternoon and there seemed little point rewinding it. My own watch is in the kitchen, and Tomorrow's slunk away, so there's only now and now and now: Seton's weight and bulk against me, keeping out the future and the night.

We're joined all along our bodies, nipples kneading nipples, his coarse hair snagging mine, our feet coiled round each other's, our tongues swapped in our mouths. I long to give him everything, as his sister, brother, lover; follow what the Pope said and break the chains of selfishness and sin; share the last crumb of my body with him; every dreg and drop of it poured out for him, like wine. I suspect he feels the same, wants to merge with me, become me, so we're one gender in one body, with no boundaries or separateness, no more Self and Other. He's never lain so still before, as if he's listening to my heartbeat, to the pulses in my wrists and neck, the musings in my mind, the slow tide of my blood as it meanders round my veins.

I suddenly ache to have my hair not short and ragged, but flowing to my waist again, so I can do a Mary Magdalen, dry not just his feet with it, but swaddle his whole nakedness, hide him here for ever in my bed. I pull away, unplug myself, kneel across his thighs, lean forward and start kissing his bare feet. I've always loved his feet. They seem so solid, powerful, grounding both of us, straight and lean and long, with dark hairs on the toes, and narrow bony fetlocks like a thoroughbred's. I suck each toe in turn into my mouth, tonguing them and drinking them, grazing with my teeth. They taste salty, like the olives; the big toe a prick itself, a small but very stiff one, forcing down my throat. Seton doesn't say a word, but I know it must excite him, because otherwise he'd shove me off, or snap at me bad-temperedly as he's done before so often. He's usually so angry – angry with the Pope, or life, or fate, or even me, but tonight he seems a different person, serene and very steady.

I release the smallest toe, slowly flick my tongue along the bottoms of his feet, then up around the ankle, up further to the knee. I think the knee must tickle because suddenly he laughs, though he's never laughed in bed before, rarely laughs at all. Laughter's catching, obviously, and we lie there shaking, stupid; doing nothing for a while but watch each other's diaphragms, then something frees in both of us because we each lunge towards the other at exactly the same moment, and he jabs in really roughly, tries so hard to fuse and lock I feel my body's being battered by the sheer force and power of his, its wish to pierce through boundaries and bone. I'm frightened for a second, then relax and just let go, accept whatever happens – fear itself, and injury. I said I'd give him everything, so how can I hold back? I think I understand him – his wildness, almost frenzy. The anger is still clogged there and he needs to hack it out, get rid of his emotion, his terror and vindictiveness, dump it all on me, so that by morning he'll be purged – nerveless, icy-calm; ready to support me, lend me his own strength, at least before we part.

All the stress and tension he's felt these last few days are being shot into my body as he heaves and slams against it. I've lost the rhythm, so we're thrusting out of time, which makes it painful, jarring, especially on the floor, with half the blankets kicked away and the thin and scratchy carpet gnawing at my spine. But pain is simply part of it and I know he needs that violence, so I accept it as my gift to him.

Suddenly, he comes, in a great gasp and shout of fury, and I'm clawed and almost winded as his groin collides with mine, and he keeps juddering and jerking, grinding me into the floor; his mouth clamped against my lips, one hand tugging roughly at my hair. I almost weep with disappointment. I wanted him to come, but not so soon, and not alone. I'd planned to give him everything, spin the night out, make it really memorable. He'll stop now, slump against me, pause a few cruel seconds to catch his breath, recover, then drag up from the bed and slink away. He never waits to see if I'll come, or lures me with his finger, or just stays around to play the loving friend. I try to cling to him and anchor him, deny the come, keep him there despite it, then I realise that he hasn't stopped, hasn't slumped at all; is still ramming, smiting into me, and now the rhythm's right, at last, so I'm part of it, part of him, taken over, kicked out of my head into his groin. He keeps moving, snaking, circling, until I'm scorching past that neat blue line where you can still think and keep control, and careening down the other scarlet side, and my body's turned right inside-out, so all the nerve-ends are exposed, and they all flinch and shock together as I come myself, arching up against him, shouting out his name.

I come again, immediately, and he still stays stiff and spurs me on, and I'm exploding like a firework, one of those wild rockets which go off in several stages – one burst, two bursts, four. I've never found it very easy to come with him, or anyone. All that training with my clients not to feel, or give; all the fear of being too exposed. But this evening's changed all that. We're both still avid, greedy, as if we haven't come at all yet, haven't even started, hardly got our clothes off. I tug the tangled rugs back, make the pile of pillows a buttress for my spine, then jack my feet right up on his shoulders, as he slides slowly in again. It feels quite different that way, especially as he's moving very teasingly – almost almost coming out, nearly breaking contact, then slicking back much faster, pressing in and down. Our two stooks of pubic hair look exactly the same colour, seem to merge into each other, share the same strong roots; my feet growing from his shoulders so we're one (strange) body now. He leans down to kiss my mouth, can't quite reach until I shift my legs, and then the angle's new again and I'm suddenly excited and churn and thresh against him, yelling crazy jumbled words which spew from somewhere older than my brain.

He waits until I've come again, then hauls me to my feet, leans against the wall and tries to do it standing up, which isn't very easy until he lifts me off the floor and I wind my legs around his waist; feel his own legs trembling as he bends forward, dovetails in, and we seem to lose all sense of whose limbs and cries are whose. I've never felt so light before – not clumsy hulking freakish Nial, but delicate and fragile Nial, whom Seton dwarfs,

504

desires still. We both collapse on to the floor again, not tired, just out of breath. I don't think we'll tire – not ever. We're pumping life and strength into each other, as if our comes are mutual blood-transfusions, so the longer we go on the more roused we are, and potent, the more part of one another.

I turn onto my side to face the wall, and Seton fits himself against me, his chest pressing in my back, then joins us lower down (which takes a while because we suddenly start laughing once again – God knows why – maybe just because we're happy, which is pretty rare for one of us, let alone for both, and both together). We take it quietly this time, a sort of slow and gentle savouring, and though I come, it's a very languid come, and Seton merely ripples. 'Running short of sperm?' I grin. He seems to see that as a challenge, because he starts thwacking at me wildly, then suddenly whips out, so he can demonstrate the sperm. I'm sticky now, all over, from sweat and heat and semen; use the corner of a blanket to blot my chest and thighs; then fling it back, lie flushed. The room feels sweaty, too; looks slovenly, dishevelled, as if it's been joining in with us. The pillows are all scattered, the chairs shoved to the wall, and there's that curdled slightly rancid smell you always get with sex – ripe bodies and stale come.

'Smoke?' asks Seton, bundling up a rug to make a cushion for our heads, and reaching for his jacket so he can find his cigarettes.

'Ssh,' I say, half-sitting up to listen. I've just heard a clock strike something from the foreign land beyond our tiny window, which is blurred now from our steamy panting breath. The quarter? The half hour? I've no idea, except it must be getting on for midnight – that sharp electric-fence between tomorrow and this evening. I suddenly cool down, as if a chill wind's blowing right into the bedroom, or my body's closed its mouths up, grown a scaly shell. It's time to stop, turn from play to pledge. I'm committed to tomorrow, to completing what I promised, and I feel I must prepare – prepare in mood and spirit. When midnight strikes this time, it won't be like New Year. We can't be whooping, laughing, knocking back champagne.

I swathe myself in Seton's coat, slip into the kitchen, find my watch amidst the debris of the peelings. Ten to twelve. I sit out those ten minutes, hearing Seton in the shower – splashing, running water, whistling some harsh tune. I don't stir or move a finger, just shift into the future in my mind, examine the alternatives – death and retribution, injury, imprisonment, interrogation, beatings-up, acquittal or escape. They all seem heavy and black-edged, except acquittal and escape, which I simply don't believe in. I get up from the table as my watch-hands clasp each other, walk slowly to the bathroom. Seton's standing naked on the mat, water streaming from his body. His skin is marked in places where it's been pressing on the floor, one elbow sore and reddened. I kiss his back a moment, seem to taste not soap, but blood – tomorrow's blood, tomorrow's fear and pain.

'Tomorrow's *here*,' I whisper, as I try to wipe my hands clean. 'Too soon.'

# 42

I stand a moment, motionless, in St Peter's crowded square. It has never seemed so vast before, so splendid and sublime. Despite the crowds, there's so much sense of space, as if the whole of teeming tangled Rome has simply disappeared, leaving one huge soaring enclave where nothing ugly, base or cramped is allowed to spoil the feeling of timelessness, immensity. Every stately column (and there must be hundreds, literally) has been given room to breathe, flaunt upwards and exult. The sky itself looks infinite, swelling out beyond the dome, beyond the gesturing statues on the roof – a whole preening tribe of Catholic saints sculpted in grey stone – some I'd never heard of until our first guided tour of St Peter's and its square.

They're so high up, I can hardly make them out, but I try to spot Saint Thecla, whom I remember in particular, since she cut off all her hair and disguised herself in man's clothes, then followed Saint Paul from Iconium to Myra and all over Asia Minor – a first-century groupie, as mad for her apostle as I was for John-Paul. She eventually stopped tagging him and retired to a rock-cave in the wilderness, where she worked miracles for seventy years, on a diet of black bread. Then some ruffians tried to rape her at the age of ninety-odd, but the solid rock-face opened up miraculously to afford her an escape. She was never seen again, vanished like a sigh. I envy her today – not the rape at ninety, but her absolute extinction. I long to disappear myself, to be rubbed out like a pencil-mark, so the page is clean and white again, undefaced, unstained.

I let my eyes fall from the statues, which are only

looming shapes, so I can't tell man from woman, or Thecla from Saint Paul. The twin colonnades below them reach out like two huge arms, embracing all mankind. And all mankind is here – pale faces and black ones, and most shades in between; flapping shoals of nuns from every country in the world; tonsured friars in fancy dress, sober-suited priests; bubbly blushing schoolgirls in pleated navy pinafores and white bows in their hair, and whole coachloadsful of English from as far afield as Sunderland and Birkenhead, judging by their accents. I'd no idea I had so many fellow countrymen in Rome. Where have they been hiding, or have they only just arrived – bluff Yorkshiremen in anoraks with polyester wives, or Surrey spinsters all dolled up in honour of their Saint?

I feel a different breed – a foreigner, an aristocrat, in my mantilla and black fur. I'm no longer a Saint Thecla, no longer wearing man's clothes, but an elegant black dress (with nothing underneath it), and stylish high-heeled shoes. God knows where Seton found the shoes, especially in my size, nor how he dug that coat out. It may be fake for all I know, though it's long and very glossy, gives me instant class. The whole thing seems a fake – not just the coat, but the very notion that our plan could ever work. They'll never let me in, never pass my camera-case, will nose out the gun immediately, arrest me as I climb the steps which lead up to the church. The police are already clustered at the bottom of those steps, the special branch security men who are so heavily armed themselves I don't stand the slightest chance.

My compact little gun weighs as heavy as a howitzer as I steer a slow and zigzag course between scrubbed and tethered children straining at their parents' arms, television cameramen dropping ash and cable, and troupes of English matrons carrying coloured silken banners proclaiming 'Guildford Catholic Widows Group' or 'Union of Catholic Mothers – Bridlington sub-branch'. I ache to swap with them, carry just a banner, or a prayer book, or a baby, and not a deadly weapon. Seton's armed the gun already, so I won't waste vital seconds doing it myself, or arouse suspicion by a sudden jerking movement. All I have to do is pull the trigger – and make sure whatever happens, I don't drop or bang the camera-case before I'm due to fire. With the safety-catch released, that impetuous Beretta is just chafing to go off.

The leather strap keeps slipping off my shoulder, sliding on the fur. I haul it back, clasp the case against my hip as I skirt around a boisterous group with Saint Edwin plastic badges, Saint Edwin carrier bags. Most of them are also carrying cameras, so I don't look out of place. Apparently, you're allowed to take photos in St Peter's, even during a solemn papal Mass. Several men are already snapping furiously, taking pictures of their smirking wives, their podgy well-fed priest. There's an air of great excitement, a sense of celebration spread so thick on everything it's like a sugar-coating, or instant spray-on tinsel; swarms of people milling round in eager restless flurries, voices bubbling over. Surely they can tell I don't belong? I'm coated not with gold, but black; carrying my banner labelled 'Death'. If you took blood-tests from us all, theirs would register exhilaration, fervour; mine reveal I'm dangerously ill. My heart isn't simply beating, it's hammering so violently I'm scared the crowds can hear it knelling like a warning above all the other racket in the square. My hands are wet with sweat, my whole body cold and clammy, despite the fur, the sun.

I squint up at the sun, implore it not to shine. It makes everything much worse, that immaculate and trusting sky, summer-blue in January and cotton-wooled with clouds – weather for a chocolate box, or a cosy Disney movie, not a callous murder. Some ironical Director seems to have set the scene today, laid on soft and sweet vignettes to underline my pain: two lovers with their rosaries entwined;

509

a skinny shaggy mongrel, all bone and bounce and tongue, leaping up to lick a toddler's nose; the child kitted out in strawberry-pink, which is colour-matched exquisitely with her strawberry ice-cream cone. I stoop down to pat the dog, more for my sake than for his – to hide my face, turn my guilty eyes away from those other fervent friendly eyes which keep meeting mine and smiling, trying to claim me as a fellow – fellow pilgrim, fellow human being.

'Don't smile,' I beg a woman who's attempting to squeeze past me with her gangling teenage daughter, her fat and freckled son – a woman twice my age with a worn but kindly face, who seems to think we're instant cronies, one happy jolly family. I dodge her, turn away, struggle back the way I've come, feeling infectious and polluted, as if I ought to wear a bell, a leper's bell which keeps tolling out 'Unclean!'. And yet I'm not wholly bad – I can't be. I'm doing this for Seton, my one perfect act, to save him, set him free. He's already made his getaway – left this morning, early, in the cold raw empty dawn; kissed me very briefly, so I was left with just his taste, my lips still smarting from last night, and the first birds breaking silence, sounding out of tune and querulous as his footsteps died away. I can't betray him, can I, change my mind (again), when he believes in me and trusts me? It's not often that I'm trusted, or given such a major part to play – the lead, the starring role.

I force my steps and body back towards the square, though my mind is still on Seton, wondering where he's gone, wondering what his feelings are – fear for me, dull horror, admiration, longing? I weave my way between the crowds, keep on going this time until I reach the crush of pilgrims seething round the steps, the impatient queue of ticket-holders who must be frisked before they're allowed into the church. Frisked. The word appals me – a jumpy, nervy, startled word, which seems to leapfrog through my stomach, judder in my chest. I remember my deep breathing, count to five as I inhale, to ten as I breathe out; try to look relaxed and almost nonchalant as I shuffle up each slow and dragging step, avoiding careless elbows, other people's bags. The queue moves very slowly, while my fear gallops, bloats, distends. I distract myself by admiring the basilica, its grand façade now rearing up in front of me; huge central marble columns dwarfing us mere mortals, more lofty statues preening from its roof. I can only think of bones – Saint Peter's bones, which were buried here in a crevice in the rock, nineteen hundred and twenty-seven years ago, before all this pomp and splendour was ever dreamed or thought of – a pathetic headless skeleton which some say is still there, crumbling in the crypt.

Death seems to smite my own bones as the security man runs his metal-detector up and down my coat, along both sleeves, down each black-stockinged leg. I'm so rigid, so shit-scared, I'm sure he'll guess there's something wrong from just the tension in my limbs; call an ambulance, if not a Black Maria. I can smell his breath – garlic doused with peppermint – see the coarse black stubble pricking through his chin, shadowing his squarish bullish jaw. I haven't brought a handbag (need one hand free, at least), but a second flint-eyed officer has just reached out for my camera-case and is checking it inside. He hasn't got a metal-detector, but even so, I realise it's all up; shut my eyes, wait to feel the handcuffs snapping on my wrists, his vicious truncheon jabbing at my back. Two minutes crawl like months, and when I dare to look again I'm still standing on the steps, but the security men are miraculously behind me, and checking someone else. My. camera-case is hanging on my shoulder. They've put the camera back all wrong, crushed my cigarettes, which I slipped in down one side, but it still weighs heavy, still bears its crucial load. I simply can't believe it. I want to shout, berate them: 'Look, you didn't find the gun. If you're so lax, so fucking casual, you'll endanger the Pope's life. Arrest me. Stop me *now*!'

No one stops me. I'm right on the top step, the bronze doors of the basilica only a pace or two away. I push the heavy central door, urged on by a marshal, step into the church, feel dazzled for a moment by its sheer overwhelming grandeur. The whole place seems to writhe with decoration. Your eye can't rest or settle, but is constantly tugged back and forth by gilding, carving, sculptures, bronze, and shimmering mosaics. Pilasters lead your gaze up to the ceiling, which is so awesomely elaborate you're forced to cast them down again, overcome and reeling; admire the complex patterns of the floor. Every surface gleams, every inch of floor and wall has been burnished, chiselled, fretted. Cherubs pout and simper, solid angels hover in mid-air, majestic Popes stretch out their hands in frozen marble blessings. There've been two hundred and sixty-three Popes since the original Saint Peter, and half of them seem buried in this church, judging by the monuments, the papal tombs and effigies. I close my eyes a second, see myself embraced not by Giovanni Paolo, but by the first apostle, Peter; the unbroken line of Popes between cementing time and history; John Paul himself the only living institution still surviving from the Roman Empire. I let my eyes drift open, almost surprised to see twentieth-century people in the pews, dressed in modern clothes and even jeans, instead of ancient Romans, wearing togas, flowing robes.

I've seen St Peter's before, of course – we've been here half a dozen times to check our plans, get our bearings, orientate ourselves. And a weird friend of Giuseppe's showed us round our second day in Rome. That was what I call our guided tour, and far better than the official ones, I reckon, since the guy spoke fluent English and talked nonstop for two hours twenty minutes; told me all the stuff about Saint Thecla, and so much else my head was almost bursting. But every time I've been here the place has been half-empty – just a few score gawping tourists, a disembodied priest (or three) penned in the confessionals, and one or two old dusty crones huddled by the candle-stands and talking to themselves. Today it's crowded, totally transformed – Saint Edwin banners fluttering from the walls; the scent of heady hothouse flowers choking down the usual smell of damp piety, cold marble. And the atmosphere's quite different – explosive and electric, as if the whole place has been charged.

I'm still standing semi-mesmerised when an usher in a stiff white shirt and what looks like morning dress checks my ticket, inclines his head most graciously, then motions me to continue up the aisle. I walk slowly on, past throngs of jam-packed pilgrims already sitting waiting in the rows and rows of chairs. They seem just blurs of colour – black swathes of silent nuns, a twitchy giggly Boys' Brigade with blue and scarlet banners; the sudden shout of purple slashed with orange as I pass a tall Swiss Guard, halberd shining, helmet scarlet-plumed. Someone suddenly jumps up from a seat beside the aisle, leans across the central wooden barrier and grabs my free left hand. I freeze in instant terror. They've realised who I am, got wind of my wild plan, are about to march me out again, clap me into jail. Half-paralysed, I turn my head a fraction, see that pretty, rather vacuous-looking woman who lent me her lace hankie when I was blubbing in that bar on New Year's Eve. What did she say her name was? I don't think I even heard it, was too lost in my problems.

'Mary,' she says, reminding me, and gesturing to herself. 'It's Nial, isn't it? I hardly recognised you.'

No, you wouldn't, I think rudely. I've changed my gender, changed my role. Trust her to be a Mary – fair and sweet and fey, and looking almost smug today, with a happy trusting smile spreading from her glowing face to her plumply rounded body. I've no wish to stop and burble sweet inanities – not now – it's far too dangerous, will only draw attention to myself, but she's already started whispered introductions, seems to have at least three scowling husbands and a whole scout-troupe of small boys. And I assumed she was a loner, like myself. 'Pleased to meet you,' I murmur *sotto voce*, as each male shams a smile.

'Perhaps we could meet afterwards,' she mouths. I nod, arrange to find her by the obelisk at noon. More sham, more empty lies. There won't be any 'afterwards', and I shan't be meeting anyone save jailers and police. I mumble something indistinct about having to find my seat, toss her a goodbye. I'm feeling strangely shaken by the whole coincidence, and still more scared to fire that shot at all. I need this congregation to be faceless and anonymous, just cardboard cutouts, stolid plaster dummies; not living feeling people with families, soft hearts. I could spatter all those boys with blood, give them nightmares, screw them up for life.

I shrug the thoughts off angrily, try to clear my mind of everything save each slow step up the aisle; fix all my concentration on my laboured hurting breathing, the dead weight on my arm. I've practised this same walk towards the altar – once with Seton, twice alone – but it never seemed so far before, so endless. Five hundred feet, Seton guessed approximately, but I've walked five miles already and still not reached the ornate *baldacchino* where I turn right at the transept for my seat. And it felt completely different when we were rehearsing it stone-cold, without the props and costumes, without the congregation, this air of sheer excitement which only fuels my fear. Another usher stops me, but flutters quite obsequiously once he sees my ticket, waves me further on. I've no idea how Seton got that ticket, a special VIP one which somehow gives me clearance to glide right to the front, upstage all those pious paid-up pilgrims. I can feel their eyes boring through my back as I'm guided to the transept, shown into the second row, which is so close to the altar, I not only have a perfect view, but feel a fraction less paranoid about missing when I shoot.

I'm surrounded not by anoraks and schoolkids, but by suave and ritzy men in formal suits; women in rich furs like mine, diamonds flashing on their hands, gold medals at their throats. My own medal's rather different – the silver salamander which the fortune-teller gave me, pinned on to my dress as my badge of courage and sanction for my mission. I touch it for a second, to give myself new strength, then try to take the scene in, eyes darting back and forth. I simply didn't realise how sumptuous it would be – even the flowers themselves arrayed in vast battalions, a whole forest of exotic blooms: gladioli, tiger lilies, forced and perfect roses, streaky two-tone tulips, double-frilled carnations, and some fantastic-looking specimens I've never seen before, with speckled purple petals, fleshy yellow tongues. And the whole display backed with fern and greenery, looped with satin ribbon, and smelling so extravagantly my own cheap perfume dies. The colours cut like knives – the sharp and stinging scarlet of poinsettias echoed by the cardinals who are sitting right behind; the deep mauve gladioli reinforced by the showy vibrant purple of the bishops. I've never seen so many churchmen – whole rows and squads and gangs of them; gashes of wild colour, sweeps of flowing robes; celibates like peacocks making up in pomp for what they lack in prick-power. And at least two hundred spare priests in simple black and white, corralled on their own behind the altar, like some huge reserve or backup, impressive in its numbers.

And now the choir are trooping in, dressed in deeper purple with frilled white smocks on top; the boys in wide white collars, the men solemn-eyed, intense. The television cameras immediately close in. I'll be immortalised myself in just another hour or so, caught on film for ever – not

515

cherubic choirboys shuffling into place, but one lone and murderous woman lunging forward with her gun. John-Paul is bound to see me, if not this actual morning, then in the rerun on the news. Will he be proud of me, I wonder; staggered by my nerve, or feel guilty and appalled that he wouldn't deign to see me when I called at his hotel?

The handsome man beside me suddenly touches my left arm. Startled, I swing round, see him smiling quite flirtatiously, offering me his binoculars, a natty little gold pair in a silk-lined leather case. I stutter out my thanks, and he answers in some language I don't recognise at all, his throaty whisper sounding near-obscene. Imagine being chatted up in the most solemn church in Rome, and when my whole mind's on Death, not Eros. I suppose he'll want to meet me afterwards, like Mary. 'Afterwards' is getting really busy, except I daren't think beyond the Mass. I wish he'd just back off and let me concentrate, instead of using the binoculars as an excuse to touch me up, leaning right across me to show me how they work. Lots of other people are whispering and gossiping, getting up to greet their friends, taking pictures, changing films. I'd no idea it would be so sort of fidgety. I'd imagined prayerful silence, a sacred reverent hush. But I can't afford to alienate my neighbour, make him either hostile or suspicious, so I smile as warmly as I can while I focus the binoculars. The vast splendour of St Peter's suddenly contracts to looming detail – an eye, a wing, a furrowed brow, leaping into close-up; emotion caught and frozen as I track into the statues, arms flung out in wild and frantic gestures, expressions dazed or agonised, robes billowing in storm-clouds.

I turn my gaze from stone to flesh, as I realise those around me are using their binoculars not to admire the carvings, but to focus on a group of pilgrims sitting near the front in the main body of the nave. At first I see just a seething mass of heads, which the sharp lenses individualise into a hat, a wart, a feather, a long fair chunky pigtail, a coarse but waxed moustache. Then, at last, I understand the reason for the scrutiny, recognise that woman who's been splashed all over the newspapers and interviewed on television – the one who claimed she was miraculously cured. It was Giuseppe who alerted me, first pointed out the headlines, jabbing with his finger and shouting 'English! English!' – one of his new words – then kept switching on the news for me, so I could follow the whole saga, salute my fellow countryman. She did stick in my mind, in fact, not just because she's English and has that absurdly inappropriate name of Mrs Lena Pain, but because she seemed so ordinary – a plain and dowdy matron, with every curve damped down: her body clamped into a corset, her hair curbed in a perm.

I also felt an envy when I read about the case; craved a miracle myself, a release from my own pain, which may not be as obvious as a swollen gammy leg, but still shrieks for help and healing. She's not even alone, as *I* am back in London, but has this doting wonder-son – a scientist, I think they said; someone really brilliant, whom she claims is so devoted to her he's refused to leave, or marry. I can see him now, hanging on her arm, his smile cracking the binoculars, his face bland and rather nothingish, like hers. If only I could swap with them, that happy special smiling pair, surrounded by admirers, picked out by God or destiny to win life's lucky draw. I feel even more an alien when I compare myself to them. I'm totally alone – isolated, terrified, not hero-worshipped by the crowds, but probably torn to pieces by them once I've fired the gun.

I rest my eyes a moment, check my watch instead; realise the great ceremony is just about to start. The basilica is packed now, and an air of tense expectancy is spreading like a fever through the craning congregation. It's like some huge royal wedding, where everyone is waiting for the bride; every head turned towards the door. Suddenly,

517

the lights strobe on, and the mosaics' brilliant colours flame still more intensely; the organ blazing gold and purple as it thunders into life. The pure voices of the choirboys soar above its baritone, and the whole church seems to pulse and throb as it welcomes the procession now flowing up the aisle. Thirty, forty bishops in sumptuous golden vestments and tall white patterned mitres follow a group of younger men in frilled white lacy gowns. The whole vast congregation has now risen to its feet and is cheering and applauding as the procession shimmers past. I struggle to my own feet, dazed and overawed. I never realised people clapped in church, but this show is so magnificent I suppose it's like a theatre-audience applauding some impressive set when the curtain first goes up. Bishop follows bishop in a swishing dazzling pageant; the first ones now so close to me I can see the appliquéd detail of their vestments – shining trumpet-lilies, grapes in velvet clusters, glossy satin vine leaves, ears of ripened wheat.

The applause is growing wilder, and there, behind the bishops, is *Sua Santità* himself, resplendent in rich gold brocade and carrying a silver cross so tall it tops his mitre. He's blessing the huge crowd, smiling, nodding, turning back and forth, as if to give everyone a share of him. *He*'s the bride, the superstar, and those pilgrims are all hungry for him, trying to press closer, reach their hands (and cameras) across the central wooden barrier which is there to stop them mobbing him. He turns slowly towards the transept and it's my turn now to eat him with my eyes – the man who dared to hold me, embraced me like a father. The choir is singing some exultant hymn of praise, voices rising with the incense which smokes round the altar; incense spreading into tree-shapes, spiralling in columns, cutting through the sunlight which streams through one high window, gold smoke meeting silver. My nose and throat are choking with its pungent musky smell, my ears

518

assaulted by the choir who seem to hurl their hymn to heaven.

I hardly know what's going on – who's speaking, praying, sermonising, though a lot of it's in English, in honour of Saint Edwin, and much of it about him, as a stately English cardinal makes the martyr's case, like a barrister or advocate listing all the reasons why his client should be canonised, then formally requesting that favour from the Pope. I have eyes only for John Paul. I fumble for the binoculars, which I've still not given back, train them on his face. His brow is creased in concentration, his eyes intent and watchful, that expression of deep suffering still etched across his features. My whole instinct is to dart across and seize him, not to blow his brains out, but to have him hold me close again. I don't want to kill this ceremony, all this dignity and ritual which I've never experienced in my life before – the slow grave solemn movements of the bishops at the altar as they bow to one another or read from precious Mass books mounted on gold lecterns; the cascade of dark and silver tongues rising from the choir; the deep faith of the organ as it underscores the hymns; the rays of sunlight streaming from the window and falling on the Pope, as if to stress his specialness, his grace.

It's his turn now to speak. He's returned to his gold chair and is declaiming in Italian to the whole rapt congregation. I can't understand the words, but I gulp them down like a famished Third World orphan starved of spiritual food. Then he switches into English, enunciating slowly like a keen and solemn child who's still a little nervous of the language, still struggles with the harder words, spits them out like prune-stones. He's eulogising Edwin, reviewing the saint's life – his miracles, his virtues, his brave and joyful death. He was martyred on Good Friday, and just before the cruel rope tightened round his neck, he said how proud and pleased he was to die on the same day as his Saviour. He welcomed death, apparently, died blessing his brute hangman, looking forward to another life, to an end of pain and suffering.

I refocus the binoculars, note how tired John Paul looks – not just sad, but drained. His hair is slightly greyer on the left side, whiter on the right, receding on the forehead; his pale skin slack and lined. He's already in his seventies, must crave for peace himself; may bless me as I fire that shot, release him into martyrdom and sleep. Suddenly, he starts to cough, stumbles on his words as he struggles to continue. The attendant bishops hover, tensing in concern. I tense myself, tempted to snatch out my gun and fire it straight away, relieve him from his misery, stop that hacking cough. But Seton's plan was to wait until Communion, when the general stir and bustle of all the people surging to receive it will cover my own movement; provide me with the perfect chance to shoot, as the Pope comes down from the altar and passes right in front of me with his ciboriumful of Hosts.

It's an hour or more till then, and I hardly know how to live through all that ache and void of time, let alone stay cool and uninvolved, when I'm continually caught up in what's going on around me, affected by it, moved by it – the soaring alleluias spilling from the choir, the sense of communion and community which welds ten thousand strangers into one united family, makes them seem at home in a vast and foreign church. I long to be a part of it, envy all these faithful who know the prayers, can join in the responses, understand the ritual, know exactly when to stand and when to sit. (I keep making errors, shuffling to my feet when other people are only genuflecting, or subsiding on my seat when my neighbours are all kneeling.)

I'm especially jealous of those who offer gifts, who are allowed to walk right up to the altar, with bread and wine, or scrolls, or precious boxes, to present them to the Pope. He doesn't have a problem like my shrink –

who regards gifts as bribes or blackmail and prefers to hand them back – but accepts them with real gratitude, even caresses those who offer them, touching children's faces, squeezing women's hands. I fight a wild temptation to walk up with my gun, present it as my tribute, and as he reaches out to take it, to fire from point-blank range. I need to get this killing over, can't endure the tension, the feeling of sick horror which is spreading through my body. The longer I'm involved in this great and solemn Mass, the worse it seems to wreck it – gag the music, smash the mystery, plunge brilliance into black.

I cling on to the chair in front, to ground myself, restrain myself; watch the Pope returning to the altar, praying silently, intently, over the chalice and the Hosts. Bread and wine. Suddenly I'm tasting Seton's mouth again, tasting our own bread and wine in Giuseppe's shabby flat; following our own ritual, at the table, on the floor. '*Sanctus, sanctus, sanctus*,' shrill the choir, but I'm hearing something else – Seton's voice beyond it, crying out in fear. His terror's rooted in me like our ugly monster-child, kicking at my stomach, wet between my legs. Fear's even in my eyeballs; hard, behind the sockets, pressing on my skull, like the cruelly hot and heavy fur which drags my body down. I grope back for my chair, the man beside me fussing, trying to touch me up again under the guise of sham concern. The woman on the other side is also looking anxious, whispers something to me, starts fumbling in her handbag, then offers me a glucose sweet, as if I were a child. I shake my head, assure her I'm all right, though I'm aware how pale I've gone; can feel the blood still draining from my face. I slump back in my seat, pinch my arm quite sharply to stop myself from fainting. Whatever happens, I mustn't draw attention to myself.

Suddenly, a bell rings out, imperious and shrill, and I glance back at the altar, see the Pope standing absolutely motionless, holding up the Host above his head; all the bishops stretching out their arms to it, every head but mine bowed low in adoration, the entire congregation kneeling. He turns slowly slowly round in a full circle, to display the Host to each section of the church. The silence is intense and almost spooky. Despite the thousands present, there's not one single sound – no careless cough or baby's cry, no rustle or cleared throat; not a murmur from the organ nor whisper from the choir. The moment feels electric, sends shivers down my spine. I bow my own head, hide my eyes, hear that urgent bell again; keep looking down, looking down, aware of some strange force or power surging through the church – holiness, or faith, perhaps – something I can't share. Then the organ starts to throb again, and after a high and straining solo from a young boy all in white, the Pope prays aloud in what I guess is Latin. The words are just a mubbled drone until he switches into English, repeating the word 'peace', spinning out its vowels in his careful stilted English, as if to stress its value.

'The p-e-a-c-e of the Lord be with you always.'

Peace isn't something I know that much about – turmoil, yes; violence, yes; bloody scraps and battles all the time. Yet I've heard the word so often in this Mass: peace in life, peace in death, peace in hearts and minds. And now the Pope is sweeping round to face us, declaring to us all: 'Let us offer each other the sign of peace.'

I watch, amazed, as he starts embracing all the bishops at the altar, and they in turn hold and clasp each other, arms around each other's necks, male enfolding male. I'm so moved, I just stand staring, until the woman on my right reaches out and clasps me in her own arms. I'm squashed right against her corset-bones, jabbed by her sharp brooch, her flowery tea-rose perfume lassoing me as well. Rose transmutes to aftershave as her husband changes places with her, pumps me by the hand. He's hardly let it go when the dark man on my other side squeezes it in his, no longer just flirtatious, but affectionate, respectful. The people in the row in front are also joining in, embracing one another, then turning round to us. A small boy in his father's arms leans across to tug my hair; his mother smiles apologies, laps my hand in hers. And it's not just our few rows. The whole vast congregation are swapping signs of peace, hands stretched out to hands, chairs scraping on the marble as people turn to either side, reach out to friends or strangers further down the rows. Two parents kiss their brood of five; two lovers almost smooch; an old crone in a see-through mac is cheek to cheek with a woman dripping mink. The Mass has broken up, or at least halted for a while, so that everybody present can greet his neighbour, offer him goodwill, display their fellow feeling and their trust.

My own hand feels quite tired. It's been pressed against great spiky rings, gripped by kids' hot fingers, snagged on old and horny skin, soothed by soft suede gloves. And people are still courting it, murmuring 'Peace be with you'; making me accepted, one of their community, a member of their church. A small girl in a corduroy coat skids up to me and offers me her cheek. My own cheeks flame as I plant a clumsy kiss on it, rigid with embarrassment. I've never kissed a child before, don't know what to say. Yet underneath I'm thrilled; thrilled to be included, made one of this whole family, a loved and wanted sibling. I'd been envying them their ties – their families and pilgrim groups, their parish clubs and unions, which allow them to belong. Now, at last, I'm part of it, can share their bonds, their peace.

I shake a final friendly hand, subside back on my seat. It's only now I realise what peace means – that sense of stillness in my gut, instead of churning tension, that sudden ease of breathing as my chest and lungs unclench, and I remove my lethal camera-case from my shoulder to the floor. I know now I can't shoot, disrupt this precious peace, abuse my family's trust. I glance up at the sun, which is still streaming through the window, the lattice of the pane patterning its beam with furrowed lines. 'Afterwards' is suddenly restored – a sunny lazy afternoon with normal things like shopping, strolling in the park, instead of Mass and morning aborted in one shot. I can even meet that Mary by the obelisk, invite her for a beer; let lunch merge into evening as I celebrate the fact there *is* an evening, and I'm free to spin it out, stay up the whole night, watch darkness switch to light again, and life.

I'm not betraying Seton – in fact I'm saving him. If I fired the shot, they'd be bound to hunt him down, hound him back for questioning, fling him in a cell. People here know that we've been lovers – Giuseppe's friends and neighbours, the couple in the flat above, that weird man in the wine-shop. I've given him his freedom, allowed him to escape. Or perhaps the plot was just a game, a symbolic killing, dressed up as a charade. I glance down at my far-fetched coat, my preposterous strappy shoes with silver diamanté on the heels. Yes – fancy-dress, a children's game, as spurious as Saint Thecla, whose cult was suppressed more than twenty years ago, her life declared a total fabrication, her story a romance.

I remove my coat, fold it on my knees, feel miraculously unburdened in my silky-nothing dress, without the weight of murder pressing on my back. My salamander sparkles, seems to dart and writhe, alive. So it *was* a lucky talisman, kept me safe in the leaping flames of danger. I let my body sag, utterly exhausted after coming through the fire. I'm the only one still sitting. The whole church seethes around me as people throng and hustle towards all the different priests who are distributing Communion in each and every part of the basilica – a score in both the transepts, dozens in the aisle; others still processing to their stations, preceded by a marshal, and holding up their sumptuous jewelled ciboriums. An endless stream of worshippers is flowing up and back, weaving round the chairs, negotiating obstacles, dodging fractious children who have strayed from parents' laps; television cameramen recording the whole hubbub. I've often had a longing to receive Communion myself, to swallow a frail wafer and feel it turn to God, but I'm too weak to move a muscle, weak with sheer relief. We've reached and passed the moment when I should have fired the shot, and instead I'm simply relaxing in my seat.

I listen to the altos slam out a wild '*Exsulta*!', exulting still myself, even trying to pray – pray for Seton, for his peace. If Saint Edwin can grant miracles to dreary frumpy widows, then why not him, as well? I want us to meet up again – Seton and myself – with no sour recriminations, no anger, violence, fury, just closeness, even love. It feels really strange to pray, makes me flushed and almost randy, as if it's affecting not my soul, but my body and my cunt. I keep my eyes fixed on the Pope, watch him giving out Communion, an infinity of taut pink tongues thrusting out in front of him as he tops each with a Host. I'm glad it takes so long. Every extra minute he's alive and functioning increases my delight. I don't need a Host myself, or bread turned into God. I'm feeding on elation, which is miracle enough.

At last, he and all the other priests glide back to the altar, where he gives his final blessing, holding up his elaborate silver crozier. The blessing seems to leave its mark quite literally, as if the precise and solemn cross he's tracing in the air has imprinted on my flesh, even etched into my bone like letters on a stick of rock. I'm safe now and protected, my gun disarmed, its bullets merely playthings, harmless children's toys. The camera-case weighs nothing as I return it to my shoulder – having slipped my coat back on – then hold it close against me as I skim up to the front. The Pope's processing out now and I want the perfect view, want to follow right behind him, monitor each step. The priests all stride out first, followed by the bishops, and lastly *Sua Santità*, moving very slowly, blessing everyone, smiling, nodding, giving of himself. The church is going wild, everyone applauding, calling out his name, scores of people in the nave climbing on their chairs, busy with their cameras, or holding up their kids to him. I'm cheering, too, and clapping, my throat hoarse from all the crazy things I'm yelling, things about my father, him being still alive. A marshal stops me pushing any closer, keeps the goggling crowds back as Giovanni Paolo makes his stately progress down the aisle. I can hardly see him now, just a glimpse of golden mitre, a glint of his tall cross.

Suddenly, a shot rings out from further down the nave, and just a fraction later, a second shot seems to explode the church away. There's a moment's total silence when sheer reeling incredulity fights with sickened shock. Then everything is uproar – people tangling, howling, Swiss Guards flashing halberds, screams of pain and panic as seething pilgrims thresh towards the doors. I kick and claw my own way not towards the exit, but in the direction of the shots, hardly caring if I'm injured I'm so wild to reach the action. It's impossible to make it to the central wooden barrier, but I leap up on a chair so I can look down on the aisle; glimpse a sight so hideous it knifes into my memory, leaves an open wound: bodies, bits of bodies, blood and brains splashed everywhere – on the chairs, the wood, the marble, even on the innocent – a child's white coat red-splattered, an old man weeping crimson. I taste vomit in my throat as I focus on the details: the Pope's right foot turned inwards as he lies bleeding on the floor, the shoe scuffed and strangely modern in contrast to his flowing golden robes, now rucked up on one side and exposing a thin leg. His grey eyes are still open, dead eyes staring upwards, looking baffled and surprised.

The second corpse is just a hump, a hump beneath a coat. I recognise the coat – the missing middle toggle, the semen stain where we used it as a mattress. I seem

526

to reel and fall towards it as a security guard thrusts me from the chair, gestures to the exit, where other guards and marshals are trying to calm the crowds, direct them safely out. I'm so appalled, so shaken, I can barely move at all, but I let the crowd walk for me, support me in their packed and jostling scrum. I listen to the babble, the brutal lying stories passed from lips to lips. 'Shot the Holy Father, then shot himself, blew his brains out, blew his evil head off.'

I shake my head, keep shaking it, tasting blood now, not just vomit. 'No,' I say to no one. 'He wasn't even here. He left – he left this morning, before anyone was up. He's not in Rome at all.' It could be someone else's coat. Duffel coats are all the same, just clones of one another. And most of them have stains or missing toggles. I close my eyes a second, see the coat again, see something else I've been trying to blank out: a bulky golf umbrella being examined by the ashen man who was kneeling by the corpses – a bodyguard, a doctor? Its colours were distinctive, not easy to forget – stripes of cream and orange, with a sturdy fretted handle which left faint patterns on my palm when I held it through that endless papal audience.

I struggle to turn round, fight the tide of pilgrims pressing on all sides. I must get that umbrella, wrest it from the man; claim it as my own, so no one can blame Seton. Of course he wasn't here. He trusted *me* to shoot, relied on me to do it, so he could leave the country, start a safe new life. I think he's in Bulgaria with Stefan, or perhaps he's gone to France, to walk in the Auvergne, or follow lonely rivers . . .

A bad-tempered marshal blocks my way, heaves and prods me back towards the exit, swears at me for causing more disruption. There's enough chaos as it is. A television cameraman has had his camera trampled and is weeping with frustration, wrestling through the crowds to try to save his work; a second one is shinning up a ledge, face contorted, feet slipping on the marble, but still doggedly recording all the action. Cardinals, policemen, are pouring in from nowhere, bossy men in uniform, nurses in blue cloaks. They're bawling through loudspeakers now, in English and Italian, trying to keep order, stop everybody panicking.

I'm very calm myself, though I don't feel well at all. There's this fierce pain in my head and heart, and I keep fearing I'll throw up. I'm forced to stop a moment, rest against a pillar; glance down at the cherub sculpted near its base, a plump and smirking baby trailing clouds of gauze. I return his marble smile. He's the only one who's happy, the only one who's real, who knows it's all a game, just a charade, a masquerade.

That marshal's bearing down on me, really hurts me this time as he shoves me in the back. He's forgotten we're all brothers, all members of one family, one loving happy family, with no evil and no death.

'P-e-a-c-e,' I tell him, smiling still, as I pass safely through the doors.

# 43

I struggle up the marble steps of the Grand Hotel Imperatore and into its huge foyer, which is like a smaller version of St Peter's, with mosaics, columns, statues, even romping cherubs. No one stops me this time, despite the fact I'm deathly pale and staggering. I'm dressed to fit the part, you see, dressed to match the hotel's pomp in my showy fur, my chic designer dress. The psychiatric conference is now well under way, judging by the notice-boards, the lists of members, lectures, the signs tacked up on pillars pointing out the meeting-rooms. It's a Sunday and it's lunchtime, so I doubt that there are lectures actually in progress, but I scan the board to check. According to their timetable, conference members should all be in the bar now – what's called the Bar Minerva, for a pre-lunch drink, reception. I follow the gold-lettered sign, turn right and right again, hear the buzz of conversation before I'm even at the door. Several hundred psychiatrists and analysts are huddled in small groups, swilling lavish drinks, gesturing with cigars, reaching out for canapés from loaded silver trays. They all look smug and shock-proofed, in well-cut pricey suits, their blue-chip voices modulated, their blank-screen faces polished, perfectly adjusted. The females seem more drab and somehow sexless – though expensive-drab like missionaries with money; their thin hair coiled or chignoned as if to give them height and power.

I slam the door behind me, stand trembling just in front of it, listening to their patter. My pain has turned to anger, my disbelief to bitter cold revenge. I sped here in a taxi, passing ambulances, police cars, all hurtling to St Peter's, a whole orchestra of sirens drowning my own

sobs. I scrub my smarting eyes as I sweep between a
would-be Freud with a beard and rimless glasses and a
suntanned dapper socialite in a perky blue bow-tie. I don't
bother to apologise as I spill the latter's drink. I'm furious
with these hypocrites, who couldn't save Seton, couldn't
even help him, just grabbed his money and paid him
back with silence, wrote out receipts in jargon. They've
all grown fat on patients' fees, which subsidise their
double gins, their expensive foreign cars, their two-week
cushy conferences at palaces like this one. What use are
windbag lectures when their abandoned frantic patients
are hoarding shotguns, blowing out their brains? These
so-called experts on the mind have minds so convoluted
they don't understand that suffering needs relieving, not
classifying, analysing, turning into seminars.

I wheel the other way, watch a breastless woman crunch
into a canapé, grains of gleaming caviar spilling down her
dress. I lick up not the caviar, but grains of conversation –
jargon once again, double-talk, obscure and arcane words.
They're all fixated on their conference, arguing absurdities
or pursuing petty feuds, while the Pope lies in a pool of
blood with a bullet through his heart. They don't even
know he's dead. And if I tried to break the news to them,
they'd assume I was deluded, stamp me with some label,
turn me into a 'case', force me into line with electric-shocks
or chemicals, or suggest I had a decade of their cruel and
specious therapy.

My breathing's harsh and laboured as I continue
searching for John-Paul, skirt the whole vast bar, scan
all its hidden alcoves, the extension at the back. No sign
of him at all, so I stride back down the passage and along
to the reception desk. It's pandemonium there. The news
of the Pope's murder has just been flashed on radio, and
the receptionist is sobbing, her male colleagues flapping
hands and tongues as they tattle in Italian.

'313,' I rap.

The weeping girl fumbles in the pigeonhole. 'That key's out,' she quavers, in broken snivelling English.

'Of course it is,' I tell her. 'My husband's got it on him. He was meant to meet me at the airport, but he got the plane-time wrong. I'm absolutely frazzled, been hanging round for hours. I'm dying for a wash and change, need the second key.'

'But . . .'

'Look, he *told* me to go up. I reached him on the phone, at last; had to have him paged, in fact, by some useless airport clerk. He was still waiting for my plane, only left a tick ago, and will be at least another hour or two, judging by the traffic. I don't intend sitting in reception half the afternoon, while he struggles with the roadblocks.' I tap impatient fingers on the desk, swish my fur irritably around me. Fur disarms suspicion, spells money, status, rank. You never keep fur waiting, or tell it to fuck off. The girl doesn't even recognise me, though she was the one who turfed me out so rudely just eight days ago. I'm a different person, not just different clothes.

A cluster of excited guests are now jostling at the desk, a frenetic clamour rising about the murder of the Pope; staff and strangers joining in in several different languages, and the radio emoting to itself. Then an impatient man behind me starts bleating for his own key – also wants his passport, his mail, his map, his bill. It's too much for the girl, who'd just started to explain to me that my husband hadn't told them he'd need a double room, nor mentioned that his wife would be arriving. She's even picked the phone up, to dial his number, check my story, check he isn't in. But the (blessed) man behind me interrupts again, sounds increasingly hysterical as he pushes to the front. The girl lets the receiver fall back on its cradle, shrugs defeat as she listens to his tirade, hands me the spare key.

My self-possession leaves me as I glide up in the lift. I'm feeling very sick again. The hump beneath the duffel coat

531

seems to have lodged in my own throat, and my hands are damp and sticky not with sweat but blood. I alight at the third floor, huddle in a corner while I fight the waves of nausea, fight to gain control. Anger's easier than pain, helps to keep the horror out: obscene and hideous images of Seton's headless body. No – it didn't happen. He wasn't there at all. It was someone else who doctored his umbrella, fired his sawn-off shotgun. I only need to slip back just one night, see him in Giuseppe's flat instead of in St Peter's, lying sated and contented on our pile of tangled rugs. It was like a consummation. I gave him everything, poured out myself like wine for him, let him drink till he was dizzy. It was *then* he died, not later, died between my legs. I remember my own suicide when John-Paul went away: that astounding perfect moment when I let go of mind and being; let go of pain and time. Seton went like that, spilled out of his body into ecstasy and void. I undo my heavy coat, let my hands stroke slowly down my breasts, trace their curving warmth beneath the clingy wisp of dress. I'm naked underneath it, naked for John-Paul. I'm widowed now, and free for him; have waited months and months to be his wife.

I prepare myself a moment before I drift along the corridor – spray my breasts with scent, smooth my tousled hair, try to calm my breathing as I pause outside his room. I insert the key so quietly it doesn't make a sound, turn it in the lock, feel the stiff door yield. I'm in a sort of antechamber and can't see much at all, save a stretch of plush gold carpet and a swathe of satin bed. I close the door behind me as softly as I can, creep a few steps in. The room is spacious, fortunately, so he doesn't even hear me; is sitting down the other end, at a desk beside the window, his back towards me, his shoulders hunched above a pile of books and papers. I admire his sense of duty, his endless diligence – the only one who's working, not propping up a bar. How could I have ignored him, even shrugged him off, allowed another father to replace my first and true one? He looks different, somehow – taller – his hair so rich and glossy it could have been stolen from a magpie, his suit a little lighter than his usual dark funereal grey. I edge up slightly closer, so I can check on all those tiny things which once held my life together, so familiar now they're old and trusted friends: his pack of kingsize Chesterfields, his snobby silver lighter which is only there for show, the deluge of dead matches, the tubes of mints and fruit-gums lined up by his ashtray, the prim pedantic fountain-pen he uses for his bills. I long to secrete them all away, start a new collection, preserve them for infinity in bullet-proof glass cases.

I watch him steer the pen across his foolscap, watch him pause a moment, deep in thought. I shouldn't interrupt him, wreck his concentration, which is so intense he's no idea I'm there. I start to back away, change my mind as I shock against the bed. He didn't book a double, that receptionist confided. I stroke its satin counterpane, cool beneath my hands. It looks big enough to me – big enough for both of us when he takes me in his arms, holds me till the sickness goes, till the bloodstains fade to white; holds me till he's sated, crying out with pleasure; the wild sheets damp, dishevelled; the blankets bucking, thrusting. I've got to make it perfect, the one great thing I promised him, the gift he can't return. I try to judge the distance, feel it's still too far, so I inch up even further, keeping every movement tiny, smiling for him, gentle for him, so he'll see how much I've changed.

At last I'm calm and ready, though I have to swallow once or twice before I dare to speak. I want my voice seductive, not stuttering or harsh. 'John-Paul,' I murmur teasingly. 'Are you glad to see your wife?'

He swings right round to face me, sees my faultless smile, sees the happy potent gun pointing at his heart; jerks up to his feet, staggers, half-collapses, clutches at a folder as if to use it as a shield. I keep completely still myself, grasp my right wrist with my left hand, to hold it absolutely steady, then slowly, slowly, slowly pull the trigger. I have to get it right this time, do what Seton asked me; not betray him, disobey him, but follow his instructions and kill John-Paul for him.

I don't flinch at the recoil, just stand motionless, watch ardent crimson petals flowering through his shirt. He falls without a sound, just crumples to the floor. I'm rather sorry, really. I wish he'd said my name, told me that he loved me.

'I loved you, too,' I whisper, as I wipe my sweaty hands, return the damp Beretta to its case. 'But Seton said we must kill the things we love.'

## 44

It's raining. Naturally. It always rains the days I see John-Paul. It's the second day of March now, so there should be signs of spring, though I can't say they're all that obvious – just overflowing drains, the odd nervous spindly daffodil shivering in a window-box. I fidget on the couch, keep wanting to turn around to check up on my doctor, see how ill he looks, or changed. I hardly dared to glance at him when I first slunk in, shaking with sick nerves. We haven't met for seven weeks six days. There were certain complications on both sides.

It's not two-ten, or lunch-time, but half past ten – a.m. I've never had appointments in the mornings, and the light seems wrong; too weak and faint and blurred. I feel weak and blurred myself, have hardly said a word yet, censored everything so far, out of embarrassment, or pain. So many words lead back to blood, or Rome.

The small things haven't changed. The clocks keep ticking ticking; the answerphone clicks on and off with its sudden throaty cracklings. The sirens sound still crueller, or perhaps I simply mind them more because they jolt me back to Rome again. John-Paul makes his usual stealthy noises: sucking cough-sweets, lighting cigarettes. I don't think he should smoke – not now – it could be very dangerous, even kill him. I choke down thoughts of death, try to focus on the pictures, see some point and purpose in their swirls of sullen brown. Rain slaps against the windowpanes, dribbles slowly down.

I wipe my hands – they're sweating – hear a muffled cough behind me, some protracted furtive business with a box of paper handkerchiefs. John-Paul has a cold, a really heavy chesty one. I caught it instantly, within minutes of arriving. I know people say you can't catch colds without an incubation period, but I willed myself to do so. He's had so much pain already, I hoped to take it from him, bear his aching head for him, his swollen scratchy throat. It didn't quite work out like that, and we're both snuffling now, and hoarse, but at least we're sharing symptoms.

We've shared them for two months. I was extremely ill myself, the time he was away; stayed in bed for several weeks, though no one was aware. I just hid beneath the covers, waiting for the summons, the hammering on the door.

There's a faint smell of eucalyptus in the room. It wafts me back to childhood – off school with tonsillitis, my mother rubbing warm oil on my chest. Or was that just a fantasy: the gentle caring Mother I invented for myself? They're dead now, anyway – my mother, my two fathers, all my gentle fantasies, both the elder brothers who died before I knew them.

'It's called the Eternal City,' I say suddenly.

John-Paul cannot speak, is fighting through a sneeze.

'So people shouldn't die there.'

The sneeze begets another. I blow my nose in sympathy. It's already sore and swollen, and my throat grates when I swallow.

'That other guy,' I mutter, almost talking to myself now. 'They gave him a life sentence.'

John-Paul clears his own throat. 'Which "other guy" d'you mean?'

'That Turk – the one who tried to kill the Pope in 1981. I can't pronounce his name.'

'Mehmet Ali Ağça.'

'Yes,' I say, impressed. 'But Seton had that anyway.'

'Had what, Nial?'

He seems a little slow today, can't follow what I'm saying. He's not as sharp, I realise, may never be again.

536

'A life sentence,' I explain. 'That's how he saw existence, like an endless spell in jail. I reckon he's much happier, released.' I'd like to add 'Don't you?', but John-Paul rarely answers questions; seems subdued today, in any case, is probably still in pain – and I don't just mean the cold. His pain ignites my own. There's a fierce stabbing in my chest, a sense of crumpling, falling. I reach out and grip the hard edge of the couch, force my mouth to work. I feel I must keep talking now I've started, dispel that aching silence we've endured the first half hour; no sound except the weeping guilty rain.

'There was this guy I used to know,' I say, groping for each word as if they're treacherous and slippery. (He was actually a client, but I keep that quiet since I've still never told John-Paul about my work.) 'He was pretty ancient, almost in his eighties, an ex-naval type who'd been commander of a minesweeper way back in the war. He had this sort of trophy-board tacked up in his study, which he'd taken from the wardroom when the ship was sent for scrap. It showed all the mines they'd scuppered – a tiny painting of each one, like a score-sheet or a tally. You ought to have one like it, fix it on the wall here, to record your patients' suicides – the successful ones, at least.'

John-Paul doesn't answer, so I close my eyes and think about my client, see his board revamped – tiny desperate people on it, instead of callous mines; all sinking, drowning, foundering; screaming out for Saviours who neither heard nor came – Seton, headless, helpless, the last one on the board. I'd like to see him up there, daubed in red and black, commemorated somehow, not stinking in a mortuary or shovelled in a hole. It hurts to think of death, though the subject keeps returning, bobbing back like a bloated stinking body after shipwreck. He died because I didn't shoot, died instead of me. I'm wearing all his clothes. They're far too big and smell of pain, but they help to make him live. They also stop me screaming, losing my control; seem to hold things in, like armour.

The silence feels oppressive now, and dangerous. My hands are damp and shaking as I light a cigarette, hear John-Paul also lighting up behind me; the sudden angry flaring of a match. He's obviously resentful that I ever mentioned suicide. Suicide spells failure as far as he's concerned, and I know how failure hurts. I failed myself, didn't I, failed in my last act, failed to make it perfect, the final consummation, the full-blown loving gift. I try to cast my mind back, remember just what happened in that hotel room in Rome, but my head is aching terribly and it's hard to work things out, disentangle fact from fiction, or plain nightmare. Probably safer really not to mention death at all, maybe break the rule completely and talk about the weather – how wet it is for spring. Though perhaps it isn't spring yet, or we'll miss it altogether; leapfrog into summer – things parching, turning brown.

I flinch as John-Paul starts to speak, expect a chilly reprimand, though his voice is quiet, impassive.

'I think what you're really saying, Nial, is that we need to do more work together, try to reach your problems at another deeper level, get in touch with your own self-destructive impulses, your own suicidal urges. Perhaps an extra session might be quite a good idea now, so that you come five times a week instead of four. I know you said you wanted that when you first began your analysis in April, and I didn't have the time then. But two other of my therapies have terminated recently, so I've got two sessions vacant on the Friday – the one day you don't come – either an appointment very early in the morning, or . . .'

I turn round to stare at him. He's offering me more sessions when I presumed he feared and loathed me, and was only waiting for the moment when he'd decide to turn me in – not now, not straight away, but playing

538

cat and mouse with me, building up the tension, spinning out the horror and suspense. I haven't dared to show my face for seven weeks six days, haven't dared be well; just cowered indoors, waiting for the footsteps, waiting for the murder charge, my whole body wrung with terror, my mind unravelling.

I scan his face a moment. It looks gaunt and deathly pale, dark eyes scorching out of it, as if they've consumed the flesh around them. How long was he in hospital, I dare to wonder now, how long and deep the scar?

'You're looking very startled, Nial. The notion of five sessions must seem frightening in some way.'

I shake my head, can't answer. He's saved me, let me go; saved me from high prison walls blocking out the spring; saved me from steel warders and starched white winter nurses with ice-chips in their hearts; saved me from the straitjacket, the electrodes on my skull, the rubber plug shoved in my mouth, so I wouldn't bite my tongue; saved me from slow needles which paralyse my body, trap it in white nightmare till I half-wake, dumb and gelded.

The pictures fade, break up. No one's ever saved me – not from death, or life. Saving's almost loving – in fact, it costs still more. Even the Prodigal Son didn't try to shoot his father.

My father. Still alive. Not dead in a basilica, slumped bleeding on white marble, but living, breathing, sneezing, just a foot or two away. I edge up on the couch so my newly-growing hair is almost spilling on his knee; long to fuse and merge with him, as I thought I had with Seton; roll up time like a length of heavy carpet, till my genes are simply *his* genes and I'm absorbed back into him.

I close my eyes a second, see that cemetery again, the one where I was buried way back in December – see my favourite gravestone there, with its intrepid Latin tag.

'*Quis separabit.*' I say the phrase out loud.

He doesn't seem to hear me, asks me to repeat myself. I

539

do so pretty desperately. He's *got* to understand. He used to pick up Latin, pick up any language, any subtle reference, any casual phrase. It's tragic he's so changed.

'*Quis separabit.*' I make it louder, slower, will him to respond.

The rain fills in the silence, the three clocks speed and snigger; a lorry in the road below crashes gears, backfires. Still he doesn't answer. There isn't any question-mark, so perhaps he sees no need. But we're separate and apart still, and those clocks are hurtling on towards the fifty-minute hour. I slew right round to face him, try to *show* him what I mean, hold out both my arms. He shifts a fraction – backwards – as if to remind me of the rules: no comfort and no contact, only words. But my words have failed to reach him, so I dare them one last time, still groping out towards him, trying to cancel any smallest space between us.

'*Quis . . . separabit.*'

A siren splits the phrase in two, severs its twin parts. My answer, I suppose. I feel tears pricking at my eyes, scour them furiously. If I start crying now, I might never stop at all, may weep until I die. I sag back on the couch, crumple up my Kleenex. I've died too much already, died and been reborn. Lazarus was better as he was. No one should have raised him, given him new life. Those New Year bells were shamming when they promised a new start. You can't throw out the old. It's part of you. It *is* you. I shan't be born again.

I curl up very small, hack off my new hair, lose my clumsy hands and feet, unscrew my hulking limbs. Then, when I'm small and smooth enough, I crawl back into John-Paul's womb, secure the catch behind me. I was happy there before, quiet and very peaceful. Every flutter that I made shock-waved through his body; every time I kicked or cried, he felt it, and responded. My blood and breath and needs and growth were part of his existence.

I should never have come out, never cut the cord, never

have been born that session in December when I imagined it was spring. I was wrong about the spring, wrong about a lot of things.

I burrow in still deeper, embed myself securely, the way I was before; start breathing John-Paul's oxygen, sucking down his food. I'm already feeling safer. The curving walls have knit and sealed around me, and all the sounds are muffled now – sirens just the rumblings of his stomach, traffic the quiet pumping of his heart. My mother's womb was scarlet steel, which bruised my pulpy limbs. John-Paul's is plush, and dark.

I float a while in darkness, getting smaller all the time. I've lost my sex, my brain-cells, and my arms are groping paddles; my legs just half-formed buds. I inhale a snort of nicotine, taste cough-sweets in my food-supply, which soothe my almost-throat – menthol balmed with honey, an after-kick of lemon. I've no longer got a cough or cold. My Mother keeps me well.

Suddenly, I'm jolted as she explodes me with a sneeze, but the cord swings me back and round again, keeps me firmly tethered. I strain my ears a moment. Her voice sounds faint and muted, but I think she's trying to speak.

'It's time.'

'*No!*' I mutter, terrified, shutting my blind foetus eyes and clinging to the handholds of her womb. Of course it can't be time. I'm hardly formed at all now, so how could I be born?

'It's time, Nial – over time now. We have to finish there.'

I decide to lose my ears, as well. Safer not to hear. I'm barely even human now, just a ball of cells, a swelling with a tail.

I feel my Mother standing up; move with her in the womb, lurching slightly, clinging on, as she walks towards the door. She opens it, stands waiting.

' "Who shall separate us," ' she murmurs almost casually, finally translating, when I thought she hadn't heard, had given up all hope that she would ever understand.

I nod my feeble pinprick head, so tiny now, it's nothing but a smile. But that smile is growing, growing.